Crocodile Creek
Rescue

ALISON ROBERTS   MEREDITH WEBBER   MARION LENNOX

MILLS & BOON

CONTENTS

The Playboy Doctor's Proposal

Alison Roberts

Dear Reader,

How lucky am I?

To have colleagues who are also my friends, whose skills I have the utmost respect for, and who share a love of the genre and a dedication to making each story the best yet.

To work together and have the challenge of a scope broad enough to link several books, along with the sheer fun of intertwining the stories of each other's characters, is an enriching experience.

So here we are, back in Crocodile Creek, and we're throwing a cyclone at our own bit of northern Australia. Scary stuff!

I'm more likely to experience a bad earthquake or maybe a tsunami where I am in New Zealand, but it's a good idea to be prepared for whatever dramatic turns nature can take, and we can get some bad storms at times.

Here's what you can do if a strong wind warning is issued:

Bring your pets inside and move stock to shelter
Secure outdoor furniture
Tape across large windows to prevent shattering
Stay inside during storm
Partially open a window on the sheltered side of the house
Stay away from doors and windows
If you have to go outside, watch out for dangling and broken power lines

Is a cyclone enough of a link for our stories? We didn't think so. There's also a little boy called Felixx....

Happy reading!

Love,

Alison

PROLOGUE

'SHH, NOW, FELIXX!'

'Hush, OK?'

'Silence. We have to have silence for Alanya to get well.'

For days this was all he'd heard, it seemed to Felixx. He crept around on the edge of Alanya's illness, too scared to ask how bad she was, shut away from seeing her except for one or two short visits to the wellness shelter each day, during which he knew he had to be silent or she wouldn't get better fast enough.

Sometimes he asked people, 'How's Mummy?' He liked to call her Mummy because that's who she was. She always wanted him to call her Alanya, because that was her spirit name, but as she couldn't hear him right now, he said 'Mummy' and it helped a little bit.

The silence helped, too. He had to stay as quiet as anything, or she might not get well. He knew that, but it was so hard. The fish on his sneaker helped. Mummy had drawn it with his felt pens. Mostly the bright orange one. She'd done it the day he'd showed her the hole.

'We can't afford a new shoe just yet,' she'd said. 'So let's make it special. The hole can be his eye, see?'

He could poke his finger in the hole. In and out. It was tight at first but now it was easy. His finger went in and out.

In and out.

It helped him to stay quiet. To stop the questions he so badly wanted to ask, like, 'Mummy… Alanya…are you feeling better? Do you need more medicine?'

She didn't seem to be eating very much. They gave her carrot juice to drink, to drain the toxins from her system. How long did toxins take to drain?

Where did they come out?

He was too scared to ask any of these questions, but he listened more than the healing sisters thought. He heard words like 'worried' and 'taking too long' and after this he stayed even quieter, stopped even asking, 'How's Mummy?' in case his talking, even outside the healing shelter, was the thing stopping her from getting well.

Late one night…he couldn't remember, maybe the sixth or seventh night of her illness…he couldn't sleep, and crept over to the healing shelter because there was light coming from its windows. It was cold and his feet were bare and he didn't dare go inside, but he listened underneath the window and heard more words. 'Getting worse' and 'I don't know' and 'ambulance'.

After this, everything got so confusing, when he thought about it he couldn't think the way it had gone. He fell asleep on the couch on the veranda of the healing shelter, and a big car came with red lights. He hid under the blanket in case he got in trouble for being there. He heard men's voices. 'Too late' and 'useless' and 'bloody quack treatments'. Someone found him—Raina, one of the healing sisters—and he pretended to be asleep and she carried him gently in her arms to his bed, and by the time he got there he must have really been asleep because he didn't remember anything else until morning.

Then there were more words—'very peaceful' and 'gone away on the most wonderful journey'—but he was so good, he didn't say anything himself in case it made Mummy…better call her Alanya…in case it made her worse. A lot of boring time went by. He wasn't allowed to see her at all. He had some meals, breakfast and lunch. Were they saying it was Alanya who had gone on the wonderful journey? When was she coming back? He didn't want to ask because that would not have been hushing and staying silent.

Raina sat him down and hugged him and kissed his forehead and told him, 'Your auntie Janey is going to come and get you, sweetheart.'

He didn't know he had an auntie Janey. He wanted to ask who she was and when she was coming but he was so, so good, he stayed quiet and silent and hushed and didn't say a word.

CHAPTER ONE

'YOU'RE *NOT!*'

'Yes, I am. What's the big deal? It's only a few days off work.'

'You never take days off work. In all the time I've known you, Hannah, and that's, what—three years? You've never missed a shift.'

Senior Nurse Jennifer Bradley collected the paper emerging from the twelve-lead ECG machine and Dr Hannah Jackson cast an experienced eye over the results.

'Bit of right heart failure—there's notching on the P waves but everything else looks pretty good for an eighty-six-year-old. No sign of infarct.'

The elderly patient, who had been sound asleep while the recording was being taken, suddenly opened her eyes.

'Give it back,' she said loudly. 'You're a *naughty* girl!'

The complaint was loud enough to attract the attention of several staff members near the central desk. Heads turned in astonishment and Hannah sighed inwardly. One of them would be her fellow senior registrar, Ryan Fisher, wouldn't it? And, of course, he had a grin from ear to ear on overhearing the accusation.

Jennifer was stifling a smile with difficulty. 'What's the matter, Mrs Matheson?'

'She's stolen my handbag! I've got a lot of money in my purse and she's taken it, the little blonde trollop!'

Hannah heard a snigger from the small audience by the central desk. It would have been a good idea to pull the curtain of this cubicle but in the early hours of a Monday morning, with the emergency department virtually empty, it hadn't seemed a priority.

'Your handbag's quite safe, Mrs Matheson,' she said soothingly. 'It's in the bag with your other belongings.'

'Show me!'

Hannah fished in the large, brown paper bag printed with the label PATIENT PROPERTY and withdrew a cavernous black handbag that must have been purchased at least forty years ago.

'Give it to me!'

Hands gnarled with arthritis fumbled with the clasp. The bag was tipped upside down and several items fell onto Doris Matheson's lap. The contents of the opened packet of peppermints rolled off to bounce on the floor and a number of used, screwed-up handkerchiefs were thrown after them.

'There, I told you! There was a *thousand* dollars in here and it's *gone!*' A shaky finger pointed at Hannah. '*She's* taken it! Call the police!'

Ryan wasn't content to observe now. He was standing at the end of the bed. Faded blue eyes peered suspiciously at the tall, broad masculine figure.

'Are *you* the police?'

Ryan flashed the ghost of a wink at both Jennifer and Hannah. 'I've had some experience with handcuffs, if that's any help.'

Hannah shut her eyes briefly. How did Ryan get away with this sort of behaviour? Sometimes, if he was any more laid back, he'd be asleep. What a shame Doris hadn't stayed asleep. She was sniffing imperiously now.

'Arrest that woman,' she commanded.

'Dr Jackson?' Ryan eyed Hannah with great interest. She

couldn't help the way the corners of her mouth twitched. This *was* pretty funny. It was just a shame it was going to give Ryan ammunition he wouldn't hesitate to use.

'She's stolen my money.'

Ryan stepped closer. He leaned down and smiled at Doris. One of those killer smiles he usually reserved for the women he was flirting with. Which was just about every female member of staff.

Except Hannah.

His voice was a deep, sexy rumble. *'Really?'*

Doris Matheson stared back. Her mouth opened and then closed. Hannah could swear she fluttered her eyelashes and stifled another sigh at the typical feminine reaction to being the centre of this man's attention. The coy smile Ryan received was only surprising because of the age of their patient.

'What's your name, young man?'

'Ryan Fisher, ma'am.'

'And you're a policeman?'

'Not really.' Ryan's tone was that of a conspirator revealing a secret. 'I'm a doctor.'

The charm he was exuding was palpable. Totally fake but, for once, Hannah could appreciate the talent. It wasn't being directed at her, was it? She didn't need to arm herself with the memories of the misery men like Ryan could cause the women who trusted them. It was certainly defusing a potentially aggravating situation here.

'Ooh,' Doris said. 'Are you going to look after me?'

'You're about to go to X-Ray, Mrs Matheson,' Hannah said. 'What for?'

'We think you've broken your hip.'

'How did I do that?'

'You fell over.'

'Did I?' The question, like the others, was directed at Ryan despite it being Hannah who was supplying the answers.

'Yes.' Hannah looped her stethoscope back around her neck.

'And we can't find any medical reason why you might have fallen.' The cause had been obvious as soon as Hannah had been within sniffing distance of her patient. She hadn't needed the ambulance officer's report of an astonishing number of empty whisky bottles lined up on window-sills.

Ryan was smiling again but with mock severity this time. 'Have you had something to drink tonight, Mrs Matheson?'

She actually giggled. 'Call me Doris, dear. And, yes, I do like a wee dram. Helps me sleep, you know.'

'I'm sure it does, Doris.' Ryan's tone was understanding. He raised an eyebrow. 'But it can make it difficult to remember some things, too, can't it?'

'Ooh, yes.' Doris was looking coy again. 'Do you know, I almost forgot where the bathroom was one night?'

'Did you forget how much money you might have had in your purse, too?'

'I *never* keep money in my purse, dear! It might get stolen.'

'It might, indeed.' Hannah got a 'there you go, all sorted' kind of glance from Ryan. She tried hard to look suitably grateful.

'I keep it in the fridge,' Doris continued happily. 'In the margarine tub.'

'Good thinking.' Ryan stepped back as an orderly entered the cubicle. 'Maybe I'll see you when you get back from X-Ray, Doris.'

'Oh, I hope so, dear.'

Hannah held up her hand as her patient's bed was pushed away. 'Don't say it,' she warned.

'Say what?' Ryan asked innocently.

'Anything about naughty girls,' Jennifer supplied helpfully. 'Or arresting them. And especially nothing about handcuffs.'

'Not even fluffy ones?'

Jennifer gave him a shove. 'Go away. Try and find something useful to do.'

They were both laughing as Ryan walked away. Relaxed. Enjoying the diversion of an amusing incident. But Jennifer could afford to enjoy Ryan's company, couldn't she? Happily married with two adorable small children at home, she was in no danger of being led astray.

Neither was Hannah, of course. She knew too much about men like Ryan Fisher. Great-looking, *fun* men like the ones who'd made her mother's life a misery after her dad died, not to mention the guy who'd broken her sister's heart not so long ago.

Hannah only ever let herself get involved with nice, trustworthy, serious men like her father had been. She'd believed herself to be totally immune to men of Ryan's ilk.

Until three months ago.

Until she'd met Ryan Fisher.

Jennifer was still smiling as she tidied the ECG leads away. 'I still can't believe you're taking time off,' she told Hannah. 'I've never even known you to be sick. You're the one who always fills in for other people like Ryan when *they* take days off work.'

Hannah glanced towards the central desk. Ryan—the king of holidays and all other good things life had to offer—was now leaning casually on the counter, talking to a tired-looking receptionist. Probably telling her one of his inexhaustible supply of dumb blonde jokes. Sure enough, a smile was starting to edge the lines of weariness from Maureen's face.

'I'm going to check the trauma room while it's quiet,' Hannah told Jennifer.

'I'll help you.' Hannah's news of taking time off had clearly intrigued her friend, who didn't consider their conversation finished. 'And there I was thinking that, if *I* didn't drag you out occasionally, you'd spend all your time off studying or something.'

Hannah picked up the laryngoscope on top of the airway trolley and pulled the blade open to check that the battery for the light was still functional. 'Are you saying I have no life?'

'I'm saying your career takes the prize as your raison d'etre.'

'I always wanted to be a doctor.' Hannah snapped the blade

back in line with its handle, switching off the light. 'Now that I *am* one, I intend to be a very good one.'

'You *are* a very good one. The best.'

'We'll see.' The glance between the two women acknowledged the growing speculation within the department over who was going to win the new consultant position. She had been the only serious contender until Ryan had thrown his hat into the ring today. Was that why she was so aware of his presence in the department tonight? Why everything about him seemed to be rubbing her up the wrong way even more than usual?

'Anyway...' The wind had been taken out of Jenny's sails, but not by much. She opened a box of syringes to restock the IV trolley. 'You don't need to prove how good you are by living and breathing emergency medicine.'

'So you're saying I'm an emergency department geek?' Hannah tilted the ceiling-mounted, operating-theatre light so it was in a neutral position. It would be fair enough if she was. Hannah loved this space. Fabulous lighting, X-ray and ultrasound facilities, every piece of equipment they could possibly need to cover the basics of resuscitation and stabilisation of a critically ill patient. Airway, breathing, circulation. To be faced with a life-threatening emergency and succeed in saving that life was all the excitement Hannah needed in her life.

Jenny caught her expression and clicked her tongue with mock exasperation. 'I'm just saying you could do with more in your life than work.'

'And that's precisely why I'm taking a few days off.'

'Touché.' Jenny grinned, magnanimous in defeat. 'OK.' She shoved the syringes into their allocated slot and then used her forefinger to stir the supply of luer plugs and IV connectors, pretending to count. 'So where the hell is Crocodile Creek, anyway?'

'Australia. Far north Queensland.'

'Oh! Has this got something to do with your sister?'

'Yes. I've been invited to a wedding.'

'Susie's getting *married*?'

'No, though I'm sure she'd be over the moon if it *was* her wedding. She's being a bridesmaid to her best friend, Emily.'

'Do you know Emily?'

'No.'

'So why have you been invited to her wedding?'

'Well…' Hannah leaned against the bed for a moment. It wasn't often they got a quiet spell, even at 2 a.m. on a Monday morning and the break hadn't gone on long enough to get boring yet. 'Susie didn't have a partner to invite and we haven't seen each other since she jumped the ditch and came to New Zealand for Christmas. I'm starting to feel guilty about how long it's been.'

'It's only March and it's a hell of a long way to go to ease a guilty conscience. Auckland to Cairns is about a six-hour flight, isn't it?'

'It sure is.' Hannah groaned. 'And then there's the little plane from Cairns to Crocodile Creek, which will take another couple of hours, I guess.'

'It must be a long way north.'

'About as far as you can get. The hospital there is the rescue base for the whole of far north Queensland. That's why I need the Friday on top of the weekend. I have to get right into the heartland of sugar and cane toads.'

'Eew!'

'Actually, it's right on the coast. It sounds gorgeous.'

'You've never been there before?'

'No, and Susie's been living there for as long as I've been working here. It's high time I checked out what my little sister is up to.'

'I thought you were twins.'

By tacit consent, the doctor and nurse were leaving the trauma room, satisfied it was ready for a new emergency. Hopefully, they'd be back in there soon with some real work to do.

'She's four minutes younger than me.'

'And she's a physiotherapist, right?'

'Yeah. She started medical school with me but she hated it. Too much pressure.'

'You must be quite different.'

'Personality-wise, definitely. To look at, no. We're identical.'

'Wow! Do you have, like, that twin thing?'

'Which "twin thing" is that?' They were near the central desk now. Ryan had disappeared, presumably into the only cubicle with a drawn curtain. The nurse on triage duty, Wayne, was sitting, drumming his fingers on the counter.

'You know, when one twin sprains her ankle, say, here in Auckland and the other twin falls over in a supermarket in central London.'

Hannah laughed, dismissing the suggestion with a shake of her sleek head. But was it so ridiculous? Was it just that she was missing a sister who had always also been her best friend or did those niggling doubts about how happy Susie was have a basis in some form of telepathic communication? Was the urge to travel thousands of miles at a very inconvenient time to attend the wedding of two people she only knew through Susie's emails just an excuse?

'Apparently this wedding is going to be great fun.' Hannah tried to find a more rational explanation for the urge she hadn't been able to resist. 'The groom, Mike, is Greek and his parents own a boutique hotel right in the cove. Susie reckons it'll be the biggest party the Creek has ever seen.'

Jennifer's peal of laughter made several heads turn.

'What's so funny?' Hannah's eye was caught by the light on the radio receiver that linked the department with the ambulance service. It was blinking.

Jennifer could hardly get the words out clearly. 'You're going to *My Big Fat Creek Wedding*!'

Grinning, Hannah still managed to beat Wayne to the microphone. 'Emergency Department.'

'Auckland four eight here. How do you receive?'

'Loud and clear,' Hannah responded, her grin fading rapidly. 'Go ahead.'

'We're coming to you from the scene of a high-speed multiple MVA. The chopper's just landing to collect a second seriously injured patient who's currently trapped, but we're coming to you with a status-one seven-year-old boy.'

The grin had long gone. Status one was as serious as it could get. Under CPR, not breathing or uncontrollable haemorrhage were all possibilities for the priority designation. This ambulance would be coming towards the hospital under lights and sirens.

'Injuries?'

'Head and facial trauma. Partially unrestrained front-seat passenger—the safety belt wasn't latched securely.'

This wasn't the time to feel angry at someone failing to strap a child into a car seat properly. Or to wonder why they were travelling at 2 a.m. in the first place.

'Vital signs?'

'GCS of 3.'

The child was profoundly unconscious. Quite possibly due to bleeding around his brain.

'Airway?'

'Unsecured.' The paramedic raised his voice as the siren came on in the background. The vehicle must be in heavier traffic now. At night, just having the beacons flashing could be enough warning of the urgency of their mission. 'There's severe facial trauma and swelling. We've got an OP airway in but that's all.'

The boy needed intubation. Securing an airway and optimising oxygen levels were a priority in a head injury. Especially in a child because they had a greater chance of neurological recovery than an adult after a head injury and therefore warranted aggressive treatment in the early stages. If the paramedics had been unable to intubate due to the level of trauma, it could mean that this was going to be a challenging case.

Hannah could feel her adrenaline levels rising and the tension was spreading. Nearby staff were all listening avidly and the curtain on cubicle 4 flicked back to reveal that Ryan was also aware of what was happening. Hannah's heightened awareness registered the interest and at some subconscious level something like satisfaction was added to the emotional mix. She was taking this call.

This would be her case, not Ryan's. Just the kind of case she needed to showcase the skills that would be a major consideration in choosing the new consultant for the department.

'What's the oxygen saturation level?' she queried briskly.

'Ninety-four percent.'

Too low. 'Blood pressure?'

'One-thirty over sixty-five. Up from one-twenty five minutes ago.'

Too high for a seven-year-old. And rising. It could well be a sign of increasing intracranial pressure.

'Heart rate?'

'One hundred. Down from about one-thirty.'

Too slow for Hannah's peace of mind. And dropping. It could also be a worrying sign. 'What's your ETA?'

'Approximately five minutes.'

'We'll be ready for you.' Casting a glance over her shoulder, Hannah could see Ryan moving towards the resuscitation area she and Jennifer had just checked. Not that she was about to decline any assistance for dealing with the incoming case but she didn't want Ryan taking over. It wasn't as though there was only one victim arriving, was it? She pushed the button on the microphone again.

'Do you know the ETA for the chopper?'

'Negative. Fire service is on scene, though.'

It shouldn't take them long to cut the second victim clear of the wreckage, then. 'And that's also a status-one patient?'

'Affirmative. Chest trauma. It's the mother of our patient.'

Ryan would be able to lead the team on that case. In resus 2.

Or they could share the main trauma room if necessary. Hannah's plan of action was forming rapidly as she replaced the microphone.

'Put out a call for an anaesthetist, please, Wayne,' she directed. 'And let's get a neurosurgical consult down here. Sounds like we might need someone from Plastics, too. Jenny, you're on the trauma team tonight, aren't you?'

'Yes.'

'And you, Wayne?'

'Yes. Resus 1?'

Hannah nodded, already moving towards the area. She pulled one of the protective plastic aprons from the large box on the wall. Ryan was already tying his behind his back.

'Could be a tricky airway management,' he said.

'Mmm. I've called for some anaesthetic back-up but I'll see how I go.' The direct look Hannah gave Ryan could leave him in no doubt that she intended to lead this resuscitation effort. The subtle twitch of an eyebrow let her know the message had been received and understood. It also hinted at amusement rather than intimidation.

'I'll stay until the mother gets here,' he said calmly. 'In case you need a hand.'

'Thanks.' The acknowledgement was perfectly sincere. There was a child's life at stake here and Hannah would never let any personal considerations affect her performance. She would stand back in a flash if she thought Ryan's skills would improve the management. Never mind that he would get the credit for managing a difficult case.

It was just annoying that people that mattered were keeping a count of those credits at present. And disappointing that a competitive edge of any kind had crept into Hannah's working environment when one of the things she loved best about her work was the way a team of people could work together and the only kudos that really mattered was a successful outcome to that work.

The decision on the consultant's position was only a week or two away. A position that represented everything Hannah was striving towards in a career she was passionate about. Why had Ryan decided to compete at the last minute like this? It wasn't as if he really *needed* the position. He didn't have a massive student loan, the repayments of which would benefit enormously from an increase in salary. He didn't need to prove himself in a field that was still dominated by males in senior positions. He was an Australian. Auckland wasn't even his home town.

She couldn't help flicking a glance towards the tall man who had now donned protective eyewear and a pair of gloves and was lounging at the head end of the bed. Why hadn't Ryan Fisher just stayed on his side of the ditch? In that Sydney emergency department where he'd honed his not inconsiderable skills? Life would be so much easier if he had. And it wasn't just due to that professional competition.

Jenny pushed the IV trolley into an easily accessible position and then stood on tiptoe to check that the tubes attached to the overhead suction and oxygen supplies were firmly in place. It was still a stretch for her short stature and Ryan was quick to step forward.

Without a word, he saved Jenny the awkward task and then gave her one of those killer smiles in response to her thanks. The senior nurse turned back to the IV trolley but Hannah noticed the extra glance that went in Ryan's direction.

Not that he had noticed. The registrar was lounging again, his keen glance taking in the mill of the gathering trauma team and registering the growing tension.

The few minutes before the arrival of a serious case was a strange time. A calm before a storm of unknown proportions. Equipment was primed and ready. Staff were wearing protective gear and waiting. Wayne stood behind a kind of lectern that had the paperwork necessary to document every moment of the resuscitation effort and he was fiddling with a pen.

Hannah had pulled on gloves and was unrolling the airway

pack on the top of a stainless-steel trolley. Others were simply standing. Waiting. There was nothing to do until their patient came rolling through those double doors. Nobody liked to speculate in too much detail on what was about to arrive because that could give them tunnel vision. A conversation that required distraction of mental focus was just as unwanted. What usually happened was a bit of gossip or a joke. Light-hearted banter that could relieve tension before it achieved destructive proportions. Something that could be abandoned as easily as begun.

And Ryan could always be counted on to provide a joke that would make everybody laugh.

Everybody except Hannah. She made a point of never laughing at Ryan's jokes because the vast majority of them were at the expense of women with blonde hair. Like hers.

Sure enough, he was telling one now.

'So this blonde—Cindy—is in desperate financial straights and she prays for help. "Please, God, let me win the lottery or I'll have to sell my car." But she doesn't win so she prays again, "Please, God, let me win the lottery. I'm going to have to sell my car *and* my house."'

Everybody was listening. Or half listening. Waiting for the distant wail of the siren that would advertise that the calm was over. Hannah kept her gaze on the trolley, checking that there was a range of paediatric-sized tubes and that the laryngoscope was still working.

She didn't have to look at Ryan to know exactly what the image would be. He would be standing completely at ease with just a hint of a smile and a twinkle in those dark eyes that advertised an upcoming punchline. It might be a terrible joke but everybody would be listening and would be prepared to laugh because Ryan commanded that sort of attention. And popularity. Without even trying.

Hannah lips pressed themselves into a thinner line as she made sure that the more serious gear that might be needed for a surgical airway was at hand. No, it wasn't just the professional competition that irked her. It was the fact that she had been as attracted to Ryan as every other woman who'd set eyes on him from the moment he'd arrived in this department three months ago.

It had been so unexpected. He was the epitome of the type of man she had always steered very well clear of. Despised, even, thanks to the collateral damage she had seen them produce in the lives of women she cared about. One of life's golden people. She had probably been the first woman ever to freeze out an advance from him. Was that why he was persevering for so long? Did she represent some kind of challenge?

'She *still* didn't win,' Ryan was continuing. 'She's down on her knees, pleading and this time God speaks to her.' His voice dropped to a deep rumble that Hannah could actually feel in her bones. 'And he says, "Work with me here, Cindy. *Buy a ticket!*"'

Sure enough, there was a wave of laughter. A wave that faded with dramatic swiftness, drowned out by the faint wail of a siren. Then the sound of the approaching siren died as it sped onto the hospital grounds with just its beacons flashing. Seconds later, the stretcher appeared. A third crew member was moving rapidly beside the stretcher, a bag-mask unit over the face of the child, trying to keep oxygen levels up on the short journey between the ambulance and the trauma bay.

The team went into action as a unit. The transfer of the small body was smooth—made easier by the fact he was strapped to a backboard with a collar to protect his neck. And although this team was well used to seeing victims of major trauma, it was a shock to get their first close-up view of this little boy.

Waiting at the head of the bed to manage the airway, Hannah sucked in a quick breath that was almost a gasp. No wonder he hadn't been intubated and it would have been far too dangerous to attempt a nasopharyngeal airway. His nose and mouth were almost lost beneath swollen and lacerated tissue. There were obvious facial fractures and the eyelids were so swollen it was impossible to open them enough to assess the pupils with a torch.

'Do we know his name?'

'Brendon,' one of the paramedics supplied. 'His mother was initially conscious enough to be calling for him.'

He was wearing pyjamas, Hannah noticed as she leaned forward. Bright red racing cars on a blue background. 'Brendon, can you hear me?' She reached over his shoulder. Why had he been in a car in pyjamas instead of safely asleep in his bed? 'Squeeze my hand if you can hear me, sweetheart.'

A response hadn't really been expected and Hannah moved swiftly to take the tip of the suction unit Jennifer was holding. The child was moving air but there was a nasty bubbling sound and the probe on his finger revealed an oxygen saturation level that was far too low to be acceptable.

'Rapid sequence intubation?'

'If it's possible.' Hannah's gaze flicked up, relieved to find one of the senior anaesthetic registrars now standing right beside her.

Ryan was on the other side of the bed and farther down, moving in to assess IV access and flow and to look for other potential injuries as the pyjamas were cut clear of the small body.

ECG electrodes were being attached. Jennifer was using a bag mask to assist the delivery of oxygen. Hannah suctioned as much blood as she could from Brendon's mouth and nose.

'I can't see anything that clearly looks like CSF,' she said. Not that that discounted the possibility of skull fractures or spinal damage.

'Saturation's down to ninety per cent. Let's go for the intubation,' the anaesthetist advised. He took the bag mask from Jennifer and began to squeeze it rapidly, increasing the amount of oxygen reserves to cover the down time for trying to get a tube into Brendon's throat. He was clearly prepared to provide back-up rather than taking over the procedure.

Hannah drew in a slow breath to dispel any nerves. She heard herself issue instructions for the drugs needed, like suxamethonium to relax muscles and atropine to prevent the heart slowing dangerously. The formula for determining the size of the endotracheal tube was there instantly—the diameter equalled the age of the child divided by four, plus four.

'I'll need a 6 millimetre, uncuffed tube,' she informed Jennifer. 'And I want you to hold his head while we ease this collar off.'

It was a challenge, easing the blade of the laryngoscope past the swollen lips, broken teeth and a badly lacerated tongue, and Hannah had to use the suction unit more than once. It was an unexpectedly easy victory to visualise the vocal cords and slip the tube into place.

'I'm in.' The tone was one of satisfaction rather than triumph, however. There was still a long way to go but at least they were on the way to stabilising a critically ill patient.

'Well done.'

With her stethoscope now on Brendon's chest to check for correct tube placement and equal air entry, the quiet words of praise were muted and, for a moment, Hannah thought they might have come from Ryan.

But he was no longer standing beside Brendon. Hannah had been concentrating so hard on her task she had managed to block the sounds of the second patient's arrival and the stretcher was now being swiftly manoeuvred to the other side of the trauma room.

'Blunt chest trauma with tachycardia and hypotension. No sign of a tension pneumothorax.' she heard Ryan stating. 'We could be dealing with an acute pericardial tamponade.'

Would Ryan attempt a procedure to drain off the fluid inhibiting the function of the young mother's heart? It would be a very impressive coup as far as patient treatment if it was successful. Hannah couldn't help casting frequent glances towards his side of the room as she worked with the anaesthetist to get Brendon's ventilator setting right, supervised the amount of IV

fluid that was being administered, started an infusion of manni-
tol, which could help reduce intracranial pressure, and arranged
transfer for an urgent CT scan of the boy's head and neck.

Sure enough, Ryan was preparing to intubate his patient,
cardiac monitoring was established and kits requested for both
pericardiocentesis and chest drainage. Ryan looked determined
and confident but less than happy about the challenge he was
about to face. And no wonder. From what Hannah could see,
the woman's condition was deteriorating rapidly.

Ominous extra beats were disrupting the line of the ECG
trace on the screen of the monitor.

There was time for one more, rapid secondary survey on
Brendon before he was taken to the CT suite.

'Some of these bruises look old,' she commented.

'Maybe he plays rugby,' Jennifer suggested.

'You reckon his mother does as well?' Wayne had been helping Ryan's team in the initial preparation of his patient. 'She's
covered in bruises as well.'

Hannah eyed the clothing remnants Wayne was putting into
a patient property bag. 'Dressing-gown?' she queried.

He nodded. 'I don't think their trip was planned.'

A police officer was standing well to one side of the now
crowded area. 'Have any relatives been contacted?' Hannah
asked him.

'We didn't need to. The car she was driving had just been
reported stolen.' The police officer's face was grim. 'By her
husband.'

Hannah absorbed the information like a kind of physical
blow. Was her patient an innocent young victim caught up in a
situation involving domestic violence? Had his mother's desperate bid to protect him ended in a disaster he might never recover from? Would he even still have a mother?

It seemed unlikely. Ryan was sounding uncharacteristically
tense as Brendon's stretcher was taken through the double doors
on the way to CT.

'We've got VF. She's arrested. Charging to 200 joules. Stand clear!' He looked up as he recharged the paddles. 'Hannah, are you free?'

Hannah's hesitation was only momentary. She had been planning to follow protocol and accompany Brendon but he already had an expert medical escort in the anaesthetic registrar. She knew what Ryan would do if the roles were reversed and *she* asked for assistance. Hannah turned back.

'I'm free,' she said quietly. 'What do you need?'

CHAPTER TWO

'WE'VE GOT SINUS RHYTHM.'

Ryan dropped the defibrillator paddles with relief. The same kind of relief he'd noted when Hannah had turned back to help before he'd delivered that last shock. Not that he'd doubted he could count on her in a professional capacity. He could see her pulling on gloves and positioning herself beside the tray containing the pericardiocentesis and chest drain kits as he reached to check his patient's pulse.

'Carotid is barely palpable,' he reported grimly.

'Systolic pressure is fifty-nine,' Wayne confirmed.

'Let's shut down the IV. Just run it enough to keep the vein open,' Ryan ordered. 'There's been no response to a fluid challenge and if we're dealing with thoracic haemorrhage it'll only be making things worse.'

'Ventricular ectopics starting again.' Hannah had an eye on the monitor screen. 'And the systolic pressure is dropping. Down to fifty-five.'

The patient was threatening to arrest again. Ryan reached for a scalpel and Hannah had the forceps ready to hand him a moment later. Then the cannula for the chest drain. In less than a minute, blood was draining freely into the bottle. Too freely. All too soon, the bottle was almost full.

'Have we got someone from Cardiothoracic on the way?'

'No.' Jennifer shook her head at Ryan's terse query. 'Sorry. They're unavailable for fifteen to twenty minutes. They're tied up in Theatre with a post-bypass complication.'

'Have we got a thoracotomy kit?' He could almost hear a collective intake of breath. 'She's exsanguinating from a chest injury and about to go into cardiac arrest again. A thoracotomy might be a long shot but it's the only hope we've got.' Ryan knew the statistics were not on his side but at least they would be doing something other than watching this woman bleed to death.

Hannah nodded once, as though she had gone through the same thought processes and was in agreement with him. 'Want me to scrub as well?'

'Yes. Thanks.'

Wayne was sent to find the rarely used sterile kit. Jennifer took over the task of manually ventilating their patient. Ryan scrubbed fast. Ideally he should have the chest opened in less than two minutes. Faster, if there was another cardiac arrest.

'Have you done this before?' Hannah squeezed soap into her hands beside him.

'Yes. You?'

'Never even seen it.'

'Know the indications?'

'Penetrating thoracic injury with traumatic arrest or unresponsive hypotension or blunt injury with unresponsive hypotension or exsanguination from the chest tube. Overall survival is between four and thirty-three per cent but higher for penetrating injury.'

'We've got VF again,' Jennifer warned. 'No...it's asystole.'

Speed was now critical. A flat-line ECG meant that the heart couldn't be shocked into producing a rhythm again. Chest compressions on someone with blunt trauma were also contraindicated because it could worsen the injury. Opening the chest was the only option with any hope at all now.

It was good that Hannah had never seen the technique. Explaining things as he started this incredibly invasive procedure somehow eased the tension of a desperate measure to save a life.

'We'll make bilateral thoracotomies in the fifth intercostal space, mid-axillary line—same as for a chest drain.' Ryan worked swiftly with a scalpel and then a heavy pair of scissors. 'I'll be ready for the Gigli saw in a sec.'

He showed her how to use the serrated wire saw, drawing a handle under the sternum with a pair of forceps and then joining the handles and using smooth, long strokes to cut through the sternum from the inside out.

Hannah was ready with the rib spreaders. For someone who hadn't done this before, her calmness and ability to follow direction was a huge bonus.

'You can see why this is called a "clam shell" thoracotomy,' he said as he spread the ribs away from the anterior incisions. 'Suction, thanks.' Ryan sucked out blood and clots from the chest cavity, hoping it would be enough for the heart to start beating again spontaneously.

It wasn't.

'Where's she bleeding from?'

'Haven't found it yet.' Ryan placed both hands around the heart. 'I'm starting internal cardiac massage. Can you find and compress the aorta against the spine, Hannah? We want to maximise coronary and cerebral perfusion. I'll clamp it in a minute.'

She was totally out of her depth here. It was a huge relief when back-up from the cardiothoracic surgeons finally arrived. They were impressed with Ryan's management of the case so far, which was hardly surprising. Hannah wouldn't have had the confidence or skill to go further than the chest drain insertion.

The thought that Ryan might deserve the consultant's position more than she did was not a pleasant one.

Edged out as people with far more experience than she had took over, Hannah could only watch. It was hard, feeling the tension and increasing frustration as they failed to get the young woman's heart started again, having controlled the haemorrhage from the damaged aorta.

Maureen's signal, with the message that Brendon was now in the paediatric ICU and an invitation to discuss the results of the CT scan with the consultant, was welcome. Hannah slipped, unnoticed, from the resuscitation area.

She couldn't afford to stand around admiring Ryan's skill and thinking how easily he might win the position she'd wanted for so long. Or to share his disappointment at the inevitable failure he was facing. Empathy would create a connection that was too personal. Even worse than laughing at one of his stupid jokes. It would only make it that much harder to maintain the necessary distance between them.

Any reduction in that distance could only make her vulnerable.

And Hannah Jackson did not do vulnerable.

She'd always been the strong one. Ever since she was ten years old and her father's sudden death had made her small family almost fall apart. Hannah had been strong for her mother. For Susie. For herself.

The lesson had been hard but valuable. Strength was protection. The only way to get through life without being scarred too deeply.

Being too tired didn't help when it came to being strong.

When Hannah entered the staffroom nearly an hour later, she could feel Ryan's dejection all too easily. He had his back to her as he made coffee but his body language said it all. Slumped shoulders. Bent head. The way he was stirring his mug so slowly. If it had been any other colleague she wouldn't have hesitated in offering commiseration. A comforting touch or even a hug. But this was Ryan. Distance was obligatory.

'No go, huh?'

'Nah.' Ryan straightened his back. 'Didn't really expect to win that one but it was worth a try. Want coffee?'

'Sure, but I'll make it.'

Ryan was already spooning coffee into a second mug. 'You take sugar?'

'No.'

'Milk?'

'No.'

He'd been in the department for three months and didn't know how she took her coffee but she was willing to bet he'd know the preferences of all the female staff who responded to his flirting. And that was every one of them.

Except her.

'So how's your little guy, then?'

'Not flash. He's in paediatric ICU but the scan was horrible. Multi-focal bleeds. If he does survive, he'll be badly brain damaged.'

'Might be better if he doesn't, then. You saw the father?'

'Yeah.' There was no need for further comment. The glance Ryan gave Hannah as he handed her the mug of black coffee told her he shared her opinion that the man she'd had to talk to about the serious condition of his child was an uncaring brute. Responsible for the death of his wife and quite likely his son, not to mention the admittedly less serious injuries sustained by the other drivers involved, and he hadn't given the impression of being overly perturbed about any of it. 'And they can't even charge him for anything.'

'No.' Ryan went and sat down on one of the comfortable armchairs dotted around the edge of the room.

The silence was heavy. Too heavy.

Ryan cleared his throat. 'Hey, have you heard the one about the blonde who didn't like blonde jokes?'

Hannah sighed. She sat down at the central table, deliberately putting Ryan out of sight behind her right shoulder. Maybe it wasn't good to sit in a depressed silence but this was going a bit too far in the other direction, wasn't it? She sipped her coffee without saying anything but Ryan clearly ignored the signals of disinterest.

'She went to this show where a ventriloquist was using his dummy to tell blonde jokes. You know, like,how do you change a blonde's mind?' He raised his voice and sounded as though he was trying to speak without moving his lips. "Blow in her ear!" And what do you do if a blonde throws a pin at you? "Run, she's still holding the grenade."'

'Yeah, yeah.' Hannah allowed herself to sound annoyed. 'I know.'

'Well, so did this blonde in the audience. She was furious. She jumps to her feet. "I've had enough of this", she shouts. "How dare you stereotype women this way? What does the colour of someone's hair have to do with her worth as a human being? It's people like you that keep women like me from reaching my full potential. You and your kind continue to perpetrate discrimination against not only blondes but women in general and it's *not* funny!"'

'Mmm.' Despite herself, Hannah was listening to the joke. So Ryan was actually aware of why someone like herself might take offence at his humour? Interesting. Did that mean he was intentionally trying to get under her skin? That his charm with her was as fake as it had been with Doris Matheson and he actually disliked her type as much as she did his?

Ryan's tone was deadpan. 'The ventriloquist was highly embarrassed. He goes red and starts apologising profusely but the blonde yells at him again. "Stay out of this, mister. I'm talking to that little jerk on your knee!"'

Hannah snorted. Somehow she managed to disguise the reluctant laughter as a sound more like derision. She didn't want to laugh, dammit! Not at one of Ryan's jokes and not when she'd just been through a gruelling, heart-breaking and probably fruitless couple of hours' work. She knew exactly why he was trying to make her laugh. It had to be the quickest way of defusing an overly emotional reaction to a case. But if she let him make her feel better, it would be worse than empathising with *him*. She could feel the connection there, waiting to happen. It needed dealing with. She had to push Ryan as far away as possible.

'You just can't help yourself, can you?'

'I thought you might appreciate that one.'

'What makes you think I'm in the mood for jokes right now?' Hannah swivelled so that she could give Ryan a direct look. 'Doesn't anything dent your warped sense of humour? Even a battered wife who died trying to get her child to a safe place?'

'That's precisely why I thought a joke might be a good idea,' Ryan said wearily. 'Sorry, maybe I should have left you to wallow in how awful it was. Maybe question your abilities and wonder endlessly what you might have been able to do better.'

'It might be more appropriate than telling jokes.'

'Really? What if another major case comes in in the next five minutes, Hannah? You going to be in a fit state to give that person the best you can?'

'Of course I am.'

'Well, lucky you. Some of us need to distract ourselves. Lift our spirits a bit. There's always time for wallowing later.'

'I don't believe you ever wallow,' Hannah snapped. She wasn't going to admit that even that stifled snort of laughter *had* done something to ease the emotional downside of this job. She'd rather believe that it was being able to channel her frustration and anger into a confrontation that had been building for some time. 'And you distract yourself often enough to be a liability in this department. You've been here, what, three months? And how many times have you taken time off to flit back to Australia? Four, five times? I should know—it's usually me that does extra shifts to cover the gaps.'

This distraction was working wonderfully well. Hannah was really hitting her stride.

'You know your problem, Ryan? You're shallow. You're so

intent on having a fun life you can't even spare the time to think about someone else.'

'Oh?' Ryan was staring at Hannah and she'd never heard him use such an icy tone. 'Shallow, am I?'

'You might find it more beneficial to your career to review cases like we've just had. You never know. Try having a professional discussion with a colleague next time instead of telling *stupid* jokes. You might learn something.'

'From you?' Ryan snorted. 'I doubt it.'

'Why?' Hannah's tone was waspish. 'Because I'm blonde?'

'No.' Ryan stood up, abandoning his cup of coffee. 'Because you're less experienced professionally and far less competent when it comes to relationships between people. You're judgmental, Dr Jackson, and you don't even bother finding out the facts before you make those judgments.'

He stalked behind Hannah and she had to swivel her head to keep glaring at him as he made his parting shot. 'And when I'm consultant, it might be nice if you made *me* coffee, babe. Not the other way round.'

'Dream on, mate!' What a pathetic rejoinder. Hannah could only hope Ryan would take it as she meant it—referring to the consultancy position and not the coffee-making.

Jennifer came in a few seconds after Ryan had left. Her eyebrows had disappeared under her fringe.

'What on earth's wrong with Ryan? I've never seen him look so grumpy!'

'He's a grumpy man.'

Jennifer laughed. 'He is not and you know it. He's a lovely man and if you weren't trying so hard not to like him you would have realised that by now.'

'I'm not trying hard,' Hannah protested. 'It's easy. Besides, it was your friend in Sydney that told you what a reputation he had for breaking hearts. The man needs an emotional health warning attached.'

Jennifer shook her head, smiling. 'Yeah...right.' She took another glance at Hannah. 'You look pretty grumpy yourself.'

'It's been a bad night. I hate cases like that—especially when they shouldn't have happened in the first place.' She sighed again. 'And I'm tired. Roll on 7 a.m.'

'Roll on Friday more like. Isn't that when you leave for a few days' R & R in the sun?'

'Sure is.' Hannah's spirits finally lifted—a lot more than Ryan's joke had achieved. 'You know, I'm finally really looking forward to this trip.'

'I could do with some time away from this place myself. Could be just what the doctor ordered. For both of us.'

'Mmm.' Hannah's agreement was wholehearted. But it wasn't the place she needed the break from. A few days away from Ryan Fisher was definitely what this doctor was ordering.

Hannah Jackson could go to hell in a hand basket.

The glimpse of a woman with sleek blonde hair disappearing into the melee of economy class was enough of a reminder to sink Ryan Fisher's spirits with a nasty jolt.

He slid his cabin baggage into the overhead locker with the same ease he slid his long body into the comfortable window seat at the rear of the business class section of the plane. Seconds later, he returned the smile of a very pretty young air hostess.

'Orange juice would be lovely,' he agreed. 'Exactly what I need.'

The frosted glass was presented while economy-class passengers were still filing past, but Ryan killed the faintly embarrassed reaction to the envious glances. Why shouldn't he travel in comfort? He had to do it often enough to make it a boring inconvenience and he'd decided he may as well make the travel as enjoyable as possible when the destination usually wasn't.

At least this time he could look forward to what lay at the other end of his journey.

'Is there anything else you need, sir?'

Ryan suppressed a wry smile along with the temptation to ask the crew member for a thousand things. How about a miraculous cure for a little girl in Brisbane that he had far more than just a bond of family with? Or perhaps freedom from the ridiculously powerful attraction he had felt for Hannah Jackson ever since he'd first laid eyes on her three months ago?

No. He was over that. As of last Monday night when she'd told him exactly what she thought of him. She hated him. He was shallow—telling jokes when he should be taking on board the misery of others. Lazy—taking time off to flit back to Australia to have fun at regular intervals. Out to win the job she felt was rightfully hers.

Ironic that he'd actually set out to catch Hannah's attention by demonstrating his clinical ability. He hadn't expected the head of department to twist his arm and put his name forward for the upcoming consultancy position but then he'd thought, Why not? The anchor of a permanent job could be just what he needed to sort out his life. And at least that way Hannah would see him as an equal.

Would really *see* him.

How idiotic would it be to waste any more time or emotional energy hankering after someone who didn't even have any respect, let alone liking, for him?

'No, thanks.' He smiled. 'I'm fine.'

Ryan sipped his chilled juice, stretching his legs into the generous space in front of him and enjoying the fact that the seat beside him was empty. So were both the seats on the opposite side of the aisle. There was, in fact, only one other occupant of business class and Ryan found himself listening to the well-dressed man with an American accent telling the air hostess that all he wanted was to go to sleep and could he have one of those eye covers? Apparently he hadn't expected a diversion to Auckland or a night in an airport hotel and he'd had more than enough of travelling for now.

'It should have been a straightforward trip to Sydney and then

Cairns,' he was saying. 'Instead, I'm bunny-hopping through the south Pacific. Inefficient, that's what it is.'

'There's been a few disruptions due to some bad weather,' the hostess responded. 'Hopefully we'll be able to bypass it on this trip.'

Ryan didn't care if they hit a few bumps. Despite what Hannah thought of him, he didn't often get a smooth ride through life. OK, so maybe he didn't wear his heart on his sleeve and go around telling everyone his problems, but it was just as well, wasn't it? Imagine how low he'd be feeling right now if he'd made it obvious just how attracted he'd been to Hannah and had been squashed like the bug she clearly thought he was?

Well, she wouldn't get the opportunity now. No way. He wouldn't have her if she threw herself at him. Wrapped up in a ribbon and nothing else.

A soft sound like a strangled groan escaped. That short flight into fantasy wasn't likely to help anything. He drained his glass and handed it back as part of the preparation for take-off. Then he closed his eyes as the big jet rolled towards the end of the runway. Maybe he should follow the example of the other occupant of business class and escape into a few hours of peaceful oblivion.

The trip promised to be anything but restful. Hannah had an aisle seat, for which she was becoming increasingly grateful. It meant she could lean outwards.

She had to lean outwards because the man beside her was one of the fattest people Hannah had ever seen. He could easily have used up two seats all by himself but somehow he had squeezed in. Apart from the parts of his body that oozed through the gaps above and below the armrests and encroached considerably on Hannah's space. Any sympathy for his obvious discomfort had been replaced by a more selfish concern about her own when the personality of her travelling companion began to reveal itself.

'Name's Blair,' he boomed at her. 'How's it going?' He certainly wasn't shy. 'They make these seats a bit bloody small these days, eh? Just want to pack us in like sardines so they make a profit.'

'Mmm.' And they were allocated the same amount of baggage weight, Hannah thought crossly. What would happen if every passenger was Blair's size? Could the plane flip over because the baggage compartment was too light? Use twice as much fuel? Drop out of the sky?

Hannah wasn't a great fan of flying. She leaned further into the aisle and gripped the armrest on that side as the plane gathered speed.

'Not keen on flying, huh?' Blair was leaning, too. 'Wanna hold my hand?'

'Ah...no, thanks.' Hannah screwed her eyes shut. 'I'm just fine.'

'It's OK. ' Blair was laughing as the wheels left the tarmac. 'I'm single.'

There was no point pretending to be asleep because Blair didn't seem to notice. He obviously liked to think aloud and kept himself amused by a running commentary on the choice of movies available, the tourist attractions of Cairns showcased in the airline magazine and the length of time it was taking for the cabin crew to start serving refreshments.

The reason for any delay was revealed when the captain's voice sounded in the cabin.

'G'day, folks. Welcome aboard this Air New Zealand flight to Cairns. We're expecting a bit of turbulence due to strong westerly winds courtesy of a tropical cyclone in the Coral Sea region going by the name of Willie. I'm going to keep the crew seated until we get through this next layer of cloud.'

Blair made a grumbling sound.

'Once we're cruising at around thirty-five thousand feet, things should get a bit smoother,' the captain continued. 'You'll be free to move around the cabin at that point but I would suggest that while you're in your seats you do keep your seat belts firmly fastened.'

Sure enough, the flight became smoother and the cabin crew began to serve drinks and meals. The steward that stopped beside Hannah cast a second glance at her companion, listened to him patiently while he complained about the delay in being fed and then winked at Hannah.

'I'll be back in a tick,' he said.

When he returned, he bent down and whispered in Hannah's ear. Then he opened the overhead locker and removed the bag she specified. Hannah unclipped her seat belt and stood up with a sigh of relief.

'Hey!' Blair was watching the removal of the bag with concern. 'Where're you going, darling?'

'We've got a bit of room up front,' the steward informed him. 'I'm just juggling passengers a bit. If you lift the armrest there, Sir, I'm sure you'll find the journey a lot more comfortable.'

Much to Hannah's astonishment, 'up front' turned out to be an upgrade to business class. Her eyes widened as she realised she was going to have a window seat—no, both the seats—all to herself.

'You're an angel of mercy,' she told the steward. 'Wow! I've never flown business class before.'

'Enjoy!' The steward grinned. 'I'll make sure they bring you something to drink while you settle in and have a look at the breakfast menu.'

Hannah sank into the soft seat, unable to contain her smile. She stretched out her legs and wiggled her toes. Not much chance of developing a DVT here. There was any amount of elbow room, as well. She tested it, sticking her arms out like wings. She even flapped them up and down a little. Just as well there was no one to see her doing a duck impression.

Or was there? Hannah hadn't yet considered the possibility of a passenger on the other side of the aisle. She turned her head swiftly, aware of a blush starting. And then she recognised the solitary figure by the window and she actually gasped aloud.

Glaring was probably the only description she could have used for the way Ryan Fisher was looking at her.

'Oh, my God!' Hannah said. 'What are *you* doing here?'

CHAPTER THREE

'I WAS ABOUT to ask you the same thing.'

'I got upgraded.' Hannah hadn't intended to sound defensive. Why did this man always bring out the worst in her? 'Things were a bit crowded down the back.'

'Here you go, Dr Jackson.' A pretty, redheaded hostess held out a tray with a fluted glass on it. 'And here's the menu. I'll come back in a minute to see what you'd like for breakfast.'

'Thank you.' Hannah took a sip of her juice and pretended to study the menu, which gave a surprisingly wide choice for the first meal of the day. There were hours of this flight left. Was she going to have to make conversation with Ryan the whole way?

It was some sort of divine retribution. Hannah had been feeling guilty ever since Monday night when she'd let fly and been so rude to a colleague. She couldn't blame him for either the retaliation or the way he'd been avoiding her for the last few days. The personal attack had been unprofessional and probably undeserved. He couldn't know where the motivation had come from and Hannah certainly couldn't tell him but…maybe she ought to apologise?

She flicked a quick glance from the menu towards Ryan. He

was still glaring. He wasn't about to use their first meeting away from work to try building any bridges, was he?

Hannah wished she hadn't looked. Hadn't caught those dark eyes. She couldn't open her mouth to say anything because goodness only knew what might shoot out, given the peculiar situation of being in this man's company away from a professional setting. Imagine if she started and then couldn't stop?

If she told him her whole life history? About the man her mother had really fallen in love with—finally happy after years of getting over her husband's tragic death. Of the way she'd been used and then abandoned. Hannah had known not to trust the next one that had come along. Why hadn't her mother been able to see through him that easily? Perhaps the attraction to men like that was genetic and too powerful to resist. It might explain why Susie had made the same mistake. Fortunately, Hannah was stronger. She might *want* Ryan Fisher but there was no way she would allow herself to *have* him.

Oddly, the satisfying effect of pushing him firmly out of her emotional orbit the other night was wearing off. Here she was contemplating an apology. An attempt at establishing some kind of friendship even.

Ryan hadn't blinked.

Hannah realised this in the same instant she realised she could only have noticed because she hadn't looked away. The eye contact had continued for too long and… Oh, *God!* What if Ryan had seen even a fraction of what she'd been thinking?

Attack was the best form of defence, wasn't it?

'Why are you staring at me?'

'I'm still waiting for you to answer my question.'

'What question?'

'What you're doing here.'

'I told you, I got upgraded.'

'You know perfectly well that wasn't what I meant. What the hell are you doing on this flight?'

'Going to Cairns.' Hannah didn't need the change in Ryan's expression to remind her how immature it was to be so deliberately obtuse. She gave in. 'I've got a connecting flight at Cairns to go to a small town further north in Queensland. Crocodile Creek.'

Lips that were usually in some kind of motion, either talking or smiling, went curiously slack. The tone of Ryan's voice was also stunned.

'You're going to *Crocodile Creek*?'

'Yes.'

'So am I.'

'Did you decide what you'd like for breakfast, Dr Jackson?'

'What?' Hannah hadn't even noticed the approach of the redheaded stewardess. 'Oh, sorry. Um… Anything's fine. I'm starving!'

The stewardess smiled. 'I'll see what I can surprise you with.' She turned to the other side of the aisle. 'And you, Dr Fisher? Have you decided?'

'I'll have the fresh fruit salad and a mushroom omelette, thanks.'

Ryan didn't want to be surprised by his breakfast. Maybe he'd just had enough of a surprise. As had Hannah. She waited only a heartbeat after the stewardess had moved away.

'Is there a particular reason why you're going to Crocodile Creek at this particular time?"

'Sure is. I'm best man at my best mate's wedding.'

'Oh…' Hannah swallowed carefully. 'That would be… Mike?'

Ryan actually closed his eyes. 'And you know that because you're also invited to the wedding?'

'Yes.'

Ryan made a sound like a chuckle but it was so unlike the laughter Hannah would have recognised she wasn't sure it had anything to do with amusement. 'Don't tell me you're lined up to be the bridesmaid.'

'No, of course I'm not. I don't know Emily that well.'

'Thank God for that.'

'My sister's the bridesmaid.'

Ryan's eyes opened smartly. Hannah could have sworn she saw something like a flash of fear. Far more likely to be horror, she decided. He disliked her so much that the prospect of being a partner to her sister was appalling? That hurt. Hannah couldn't resist retaliating.

'My twin sister,' she said. She smiled at Ryan. 'We're identical.'

Ryan shook his head. 'I don't believe this.'

'It is a bit of a coincidence,' Hannah agreed, more cheerfully. Ryan was so disconcerted that she actually felt like she had control of this situation—an emotional upper hand—and that had to be a first for any time she had spent in Ryan's company, with the exception of Monday night. Maybe this wouldn't be so bad after all. 'So, how come you know Mike so well?'

But Ryan didn't appear to be listening. 'There are two of you,' he muttered. 'Unbelievable!'

Their conversation was interrupted by the arrival of their food. Hannah was hungry enough to get stuck into the delicious hot croissants and jam she was served. Ryan was only halfway through his fruit salad by the time she had cleaned her plate and he didn't look as though he was particularly enjoying the start of his meal.

Hannah had to feel sorry for him but she couldn't resist teasing just a little. She adopted the same, slightly aggrieved tone he had been using only a short time ago.

'You didn't answer my question.'

'What question?' Ryan wasn't being deliberately obtuse. He looked genuinely bewildered.

'How do you know Mike? The groom at this wedding we're both going to.'

'Oh… I was involved in training paramedics in the armed forces for a while, years ago. Mike was keen to add medical training to his qualifications as a helicopter pilot, having been in a few dodgy situations. We hit it off and have stayed in touch ever since.' Ryan stirred the contents of his bowl with the spoon. 'I was really looking forward to seeing him again,' he added sadly. 'The last real time we had together was a surfing holiday in Bali nearly three years ago. After he got out of the army but before he took himself off to the back of beyond.'

'Crocodile Creek does seem a bit out of the way,' Hannah had to agree. Besides, thinking about geography was a good way to distract herself from feeling offended that Ryan seemed to think all the pleasure might have been sucked from the upcoming weekend. 'It was easy enough to hop on a plane to Brisbane to spend a day or two with Susie.'

'I got the impression you never took time off.'

'I don't take rostered time off.'

'Unlike me.' Ryan said it for her. ''Cos you're not lazy.'

Hannah wasn't going to let this conversation degenerate into a personality clash. Here was the opportunity she had needed. 'I never said you were lazy, Ryan. You work as hard as I do. You're just more inclined to take time off.'

'For the purposes of having fun.'

'Well…yes…' Hannah shrugged. 'And why not?' Would this count as an apology, perhaps? 'All work and no play, etcetera.'

'Makes Jack a dull boy,' Ryan finished. 'And Jill a very dull girl.'

Was he telling Hannah she was dull? Just a more pointed comment than Jennifer telling her she was an ED geek? If he saw her as being more *fun*—say at a wedding reception—would he find her more attractive?

Hannah stomped on the wayward thought. She didn't want Ryan to find her attractive. She didn't want to find *him* attractive, for heaven's sake! It was something that had just happened. Like a lightning bolt. A bit of freak weather—like the cyclone currently brewing in the Coral Sea, which was again causing a bit of turbulence for the jet heading for Cairns.

The two cabin-crew members pushing a meal trolley through to economy class exchanged a doubtful glance.

'Should we wait a bit before serving the back section?'

'No.' The steward who had been responsible for Hannah's upgrade shook his head. 'Let's get it done, then we can clear up. If we're going to hit any really rough stuff, it'll be when we're north of Brisbane.'

Hannah tightened her seat belt a little.

'Nervous?' Ryan must have been watching her quite closely to observe the action.

'I'm not that keen on turbulence.'

'Doesn't bother me.' Ryan smiled at Hannah. Or had that smile been intended for the approaching stewardess? 'I quite like a bumpy ride.'

Hannah and Ryan both chose coffee rather than tea. Of course the smile had been for the pretty redhead. Likewise the comment that could easily have been taken as blatant flirting.

'I don't know Emily,' Ryan said. 'Maybe you can fill me in. She's a doctor, yes?'

'Yes. She's Susie's best friend.'

'Susie?'

'My sister.'

'The clone. Right. So how long has she been in Crocodile Creek?'

'About three years. She went to Brisbane to get some post-grad training after she finished her physiotherapy degree and she liked it so much she decided to stay.'

'I thought she was a doctor.'

'No. She started medical school with me but it wasn't what she wanted.'

'How come she lives in that doctors' house that used to be the old hospital, then?'

'She doesn't.'

'That's not what Mike told me.'

'Why would Mike be telling you about my sister?'

'He wasn't. He was telling me about his fiancée. Emily.' Ryan groaned. 'We're not on the same page here, are we?'

'No.' And they never would be. 'Sorry. I don't know much about Emily either, except that she's a really nice person and totally in love with Mike and his parents are thrilled and hoping for lots of grandchildren.'

Ryan was still frowning. 'If you don't know Emily and you don't know Mike, why have you been invited to their wedding?'

'As Susie's partner, kind of. We haven't seen each other since Christmas.'

'That's not so long ago.'

Hannah shrugged. 'It seems a long time. We're close, I guess.'

'Hmm.'

Ryan's thoughts may as well have been in a bubble over his head. As best man, he would have to partner Hannah's clone. Another woman who wouldn't be on the same page. Someone else who would think he was shallow and lazy and a liability.

Hannah opened her mouth to offer some reassurance. To finally apologise for losing it on Monday night in such an unprofessional manner. To suggest that they would both be able to have a good time at the wedding despite having each other's company enforced.

She didn't get the chance.

Her mouth opened far more widely than needed for speech as the plane hit an air pocket and seemed to drop like a rock. The fall continued long enough for someone further down the plane in economy to scream, and then they got to the bottom with a crunch and all hell broke loose.

The big jet slewed sideways into severe turbulence. The pitch of its engine roar increased. The water glass and cutlery on Hannah's tray slithered sideways to clatter to the floor. The seatbelt sign on the overhead panel flashed on and off repeatedly with a loud dinging noise. Oxygen masks were deployed and swung like bizarre, short pendulums. Children were shrieking and someone was calling for help. The stewardess who had been

pushing the meal trolley staggered through the curtain divid-
ing business class from the rest of the cabin, her face covered
in blood. She fell into the seat beside Hannah.

'I can't see anything!'

Hannah was still clutching her linen napkin in her hand.
She pushed the tray table up and latched it, giving her space
to turn to the woman beside her, who was trying to wipe the
blood from her eyes.

'Hold still!' Hannah instructed. She folded the napkin into
a rough pad. If her years of training and practice in emergency
departments had done nothing else, Hannah would always bless
the ability to focus on an emergency without going to pieces
herself. 'You've got a nasty cut on your forehead.' She pressed
the pad against the wound as best she could, with the plane continuing to pitch and roll.

'I came down on the corner of the trolley.'

'What's happening?' Ryan was out of his seat, hanging onto
an armrest for support.

By way of answer, calmly overriding the noise of the engines
and distressed passengers, came the voice from the flight deck.

'Sorry about this, folks. Bit of unexpected rough stuff. We
should be through this pretty fast. Please, return to your seats
and keep your belts firmly fastened for the moment.'

Ryan ignored the direction. 'Anyone else hurt back there?'

'I don't know.' The stewardess was leaning back in the seat,
her face pale beneath smeared blood. 'We were still serving
breakfast. It'll be a mess. I should go and help.'

Ryan held back the curtain to look into the main body of the
cabin. Clearly, he was trying to see where he might be needed
most urgently. Forgetting one's own fear and helping someone
who'd happened to land in the seat beside her was nothing com-
pared to the courage it would need to take command of the kind
of chaos Hannah could imagine Ryan assessing.

Mixed in with her admiration of his intention was a desire

to prove she could also rise to the occasion. Ryan's courage was contagious.

'Hold this.' Hannah took the hand of the stewardess and placed it over the pad. 'Keep firm pressure on it and the bleeding will stop soon. I'll come back and check on you in a bit.' She unclipped her seat belt and stood up. The oxygen mask bumped her head but Hannah ignored it. The jolt from the air pocket must have caused their deployment because she wasn't at all short of breath so the oxygen level had to be OK. Lurching sideways to get past the knees of the stewardess, Hannah found her arm firmly gripped by Ryan.

'What *do* you think you're doing, Hannah? Sit down and belt up.'

'Help!' A male voice was yelling loudly. 'We need a doctor!'

'Stay here,' Ryan ordered crisply. 'I'll go.'

But Hannah knew that her own courage was coming from the confidence Ryan was displaying. If he left, she might be tempted to strap herself safely back into her seat and wait for the turbulence to end.

People needed help.

'No,' she said. 'I'm coming with you.'

Something unusual showed in Ryan's eyes. Did he know how terrified she was? What an effort trying to match his bravery was?

Maybe he did. The glance felt curiously like applause. He let go of her arm and took her hand instead, to lead her through the curtain. Hannah found herself gripping his fingers. He'd only done it to save her falling if there was more turbulence, but she was going to allow herself to take whatever she needed from this physical connection. What did it matter, when it felt like they might all be going to plunge to their deaths at any moment?

She followed Ryan through the curtain to become the new focus for dozens of terrified passengers as they moved down the aisle. Some were wearing their oxygen masks, others trying to get them on. She saw a young woman with her face in her hands, sobbing. A much older woman, nursing what looked like a fractured wrist. A nun, clutching her crucifix, her lips moving in silent prayer. The steward was waving at them from the rear of the aircraft.

'Here! Help!' he shouted. 'I think this man's choking.'

'It's Blair!' Hannah exclaimed.

Her former seat neighbour was standing, blocking the aisle. His hand was around his neck in the universal signal of distress from choking and his face was a dreadful, mottled purple.

Ryan was moving fast. He let go of Hannah's hand to climb over the empty seat that had initially been hers to get behind Blair.

'I've tried banging him on the back,' the steward said unhappily.

Ryan put his arms around Blair but couldn't grasp his fist with his other hand to perform an effective Heimlich manoeuvre. There was just too much of Blair to encompass and there was no time. The huge man was rapidly losing consciousness and there was no way Ryan could support his weight unaided.

Blair slumped onto his back, blocking the aisle even more effectively. There was no way for anyone to move. Ryan looked up and Hannah could see he was aware of how impossible it was going to be to try and manage this emergency. She could also see that he had no intention of admitting defeat. It was a very momentary impression, however, because the plane hit another bump and Hannah went hurtling forward to land in a most undignified fashion directly on top of Blair.

She landed hard and then used her hands on his chest to push herself upright. Blair gave a convulsive movement beneath her and Hannah slid her legs in front of her old empty seat to try and slide clear. Ryan grabbed Blair's shoulder and heaved and suddenly Blair was on his side, coughing and spluttering. Ryan thumped him hard between his shoulder blades for good measure and the crisis was over, probably as quickly as it had begun, as Blair forcibly spat out what looked like a large section of a sausage.

'Let's sit you up,' Ryan said firmly.

Blair was still gasping for air and had tears streaming down his face but somehow, with the help of the steward and another passenger, they got him back into his seat. Hannah jerked the oxygen mask down to start the flow. At least one person was going to benefit from their unnecessary deployment.

'We're through the worst of it now, folks. Should be plain sailing from now on.'

The timing of the captain's message was enough to make Hannah smile wryly. Catching Ryan's gaze, her smile widened.

'He doesn't know how right he is, does he?'

Ryan grinned right back at her, with the kind of killer smile he gave to so many women. The kind that old Doris Matheson had received the other night. But it was the first time Hannah had felt the full force of it and for just a fraction of a second it felt like they had connected.

Really connected. More than that imaginary connection Hannah had taken from the hand-holding.

And it felt astonishingly good.

Good enough to carry Hannah through the next hour of helping to treat the minor injuries sustained. Splinting the Colles' fracture on the old woman's wrist, bandaging lacerations and examining bruises.

The other occupant of business class had been woken by the turbulence and offered his services.

'I'm a neurosurgeon,' he said. 'Name's Alistair Carmichael. What can I do to help?'

'We've got a stewardess with a forehead laceration,' Hannah told him. 'You're the perfect person to check and make sure she's not showing any signs of concussion—or worse. Mostly, I think it's going to be a matter of reassuring people.'

Hannah made more than one stop to check that Blair wasn't suffering any lingering respiratory distress.

Ryan worked just as hard. The first-aid supplies on the plane were rapidly depleted but it didn't matter. The plane was making a smooth descent into Cairns and Blair, who had been the closest to a fatal injury, was beaming.

'You saved my life, darling,' he told Hannah when he was helped from the plane at Cairns by paramedics who would take him to hospital for a thorough check-up.

'Yes.' Ryan's voice seemed to be coming from somewhere very close to Hannah's ear and she gave an involuntary shiver. 'Interesting technique, that. You should write it up for a medical journal.'

Hannah turned her head. Was he making fun of her?

'The "Jackson manoeuvre",' Ryan said with a grin.

Hannah was too tired to care whether he was laughing at her. And the incident *had* had a very funny side. 'Yeah,' she said. 'Or maybe the "Blonde's Heimlich"?'

Much to Ryan's disappointment, they weren't sitting anywhere near each other on the connecting flight to Crocodile Creek, despite the much smaller size of the aircraft. It seemed to have been taken over by a large contingent of rather excited Greek people who had to be part of Mike's family. They were too busy talking and arguing with each other to take notice of strangers, and that suited Ryan just fine. He was tired and felt like he had too much to think about anyway.

Fancy Hannah being able to laugh at herself like that! Or had it been some kind of dig at him? Ryan knew perfectly well how his blonde jokes got up her nose. They had become a kind of defence mechanism so that no one would guess how disappointed he was when Hannah took no notice of him. He might get a negative reaction to the jokes but at least she knew he existed.

And what about the way she hadn't hesitated to go and help others when she had clearly been terrified herself by the turbulence. That had taken a lot of courage. She obviously didn't like flying. Ryan had seen the way she'd looked at the size of their connecting aircraft. He hoped she was as reassured as he had been by the information that the tropical storm was now moving out to sea and their next journey would be much smoother. They were even forecasting relatively fine weather for the rest of the day.

'But make the most of it,' the captain warned. 'It could turn nasty again tomorrow.'

That caused the volume of conversation around him to increase dramatically as the Greek wedding guests discussed the ramifications of bad weather. Ryan tuned out of what sounded like superstitious babble of how to overcome such a bad omen.

Hannah was sitting as far away as it was possible to be down the back of the cabin. Had she arranged that somehow? She was beside the American neurosurgeon, Alistair, who had proved himself to be a very pleasant and competent man during the aftermath of the turbulence. Distinctive looking, too, with those silver streaks in his dark hair. He had put the jacket of his pin-striped suit back on but he was asleep again.

There was an odd relief in noticing that. Surely any other man would find Hannah as attractive as he did? And he hadn't known the half of it, had he? No wonder he hadn't recognised her from behind on the larger plane. He'd only seen her with her sleek blonde hair wound up in a kind of knot thing and baggy scrubs covering her body. The tight-fitting jeans and soft white shirt she was wearing today revealed a shape as perfect as her face.

Impossible to resist the urge to crane his neck once more and check that the American was still asleep. He was. So was Hannah, which was just as well. Ryan wouldn't want her to know he'd stolen another glance. He settled back and dozed himself and it seemed no time until the wheels touched down on a much smaller runway than the last one.

He was here. At the back of beyond, in Crocodile Creek. For three whole days. With Hannah Jackson. What had happened to that fierce resolve with which he had started this journey? That

Hannah could go to hell because he was no longer interested? That he was completely over that insane attraction?

It had been shaken by that turbulence, that's what. It had gone out the window when he'd taken hold of her hand and she hadn't pulled away. Had—amazingly—held his hand right back.

Ryan sighed deeply and muttered inaudibly.

'Let the fun begin.'

CHAPTER FOUR

HEAT HIT HER like a blast from a furnace door swinging open.

Thanks to the early departure from Auckland and the time difference between Australia and New Zealand, it was the hottest part of the day when they arrived in Crocodile Creek.

The bad weather that had made the first leg of the journey so memorable seemed to have been left well behind. The sky was an intense, cobalt blue and there were no clouds to filter the strength of the sun beating down. It was hot.

Very hot.

Descending the steps from the back of the small plane onto the shimmering tarmac, Hannah realised what a mistake it had been to travel in jeans.

'I'm cooking!' She told Susie by way of a greeting as she entered the small terminal building. 'How hot *is* it?'

'Must be nearly forty degrees.' Susie was hugging Hannah hard. 'What on earth possessed you to wear jeans?' She was far more sensibly dressed, in shorts, a singlet top and flip-flop sandals.

'It was cold when I got up at stupid o'clock. Our flight left at 6 a.m.' Hannah pulled back from the hug. 'You've let your hair grow. It looks fabulous.'

Susie dragged her fingers through her almost shoulder-length golden curls. 'It'd be as long as yours now, if I bothered straightening it.'

'Don't!' Hannah said in mock alarm. 'If you did that, nobody would be able to tell us apart and it would be school all over again.'

'Yeah...' Susie was grinning. 'With you getting into trouble for the things I did.'

The noise in the small building increased markedly as the main group of passengers entered, to be greeted ecstatically by the people waiting to meet them. The loud voices, tears and laughter and exuberant hugging made Susie widen her eyes.

'That's *another* Poulos contingent arriving. Look at that! This wedding is a circus.'

Why did Hannah's gaze seek Ryan out in the crowd so instantly? As though the smallest excuse made it permissible? She turned back to Susie.

'What's your bridesmaid's dress like?'

'Pink.'

'Oh, my God, you're *kidding!*'

'Yeah. It's peach but it's still over the top. Sort of a semi-meringue. Kind of like you'd expect some finalist in a ballroom dancing competition to be wearing. I could keep it to get married in myself eventually—except for the lack of originality. Five other girls will have the same outfit at home.'

'*Six* bridesmaids?'

'Yes, but I'm the most important one. Poor Emily doesn't have any family and she only wanted two bridesmaids—me and Mike's sister, Maria, but there were all these cousins who would have been mortally offended if they hadn't been included and, besides, Mike's mum, Sophia, is determined to have the wedding of the century. I think she only stopped at six because it was getting hard to find the male counterparts. Funnily enough, they weren't so keen.'

'How's Emily holding up?'

'She's loving every minute of it but going absolutely mad.

And she'll need a lot of make-up tomorrow to cover red cheeks from all the affectionate pinching she's getting.' Susie's head was still turning as she scanned the rest of the arrivals. 'Let's go and find your bag before we get swamped. If Sophia starts introducing me as the chief bridesmaid, I'll probably get *my* cheeks pinched as well. Oh, my God!' Susie did a double take as she lowered her voice. 'Who is *that*?'

There were two men standing a little to one side of the crowd, their attention on the signs directing them to the baggage collection area. One of them was Ryan. His head started to turn as though he sensed Hannah's gaze so she transferred it quickly to the other man. It was easy to recognise the person who had been dozing in the seat beside her on the last leg of her long journey. In that suit, he had to be even hotter than Hannah was in her jeans.

'He's an American,' she told Susie. 'A neurosurgeon. Alistair... someone. He's here for the wedding but he didn't say much about it. I got the impression he wasn't that thrilled to be coming.'

'That's Gina's cousin, then. Gorgeous, isn't he?'

'I guess.' Hannah hadn't taken much notice. Who would, when someone that looked like Ryan Fisher was nearby? 'Gina?'

'Also American. A cardiologist. She's getting married to Cal next weekend. I told you all about her at Christmas. She arrived with her little boy, who turned out to be Cal's son. Cal's one of our surgeons.'

'Right. Whew! *Two* weddings in two weeks?'

'Wedding city,' Susie agreed. She was leading the way past where the men were standing. Hannah could feel the odd prickle on the back of her neck that came when you knew someone was watching you. She didn't turn around because it was unlikely that she'd feel the stare of someone she didn't know with such spine-tingling clarity.

'Some people are going to both weddings,' Susie continued, ' and they've had to travel to get here so everybody thought they might like to just stay and have a bit of a holiday in between.'

'He won't have much of a holiday if he stays in that suit. And I thought I was overdressed!'

'Oh! The guy in the suit is the American?' Susie threw a glance over her shoulder. 'So who's the really gorgeous one who's staring at you?'

Hannah sighed. 'That'll be Ryan.'

'Ryan Fisher? The best man?'

'Yes.'

'Wow!' Susie's grin widened. 'My day's looking up! Mike told me what a fabulous guy he is but he forgot to mention he was also fabulous looking.'

'Don't get too excited,' Hannah warned.

'Why? Is he married?'

'No, but he might not be too friendly.'

Susie's eyebrows vanished under the curls on her forehead. 'Why not?'

Hannah sighed inwardly, feeling far too hot and weary to start explaining why her sister could well have to deal with unreasonable antipathy from someone because he disliked her mirror image.

'I'll fill you in later.' It was much easier to change the subject. Very easy, in fact. 'Good grief!'

'What?' Susie's head turned to follow the direction of Hannah's astonished stare at the small, dark woman wearing black leather pants, a top that showed an amazing cleavage and... red stiletto shoes. 'That's Georgie.' She smiled. 'You'll meet her later.'

As though that explained everything! 'She must be as hot as hell in those clothes.'

'She's got super air-con for travel. She rides a Harley.'

'In *stilettos*?' Hannah's peripheral vision caught the way Ryan was also staring at the woman. There was no mistaking the appreciative grin on his face. 'Good *grief*,' she muttered again.

'I guess Georgie's here to meet Alistair. Georgie's Gina's

bridesmaid and Alistair's here to give Gina away. He was supposed to arrive yesterday but his flight from the US was delayed by bad weather, and Gina and Cal are on one of the outer islands today, doing a clinic. So wow! Georgie and Alistair...' Susie shook her head. 'Leathers and pinstripes. They look a perfect couple. Not! Is that your bag?'

'Yes. Coming off first for a change.'

'Let's go, then.'

While it was a relief to escape the terminal building—and Ryan—it was a shock to step back out into the heat. And the wind. Huge fronds on the palm trees were bowing under its strength and Hannah had to catch her hair as it whipped into her face.

'Hurry up, Hannah! My car's over here and we're going to run out of time if we don't get going.'

'But the wedding's not till 4 p.m. tomorrow.' It was too hot to move any faster. 'What's the rush?' Hannah climbed reluctantly into the interior of a small hatchback car that felt more like an oven and immediately rolled down her window.

Susie started the engine and fiddled with the air-conditioning controls. 'It's all a bit frantic. I'm sorry. There's a rehearsal later this afternoon and I've got a couple more patients I just have to see before then.' She turned onto the main road and the car picked up speed rapidly. 'If you roll up your window, the air-con will work a lot better.'

Hannah complied and a welcome trickle of cool air came from the vents.

'Are you seeing your patients at your rooms?'

'No, I've finished the private stuff for today. These are hospital cases. Old Mrs Trengrove has had a hip replacement and absolutely refuses to get out of bed unless I'm there to hold her hand, and Wally's been admitted—he's one of my arthritis patients and it's his birthday today so I'll have to go and say hello.'

'Do you want to just drop me off at your place? I'm sure I could find my way to the beach and have a swim or something.'

'No, you can't swim at the beach. The water's all horrible because of the awful weather we've had in the last few days and it's stinger season. With the big waves we've been getting, the nets might not be working too well. Besides, I want to show you around the hospital. If you take your bathing suit, you could have a dip in the hospital pool.'

'Sounds good.' Hannah tried to summon enthusiasm for the busman's holiday delight of visiting the hospital.

'It's fabulous. You'd love it, Hannah. Hey...' Susie turned to look at her sister. 'They're always short of doctors. You could come and live with me for a while.'

'I couldn't stand working in heat like this.'

'It's not always like this.'

'It *is* beautiful.' Hannah was looking past sugar-cane plantations and the river towards rainforest-covered mountains in the distance.

'Wait till you see the cove. You'll fall in love with it just like I did.'

'The roads are quieter than I expected.'

'Bit quieter than usual today. I expect it's got something to do with the big fishing competition that's on.'

They crossed the river that gave Crocodile Creek township its name, drove through the main part of town and then rattled over an old wooden bridge to cross the river again. Rounding the bend on a gentle downhill slope, Hannah got the postcard view. The picture-perfect little cove with the white sandy beach and the intriguing, smudged outlines of islands further out to sea.

'The sea's the wrong colour at the moment,' Susie said apologetically. 'It's usually as blue as the sky. That's the Athina.' She pointed at the sprawling white building with Greek-style lettering on its sign that advertised its function as a boutique hotel. 'That's where the reception is being held tomorrow. And that rambling, huge house on the other side of the cove is the doctors' house.'

'Ah! The original hospital which is now the hotbed of romance.'

'Don't knock it!' Susie grinned at her sister. 'You could live there if you didn't want to squeeze into my wee cottage. Who knows? You might just find the man of your dreams in residence.'

'Doubt it.'

'Yeah.' Susie chuckled. 'The man of *your* dreams is probably buried in a laboratory somewhere. Or a library. Or an accountant's office.'

'Dad was an accountant,' Hannah reminded her. 'It didn't stop him being a lot of fun.'

'True.' Susie was silent for a moment. 'And Trevor was a brain surgeon and had to be the most boring man I'd ever met.'

'Hey, you're talking about the man I was engaged to for three years.'

'And why did you break it off?'

Hannah laughed. 'Because I was bored to tears. OK, I agree. There should be a happy medium but I haven't found it yet.'

'Me neither,' Susie said sadly. 'There always turns out to be something wrong with them. Or, worse, they find something wrong with me.' She screwed up her nose as she turned towards her sister. 'What *is* wrong with me, Hannah?'

'Absolutely nothing,' Hannah said stoutly. 'The guys are just idiots and don't deserve you. You're gorgeous.'

'That makes you gorgeous as well, you realise.'

'Of course.' Hannah grinned.

This was what she missed most about not having Susie living nearby any more. The comfort of absolute trust. Knowing you could say anything—even blow your own trumpet—without having it taken the wrong way. Not that they didn't have the occasional row but nothing could damage the underlying bond. And nothing else ever came close to the kind of strength a bond like this could impart.

'We're both gorgeous,' she said. 'Smart, too.'

'I'm not as smart as you. You're a brilliant doctor, soon-to-be emergency medicine specialist. I'm only a physiotherapist.'

'You could have easily been a doctor if you'd wanted, as you well know, Susan Jackson. You're doing what you want to do and you're doing it brilliantly. Anyway, being seen as clever isn't an advantage when it comes to men. It intimidates them.'

Although Hannah had a feeling that Ryan Fisher would be stimulated rather than intimidated by an intelligent woman if he ever bothered trying to find out.

'Look!' Susie was distracted from the conversation now. 'That's the Black Cockatoo, our local. And that's Kylie's Klipz. Kylie's amazing—looks like Dolly Parton. She's our hairdresser and she'll be doing all the hair and make-up for tomorrow. That's the Grubbs' place with that rusty old truck parked on the lawn and...here's my place.'

Susie parked outside a tiny cottage with two front windows in the shade of a veranda that was almost invisible beneath bougainvillea.

'Cute!'

'Speaking of cute.' Susie was unlocking her front door as Hannah carried her bag from the car. 'What's wrong with Ryan Fisher? Was he rude to you on the plane or something?'

'Not exactly. I just happen to know he's a player.'

'How do you know that? Do you know someone that works with him in Sydney?'

'He doesn't work in Sydney any more. He works in Auckland.'

'As in the same place you work?' Susie had opened the door but hadn't made any move to go inside.

'Exactly.'

'He's in your ED?'

'He's the guy who's after my job. I told you about him.'

Susie's jaw dropped. '*Ryan's* the holiday king? The Aussie playboy who's been driving you nuts with all those blonde jokes?'

'That's him.'

'The one who's out to date every nurse in the department in record time?'

'Yep.'

'So why have you been calling him Richard the third in your emails?'

'Because he reminds me of that bastard that Mum fell in love with when she'd finally got over Dad's death. *And* the creep who dumped you just before you went to Brisbane. He's a certain type. Skitters through life having a good time and not worrying about hurting anyone along the way. A flirt.'

'I'll bet he doesn't have any trouble getting a response.'

'He drives a flashy car. A BMW Roadster or something.'

'Nice. Soft top?'

Hannah ignored the teasing. 'He knows I can see right through the image. He hates *me*, too.'

Susie finally moved, leading the way into one of the bedrooms at the front of the cottage. 'I didn't get that impression from the way he was staring at you at the airport.'

'He was probably staring at you. At *us*. Wondering how he could be unlucky enough to be partnered with my clone.'

'That bad, huh?'

'Yep.' Hannah threw her suitcase onto the bed and snapped it open. 'No time for a shower, I don't suppose?'

'Not really. Sorry. Put your togs on under your clothes and take a towel. You can swim while I do my patient visits.' Susie made for the door. 'I'd better throw a shirt over this top so I look more respectable to go to work. It's lucky we don't stand on ceremony much around this place.'

It was blissful, pulling off the denim and leaving Hannah's legs bare beneath the pretty, ruffled skirt that she chose. The lacy camisole top was perfectly decent seeing as she was wearing her bikini top instead of a bra. Hannah emerged from the room a minute later to find Susie looking thoughtful.

'I just can't believe that the guy Emily was telling me about is the same guy you've been describing. As far as Mike's concerned, he's a hero. Practically a saint.'

Hannah dampened the image she had of Ryan when he was about to ignore the captain's direction to stay safely seated during severe turbulence to go and help where he was needed. He certainly had the courage that provided hero material. But a saint? No saint could get away with emitting that kind of sexual energy.

'Mike's not a woman,' she said firmly. 'I doubt there's a saintly bone in that body.'

'You could be right.' Susie's forget-me-not blue eyes, the exact match of Hannah's, were still dreamy. 'He's got that "bad boy" sort of edge, hasn't he?'

'I wouldn't say it like it's a compliment.'

Susie closed the front door behind them. 'Shall we walk? It's only a few minutes if you don't mind being blown about.'

'Yes, let's blow the cobwebs away. I could do with stretching my legs after all the sitting in planes.'

With a bit of luck, the wind might blow the current topic of conversation away as well.

No such luck.

'You have to admit, it's attractive.'

'What is?'

'That "bad boy" stuff. The idea that some guy could give you the best sex you've ever had in your life because he's had enough practice to be bloody good at it.'

Hannah laughed, catching her skirt as it billowed up to reveal her long legs. A car tooted appreciatively as it shot past. Thank goodness she was wearing a respectable bikini bottom instead of a lacy number or a thong and that her summer tan hadn't begun to fade yet. Despite being blonde and blue-eyed, she and Susie both tanned easily without burning.

'I don't do one-night stands or even flings,' Hannah reminded Susie. 'You know perfectly well the kind of trouble they lead to.'

'Yeah.' But Susie seemed to have finally got over her last

heartbreak. 'But you always think you might just be the one who's going to make them want to change. And they're such *fun* at the time. To begin with, anyway.'

They walked in silence for a minute and Hannah looked down the grassy slope dotted with rocks and yellow flowers that led to the beach. A quite impressive surf from the murky sea was sending foamy scum to outline the distance up the beach the waves were reaching.

'You've never done it, have you?' Susie asked finally. 'Let your hair down and gone with sheer physical attraction? Slept with someone on a first date or fallen in love just because of the way some guy *looks* at you.'

'Never.' If she said it firmly enough she could convince herself as well, couldn't she? She couldn't admit, even to Susie, how often Ryan infiltrated her thoughts in the small hours of the night. It was lust she felt for the man. Nothing more.

Or should that be *less*?

'Sometimes I wish I were as strong as you,' Susie said wistfully.

'Someone had to be, in our family. The voice of reason, that's what I was. The devil's advocate.'

'You were always good at picking out what was wrong with the men Mum brought home.'

'Just a pity she never listened to me. She lost the house because she went ahead and married that slimeball, Richard the first.'

'Yeah. At least she's happy now. Or seems to be. Jim adores her.'

'And he's comfortably off and perfectly sensible. I'm sure Mum's learned to love fishing.'

'Hmm.'

Hannah couldn't blame Susie for sounding dubious. She made a mental note to ring her mother as soon as she got home.

'Come this way.' Susie pointed away from the signs directing people to the emergency and other departments of Crocodile Creek Base Hospital. 'We'll cut through the garden to the doctors' house and I can show you the pool and then shoot off and see those patients. Might be better if we leave the hospital tour until Sunday. Your flight doesn't leave till the afternoon, does it?'

'3 p.m.'

'Bags of time. I'll be able to introduce you properly to every hungover staff member we come across instead of confusing you with too many names.'

'I'll meet them at the wedding in any case.'

'You'll meet a few of them tonight. We're hoping to whisk Emily away after the rehearsal and take her out to dinner to give her a kind of hens' night. Which reminds me, I need to pop into the house and see who's going to be around. Gina might be there and Georgie should be back by now.'

'Is the dinner going to be at the Athina?'

'Heavens, no! Sophia already has the tables set up and about three thousand white bows tied to everything. She'll be making the family eat in the kitchens tonight, I expect—or they'll be roasting a lamb on a spit down on the beach. Such a shame about this weather.'

The lush tropical garden they were entering provided surprisingly good shelter from the wind thanks to the thick hibiscus hedges, and Hannah found she was too hot and sticky again. Her head was starting to throb as well, probably due to dehydration.

'Any chance of a glass of water?'

'Sure. Come up to the house with me.'

Skirting a sundial in the centre of the garden, Hannah could hear the sound of laughter and splashing water. An irresistibly cool, swimming pool sort of sound. The pool was behind a fenced area, screened by bright-flowered shrubs that smelt gorgeous, but Hannah didn't get time for a proper look because Susie was already half way up a set of steps that led to the wide veranda of a huge old two-storey building. Following her, Hannah found herself in a large kitchen and gratefully drank a large glass of water while Susie dashed off to see who was at home.

'There's nobody here,' she announced on her return. 'Come on, I'll bet they're all in the pool as it's still lunchtime.'

The air of too much to get done in the available time was contagious and Hannah hurriedly rinsed her glass and left it upside down on the bench amongst plates that held the remains of what looked like some of Mrs Grubb's legendary chicken salad sandwiches. Susie was a woman on a mission as she sped out of the house and she was only momentarily distracted by the bumbling shape of a large, strangely spotty dog that bounded up the steps to greet her.

'Rudolf!' Susie put her arm out as though she intended to pat the dog, and Hannah had no idea what happened. A split second later, Susie was tumbling down the steps with a cry that was far from the delighted recognition of the dog and then—there she was—a crumpled heap at the bottom.

'*Susie!* Oh, my God! Are you all right?'

Hannah wasn't the only one to rush to her sister's rescue. More than one dripping figure emerged through the open gate in the swimming-pool fence.

Two men were there almost instantly. And one of them was Ryan.

'What's happened?'

'She fell down the steps. There was this dog.'

'Damn, who left the gate open?' Another dark-haired man with a towel wrapped around his waist appeared behind the others. 'CJ, you were supposed to be watching Rudolf.'

'I was being a *shark!*' A small wet boy wriggled past the legs of the adults to stare, wide-eyed, at Susie. 'I had to be underwater,' he continued excitedly. 'With my fin on top—like this.' He stuck a hand behind his neck but no one was watching.

'It wasn't Rudolf's fault.' Susie was struggling into a sitting position. 'It's all right. I'm all right.'

'Are you sure?' A man with black curly hair and a gorgeous

smile was squatting in front of Susie. 'You didn't hit your head, did you?'

'No. I don't know what happened, Mike. I just... Oh-h-h!'

'What's wrong?' Ryan moved closer. 'What's hurting?'

'My ankle,' Susie groaned. 'I think it's broken.'

'Just as well Luke's here, then,' Mike said, turning to another man who had approached the group. 'And they say you can't find an orthopaedic surgeon when you need one?'

'I *don't* need a surgeon,' Susie gulped. 'I hope.'

'I'll just be on standby,' Luke assured her. 'I am on babysitting duties after all.'

'*I'm* not a baby,' CJ stated. His hand crept into Luke's. 'You said I was your *buddy*.'

'You are, mate. You are...'

'Let *me* have a look.' Ryan's hands were on Susie's ankle. He eased off her sandal before palpating it carefully. 'I can't feel anything broken.'

'Ouch!'

'Sorry. Sore in there, is it? Can you wiggle your toes?'

There was a small movement. 'Ouch,' Susie said again. She looked close to tears and Hannah crouched beside her, putting an arm around her shoulders. 'I don't believe this. How could I have done something this stupid?'

'Accidents happen,' Ryan said calmly. He laid his hand on top of Susie's foot. 'Can you stop me pushing your foot down?'

'No. Oh, that *really* hurts.'

'It's starting to swell already.' Hannah peered anxiously at Susie's ankle. She might not have been very impressed if this injury was in front of her in the emergency department, but this was no professional environment and this was her sister. And Ryan looked nothing like he did in the ED. Hannah's gaze swung back to her colleague for a moment. He was practically naked, for heaven's sake. Tanned and dripping and...gorgeous. And giving Susie that killer smile.

'I think it's just a bad sprain but we'll need an X-ray to be sure. At least you chose the right place. I believe there's an X-ray department not far away.'

'It's not funny,' Susie wailed. 'I've got to wear high heels tomorrow. Little white ones with a rose on the toe. My dress is nowhere long enough to cover an ankle the size of an elephant's. I need some ice. Fast.' Susie leaned down to poke at the side of her ankle. 'What if it's broken and I need a cast? Oh, Mike, I'm so sorry! This is a *disaster!*'

'Forget it,' the curly haired man told her. 'The only thing that matters right now is making sure you're all right. Let's get you over to A and E.'

'I'll take her,' Ryan offered. 'Isn't Emily expecting you back at the Athina?'

Mike glanced at his watch and groaned. 'Ten minutes ago. And I'm supposed to have all the latest printouts from the met bureau. The women are all petrified that Willie's going to turn back and ruin the wedding.'

'As if!' Luke was grinning. 'There's no way Sophia's going to let a bit of weather undermine a Poulos wedding.'

Hannah could feel an increasing level of tension curling inside her. This was no time to be discussing the weather. Or a wedding. Susie needed attention. Her sister's face was crumpling ominously.

'*I'm* ruining the wedding,' she wailed forlornly. 'How could I have been so *stupid*?'

Hannah glared at Ryan. If he made even one crack about anything blonde, he would have to die!

Ryan's eyebrows shot up as he caught the force of the warning. Then he looked away from Hannah with a tiny, bemused shake of his head.

'Nothing else hurting?' he asked Susie. 'Like your neck?'

She shook her head.

'Right. Let's get this sorted, then.'

With an ease that took Hannah's breath away, Ryan took

charge. He scooped Susie into his arms as though she weighed no more than the little boy, CJ. 'Emergency's that way, yes?'

'Yes,' Luke confirmed. 'Through the memorial garden.'

'Can I go, too?' CJ begged. ' I want to watch.'

'No,' Luke said. 'We told Mom we'd be waiting here when she got back.'

Mike was grinning broadly. 'You sure you want to go in like that, mate?'

'No time to waste.' Ryan was already moving in the direction Hannah had approached earlier. 'We need ice. And an X-ray.'

Hannah was only too pleased to trot behind Ryan. This was exactly the action that was required and there was no way she could have carried Susie herself.

'I'll bring your clothes over,' Mike called after them. 'I'll just call Emily and let her know what's happening.'

What was happening was a badly sprained ankle.

Despite ice and elevation and firm bandaging, Susie's ankle was continuing to swell impressively and was far too painful to put any weight on at all.

'Crutches.' An older and clearly senior nurse appeared in the cubicle Susie was occupying nearly an hour later. 'At least I won't need to give you a rundown on how to use them, Susie.'

'Thanks, Jill.' But Susie took one look at the sturdy, wooden, underarm crutches and then covered her face with her hands as though struggling not to burst into tears.

There was a moment's heavy silence. The cubicle was quite crowded what with Hannah standing by the head of Susie's bed, Ryan—now dressed, thankfully—and Mike leaning on the wall and Jill at the foot of the bed, holding the horrible accessories Susie was not going to be able to manage without.

Then the silence was broken.

'What are you saying?' came a loud, horrified, female voice. 'She can't *walk*? How can we have a bridesmaid who can't *walk*?'

'Oh, no!' Susie groaned. 'Sophia!'

'I was wondering how she'd take the news,' Mike said gloomily. 'Em didn't sound too thrilled either.'

A young woman with honey-blonde hair and rather serious grey-blue eyes rushed into the cubicle.

'Susie, are you all right? Is it broken?' She leaned over the bed to hug her friend. 'You poor thing!'

Hannah's eyes widened as the curtain was flicked back decisively. It wasn't just Mike's mother who had accompanied Emily. There were at least half a dozen women and they were all talking at once. Loudly. Anxiously.

'Susie! Darling!' The small, plump woman at the forefront of the small crowd sailed into the cubicle and stared at Hannah. 'What *have* you done to your hair?'

'I'm not Susie,' Hannah said weakly, as her sister emerged from Emily's hug. 'I'm her twin, Hannah.'

'Oh, my God!' The young, dark-haired woman beside Sophia was also staring. 'You *are* identical. Look at that, Ma! You wouldn't be able to tell them apart.'

An excited babble and an inward flow of women made Hannah back into the corner a little further. Alarmed, she looked for an escape route, only to catch the highly amused faces of both Mike and Ryan. There was nothing for it but to hold her breath and submit to the squash of people both wanting to pat and comfort Susie and to touch Hannah and see if she was actually real.

Jill looked as though she knew even her seniority would be no help in trying to evict this unruly mob from her emergency department and was taking the crutches out of the way for the moment, but the movement attracted Sophia's attention.

'What are those?'

'Susie's crutches.' Jill picked up speed as she backed away.

'She needs *crutches*?' Sophia crossed herself, an action that was instantly copied by all the other relatives. 'But we can't have crutches! The photographs!'

'It's all right, Ma.' The woman who had to be Mike's sister, Maria, was grinning. 'It doesn't matter if Susie can't walk.'

'It doesn't matter? Of course it matters!' Sophia's arms were waving wildly and Hannah pressed herself further into the corner. 'There are six dresses. We have to have six bridesmaids and Susie is Emily's best friend. She has to be in the photographs. In the ceremony.' A lacy handkerchief appeared from someone's hand and Sophia dabbed it to her eyes. 'But with crutches? Oh, no, no, no...' The sympathetic headshakes from all directions confirmed that this event was cataclysmic.

'Never mind Willie,' Mike murmured audibly to Ryan. 'This is going to be worse than any cyclone, believe me.'

'Ma, listen!' Sophia's shoulders were firmly grasped by Maria. 'We can use Hannah instead.'

'What?' The word was wrenched from Hannah and everybody was listening now. And staring. And then talking, all at once.

'No, her hair's all wrong.'

'She's the same size. She'll fit the dress.'

'Nothing that curling tongs couldn't fix.'

'No crutches!'

'Nobody will know the difference.'

'I'll know,' Emily said emphatically. 'And so will Susie.' She still had her arms protectively around her friend.

'Would it matter?' Susie spoke only to Emily. 'I'd rather it was Hannah than me in the photos, Em. I'd just spoil them.'

'No, you wouldn't.'

'Yes, I would. It would be the first thing anyone would notice when they looked at the pictures. Or when they're sitting in the church. Instead of saying, "Look at that gorgeous bride," they'd be saying, "Why is that girl on crutches? What's wrong with her?"'

The chorus of assent from the avid audience was unanimous. Emily looked appealingly at Mike but he just shrugged sympathetically and then grinned.

'Up to you, babe,' he said, 'but it does seem fortuitous that you chose a chief bridesmaid that's got a spare copy of herself available.'

Hannah looked at Ryan. If this crazy solution was going to make everybody happy then of course she would have to go along with it. But would Ryan?

Clearly, it *was* going to make everybody happy. Especially Susie.

'I'll still be there,' she was telling Emily. 'And Hannah's like part of me anyway.'

'Hannah? Are you OK with this?'

'Sure.' Hannah smiled warmly at Emily. 'I'd be honoured.'

'Hannah! Darling!' Sophia was reaching to squeeze Hannah's cheeks between her hands. 'Thank you! Thank you!'

Nobody asked Ryan if he was OK with the plan. Hannah caught his gaze and for a moment they just stared at each other. Another moment of connection. They were the two outsiders. Caught up in a circus over which they had no hope of exerting the slightest control.

It was a bit like dealing with the turbulence on that plane trip really. Had that been only this morning? Fate seemed determined to hurl them together. As closely as possible.

Ryan's expression probably mirrored her own. There was nothing they could do about it so they may as well just go with the flow.

There was something else mixed in with the resignation. Maybe it was due to the almost joyous atmosphere in the cubicle at having solved a potentially impossible hitch to the perfect wedding. Or maybe, for Hannah, it was due to something she didn't want to analyse.

It was more than satisfaction.

Curiously, it felt more like excitement.

CHAPTER FIVE

Clouds were rolling in towards the North Queensland coast by 5 p.m.

Stained-glass windows in the small, Greek Orthodox church in the main township of Crocodile Creek were rattled with increasing force by the sharp wind gusts.

'Did you hear that?' Emily tugged on Mike's arm. 'It's getting worse.'

'Last report was that Willie's heading further out to sea. Stop fretting, babe. Spit for luck instead.'

'I've given up spitting, I told you that.' The smile Emily shared with her fiancé spoke of a private joke and Hannah found herself smiling as well. Emily and Mike had the kind of bond she had only ever found with her sister. One where an unspoken language said so much and just a look or a touch could convey a lot more than words.

If she was ever going to get married herself, Hannah would want that kind of a bond with the man she was going to spend the rest of her life with. She had known it wouldn't be easy to find a man she could trust to that extent. No, that wasn't quite true. Trevor had been as reliable and trustworthy as it was possible to be—perhaps because he was so hard working and scientific and couldn't tolerate anything that required imagination or spontaneity.

The relationship had gone from one of comfort to one of predictability. And then boredom had set in. In the end, Hannah had been quietly suffocating. The opportunity that moving to Auckland to take up her first registrar position had afforded had been too good to miss. Much to poor Trevor's unhappy bewilderment, she had also moved on from their relationship.

She hadn't been in another relationship since. Hurting another nice, kind, trustworthy man was not on the agenda. Risking personal disaster by trying the kind of man who was fascinating was also a place Hannah had no intention of going. Of course Susie was right. That 'bad boy' edge was attractive. It would be all too easy to think like most women—that *they* would be the one to make the difference—but it never happened like that. Not in real life.

Emily tore her eyes away from Mike to smile apologetically at Hannah. 'I must sound like a real worry wart,' she said, 'but I've got a long veil. Can you imagine what it's going to be like in gale-force winds?'

'There are six of us.' Hannah glanced at the lively group of young women milling behind her that included Mike's sister, Maria. 'I'm sure we'll be able to keep your veil under control.'

Sophia put the finishing touches to yet another of the large, alternating peach and white bows she was tying to the ends of the pews and then clapped her hands.

'Another practice!' she ordered. 'Michael! What are you doing? Go back up to the front with the others. Ryan! You're supposed to be making my son behave.'

'That'll be the day,' Ryan muttered. 'Come on, mate. Let's get this over with and then we can hit the bright lights of Crocodile Creek for a stag party, yes?'

'That really *would* be the day,' Mike responded with a grimace. 'There's a lamb on a spit turning as we speak and every member of the family has about six jobs to do later. I think

you're down for potato-peeling duties. Or possibly painting the
last of the damn chicken bones.'

'Chicken bones?'

'Quickly!' Sophia's tone suggested that there would be trouble if co-operation did not take place forthwith.

The two men shared a grin and then ambled up the red carpet of the aisle, and the rear view made Hannah realise how
similar they were. Both tall and dark and handsome. They were
wearing shorts and T-shirts at the moment but Hannah could
well imagine what they'd look like tomorrow in their dark suits,
crisp white shirts and bow ties. Just…irresistible.

Emily was watching the men as well and she sighed happily.
'I can't believe this is really going to happen,' she whispered.
'It's just too good to be true.'

Her eyes were shining and Hannah could feel the glow. What
would it be like, she wondered, to be *that* happy? To be so sure
you'd chosen the right person and that that kind of love had a
good chance of lasting for ever? Mike looked like Ryan in more
than an outward physical sense. They both had that laid-back,
mischievous gleam that advertised the ability to get the most
enjoyment possible out of life. And that did not generally in-
clude settling down with one woman and raising a family. Had
Emily been the one to change Mike? Did being Greek make the
difference? Or was she heading for unimaginable heartbreak?

No. Hannah didn't believe that for a moment. She had seen
the way Mike and Emily had looked at each other. They had
found the real thing, all right. Standing in this pretty church,
about to rehearse the steps for a ceremony to join two lovers in
matrimony, Hannah couldn't help a flash of envy. It was a bit
like winning the lottery, wasn't it? Only it was a human lottery and you couldn't buy tickets. And even if you were lucky
enough to find one, you might forget to read the small print and
think you'd won, only to have the prize snatched away. It had
happened to both her mother and to Susie, and Hannah knew

why. Because 'the Richards' had had that hint of a 'bad boy' edge. They had been playboys. Fun-seekers. Like Ryan.

The pageboys and flower girls were being rounded up from their game of chase between the empty pews. They were holding plastic beach buckets as a prop to represent the baskets of petals they would hold tomorrow. Sophia herded them into place and repeated instructions they had apparently misheard on the first rehearsal.

'Gently!' she insisted. 'You are throwing rose petals, CJ, not sticks for Rudolf!'

Maria was examining her nails. 'They're full of silver paint,' she complained. 'I never want to see another chicken bone in my life.'

'What's with the chicken bones?' Hannah queried. 'I heard Mike saying something about them as well.'

'Wishbones.' Emily was moving to take her place in the foyer. 'Painted silver. Sophia's planning to attach them to the little bags of almonds the guests will be given. Not that anyone's found time to put the almonds in the bags yet, let alone attach the wishbones.'

'They're for fertility,' Maria added. 'The almonds, that is. And boy, do I wish they hadn't been scattered around at my wedding. Watch out for the ones in your bed, Em. I'd sweep them out if I were you or you might end up like me, with four little monsters under five.' She was peering anxiously past Hannah to see if her small children were doing what they were supposed to on reaching the end of the petal-throwing procession.

'Uncle Mike!' one of them shrieked. 'Did you see me pretending to throw petals?'

Mike swept the small girl into his arms and kissed her. Ryan held out his hands and got high-fives from two small boys—a gesture that was clearly well practised. Then he pulled them in, one on each side of his body, for a one-armed hug.

'Good job, guys,' Hannah heard him say.

When did Ryan get to spend enough time with young children to be that at ease with them? Did he have a big family with lots of nieces and nephews? Maybe he'd been married already and had his own children. The notion was quite feasible. It would explain his frequent trips back to Sydney. Not that it mattered to Hannah. She was just aware of how little she knew about her colleague. Aware of a curiosity she had no intention of satisfying.

'I hope the aisle's going to be wide enough.' Emily had come back to her cluster of bridesmaids. 'My dress is *huge*. A giant meringue. Do you think there'll be room for a wheelchair beside me?'

'A wheelchair?' Hannah was glad she'd paid attention to Susie's emails. 'Is Charles Wetherby giving you away?'

'Yes. He's the closest thing to a father figure I've got.'

Reading between the lines of those emails, Hannah had the impression that Charles was a father figure to more than just Emily. With an ability to know more about what was happening within the walls of the hospital he directed than his staff were always comfortable with. A man with a quiet strength and wisdom that provided the cement for a remarkable small community of professional medics. A community that her sister was very much a part of now.

'I'm sure there'll be room,' she said confidently.

'Susie!' Sophia was sounding flustered. She was waving frantically from the altar end of the aisle. 'Pay attention, darling!'

'It's Hannah, Ma, not Susie,' Maria shouted.

'I knew that. You know what I mean. Come on, girls. In your pairs.'

Hannah and Maria were first. They walked along the red carpet beneath the elaborate chandelier, the gilt frame of which had miniature copies of the paintings of various saints that decorated the walls of this church between the stained-glass windows. The tiny crystals tinkled musically overhead as another gust of wind managed to shake the solid brick building.

Maria glanced up at the chandelier and muttered something under her breath that could have been either a curse or a prayer. Maybe a bit of both, Hannah decided, as Mike's sister flashed a grin at her.

'It's going to be a wild wedding at this rate!'

Hannah nodded agreement but found herself swallowing a little nervously. Even if Willie was out to sea and moving in a safe direction, this was still as close to a tropical cyclone as she felt comfortable with.

The first rehearsal made it easy to remember what to do this time. Hannah and Maria climbed to the top of the three steps and then waited until the other pairs of bridesmaids were on the lower steps before they all turned gracefully in unison to watch the bride's entrance.

Hannah felt a complete fraud. If only Emily and Susie weren't so set on her standing in. She couldn't even follow someone else's lead. She was the chief bridesmaid. It was up to her to make sure all the others did the right thing at the right time. There was a point when she would actually be a closer part of this ceremony, too. When the bride and groom were wearing the matching orange-blossom wreaths on their heads that were joined by satin ribbons, they would take their first steps as man and wife with a tour three times around the altar. It would be Hannah's job to hold up the train of Emily's dress and keep her veil in order. As best man, Ryan would be right beside her, holding up the ribbons joining the wreaths.

He would be wearing his tuxedo and Hannah would be so dressed up and groomed she wouldn't even feel like herself. She would have to be Ryan's partner in this ceremony and probably at the reception. She might even have to dance with him, and she was going to feel so uncomfortable she would be hating every minute of it.

And you'll look miserable, a small voice at the back of her mind warned. You'll make Susie miserable and probably Emily and definitely Ryan, and they'll all wish you'd never been invited to this wedding. Hannah noticed the nudge that Mike gave his best man by bumping shoulders. There was a whispered comment and then a frankly admiring stare from both men as the girls behind Hannah proudly arranged themselves on the steps. The men grinned approvingly. The girls giggled. They were all enjoying every moment of this circus.

And why not? It was going to be a huge party. The wild weather would probably only enhance the enjoyment of those safely tucked away inside. It was play time, not work time. Why couldn't she just relax and have fun, like they were?

Everybody thought she was boring. Too focussed on her career. Too ready to troubleshoot problems before they even occurred. It should, and probably did, make her a very good doctor, but too many people had criticised that ability in the last few days. Jennifer thought she had no life of her own out-side work. Ryan thought she was dull. Even her own sister had commented on her lack of spontaneity or willingness to reap the rewards of taking a personal risk.

Hannah had never allowed sheer physical attraction to be the deciding factor when it came to men. Or slept with some-one on a first date. Not that she intended to jump Ryan's bones, of course. Or fall in love with him because of a look, or, in his case, more likely due to the kind of smile she'd experienced in the plane that morning. The kind her junior bridesmaids were enjoying right now.

She could, however, throw caution to the winds for once, couldn't she? Given the current weather conditions in Croco-dile Creek, it would be highly likely to be blown a very long way away, but would that be so terrible?

For the next twenty-four hours or so, she was going to have to pretend to be Susie. Someone with a rather different perspec-tive on life and taking risks. This could be the perfect oppor-tunity to step outside her own comfort zone. To really let her guard down and simply enjoy the moment, without trying to see down the track to locate potential hazards.

What did she have to lose? On Sunday she would get on a plane again to go home. Back to being herself. Back to working hard enough to ensure the success she craved. Hopefully, back to a new position as an emergency department consultant. And how much time would she get to have fun after that? This weekend could be seen as a kind of hens' party really. A final fling before Hannah became wedded to a new and intense phase of her career.

And it wouldn't hurt to show Ryan Fisher that she *did* know how to enjoy herself. That she wasn't all work and no play and as dull as ditchwater.

Yes!

Hannah hunched her shoulders and then let them drop to release any unconscious tension.

And then she smiled at Ryan. Really smiled. Here we are, then, her smile said. Let's have fun!

Good grief!

What had he done to deserve a smile like that? One that actually touched Hannah's eyes instead of just being a polite curve of her lips.

Ryan had to fight the urge to glance over his shoulder to see whether the real recipient of the smile was standing nearby.

Hell, she was gorgeous. It was going to be more than rather difficult to stick to his resolution if she was going to do things like smile at him like that. Almost as bad as discovering it had been Hannah and not Susie wearing that frilly skirt. The one that the wind had whipped up to reveal a pair of extremely enticing legs as he and Mike had driven up to the hospital earlier that afternoon. He'd never be able to see her wearing scrubs trousers in the ED again without knowing what lay beneath the shapeless fabric.

Mind you, that hadn't been half as disconcerting as what had happened later. Ryan had been entertaining hopes of finding Susie's company perfectly enjoyable. Of maybe being able to learn why his attractive colleague was so uptight and had taken such an instant dislike to him.

To have Susie incapacitated and Hannah stepping in to fill the breach had been a cruel twist of fate. Not that he'd allowed his disappointment to show, of course. Not when Emily had looked so happy. When Emily looked that happy, Mike was happy. And if his best buddy was happy, Ryan certainly wasn't going to do anything to tarnish the glow.

He'd go through with this and he'd look as if he was enjoying every moment of it. It would be hard *not* to enjoy it, in fact, and if he could only make sure his resolution regarding Hannah Jackson didn't go out the window, he could be sure he wouldn't spoil that enjoyment by getting some kind of personal putdown.

But it would help—a lot—if she didn't smile at him like that. As though she had put aside her preconceived and unflattering opinions. Opened a window in that wall of indifference to him and was seeing him—*really* seeing him—for the first time.

She did look a bit taken aback when he offered to take her home after the rehearsal but she rallied.

'Sure. I guess it's on your way, seeing as you're staying in the doctors' house. I might even go as far as the hospital and check on Susie.'

'It's good that she decided she would stay in overnight and get that intensive RICE treatment. It should help a lot.'

'Mmm.' Hannah's tone suggested that nothing would help enough unless, by some miracle, Susie awoke after a night of compression bandages and ice and elevation to find her foot small enough to wear her shoe and the ability to stand and walk unaided, which was highly unlikely. 'I need to stop at her house and collect a few things she might need, if you're not in too much of a hurry.'

'Not at all.' Ryan lowered his voice. 'With a bit of luck, I'll arrive at the Athina *after* all the potatoes are peeled.'

Hannah made no response to that and Ryan kicked himself

mentally. What was he trying to do here? Prove how shallow and lazy he was?

'Tell Susie I'll be up to see her later,' Emily said as they left the church. 'If she can't come to the hens' party, we'll just have to take the party to her.'

'I think Jill might have something to say about that,' Mike warned. 'She's not big on parties happening in her wards.'

'Yeah.' Emily nodded sadly. 'She'd say that I should know the R in RICE stands for rest. Tell Susie I'll come and get her later in the morning, then, so she can come and supervise. Kylie can still do her hair and make-up.'

To Ryan's disappointment, Hannah was ready for the wind when they stepped outside. She had wrapped her skirt firmly around those long brown legs and was holding it in place. On the positive side, the action affected her balance and a good gust sent her sideways a few moments later to bump into Ryan. She could have fallen right over, in fact, if he hadn't caught her arms.

Bare arms.

Soft skin.

Enough momentum in the movement for Ryan to feel the press of her breasts against his hands. It wasn't the first time he had touched her skin but the tension of that incident in the plane hadn't really afforded an opportunity to analyse the effect. It was, quite simply, electrifying. Or was that because this contact had come about so unexpectedly?

No. He'd known, all along, that there would be something very different about touching this woman.

Something very special.

He didn't want to let go. The urge to pull her even closer and kiss her senseless was as powerful as what felt like hurricane-force winds funnelling through the church car park, whipping their hair and buffeting their bodies.

Simply irresistible.

* * *

Oh… *God!*

The strength of the grip Ryan had on her arms was sending shock waves through Hannah, not to mention the delicious tingle of what had to be that latent lust kicking in.

And he looked…as though he wanted to *kiss* her!

Even more shocking was the realisation that she *wanted* him to.

Letting her hair down and being prepared to enjoy this weekend was one thing. Making out with Ryan Fisher in a church car park was quite another. And quite unacceptable.

Hannah wrenched herself free. 'You've got Mike's car?'

'Yes. That Jeep over there.'

The vehicle was vaguely familiar. Hadn't that been the one that had hooted when her skirt had blown up around her neck on that walk around the cove? Had it been Ryan getting a close-up view of her legs?

The tingle became a shaft of something much stronger that was centred deep in Hannah's abdomen but sent spirals all the way to the tips of her fingers and toes. Battling with the door of the Jeep so it didn't catch in the wind and fly outwards was a welcome diversion. Why was she feeling like this? Had she somehow flicked a mental switch back there in the church that could lead her rather too far into temptation?

How inappropriate.

But intriguing.

Ryan wouldn't think twice about following his inclinations, would he? Sleeping with someone on a first date or having a little weekend fling? Hannah couldn't help casting a speculative glance at her companion as he started the Jeep and they moved off. His hands gripped the steering-wheel with enough strength to keep the vehicle straight despite the strong winds but they didn't look tense. Strength and a capacity to be gentle. What had Susie said about bad boys and getting the best sex you ever had?

Maybe her thoughts were too powerful. Something made Ryan turn his head. He held her gaze for only a heartbeat and then gave her one of those smiles.

Oh…help! Hannah spent the next few minutes until they were driving over that rickety bridge wondering if Ryan was discreet. Whether what happened on camp would stay on camp. Seeing as she'd never actually heard any firsthand gossip about his previous conquests, it seemed likely that the answer was yes. The added bonus of dealing with that distracting attraction as well as proving she could be fun might well mean that her working relationship with Ryan could be vastly improved. Even when she got the consultancy position and, effectively, became his boss.

It was quite difficult to rein in her thoughts and focus on her immediate intentions.

'I might change my clothes before I go and visit Susie.' Thinking out loud was partly to ensure Ryan didn't know what she'd really been thinking about. 'I've still got my bikini on under this and it's not as if I'm going to get a chance to swim.'

'That's a shame. The pool's great. Very refreshing.'

'It has been a long day, hasn't it?' Hannah agreed. 'Feels like for ever since we left Auckland.' A different time. A different place. Different rules were definitely allowable.

'You could have a swim after you've been visiting.'

'I'd still need a change of clothes and, besides, it gets dark early here, doesn't it?'

'About eight, I think. But there are lights around the pool. People often swim at night over summer from what Mike was telling me.'

'Tempting. I might just do that. This heat is really getting to me.' It wasn't the first time that day that Hannah had lifted the weight of hair off her neck to try and cool down a fraction. 'I don't think I've ever felt this hot in my life.'

'Mmm. You look pretty hot.' Ryan's grin suggested that he was commenting on her sexual appeal rather than her body temperature but, for once, Hannah wasn't put off. Was that because the flirtatious comment was acceptable under the new rules that seemed to be forming?

She laughed. 'You're hopeless, Ryan.' Then she pointed ahead. 'Stop here—that's Susie's cottage.'

Ryan followed her as far as the veranda. When Hannah emerged a few minutes later, wearing light cargo pants and a shirt over her bikini and with a towel and underwear and things for Susie in a carry bag, he was lounging against one of the posts framing the steps. Strands of bougainvillea snapped in the wind and a shower of dark red petals had left blooms caught in the dark waves of his hair.

'Why am I hopeless?'

Had he been stewing over the casual reprimand the whole time he had been waiting for her?

'Because you're an incorrigible flirt,' Hannah informed him. 'You can't talk to women without...' She had to leave the sentence unfinished. 'Without making them feel like you're attracted to them' had been the words on the tip of her tongue but what would happen if he responded by saying he *was* attracted to her? In theory, letting her hair down was great, but this was actually quite scary. What if he said she had nothing to worry about because there was no way he could be attracted to her? Hannah's mouth felt oddly dry.

'Most women appreciate a compliment,' Ryan was saying. 'I try to be nice. To establish a good rapport with the people I work with.'

'Hmm.' Hannah didn't have to try and make the sound less than understanding. Professional rapport had boundaries that Ryan clearly took no notice of.

He hadn't moved from the support of the post. To get to the car, Hannah had to go down the steps, which meant moving closer to the stationary figure.

'I work with you, Dr Jackson.'

'You do, Dr Fisher.' Hannah gripped the handles of her carry bag more firmly and made the move to the top of the steps.

'I'd like *us* to establish a good rapport. I don't think we've really got one yet, have we?'

'No.' She was close to Ryan now. She could almost have reached out and plucked petals from his hair.

'Why is that, Hannah?'

'I...ah...' It had been a mistake to make eye contact at this proximity. Words totally failed Hannah.

'Maybe we could try again,' Ryan suggested softly. 'We're in a new place that has nothing to do with work. We could make this weekend a new start.'

'Ah...' Something had already started. Hannah watched the way Ryan's gaze slid from her eyes to her mouth. The way his head was tilting slightly. She had to close her eyes as a wave of desire threatened to make her knees wobble and send her down the steps in an undignified stagger.

Had she mirrored that tilt of his face? Leaned closer to Ryan? Or had he just closed the gap of his own accord so that he could kiss her?

Not that it mattered. The instant his lips touched hers, *nothing* else mattered.

Yes, it was the start of something new, for sure. Something Hannah had never experienced. The first brush of paint on a totally new canvas.

Soft lips. A gentle pressure. Long enough to be intensely arousing but not nearly long enough. Hannah wanted more.

A *lot* more.

She wanted to taste this man. To touch him. To have him touch her. To fill in more of that canvas because she had no idea what colours and textures it would encompass or what the finished picture might be like. What that brief kiss *had* told her, however, was that the picture would be bigger and more exciting than any she'd ever seen.

It was Ryan who bent to pick up the carry bag, which had slipped, unnoticed, from Hannah's fingers.

'This way, Dr Jackson,' he murmured. 'Your chariot awaits.'

Hannah didn't want to move. Unless it was to go back into the cottage and take Ryan with her. It was disappointing that he hadn't suggested it himself. Surely he would normally follow through on a kiss like that?

Perhaps he intended to. He smiled at Hannah.

'Maybe,' he said lazily, 'we can do something else about establishing that rapport later.'

'Rapport, huh? That's a new word for it.' Susie lay on her hospital bed with her leg elevated on pillows, bandaged and packed in ice. 'So what was it like, then?'

'The kiss?' Hannah chewed the inside of her cheek. 'Not bad, I guess.'

Susie pulled a pillow from behind her back to throw at her sister.

'OK, it was great. Best kiss I've ever had. Satisfied?'

'No. Are you?'

Hannah smiled wryly. 'No.'

'So what are you going to do about it?'

'What can I do? OK, he might have been tempted to kiss me for some reason but I can't see it going any further. He doesn't even like me. I don't like him. I'm just…attracted to him physically.'

'Maybe he's pretending not to like you because he's really attracted to you and you haven't given him any encouragement.'

'I kissed him! What more encouragement could he need?'

'Maybe he likes to take things slowly.'

'Ha!'

'Yeah.' Susie grinned. 'He doesn't look the type to take things slowly. Never mind, you've got the whole weekend in a tropical paradise. Something's bound to happen.'

'Forty-eight hours isn't that long.'

'But weddings are very romantic. And it's not as if you won't be seeing each other after you go home.'

'We won't be "seeing" each other when we go home. This is purely physical, Susie. An opportunity to get it out of my system. I mean, what if I'm sitting in a rest home when I'm ninety-five and I regret never trying a one-night stand? Doubt that I'd have the opportunity then.'

'So Ryan's not a long-term prospect, then?'

'Are you kidding? Would you take up with Richard the second with the benefit of hindsight?'

'No… Yes… Maybe…' Susie sighed. 'But Ryan might be different. He might not take off as soon as he spots greener pastures.'

'*Ha!*' Hannah put even more feeling into the dismissive response this time.

'Will you be seeing him again tonight?'

'No. I'm going to finish watching this movie with you, go and have a quick dip in the pool and then go home to sleep. I'm stuffed.'

'Why don't you skip the movie and see if you can find him over at the doctors' house? I've got some stuff about Emily I was going to tell him so he could put it in his best man's speech.'

Hannah groaned. 'He's probably got it written already. One long string of blonde jokes.'

'It's a good excuse to talk to him.'

'He'll be at the Athina. Peeling potatoes or something.'

'He might be back by now. He got up as early as you did so he's probably equally stuffed.'

'I could go and have a swim.'

'What's the weather like out there now?'

'Horribly windy but still hot. It's not raining.'

'The pool's nice and sheltered. You probably won't be the only one there. Lots of people like to cool off before they go to bed. You sleep a lot better that way.'

* * *

Hannah wasn't the only one in the pool.

Ryan was there.

'I've done my potato-peeling bit,' he told Hannah. He was watching her shed her outer clothing. 'I really needed to cool off.'

Hannah slid into the water with a sigh of pleasure. The pool area was sheltered but it was still windy enough to make the water slightly choppy and the wind on wet skin pulled the heat out quickly enough to raise goose-bumps when Hannah stood up at the shallower end of the pool. She ducked down and swam breaststroke into deeper water. 'This is gorgeous.'

'Isn't it?' Ryan was swimming towards her. Only his head was showing but, thanks to Susie's accident, Hannah was only too well aware of what the rest of Ryan looked like. She took a determined breath.

'Susie's been telling me things about Emily that might be useful for your best man's speech. Or have you finished writing it?'

Ryan grinned. 'No. Haven't started. Thought I might just wing it.'

'Well, there's a funny story about her spitting on Mike's helicopter.'

'Why did she do that?'

Hannah trod water, edging further away from Ryan. 'She was terrified of flying in helicopters and there's this Greek thing of spitting for luck. Only when the Greeks do it, it's kind of a token spit.' Hannah turned and swam a few strokes before shaking wet strands of hair from her eyes and taking another breath. 'When Emily did it, Mike had to clean the helicopter and there's a long-standing joke between them now about the paint-work getting corroded.' Hannah trod water again and turned. She should be a safe distance away from Ryan now.

She wasn't. He had kept pace with her.

'Interesting,' he said. 'I did know that Em hated helicopters. The night Mike proposed to her, they'd been sent on a mission that got cancelled and he landed them on a secluded beach. She thought they were crashing so she was really angry but Mike said that emergency measures had been necessary because he really needed to talk to her.'

'It all worked out, then.'

'Mmm. They have a very good rapport.' Ryan twisted his body in the water so that he was floating on his back. 'How's our rapport coming along, Dr Jackson?'

'Pretty good, I think.' Was it a feeling of insecurity that made it a relief to find her feet could touch the bottom of the pool here?

'Could be better, though, couldn't it?' With a fishlike movement, Ryan turned again, moving sideways at the same time so that he was within touching distance of Hannah. He caught her shoulders and Hannah seemed to simply float into his arms.

Not that she tried to swim away. She could have. Her feet were secure on the tiles at the bottom of the pool as she stood up and it would have been possible to get enough momentum to escape.

But she had no intention of escaping. This was it. She just had to get over the fear of doing something so out of character. Falling into what looked like a matching desire in Ryan's dark eyes, it became possible to step over that boundary.

'Yes,' she managed to whisper.

And then he was kissing her again and it was totally different to that kiss on the veranda. This one had a licence to continue. This one rapidly deepened so that Hannah had to wind her arms around Ryan's neck to keep her head above water. She could feel his hands on her bare skin, along with ripples from the disturbed water that seemed to magnify the sensation. His fingers trailed from her neck down her back, held her waist and then stroked their way up to cup her breasts.

At the same time, his lips and tongue were doing things that were arousing Hannah more than she would have believed possible. His face and lips were cool, thanks to the relentless wind, but the inside of his mouth was far from cool. It was hot enough to fuel an already burning desire. Hannah kissed him back, sucked headlong into that desire until she totally forgot herself. When he held her closer, Hannah found herself winding her legs around Ryan so that she couldn't float away.

Ryan groaned. 'God,' he murmured, pulling her hips even closer with an urgent strength to his grip. 'I want you, Hannah. You know that, don't you?'

Hannah tried to swallow, but couldn't. 'I want you, too.'

'Not here. Somewhere dry.'

Hannah had all the incentive she needed to throw caution to the winds for at least one night of her life. She even managed to sound as though she was quite used to being carried away by physical passion.

'Your place or mine?' she asked with a smile.

'Mine's closer. Just up those steps. It's Mike's old room. You can get in through a door on the veranda so nobody will see us.' Ryan bent to kiss her again and then he took her hand in his to lead her from the pool. 'You sure about this, Hannah?'

'What's not to be sure of? As you said, it's important to establish a good rapport with the people you work with.' She tightened her fingers around his, shivering as she climbed the steps of the pool and the wind caught at more of her exposed skin. Or was it the thought of where she was going and what she knew they would do that caused that shiver? Not that she had any intention of backing out. No way.

'Lead on, Dr Fisher.'

CHAPTER SIX

IT WAS THE curious howling sound that woke Ryan.

The first fingers of light were stretching under the roof of the wide veranda to enter his room and he could just make out the smooth hump of the feminine shoulder beside him.

Without thinking, Ryan touched the skin with his lips. A butterfly kiss that was as gentle as the way he traced the delicious curve of Hannah's hip with his hand, loving that dip to her waist that was accentuated by her lying on her side.

Loving everything about this woman. This new version of Hannah Jackson.

Her intensity. Softness. Suppleness. The way she accepted everything he had to offer and had responded in kind.

Thank God he hadn't stuck to that resolution to stay well away from her.

If he had, he would have missed out discovering just how good it was possible for sex to get. His experience last night had been the best he'd ever had in his life.

And Ryan knew what had made the difference. It was knowing he'd been right the moment he'd first laid eyes on Hannah. That there was a reason why the attraction had been so powerful. It was just possible he had found what he desperately needed in his life.

More of an anchor than a permanent job represented. The haven of a relationship that could be trusted. Could grow into something strong enough to last a lifetime. Could become a whole family even.

Something *good*. Love that wasn't darkened by the grim side of life. He was so tired of being strong for the people he loved. Not that he'd ever stop, but he badly needed something that would let the sunshine back into his own soul.

Someone he could be totally honest with. Someone that he could actually allow to see that things ripped him apart sometimes. He was fed up with hiding. Being flippant because he couldn't afford to share how he really felt. Making other people laugh because he'd discovered that was the best way to escape his own fear or misery.

Not that he'd ever made Hannah really laugh and, in a way, that was scary. Could she see through him? Despise him for being less than honest with himself and others? Had she been hurt in the past by a man who hadn't been able to connect on an emotional level and was that why that prickly barrier had been between them since that first meeting? If so, he could understand. Forgive and forget any of the putdowns.

Ryan pressed another soft kiss to Hannah's shoulder. Then he lifted her hair to kiss the side of her neck. She'd dropped that barrier last night, hadn't she?

One night.

A perfect night.

Ryan let his breath out in a contented sigh. Never mind that dawn was breaking. Last night had been just the beginning. The connection had been established and it could be the foundation for something that was going to last for ever.

Right now, Ryan had no doubt that it was entirely possible he could spend the rest of his life loving Hannah—in bed and out of it.

The dream took on colours that were so beautiful they took Hannah's breath away. She could actually *feel* them and the building excitement was something she remembered from child-hood, waking up to a longed-for day that was going to bring something very special.

She was flying in her dream. Soaring over some incredible tropical landscape towards the place she most wanted to be. But she wasn't going to reach her destination because the edges of reality were pushing the dream away. The sense of loss was only momentary, however, because the reality was the touch of Ryan's lips. They were on the side of her neck, delivering a kiss so gentle it made her want to cry. Instinctively, she turned towards him, seeking the comfort of being held, only to find his lips tracing a line from her neck all the way to her breast. Stopping when they reached the apex and the cool flick of his tongue on her nipple took Hannah's breath away for real.

There was still a dreamlike quality to this, though, and Han-nah kept her eyes closed even as her hands moved to find and touch Ryan where she now knew he most liked to be touched. The whole night had been a dream—the stuff of erotic fan-tasy—so why not keep it going just a little longer?

Thank God she had given in to that urge to experience some-thing new. To find out if Susie was right and she'd discover the best sex of her life. Even in her wildest dreams until now, she hadn't had any idea what it could be like. Hannah could under-stand perfectly what had drawn her mother and her sister and probably countless other women into relationships that could only end in heartbreak.

Not that she was going to allow this to go that far. This was just a perfect ending to a perfect night. A one-night stand that Hannah could treasure the memory of for the rest of her life.

With a small sound of absolute pleasure, she slid her arms completely around Ryan to draw him closer.

It was raining when they woke again. Rain driven sideways by a wind that hadn't abated at all during the night. If anything, it was worse.

'What's the time?'

Ryan reached to collect the wristwatch he'd dropped by the side of the bed. 'Nearly nine.'

'Oh, my God, I can't believe we've slept in!' Hannah slid out from the tangled sheets, covering her bare breasts with her hands while she looked for her clothes. 'I've got to get back to Susie's place and get sorted. We're supposed to be at Kylie's salon by nine-thirty. It's probably chaos out there by now.'

'It would be chaos whatever time it is.' Ryan put his arms behind his head, clearly intending to watch Hannah getting dressed. 'Don't worry about it.'

'Where's my phone?' Hannah felt more in control now that she had her underwear on. 'Susie's probably been trying to text me. I put it on silent mode at the rehearsal yesterday and I completely forgot to reset it.'

'You got distracted,' Ryan said with satisfaction. 'The wedding's not till 4 p.m. Don't stress.'

Hannah pulled on crumpled cargo pants. Impossible not to feel stressed with the sound of rapid footsteps on the wooden boards of the veranda behind the thin curtain and then the excited bark of a dog.

'I need to get out of here without anyone seeing me.'

'Why?'

'It would be embarrassing if everyone knew I'd spent the night here.'

'Why?' Ryan repeated. 'It's nothing to be ashamed of. We're both single, consenting adults, aren't we?'

'Yes...' But there was an element of shame as far as Hannah was concerned. She'd never done anything like this in her life. This kind of selfish physical indulgence might be normal for Ryan and the women he chose, but it couldn't be more out of character for her. She'd always made sure she was ready to commit to an exclusive relationship before going to bed with someone.

'And it was fun, yes?' Ryan wriggled his eyebrows suggestively. 'I certainly enjoyed it.'

'Mmm.' Hannah tore her eyes away from the sight of Ryan getting out of bed. He obviously felt no need to cover himself. This was a man who was quite comfortable in his own skin. An enviable confidence that Hannah could only aspire to. She did her best. 'Me, too,' she added with a smile.

Ryan covered the floor space between them with an easy couple of strides. He drew Hannah into his arms and kissed her. 'I *really* enjoyed it,' he murmured. 'You're amazing.'

'Mmm.' The sound was a little strangled this time. Hannah wasn't so sure about daylight kisses. Sexual fantasy needed the cover of dark. She drew away. 'Could you keep an eye out and tell me when the coast is clear on the veranda? I can go down the other end, away from the kitchen, can't I?'

'Yeah.' Ryan turned away and picked up his shorts. 'I'll come with you.'

'No need. It'll only take me a few minutes to walk and I could do with the fresh air.'

'It'll be fresh all right. Might feel quite cold after yesterday with this rain. Did you bring a jacket?'

'No.'

'Then why don't you let me drive you home? I've got to take Mike's Jeep back up to the Athina, anyway. I'd better check in and see what my best-man duties involve. I suspect I'll have to stick with Mike for the rest of the day.'

And Hannah would need to be with Emily. She probably wouldn't see Ryan again till later that afternoon. No more daylight kisses to contend with. The odd sensation in her stomach had to be relief, rather than disappointment, surely?

'A ride would be good,' she said. 'That way I can get sorted faster.'

The veranda was deserted and no one interrupted their journey through the garden to the car park. As they scrambled from the end of the veranda, Ryan took hold of Hannah's hand and it felt so natural it would have been rude to pull hers away. As they left the gardens behind them, Hannah glanced at the hospital buildings but there had been no message from Susie yet and she would be back here in no time. Would she tell her sister about last night?

Maybe not. Not yet, anyway. The experience was still too fresh. Private and...precious?

Would Ryan say anything?

Maybe not. The way his hand still held hers was comforting. As though he shared a reluctance to break the illusion of a bond they'd created last night. Hannah was even more confident he could be discreet when he dropped her hand at the sight of someone running towards them.

Wet curls of black hair were plastered around Mike's face. 'I was just coming to find you, mate. Hi, Hannah.'

'What's up?' Ryan wasn't smiling. Neither was Mike.

'There's been an accident up at Wygera. Harry called me to see if I can do a first response with the Jeep. I've got a good paramedic kit in the back.' Mike was still moving and both Ryan and Hannah followed. 'I was on the way to the house to find a doc to come with me, but you'll do just fine.'

'Do you want me to come as well?' Hannah queried.

'Please.' Mike caught the keys Ryan threw and unlocked the doors of the Jeep. 'Sounds like there are at least three casualties. All teenagers.' He opened the back of the vehicle and pulled out a light, which he stuck to his roof. A cord snaked in through his window and he plugged the end into the cigarette lighter. A bright orange light started flashing as he turned on the engine.

'Where's Wygera?' Ryan pulled his safety belt on as Hannah climbed into the backseat.

'It's an aboriginal settlement about fifty miles from here. We'd normally get the chopper out for something like this but there's no way anyone's going to be flying today.' Gears crunched and the Jeep jerked backwards as Mike turned with speed and they took off. Hannah clicked her safety belt into its catch.

'What's happened?' she queried. 'And don't you have an ambulance available?'

'They're all busy on other calls right now and it'll take time to get a vehicle on the road. There's been trouble with the bloody bulls, by the sound of it—thanks to this weather.'

They were on the main road now, and Hannah could feel how difficult it was going to be, driving fast in the kind of wind gusts they were being subjected to. The windscreen wipers were on high speed but the rain appeared to be easing a little. Hannah shivered. She was damp and still hadn't had the opportunity to get any warmer clothing. Wrapping her arms around herself for warmth, she listened as Mike continued filling them in.

'There's a guy up at Wygera by the name of Rob Wingererra. They've acquired a few rodeo bulls. Long story, but they're a project for the teenagers up there. Huge animals with wicked horns. Apparently the wind caused some damage last night and brought a fence down and damaged a shed. The kids went out to try and get the bulls rounded up and into shelter and they got out of hand. Some kid's been cut by corrugated iron, one's been gored by a bull and another sounds like he might have a crush injury of some kind after getting caught between a bull and a gate.'

'How long will it take us to get there?'

'It's an hour's drive on a good day but I'm hoping to get there sooner than that. Hang on tight back there, Hannah, but don't worry. I know this road like the back of my hand. We'll just need to watch out for slips or rubbish on the road.'

He certainly knew the road. Having gone over the bridge and through the township, Mike headed towards the foothills of the mountains that divided the coastal plain from the cattle country Hannah knew was further inland. At the speed they were going, they would arrive there as fast as any ambulance was capable of. As they rounded one corner, Ryan threw a glance over his shoulder.

'You OK, Hannah?'

The tone was caring. How long had it been since a man had been this concerned for her well-being? It was dangerous to allow it to matter.

'I'm fine,' she said hurriedly.

'No, you're not—you're freezing!' Ryan twisted his body beneath the safety belt, pulling off the lightweight jacket he was wearing. 'Here. Put this on. '

'Thanks.' Hannah slid her arms into sleeves that were still warm from Ryan's skin. 'Are you sure you don't need it?'

But Ryan wasn't listening. 'What information have you been given about these kids so far?'

'There's a health worker at the settlement, Millie, who's very good. Rob called her after he found the kids and they've got them inside at his place. She's controlled the bleeding on the boy that got cut but it sounds like he might have lost quite a bit of blood. The one who got poked by a horn isn't feeling too good. He's been vomiting but Millie thinks that might have something to do with a heavy night on the turps. The other one has sore ribs, maybe a fracture, so he's finding it painful to breathe.'

'Sounds like a mess.'

'I'm glad I've got you two along.' Mike flashed a grin over his shoulder at Hannah. 'Not the chief bridesmaid duties you were expecting this morning, eh? Sorry about that.'

Hannah smiled back. 'Actually, this is probably more within my comfort zone.'

'We'll have back-up pretty fast. There'll be an ambulance not far behind us and they'll send another one as soon as they're clear. We just need to do the initial triage and make sure they're stable for transport. Couldn't ask for more than two ED specialists on my team.'

'Let's hope it's not as bad as it sounds,' Ryan said. 'At least the rain's slowing down.'

'I've put in a good word to try and get some sunshine for Em this afternoon.'

Ryan laughed. 'You think the big guy's going to listen to you?'

'Hey, I've collected a few brownie points in my time. At least as many as you. Or maybe not.' Mike glanced at his friend. 'How's your dad doing?'

'Not so great. It's hard on Mum.'

'She must be delighted to have you in Auckland now.'

'Yeah.'

'Few trips to Brisbane still on the agenda, though, I guess? How's Michaela?'

Ryan shrugged. 'You know how it is,' was all he said.

'Yeah, buddy.' Mike's response was almost too quiet for Hannah to catch. 'I know.'

What was wrong with Ryan's father? And who was Michaela? An ex-wife? Hannah slumped back a little in her seat. How ridiculous to feel jealous. A timely reminder that this was just one weekend of her life; she didn't need to get caught up in Ryan Fisher's personal business. That was the road to the kind of emotional disaster Hannah had carefully avoided in her life thus far.

Caught up in her own thoughts and then a text conversation with Susie, who had heard about the drama at Wygera and was happy to wait for Emily to collect her, it seemed only a short time later that a tall water tower came into view. The cluster of houses nearby had a sad, tired air to them, with the rusting car bodies on the sparse greenery of surrounding land adding to an impression of poverty.

The eucalyptus trees were huge. They had been here far longer than the housing and would no doubt outlast most of these dwellings. Right now, the majestic trees were dipping and swaying in the strong wind, participating enthusiastically in a form of elemental ballet. Small branches were breaking free, swirling through the air to join the tumble of leaves and other debris on the bare ground. A larger branch caught Ryan's attention as it landed on the steep roof of the tidiest building they'd seen so far.

'It's the local hall,' Mike told him. 'Built to withstand snow, from what I've heard.' He grinned. 'Really useful, huh? It should manage the odd branch or two, anyway. We've got a turn-off up here and then we should almost be at Rob's place.'

A young woman could be seen waving frantically as they turned onto a rough, unsealed road.

'Target sighted,' Mike said. 'One windmill!'

Hannah was amazed he could sound so relaxed. And that Ryan could share a moment of amusement. She felt completely out of her depth here. They had one paramedic kit between the three of them and three potentially seriously injured teenagers. Hannah had never worked outside a well-equipped emergency department before.

'Hell, you took a long time,' the young woman told them. 'The boys are hurt bad, you know.' She led the way into the house. 'Stupid bulls,' she added with feeling.

'They weren't being nasty,' an older woman said. 'They were scared by the wind and that flapping metal on the shed. Hi, Mike!'

'Hi, Millie.' Mike smiled at the health worker and then at a man who was holding bloodstained towels to the leg of a boy on the couch. 'G'day, Rob. How's it going?'

'I'll let you tell me,' Rob said. His weathered face was creased with anxiety. 'I think I've finally managed to stop the bleeding in Jimmy's leg now, anyway. I've been sitting on the damn thing for an hour.'

Mike had set his backpack-style kit down on the floor and was unzipping it to pull out a stethoscope. 'This is Ryan,' he said, 'and that's Hannah. They're both doctors.' He glanced at the two other boys, who were sitting on the floor, leaning against the wall. They both had a rug over their legs and they both looked miserable. One had a plastic basin beside him. He shifted his gaze to Millie questioningly.

'Hal's got the sore ribs and Shane's got the puncture wound.' She smiled at Hannah and Ryan. 'Guess you've all got one patient each. Who wants who?'

Hannah swallowed a little nervously. An abdominal goring from a long bull's horn could have resulted in nasty internal injuries that would be impossible to treat in the field. Broken ribs could result in a tension pneumothorax and there were no X-ray facilities to help with diagnosis. A cut leg seemed the safest option. Even if Jimmy had lost enough blood to be going into shock, the treatment was easy. Stop the bleeding, replace fluid and supply oxygen.

'I'll have a look at Jimmy,' she said quickly. 'Have you got a sphygmomanometer in that kit, Mike?'

'Yep.' Mike pulled it out. 'You want to check Shane, Ryan?'

'Sure.'

'Mary?' Mike spoke to the girl who'd shown them inside. 'Could you go back to the road, please? There should be an ambulance arriving before too long and it was really helpful to have you show us where to stop.'

'But I wanted to watch,' Mary protested. 'Are you going to sew Jimmy's leg up?'

'Probably not,' Hannah responded. 'Not until we get him to hospital anyway.'

'Do as you're told,' Millie added firmly.

Hannah moved towards Jimmy, who looked to be about fourteen. 'Hi.'

The youth stared back silently for just a second before averting his eyes, which gave Hannah the impression he'd taken an instant dislike to her.

'I'm going to be looking after you for a bit, Jimmy,' she said. 'Have you ever had your blood pressure taken?'

He shook his head, still avoiding eye contact.

'It doesn't hurt. I'm going to wrap this cuff around your arm. It'll get a bit tight in a minute.'

Ryan had gone to Shane who looked younger than the other two. He was holding a teatowel to his side and it, too, was blood soaked.

Hannah unwound the blood-pressure cuff from Jimmy's arm. His baseline recording for blood pressure was within normal limits but he was young enough to be compensating well for blood loss. She would need to keep monitoring it at regular intervals.

'I'm going to put a small needle in the back of your hand,' she warned Jimmy. 'OK?'

'Why?'

'You've lost a fair bit of blood. We need to give you some fluid to get the volume back up. Blood doesn't work as well as it should if there isn't enough of it going round. Is your leg hurting?'

'Yeah, course it is. It's bloody near chopped off.'

'Can you wiggle your toes?'

'Yeah.' The tone was grudging and Jimmy still wouldn't make eye contact. Was it just her or were all strangers not welcomed by these teens?

'I don't think it's in too much danger of dropping off, Jimmy,' she said calmly. 'I'll check it properly in a minute. When I've got this needle in your hand, I'll be able to give you something to stop it hurting so much.'

Ryan seemed to be getting a similar suspicious response for being a stranger. Shane didn't look too happy when he put his hand out to touch the teatowel.

'Mind if I have a look, buddy?'

'Are yous really a doctor?'

'Sure am. Just visiting from New Zealand.'

'He's a mate of mine,' Mike told the boys. 'He's going to be the best man at my wedding.'

'Oh, that's right!' Millie exclaimed. 'You're getting married today, Mike. Crikey, I hope you're not going to be late for your own wedding. Dr Emily would be a bit cheesed off.'

'We'll get sorted here in no time,' Mike said calmly. 'Hal, I'm just going to listen to your chest while you take a few breaths, OK?'

'But it hurts.'

'I know, mate. I want to make sure those ribs haven't done any damage to your lung, though. Try to lean forward a bit.'

Hannah had the IV line secured and a bag of fluids attached and running. She got Rob to hold the bag. Having been given the kudos of being Mike's best friend, Ryan now had a more co-operative patient.

'Does it hurt if you take a deep breath?'

'Yeah.'

'Can I have a look at it?'

'I guess.'

'Wow, that's a pretty impressive hole! These bulls must be big fellas.'

'Yeah.'

'Does it hurt if I touch here?'

'Nah. Not much.'

For the next few minutes a rather tense silence fell as they all worked on assessing and treating their patients. Hannah didn't want to disturb the makeshift dressing on Jimmy's leg in case the bleeding started again, but she made a careful examination of his lower leg and foot to check for any serious damage to blood supply and nerves.

Mike was worried about a possible pneumothorax from Hal's broken ribs and got Ryan to double-check his evaluation.

'I think you're right,' Ryan said. 'Breath sounds are definitely down on the left side but it's not showing any signs of tensioning. One of us should travel with him in the ambulance, though.'

The need for constant monitoring and the potential for serious complications from the injury went unspoken, but Hannah could feel the level of tension in the room creep up several notches.

Ryan glanced around him. 'Anyone heard the one about the blonde and the bulls with big horns?'

Hannah almost groaned aloud. Just when she'd been impressed by the professional, *serious* manner in which Ryan was approaching a job that should have been as much out of his comfort zone as it was for her, he was about to revert to type and tell one of his stupid jokes. Make light of a serious situation.

And then she caught Ryan's gaze.

This was deliberate. He knew exactly what he was doing. This was a ploy—as much of a skill as applying pressure to stop heavy bleeding, only it was intended to work in the opposite direction. A safety valve to relieve pressure. A way of defusing an atmosphere that could be detrimental if it was allowed to continue.

What if Hal picked up on how dangerous a pneumothorax could be and got frightened? He would start to breathe faster, which would not only hurt but interfere with his oxygen uptake. Shane might start vomiting again and exacerbate an internal injury. Jimmy might get restless and open the wound on his leg, with further blood loss.

They were all listening already.

'So, she tells him exactly how many bulls there are in this huge paddock and demands that he honours his side of the bargain and gives her the cute baby one.'

If this was a practised skill, as that almost defensive glance had suggested, what did that tell her about the man Ryan *really* was? Was the fun-loving, laid-back image simply a veneer?

'And the farmer says, "If I can tell you the real colour of your hair, will you give me back my baby bull?"'

Maybe the times Hannah saw Ryan so focussed on his patients—as he had been with Brendon's mother on Monday night and with Shane only minutes ago—said more about who he really was. Or the concern she'd heard in his voice when he'd asked if she was OK on the trip up here. Or…that incredible ability to be so gentle she'd discovered in his touch last night.

No. Hannah couldn't afford to believe in the serious side Ryan was capable of presenting. That was the short cut to disaster that her mother and sister had followed so willingly. She was stronger than that. She could push it away. It was easy, really. All she had to do was remember the way he flirted. The way women flocked to queue up for a chance to go out with him.

He might have the ability to be serious but it couldn't be trusted to last. Serious stuff couldn't be allowed to continue for too long. It just had to be broken by the injection of fun.

"'Now...give me back my dog!'"

Even though she'd only been half listening, Hannah found herself smiling. Shane and Jimmy were giggling. Hal groaned because it hurt, trying to laugh, but he still managed a big grin. Rob and Millie were still laughing when two ambulance officers came through the door with Mary. Eyebrows shot up.

'We heard there was an accident here,' one of them said, 'not a party!'

How many doctors would be able to achieve that? Hannah wondered. Then her own smile broadened. How many doctors had such a supply of awful jokes that could seemingly be adapted to suit the situation? As a demonstration of how useful it could be to be so laid back, this had been an eye-opener. The tension that had filled this room when Hannah had arrived and had threatened to get worse later had gone. Much of the anxiety had left the faces of Rob and Millie and even the boys were all still grinning, even when faced with imminent transport to hospital.

It didn't take long to sort out the transport arrangements. Mike would travel in the ambulance with Hal and Jimmy. Shane demanded to travel with Ryan in the Jeep.

'You can't do that,' Millie said. 'You'd better wait for the other ambulance. You've got a hole in your guts.'

'It's pretty superficial, luckily,' Ryan told her. 'It's going to need a good clean-out and examination under local, but I don't see any harm in Shane riding in the Jeep to start with, anyway. We can meet the other ambulance on the road and transfer him then.'

'Guess that'll be quicker.' Millie waved at Mike as he climbed into the back of the ambulance. 'You'd better get back in time to get your glad rags on, eh?'

Hannah was in the backseat of the Jeep again and Ryan kept up an easy conversation with Shane, interspersed with the occasional query and frequent glance that let Hannah know how closely he was monitoring the lad's condition.

They got back to Crocodile Creek before a rendezvous with the second ambulance. Hannah gave herself a mental shake when she realised that she was disappointed. It wouldn't do to be shut in the confines of a vehicle with no company other than Ryan's, she told herself firmly. It would make it impossible not to feel the strength of the connection that daylight and even a semi-professional working environment had failed to dent.

Disturbingly, it seemed to have become stronger. Hannah stood back in the emergency department of Crocodile Creek Hospital after doing a handover for Jimmy. When Ryan finished transferring the care of Shane to the hospital staff, he turned to look for her. When he spotted her, standing near the water cooler, he smiled.

A different sort of smile. It went with a questioning expression that suggested he really cared about whether she was OK. Like his tone had been when he'd given her his jacket to keep her warm. It touched something deep inside Hannah and made it impossible not to feel happy.

Dangerous, dangerous territory.

She wasn't going to fall in love with Ryan Fisher.

Hannah simply wasn't going to allow it to happen.

CHAPTER SEVEN

WHEN HAD IT HAPPENED?

How had it happened?

It wasn't just the atmosphere. The way Mike and Emily were looking at each other as they walked around the altar, taking their first steps as man and wife. Or the chanting of the priest as he gave them his blessing. Or the collective sigh of approval coming from the packed church pews.

There was no question it *had* happened, however.

With her arms full of the white silk train of Emily's dress and the soft tulle of her veil, Hannah was walking very slowly, her arm touching Ryan's as he held the silk ribbons joining the wreaths on the heads of the bridal couple. They got a little tangled at the last corner and there was a momentary pause.

And Ryan looked at her.

There could be no mistaking that sensation of free-fall. The feeling that all the cells in her body were charged with some kind of static electricity and were desperately seeking a focus for their energy.

Or that the focus was to be found in the depths of the dark eyes that were so close to her own. This was a connection that transcended anything remotely physical. The caress of that eye contact lasted only a heartbeat but Hannah knew it would haunt her for life.

It was a moment of truth.

A truth she hadn't expected.

One she most certainly didn't want.

She was in love with Ryan Fisher. She could…incredibly… imagine that this was a ceremony to join *them* in matrimony, not Mike and Emily and the notion only increased that delicious sensation.

Fortunately, Hannah had a huge armful of fabric she could clutch. It brought back memories of the cuddly blanket Susie had dragged around with her for years as a small child, much to Hannah's disgust. The fleecy square had become smaller and smaller over the years and was finally abandoned but somehow the last piece had emerged just after their father had died and Susie had slept with it under her pillow and had genuinely seemed to derive comfort from the limp rag.

Hannah had never needed an inanimate object for comfort.

Until now.

How stupid had it been to go to bed with Ryan?

She *knew* she didn't do one-night stands. She had always believed that that kind of intimacy should be reserved for a relationship that meant something because it was too hard to separate physical and emotional involvement.

Had her subconscious tricked her into believing that, for once, she could do just that? Or had she known all along that her attraction to Ryan had only needed a push to become something far deeper and she had been drawn towards it as inevitably as her mother and sister had been drawn to involvement with the Richards? Had she despised his flirting because, deep down, she had been jealous?

Stupid, stupid, stupid!

How horrified would Ryan be if he guessed how she was feeling? Or, worse, would he take advantage of it, in the Richards style, making the most of having some female fall at his feet—just until he got bored and moved on to a more exciting playground?

Any of those wayward thoughts, generated by the chaos and excitement of the afternoon's preparation for this ceremony, of allowing her one-night stand to become a one-weekend stand had to be squashed.

This had all the makings of a painful ending already. If even a tiny bit more was added to the way Hannah was feeling, it could be just as disastrous as spending weeks or months in a relationship, only to have it end. She might have had no intention of making an emotional investment but something had been automatically deducted from her account without her realising.

Hannah liked that analogy. It wasn't possible to withdraw the sum but she could, at least, stop throwing good money after bad and pull the plug.

Firmly enough to break the chain so she could throw it away.

Facing the congregation as they made their final circuit, Hannah looked up, finally confident she had control again. There was a woman in the second row in the most extraordinary hat she had ever seen. A vast purple creation with bright pink artificial flowers, like giant gerberas, around its brim.

In front of the hat sat Mike's mother, a handkerchief pressed to her face to mop up her tears of joy. His father was using his sleeve to wipe his. Beside them sat a little row of children— the pageboys and flower girls who had done a wonderful job of petal-strewing and had had to sit quietly for the more serious part of the proceedings.

As a sensible insurance policy, Susie sat at the end of the pew, hemming the children in, her crutches propped in front of her, and beside her, in the aisle, was Charles in his wheelchair with one of the flower girls sitting on his lap. The adults were both smiling happily but there was an almost wistful element in both their expressions.

It *had* been a gorgeous service. Sophia must be thrilled that everything had gone so perfectly despite the worry that the worsening weather that afternoon had caused.

Not that any of the bridal party had had time to fret. Kylie, the gum-chewing, self-confessed gossip queen, had worked like a Trojan to make them all as beautiful as possible. Hannah had been startled by how she looked with her soft, natural curls bouncing on her shoulders and more make-up than she would normally have worn. By the time she was encased in her peach silk, sheath dress with the big flower at the base of a plunging halter neckline that matched the explosion of froth at knee level and the sleeveless, silver bolero jacket, Hannah felt almost as gorgeous as Emily looked in her cloud of white lace and flowers.

The men had peach silk bow ties to match the bridesmaids' dresses and silver waistcoats to match their jackets. Hannah hadn't been wrong in thinking they would look irresistibly handsome in their dark suits and white dress shirts. And Ryan, of course, was the best looking of the lot, with his long, lean frame encased in tailored elegance and his dark hair groomed to keep the waves in place. Even a very recent shave hadn't been enough to remove the dark shadow, however, and Hannah couldn't help remembering the scratch of his face that morning on some very tender areas of her skin.

With some difficulty, she dragged her thoughts back to the present. Yes. It had been an over-the-top, fairy-tale wedding ceremony for two people who were obviously very deeply in love and that had the potential to make any single person like Susie or Charles Wetherby reflect on what was missing from their own lives.

It had to be contributing a lot to Hannah's own heightened emotional state. With a bit of luck, she would see things quite differently once they were away from the church.

It was nearly time for the bridal procession. Hannah could see Charles moving his wheelchair and Susie whispering to the children to give them their instructions. They would come at the end of the procession after each pair of bridesmaids and their male counterparts had moved into the aisle. Hannah's partner was, of course, Ryan. She would have to take his arm at least until they got to the foyer, where she would need both hands to help Emily with her veil.

It might take all twelve available bridesmaids' hands, judging by the howl of the wind that could now be heard over the trumpet music. The blast of air inside that came as someone opened the main door of the church was enough to catch Emily's veil and threaten to tear it from her head. The chandelier overhead rattled alarmingly and a crashing sound brought a gasp from everybody standing to watch the procession.

People were craning their necks to see what had happened but they were staring in different directions.

'It was the flowers!' someone near Hannah exclaimed. 'Look!'

Hannah looked. She could see the huge vase of exquisitely arranged peach and white blooms that had toppled from its pedestal near the altar. A large puddle was spreading out from the mound of scattered blooms amongst the shards of broken china.

'No, it came from outside,' someone else shouted. 'Everybody, sit down!'

The priest was looking as alarmed as his congregation. Hannah caught a glimpse of Sophia crossing herself as the priest hurried down the side aisle. Another loud splintering noise was heard as he reached the foyer and his robes were whipping around his legs.

'Close the door,' they heard him order. He came back to where Emily and Mike had halted a few seconds later. 'There are slates coming off the roof,' he reported. 'You can't go out that way.'

A buzz of consternation rippled through the crowded pews. What was happening? Was this a bad omen for the bridal couple? The noise level continued to increase as the priest spoke to Mike and Emily, pointing towards another door at one side of the church.

'You'll have to go out through the vestry. It's not safe this way.'

'No, no, no!' Sophia was powering down the side aisle, gesticulating wildly. Hannah saw a pretty young woman in a dark blue dress with a matching ribbon in her curly hair get up hurriedly to follow her. 'They can't go backwards,' Sophia cried. 'It's bad luck!'

A chorus of assent came from the congregation nearby. The priest was looking deeply concerned and even Mike and Emily exchanged worried glances.

'How about "take two"?' Ryan suggested calmly. 'We'll push rewind. You guys go back to the altar, have another snog and then go down the side and out the vestry door. That way, you won't be going backwards before you leave the church.'

'How about it, Ma?'

'It's a great idea,' the young woman beside Sophia said firmly. 'Isn't it, Mrs P.?'

'I don't know. I really don't know. This is bad....'

'Don't cry, Ma,' Mike ordered. 'Have you got a spare hanky there, Grace?'

The sound of more slates crashing into the courtyard decided the matter. As one body, the bridal party turned and moved swiftly back towards the altar. The sound of spitting for luck from everybody at the end of the pews was clearly audible despite continuing, excited conversation.

'Hey!' Ryan leaned towards Hannah. 'Aren't you supposed to be hanging on my arm?'

'I don't think we rehearsed this bit.' But Hannah obligingly took the arm being offered.

'I haven't had a chance to tell you but you look fabulous in pink.'

'It's peach, not pink.'

The second kiss that Mike and Emily shared in front of the

altar was a little more hurried than the first. They were all aware of the priest now standing by the vestry door, virtually wringing his hands with anxiety. He wanted his church emptied, preferably without anyone being decapitated by flying slates.

Sophia looked as though she would benefit from smelling salts. Unplanned happenings were threatening to disrupt the most carefully orchestrated wedding that Crocodile Creek was likely to experience.

The loose slates weren't the only surprise. Hannah was close behind the bride and groom as the priest opened the vestry door and there, in front of them, was a couple locked in a rather passionate embrace.

It had to be that girl, Georgie, she had seen at the airport. Hannah would have recognised those red stiletto shoes anywhere.

Ryan nudged her. 'Isn't that Alistair—that American neurosurgeon?'

'Yes, I think so.'

'Seems like they've been having their own little ceremony.'

'Mmm.' What was it about this place? Something in the tropical air? Romance seemed to be around every corner.

Maybe *that* was the problem. She'd get over Ryan in a flash once she was breathing nice clean, sensible New Zealand air again. Not that there was time to think even that far into the future. Some of the male guests had braved the front entrance to make sure it was safe to leave the church from this side. Vehicles were being brought right to the door and the mammoth task of shifting the whole congregation to the Athina for the reception was under way.

Any hint of blue patches between the boiling clouds had long gone. It looked as though another heavy, squally rain shower was imminent.

'Quickly, quickly,' Sophia said to everyone passing her at the door. She had clearly abandoned her carefully thought-out transport arrangements and was planning to move everybody as fast as possible. 'We must get home!'

She made Emily, Mike, Ryan, Hannah and Susie squeeze into the first of the limousines. 'The bride mustn't get wet!' she warned. 'It's bad luck!'

Sophia spat three times as Emily and Mike climbed into the spacious rear of the car. What with the huge wedding dress and then Susie's crutches, there wasn't much room left for Ryan and Hannah. They ended up on the same side as Susie with Hannah in the middle. A crutch pressed against her thigh on one side but that discomfort paled in comparison to the disturbing effect of having such close contact with Ryan's thigh on the other side.

'Well, that was fun.' Mike had a huge grin on his face. Then he turned to Emily and his smile faded before he kissed her tenderly.

'Don't mind us,' Ryan drawled.

Mike surfaced reluctantly. 'You should try this some time, mate. It's not that bad.'

'Mmm.' Ryan's sidelong glance at Hannah involved a subtle quirk of an eyebrow. *I know,* the glance said. *I've enjoyed that particular pastime quite recently myself.*

'Hey!' Mike was grinning again. 'If you got around to it soon enough, we could give these suits another airing. I'll return the favour and be *your* best man.'

'I'll keep that in mind.'

Why did Ryan choose that moment to slide his hand under the peachy froth of Hannah's skirt to find her hand? To hold it and give a conspiratorial kind of squeeze?

Had he got some crazy notion himself during that cere-mony—as she had? Was Hannah going to be tricked into be-lieving she was a candidate for his bride?

No!

She pulled her hand free but the gesture lost any significance because the driver of the limousine chose precisely that moment to slam on his brakes and she, Ryan and Susie tumbled forward.

'Ouch!' Susie cried.

'Are you all right?' Ryan helped her back onto the leather seat.

Mike slid the glass partition behind his head open. 'What's going on?'

'Rubbish bag flying around in this wind,' the driver told him. 'Sorry—but it landed on the windscreen and I couldn't see a thing. You guys OK back there?'

'Fine,' they all chorused.

Including Hannah. She *was* fine now that Ryan wasn't holding her hand. Now that they'd all been shaken out of the romantic stupor emanating from the bridal couple.

'Crikey!' The car slowed again as it crossed the old wooden bridge into the cove. 'If that water comes up any more, this'll get washed out to sea.'

The creek was more like a raging torrent and the wind was whipping up small waves on its swift-moving surface. The strings of fairy-lights adorning the exterior of the Athina were seriously challenging the staples holding them in place and Mike heroically gathered Emily's dress together to scoop his bride into his arms and carry her the short distance from the car to the restaurant doors.

Huge, fat drops of rain were starting to fall but Mike moved fast enough to prevent Emily's dress getting damp.

'Thank goodness for that.' She laughed. 'Sophia will be feeling my dress the moment she walks in.'

'Let me check.' Mike ran his hands down the embroidered bodice of the dress and then yanked Emily close. Laughing again, she wrapped her arms around his neck and lifted her face for a kiss.

Ryan's voice was close to Hannah's ear. Too close.

'They have a good rapport, don't they? Just like us.'

Hannah swallowed hard. Even his voice was enough to stir desire. A sharp yearning that was painful because she couldn't allow herself to respond.

'Later,' Ryan murmured. The word was spoken too softly for anyone else to overhear.

'No!'

She hadn't expected her response to come out with such vehemence but the promise Ryan's word had contained was too much. *Pull the plug,* her brain was screaming. *Now!*

The momentary freezing on Ryan's part was strong enough for Hannah to sense his shock at the rebuttal but there was no time to try and soften the rejection with any kind of explanation or excuse. The second and third cars from the church had pulled up and Mike's parents spilled out, along with several more clouds of peach-tulled women and dark-suited men.

'Your dress!' Sophia wailed. 'Let me feel your dress, darling! Is it wet?'

'No, it's completely dry. See?' Emily did a twirl in front of the mass of wedding presents piled up in the restaurant entrance.

Mike's father, George Poulos, beamed happily. 'Inside. Everybody inside. Our guests are arriving. It's time to eat, drink and be merry!'

The next hour was a blur of posing for the photographer and then introductions amongst a loud, happy crowd who were determined to ignore the shocking conditions outside. The howl of the wind, the intermittent thunder of rain on the roof and the crash of huge waves on the beach below the restaurant windows were largely drowned out by the enthusiastic live band and even more enthusiastic guests.

Hannah did her best to ignore the rather dark glances that were coming her way from Ryan. It was easy to avoid him by talking to other people. Like Grace, the young nurse with the blue ribbon in her hair.

'It's been my job to try and keep Mrs P. calm,' she told Hannah. Blue eyes that matched her ribbon rolled in mock exasperation. 'As if! Don't be at all surprised if there are a few doves flying around in here later.'

'Plates!' Mike's father carried a stack past them, weaving through a circle of dancers. 'For later,' he threw over his shoulder at Hannah and Grace. 'Don't tell Sophia.'

'I'd better distract her. Excuse me.' Grace hurried away.

'Opa!' someone shouted.

A chorus of echoes rippled through the room and Hannah saw a lot of small glasses being raised to lips.

'Ouzo?' A waiter had a tray of the small glasses, as well as the more traditional champagne flutes.

'Maybe later.' Hannah was having trouble trying to keep her head clear enough to remember all the names and she knew she would have to keep it clear to deal with the conversation that was bound to occur with Ryan.

He was right behind the waiter. 'What did you mean, "No"? "No", what?'

'I meant "no" to later,' she said with a resigned sigh.

'But I thought…is something wrong, Hannah?'

'Not at all.' Hannah smiled—reassuringly, she hoped. She would have to work with Ryan. She didn't want to offend him. 'Last night was lovely. Great fun.'

'Fun?' Ryan was staring at her. He had no right to look so shocked. Surely he did this kind of thing all the time? A bit of fun. Move on.

'This is Harry.' Grace had returned to where Hannah was standing, staring dumbly back at Ryan. 'He's our local policeman here in the cove. Hi.' She smiled at Ryan. 'You did a good job as best man.'

'I do an even better job at dancing.' Ryan's killer smile flashed as he extended his hand. 'Come on, let me show you.'

It was a snub, Hannah realised as Ryan turned away with Grace on his arm without a backwards glance. He was offended for some reason.

Harry was staring after the couple as though he didn't approve any more than Hannah did, but then they managed to smile at each other. In fact, it wasn't that difficult for Hannah to smile. A glow of something like pleasure curled within her. He had liked being with her, then. It had been good enough for him to want more.

If she wasn't so weak, she would have wanted it herself. How wonderful would it be to sink into a relationship with someone like Ryan and enjoy it for what it was? An interlude. One that would set the standard for the best that sex and probably companionship could offer. But to do it without losing too much of her heart and soul?

Impossible.

He would wreck her life eventually.

She would end up like her mother, settling for something that was better than nothing. Learning to enjoy fishing.

Or alone, like Susie, unable to find anyone that excited her as much as the first man who had really stolen her heart.

Harry was telling her something. Hannah made an effort to focus on the tall, good-looking man with a flop of black hair and a worried expression.

'I'm trying to keep tabs on what's happening with Willie,' he told her. 'They're making noises about upgrading it from a category 3 to a 4.'

'Is that serious?'

Harry nodded. 'Cyclones are all dangerous. 'Specially Aussie ones—they're known for exhibiting a more erratic path than cyclones in other parts of the world. The higher the number, the more danger they represent. A category 3 is a severe tropical cyclone. You can get wind gusts up to 224 kilometres per hour and can expect roof and structural damage, and a likely power failure.'

'The slates were certainly flying off the church.'

'There's a few people with tarps on their roofs already. They'll lose them if things get any worse.'

'And they're expected to?'

'It's been upgraded to a 4. It's running parallel to the coast at the moment but if it turns west we'll be in trouble. A 4 has winds up to 279 kilometres per hour. You'll get significant structural damage, dangerous airborne debris and widespread power failures.'

As though to underline Harry's sombre tone, the lights inside the Athina flickered, but there was still enough daylight for it not to matter and they came back on almost immediately.

'I'm with the SES—State Emergency Services,' Harry finished. 'In fact, if you'll excuse me, I should make a call and see what's happening.'

Just as Harry disappeared, Ryan emerged from an animated group of Greek women nearby.

'*Fun?*' he queried with quiet menace. 'Is that all it was for you, Hannah? *Fun?*'

This was disconcerting. She would have expected a shrugged response from Ryan by now. A 'there's plenty more fish in the sea' kind of attitude.

'It *was* fun.' She tried to smile. To break the tension. 'But we both know it could never be any more than that.'

'*Do* we?' Ryan held her gaze. Challenging her. 'Why is that?'

'Oh, come on, Ryan.' Hannah looked for an escape. Someone to talk to. A new introduction. Where was Susie when she needed her? Nothing seemed readily available. They were marooned. A little island of hostility that was keeping all the happy people away with an invisible force field. 'We're not on the same page, remember?'

'Obviously not,' Ryan snapped. 'There I was thinking that we had made a fresh start. The start of something that could actually be meaningful.'

Meaningful? Oh, help! It would be so easy to believe that. Hannah so *wanted* to believe it. To believe *she* could be the one to tame this particular 'bad boy'. To have him love her so much he would be content to settle down and never get bored.

The wheelchair arrived beside them so smoothly neither had noticed.

'I'm Charles Wetherby,' the man said unnecessarily. 'I must

apologise for this awful weather Crocodile Creek is turning on for you. I hope you're still managing to enjoy yourselves.'

Hannah had the weird feeling that Charles had known exactly how much they were enjoying themselves and was there to do something to defuse the atmosphere.

Ryan controlled the flash of an ironic smile and managed to introduce both himself and Hannah to Charles without missing a beat.

And then he excused himself, as though he couldn't stand being in Hannah's company any longer.

He was hurt, she realised. She hadn't expected that at all. It was confusing. Why would he be hurt…unless he was being honest. Unless he really had thought there was something meaningful going on.

No. He might think that—for now. He might even believe it long enough for Hannah to trust it, but he was a type, wasn't he? He was, what, in his mid-thirties? At least a couple of years older than she was, given his professional experience. If he was into commitment he wouldn't still be playing the field. And what about Michaela? Was she someone who had believed in him and had now been discarded?

Hannah had to paste a smile onto her face to talk to Charles.

'You look so like Susie,' he was saying. 'It's a real treat. Must be wonderful to have a sibling that you're so close to.'

'It is.'

'Uncle Charles! Look at me! I'm dancing!'

The small blonde flower girl who had been sitting on Charles's knee during the ceremony was part of a circle of dancers, between two adults. She wasn't watching the steps any more because her head was twisted in Hannah's direction and she had a huge smile on her face.

'This way, Lily.' Mike's sister, Maria, had hold of one of Lily's hands. 'We go this way now.'

'Opa!' The cry to signal a new round of toasting the bridal couple rang out.

'Ouzo?'

'No, thanks.' Hannah shook her head at the attentive waiter. Lily had given her an excuse to watch the dancers and Ryan was now part of the circle. So was Mike. And then the circle disintegrated as Sophia bustled through.

'Eat! Eat! The food will be getting cold.'

Ryan and Mike took no notice. With an arm around each other's shoulders and their other arms extended, they were stepping in a dance of their own. Happy. Relaxed. The bond of a deep friendship was obvious to everyone and they all approved. They were clapping and stamping their feet in time with the music and calling encouragement.

And then George was on the dance floor, a plate in each hand.

'No!' Sophia cried.

But the sound of smashing crockery only brought a roar of approval and more people back to the dance floor.

Hannah turned away. She spotted Susie sitting with a very pregnant woman. They had plates of food from the buffet.

Not that Hannah felt hungry. Watching Mike and Ryan dance had left her with a curious sense of loss. How long had Ryan known his best friend? Ten years? More? Their bond appeared unshakable. Mike trusted him completely.

But Mike wasn't a woman. The ending of a friendship, however close, could never destroy someone as much as the ending of the most intimate relationship it was possible to have.

It was really quite straightforward so why was her heart winning the battle with her head right now?

Why did she feel this sense of loss? As though she had just made a terrible mistake?

Because it was already too late. She was in love with this man.

She was already prepared to believe in him.

And if he gave her another chance, she would take it.

Take the risk.

Do whatever it took to spend as much time as possible with him. In bed and out of it.

The rest of her life, even.

CHAPTER EIGHT

THIS HAD TO be the ultimate putdown.

And he had only himself to blame.

It had only been one night. Hannah Jackson was only one of hundreds of women Ryan had met since he'd grown up enough to be interested in the opposite sex. Thousands, even, and he'd dated a fair few in those early years. Slept with enough to know how rare it was to find a woman who could be both intellectually and physically stimulating.

He could have dealt with that attraction, however powerful it had been, when that was all it was. Moved on with maybe just a shrug of regret. But Hannah had taken down that barrier. Taken him by the hand and shown him a place he had never been to before. A place he didn't want to leave.

And now she was shoving him out. Had put that barrier back up and.....it *hurt*, dammit! Nobody had ever treated him like this before—and she'd accused *him* of being shallow? What reason did she have? She might have been hurt in the past, he reminded himself. Some bastard might have treated her badly enough to leave scars that hadn't healed yet.

No. It didn't matter how good the reason might be. Or how fresh the scars. Why the hell would he set himself up for another kick in the guts like the one she'd just delivered? With a smile, no less. A damning with faint praise.

Fun? Like a night out? A party? A game of tennis?

'What's up, mate?' Mike's fingers dug into his shoulder. 'You look like you're at a funeral, not a wedding.'

'Sorry. Miles away.'

'Not in a happy place, by the look of that scowl. Forget it. Come and eat. The lamb's wonderful and Ma will be force-feeding you soon if she doesn't see you holding a plate.'

'Good idea. And I think a drink or two is overdue as well.'

'Just don't get trollied before you have to make that speech and tell everyone how wonderful I am.'

Ryan laughed. 'More like seeing how many stories of your disreputable past I can dredge up. What time am I on?'

'Just before the cake-cutting. I think Ma's got it down for about 8:30 p.m.'

'Cool. Gives me half an hour to see how much I can remember. What was the name of that girl in Bali? The one with all the tattoos?'

'Don't you dare! You might get Em worried I haven't settled down.'

'And have you?'

'No question, mate. I'll never look at another woman. I've found the one for me. Oh, great—a slow song! Catch you later. Go and eat. I'm hanging out for a waltz with my wife.'

Lucky man, Ryan thought, watching Emily's face light up as Mike reached her and the way she seemed to float dreamily in his arms as they found a space on the dance floor.

Lucky, lucky man.

The lights had flickered more than once in the last hour but this time they went out and stayed out.

Hannah, sitting with Susie, the very pregnant doctor called Christina and her gorgeous, dark-skinned husband Joe, who had turned out to be a fellow New Zealander, had also been watching the bridal couple dance. And Harry and Grace, who were dancing towards the edge of the crowd. And the woman who hadn't taken off that extraordinary purple hat with the huge flowers.

'That's Dora for you,' Susie was saying. 'She's so proud of that hat she'll probably wear it when she's polishing floors at the hospital for the next week or—'

She stopped as the room plunged into semi-darkness. The candles on tables provided only a dim light that would take a few moments to adjust to. People were just shadowy figures. The dancing had stopped and there was an uncertain kind of milling about, both on the dance floor and around the tables. The couple who were not moving at all in the corner caught more than Hannah's attention.

'Who *is* that?' Susie whispered loudly. 'I can't see in this light.'

'Whoever they are, they seem to like each other.' Joe grinned.

Susie winked at Hannah. 'Yeah. I'd say they've got a pretty good rapport all right.'

Hannah elbowed her sister. A reminder of what had started this small life crisis she was experiencing was not welcome.

They found out who the male of the pair was almost immediately, as Charles Wetherby rolled past their table accompanied by a young police officer who was holding a candelabrum. The flames on several candles were being dragged backwards to leave little smoke trails due to the speed with which the men were moving.

'Harry Blake!' The tone was urgent enough for conversation to die amongst everyone within earshot and the reaction to it spread rapidly. A lot of people could hear what Charles had to say as Harry seemed to attempt to shield the woman he'd been kissing so passionately by steering her further into the dark corner and then striding forward to meet the hospital's medical director.

'Bus accident up on the mountain road,' Hannah heard him say.

'I think it was *Grace* he was kissing,' Susie whispered. 'Woo-hoo!'

'Shh!' Hannah warned. 'This sounds serious.'

Joe's chair scraped as he got up and moved towards the knot of men. Christina's bottom lip was caught between her teeth and she laid a protective hand, instinctively, on her swollen belly. Tension and urgency were radiating strongly from their centre of focus.

Everybody who could hear was listening avidly. Others were trying to find out what was being said.

'What's going on?' someone called.

'Why are the police here?'

'Why haven't the lights come back on?'

'The hospital's four-wheel drive is on its way here to pick up whatever hospital staff you think you might need on site. Have you seen Grace? If we've got to set up a triage post and then get people off the side of the mountain, we'll probably need an SES crew up there, as well....'

Mike was heading towards the expanding knot of male figures. So was Ryan. Hannah got to her feet. If this was a major incident, they would need all the medical expertise available.

Charles would be magnificent in any crisis, Hannah decided. So calm. So in touch with what was happening everywhere in his domain.

'We've been on standby to activate a full code black disaster response, thanks to the cyclone watch on Willie,' he told the cluster of medics now around him. 'I'm going to go ahead and push the button. We have no idea how many casualties we might get from this bus but it looks likely we're in for trouble from Willie so it'll give us a few hours' head start. A dry run, if you like.'

'What's happening?' Sophia pushed her way towards Charles.

Dora Grubb was not far behind her, the pink flowers on her hat wobbling nervously.

'There's been an accident, Sophia,' Charles said. 'A bus full of people has vanished off the road near Dan Macker's place. Big landslide, thanks to all the rain we've had this week.'

'Oh... *Oh!*' Sophia crossed herself, her face horrified. 'This is bad!'

'I'm going to have to call in all available medical staff, starting with everyone here. Including Mike and Emily. I'm sorry, Sophia.'

'*Oh!*' Sophia looked stricken now. 'But the cake! The speeches!' Then she rallied, visibly pulling herself together. She stood as tall as possible for a short, plump person. 'Of course you need my boy,' she said proudly. 'And our Emily. Who else can look after those poor people if they need an operation? Emily! Darling! Let me help you find something else to wear.'

Hannah looked down at the froth of peach tulle around her knees and on to the flimsy white shoes with the flowers on the toes.

Mike noticed the direction of her glance. 'I've got spare flight suits in our room and Em's probably got a spare set of boots. Ryan? You'd better come and grab a suit, too.'

'Thanks, mate.'

'At least you won't have to roll up the sleeves and legs. Come with me, you guys. Let's get kitted up.'

It was Susie's turn to look stricken. 'I want to help but I'm useless with these crutches!'

'Not at all,' Charles said. 'You can stay with me and Jill. There's a lot of admin we'll need to do at the hospital. Code black means we've got to empty as many beds as we can. Set up a receiving ward. Mobilise stores. Reorganise ED...'

The list was still continuing as Hannah hurried in the wake of Mike and Ryan. She could also hear Dora Grubb talking excitedly to Sophia.

'They'll need food, all these rescue people.'

'We *have* food. Too much food. All this lamb! I'll tell the chef to start making sandwiches.'

It took less than ten minutes for the four young medics to encase themselves in the helicopter service issue overalls.

Emily sighed as she took a glance over her shoulder at the mound of white lace and silk on the bed. 'It was nice while it lasted,' she said, 'being a princess.'

'You'll always be a princess, babe,' Mike assured her. 'And I reckon you know how sexy I think you look in those overalls.'

Hannah carefully avoided looking anywhere close to Ryan's direction. She could understand the look that passed between Mike and Emily because she had stolen a glance at Ryan moments before, when he'd bent to lace up the spare pair of Mike's heavy steel-capped boots, and there had been no danger of him catching her glance.

It was a completely different look to civvies. Or scrubs. Or the white coat that doctors never seemed to bother with any more. He looked taller, somehow. Braver. Ready to get out there and save lives. And there was a very determined tilt to his chin that she hadn't seen before. Tension that visibly knotted the muscles in his jaw.

Was he anticipating a tough job at the scene of the bus crash or was it controlled anger? Directed at her?

Whatever.

Sexy didn't begin to cover how he looked.

Hannah scraped back her carefully combed curls and wound an elastic band to form a ponytail. Would Ryan see *her* as looking adventurous and exciting in these overalls with the huge rolled-up cuffs on the arms and legs?

Not likely.

Especially as he appeared determined not to actually look directly at her at all.

Even in the back of an ambulance a commendably short time later, when they had collected gear and co-ordinated with other personnel at the hospital, he was avoiding anything as personal as direct eye contact.

Mike was with them. Emily had ended up staying behind at the hospital to oversee the set-up and preparation of Theatres. Because of the weather conditions, with injured people exposed to the rain and wind, she needed to organise fluid warming devices and forced-air warmers on top of making sure she was ready to administer a general anaesthetic at short notice.

A second ambulance was following with another crew and all Crocodile Creek's available fire appliances had gone on ahead. Police had been first on scene, and by the time Hannah arrived, the road was lined with vehicles—a chain of flashing lights they had glimpsed from miles away as they'd sped up the sometimes tortuous curves of the mountain road. Lights that had haloes around them right now thanks to the heavy curtain of rain.

A portable triage tent was erected on the road to one side of the massive obstacle of mud, rocks and vegetation. Guy ropes had it anchored but the inflatable structure was looking alarmingly precarious in the high wind and its sides were being sucked in and then ballooning out almost instantly with a loud snapping sound.

The generators used to fill the outlines of the tent with compressed air were still running, powering lights, including some that were being directed downhill from the point where large skid marks were visible. There was more noise from the fire engines whose crews were rolling out winch cables from the front of the heavy vehicles. Pneumatic tools like the Jaws of Life were being primed and tested. As a background they were already tuning out, the wind howled through the treetops of the dark rainforest around them.

Harry Blake, wearing a fluorescent jacket that designated him as scene commander, met the ambulance, framed by the back doors Mike pushed open and latched.

'Who's in charge?' he queried briskly.

'I'm liaising with the medical director at the ED.' Mike clipped his radio to his belt. 'What frequency are we using on site?'

'Channel 8.'

Mike nodded. 'Channel 6 is the hospital link.' He leapt out of the back of the ambulance. 'I'll go down and triage with these two doctors and then we'll deploy all the other medical crews we get. What's it looking like down there?'

'It's a bloody mess,' Harry said grimly. 'The bus must have come off the road at speed and it rolled on the way down. The windows have popped out and we've got people and belongings all over the place. Some of the seats have come adrift inside and there's people trapped, but we can't get inside until the fire boys get a line or two onto the bus.'

'It's not stable?' Mike was sliding his arms into the straps of his backpack containing medical supplies.

'Hell, no. It could slide farther, especially if it keeps raining like this.'

Hannah and Ryan were out of the ambulance now, standing beside Mike. 'Don't forget your helmets,' he reminded them. Then his attention was back on Harry. 'Any fatalities?'

'At least one.' Harry raised his voice to a shout to be heard as they started walking and got closer to the generators. 'There's a guy who's been thrown clear and then caught under the bus. He's at the front and we think he's probably the driver. We won't be able to shift him until we can jack up the front corner somehow.'

'The fire guys going to be able to use their cutting gear down there? Is it safe to have them clambering around?'

'We've got nets anchored on the slope. It's not too bad for climbing. There's an SES crew down there at the moment, trying to clear the scene of everybody who's able to move.'

'How many are we dealing with?' Ryan had jammed his hard hat on and was pulling the strap tight.

Harry shook his head. 'Haven't been able to do a head count yet. There's injured people over quite a wide area. We think there's two or three still trapped in the bus, from what we can see. One of the passengers who's not hurt thinks the bus was quite full. There's about ten people we can bring up now. Could be fifteen or twenty still down there needing attention.'

Mike and Ryan shared a glance. This was huge. It was going to stretch their resources and everybody's skills.

'Let's do it.' Ryan pulled on latex examination gloves and then heavier ones for climbing. He gave Mike a thumbs-up and Mike responded with a terse nod and another shared glance. They had faced difficult situations before. They were more than ready to tackle this one. Together.

Hannah felt oddly excluded. Even when Mike put her after Ryan and before himself to protect her as she climbed down the steep, slippery slope, she didn't really feel a part of this small team.

Ryan hated her. He didn't want her there.

Within the first few metres of their climb, however, any thoughts of personality clashes or anything else that could affect a working relationship were forgotten.

A woman lay, moaning. 'My leg,' she groaned. 'I can't get any further. Help...'

This was an initial triage. No more than thirty seconds could be allocated for any patient to check for life-threatening injuries like uncontrolled haemorrhage or a blocked airway. Mike had triage tags in his pocket. Big, brightly coloured labels with an elastic loop that would alert all other personnel to the priority the victims had for medical attention. This woman was conscious and talking. It took less than thirty seconds for Ryan to examine her.

'Fractured femur. Closed. No external bleeding. Airway's clear.'

Mike produced a yellow label. Attention needed but second priority. 'Someone will be with you as soon as possible,' he reassured the woman as they moved on. 'We've got to check everybody else first and then we'll be back.'

'But it *hurts*... Oh-h-h....'

It was hard, leaving her to keep descending the slope. A huddle of people near the base of the nets were bypassed. They were all mobile and being looked after by SES people. Grace was there, organising the clearance of the less injured from the scene. Mike gave her a handful of green triage tags that designated the lowest priority. Hannah saw a young Asian couple clinging to each other, looking terrified, and she could hear someone talking in a foreign language that sounded European. Had the bus been full of tourists? It could make their job more difficult if they couldn't communicate with their patients.

A young woman lay, unconscious, against the base of a huge eucalyptus tree.

'Hello, can you hear me?' Hannah pinched the woman's ear lobe. 'Non-responsive,' she told Mike. She laid a hand on the woman's neck and another on her belly. 'She's breathing. Good carotid pulse. Tachy.'

The elastic of a pink triage label went over her wrist. Highest priority. This case was urgent, with the potential to be saved and the likelihood of rapid deterioration if left. They moved on.

'There's one over here,' a fire officer yelled at them. 'He's making a weird noise.'

'Occluded airway.' Mike repositioned the man's head and the gurgling sound ceased. Another pink tag.

Winch hooks were being attached to the bus. There were no big lights down here and the rescue workers had to make do with the lamps on their helmets. A curious strobe effect to viewing the disaster was evident as lights intersected and inspected different areas. It made it easier to deal with, Hannah decided, because you could only see a patch at a time. A single patient, a broken window, dented metal, broken tree branches, strewn belongings and luggage.

Just the top half of the unfortunate man who had been caught beneath the front wheel of the bus. It took only a moment to confirm the extinction of life and give the man a white tag to signify a fatality so that nobody would waste time by checking him again.

'Don't go downhill from the bus.' A fire officer with a winch hook in his hand shouted the warning. 'We haven't got this thing stable yet.'

The doors of the bus were blocked because it was lying, tilted, on that side. The emergency hatch at the back was open, however, and must have been how some of the less injured had escaped the wreckage.

Mike saw Ryan assessing the access. 'Not yet, buddy,' he said firmly. 'You can just wait until it's safer.'

Safer, Hannah noted. Not *safe.* It could never be really safe to do something like this, could it? And yet Ryan was clearly frustrated by having to hold back.

Hannah shook her head to clear the water streaming down her face from looking up at the hatch. She was soaked now and the wind was chilling. She flexed increasingly stiff fingers and cast a glance at her colleagues.

There was certainly no doubting Ryan's commitment to his work and the people he cared for. How many ED specialists would be prepared to work in conditions like this? To risk their own lives without a moment's hesitation to try and save others?

Mike might have been off the mark in making people think Ryan was some kind of saint, but he hadn't been wrong in advertising him as a hero. They both were. The way these two men worked together suggested they had been in situations before that had not been dissimilar. There was a calm confidence about the way they worked that was contagious.

Like Ryan's courage in that plane turbulence had been.

What if she couldn't redress the antipathy Ryan now held towards her and the one who didn't win that consultancy position in ED felt obliged to go and work elsewhere? If she never had the chance to work with him again?

The sense of loss she had experienced watching him dance with Mike came back strongly enough to distract Hannah for several seconds. Was it always going to haunt her? Did she have to be ruthlessly squashed at frequent intervals in order for her to perform to her best ability? Like now?

Hannah continued the triage exercise with grim determination. They found another five people with fractures and lacerations who needed yellow tags. One more pink tag for a partially amputated arm and severe bleeding. An SES worker had been doing a great job of keeping pressure on the wound. Then they were given the all-clear to check out the bus.

'Not you, Hannah,' Mike stated. 'You can check in with the SES guys. Make sure we haven't missed anyone. Get someone to check further afield as well. We've got debris over a wide area and injured people could have moved or even fallen further down the slope.'

Hannah moved to find someone to talk to but she couldn't help stopping for a moment. Turning back to watch as the two men climbed into the bus.

Turning back again a moment later, when alarmed shouting heralded a noticeable shift in the position of the bus.

'Oh, my God...' Was the bus going to move with the extra weight? Slide and possibly roll again down the side of this mountain?

Remove any possibility of repairing the rift she'd created with Ryan?

Remove Ryan from her life with the ultimate finality of death?

'No-o-o!'

It was a quiet, desperate sound, snatched away and disguised by the howl of the wind. If it was a prayer, it was answered. Having taken up some slack from one of the winch cables, the movement stopped. Mike actually leaned out a broken window with his thumb and forefinger forming the 'O' of a signal that they were OK.

It was only then that Hannah realised she had been holding her breath. A couple of minutes later and Ryan and Mike emerged from the bus.

'One pink, one yellow, one white,' Mike reported. 'One's unconscious and another's trapped by a seat.' He reached for his radio. Medical crews could now be co-ordinated, specific tasks allocated, patients treated and evacuated. The most seriously injured patients would be assigned a doctor who would stabilise and then escort them to hospital.

Hannah was joined by a paramedic by the name of Mario, issued a pack of gear and assigned the case of the woman who had been pink-ticketed at the base of the eucalyptus tree. Mike and Ryan were going to work on the pink-ticket patient inside the bus. Hannah watched them climb inside again. A scoop stretcher was passed in along with the pack of resuscitation gear by firemen who then waited, knowing their muscle would be needed to assist with extrication.

Once again Hannah felt that sense of loss as Ryan vanished from view and this time she couldn't quite shake it off.

She *needed* him, dammit! This was so far out of her comfort zone, it wasn't funny. The rain might be easing but she was still soaked and cold and her fingers felt uselessly stiff and clumsy.

The effort to concentrate seemed harder than it had ever been. Hannah was trying to recall the workshop she'd attended at a conference once, on the practice of emergency medicine in a hostile environment. Control of the airway was the first priority, of course, with cervical spine control if appropriate.

It was appropriate in this case. Hannah's gloved hand came away streaked with blood after touching the back of the young woman's head. Had she been thrown clear of the bus and hit the tree she now lay beside? If the blow had been enough to cause her loss of consciousness, it had potentially caused a neck injury as well.

'I need a collar,' she told Mario. She placed her hand, side on, on the woman's shoulder, making a quick estimate of the distance to her jaw line. 'A short neck, please. And a dressing for this head wound.'

It was difficult, trying to assess how well their patient was breathing. Hard to see, given the narrow focus of the beam of light from her helmet. Hard to feel with her cold hands and impossible to hear with the shouting and noise of machinery. And over it all, the savage wind still howled. Large tree branches cracked ominously and small pieces of debris like broken branches flew through the air, occasionally striking Hannah in the back or hitting the hard helmet she wore with a bang, magnified enough to make her jump more than once.

'I don't think we can assess her for equal air entry until we get her into an ambulance, at least,' she said. 'She's certainly breathing on her own without any respiratory distress I can pick up.'

Which was a huge relief. While this woman was probably unconscious enough to be able to be intubated without a drug regime, the lecturer at that conference had discussed the difficulties of intubation in a situation like this. Often, the technique of cricothyroidotomy was more appropriate and that wasn't something Hannah wanted to attempt with limited light and frozen fingers.

IV access was more manageable. Hannah placed a large-bore cannula in the woman's forearm and started fluids. She remembered to use extra tape to secure both the cannula and the IV fluid lines. The lecturer's jocular warning was what she'd remembered most clearly about that workshop. "If it can fall out," he'd said, 'it *will* fall out.'

Mario had the expertise and strength to move the woman onto a backboard and strap her securely onto it. And then the firemen took over, inching their way up the mountainside with the help of ropes and the net.

Moving to follow them, the beam of Hannah's light caught something that made her stoop. She picked the object up. It was a shoe. A rather well-worn sneaker with a hole in the top and what looked like a picture of a bright orange fish done in felt pen or something similar. What startled her was its size. It was small.

Very small.

A child's shoe.

But they hadn't come across any children in their triage, had they? Hannah had the awful thought that it could be the fatality inside the bus. But maybe the owner of this shoe was uninjured? Not seen amongst that huddle of frightened people who had been waiting for help up the slope? Hannah certainly hoped so. And if they were, they might have one bare foot and be grateful to see that shoe. Hannah stuffed it into the large pocket on the front of her overalls.

It wouldn't have been easy for a child to climb, even with the hand- and footholds the net provided. They were wet now and very muddy. Hannah slipped, more than once, and had to save herself by grabbing the netting or a tree root or branch.

How could fifty metres seem such a long way? And how long had they been on scene? Certainly no more than an hour, but she felt as though she had just completed a full night shift in the ED and a busy one at that.

The third time she slipped, Hannah might well have fallen but she was caught by her arm in a vice-like grip.

'Are you OK?' Ryan asked.

It had to be her imagination that she could hear the same kind of caring in the query that she had heard in the car on the way to Wygera that morning. An aeon ago. In her current state it was enough to bring the sting of tears to her eyes. She blinked them away.

'Yeah...thanks...'

'Not easy, this stuff, is it?' Ryan was climbing beside her. Just below them, the scoop stretcher containing his patient was making slow progress upwards. 'How's your woman?'

'Still unconscious but breathing. A head injury but I have no idea how bad it is yet.'

'You'll be able to do a more thorough assessment in the ambulance. We won't be far behind you if you run into trouble. Mike says they're going to stage departures so we arrive at the ED at about six-minute intervals. Just pull over and keep your lights on and we'll stop to help.'

'Thanks,' Hannah said again. Professional assistance but at least he was talking to her. She was almost at the top of the slope now. A fire officer had his hand out to help her onto the road and the noise level increased markedly. She could still hear Ryan's call, though.

'Hey, Hannah?'

'Yeah?'

'You're doing a fantastic job. Well done.'

Those tears were even closer all of a sudden. They couldn't be allowed to spill. Hannah clenched her fists as she got to her feet on the road and her hand struck her bulky pocket. She peered down at Ryan.

'Hey, did you come across any children in the bus?'

'No. Why?'

'I found a shoe. A kid's size shoe.' She pulled it from her pocket. 'See?'

'Could have come from anywhere,' Ryan said. 'Maybe there's a kid amongst the green tickets.'

'Yes, I thought of that. I'll check with Grace later.'

'It could have come from spilled luggage as well. Or even been thrown away. Looks pretty old.'

'Hannah?' Mario, the paramedic, was calling. She could see the backboard supporting her patient being lifted into the back of an ambulance. 'We're nearly ready to roll.'

'On my way.' Hannah turned to give Ryan a smile of thanks for his help but he wasn't watching. He had already turned back to his patient.

'I'll take over the ventilations there, Mike. You've done a fantastic job up the hill.'

A fantastic job. Like her. So the praise hadn't really been

personal, had it? The doors of the ambulance slammed shut behind her and someone thumped on the back to give the officer driving the signal to go. Hannah took a deep breath.

'Let's get some oxygen on, Mario. A non-rebreather mask at ten litres a minute. And I want a slight head tilt on the stretcher. Can we do that with a backboard in the way?'

'Sure, we'll just use a pillow under this end.'

'Let's get some definitive baseline measurements, too. Blood pressure, heart rate and rhythm, oxygen saturation.' She pulled a stethoscope from the kit. 'I'm going to check her breathing again.'

It felt good to be on the move towards a fully equipped emergency department and hospital. Hannah would feel far more in control then. Far less likely to be thrown off balance by overly emotional reactions to someone else's words or the way they looked at her. Or *didn't* look at her.

It helped to know that Ryan would be on the road within minutes, though. Travelling in the same direction she was. Sharing the same experiences and goals that had arrived in their lives so unexpectedly. To get through this ordeal and help as many people as possible.

They were on the same page now, weren't they?

What a shame it was just too late.

CHAPTER NINE

THE CONTRAST COULDN'T have been greater.

The Poulos wedding had been a happy circus. Crocodile Creek Base Hospital was hosting a miserable one.

Injured, bewildered people filled the cubicles and sat on chairs. A moving sea of professional staff was doing everything necessary. Doctors, nurses, clerks, radiographers and orderlies were doing their jobs. And more. The fact that it was late at night and the majority of people here were not rostered on duty meant nothing. A disaster response had been activated and there was nobody associated with this medical community who wasn't prepared to do whatever they could to help.

There was a lot to be done. Hannah's case was the first serious one to arrive so she had the initial advantage of all the staff she could possibly need to assist.

Luke hadn't yet gone to the receiving ward where he would be available on the surgical team, along with Cal and Alistair. Emily was still in the department as well, because minor cases needing surgery were going to have to wait until all the majors had been dealt with. They both came to assist Hannah. Charles wasn't far behind.

'You should get changed out of those wet overalls,' he told

Hannah. 'There's plenty of people here to take over. Susie can show you where the scrubs are kept.'

'Soon,' Hannah promised. 'I just want to make sure she's stable.' Having come this far with the injured woman, Hannah was reluctant to hand over. 'If that's OK with you, Dr Wetherby?'

Ryan might be registered to work in Australia but Hannah wasn't. It was Charles who could give her permission. It was up to him whether he trusted that she was competent enough not to cause problems he would have to take ultimate responsibility for.

The look she received was assessing but Charles had obviously seen enough to make a decision.

'Go ahead,' he said.

Mario and a male nurse had moved the woman, still strapped to her backboard, onto the bed.

'Right.' Hannah nodded, tucking away the pleasure that someone like Charles Wetherby was prepared to trust her. 'This woman was apparently thrown clear of the bus and was found unconscious. There's been some response on the way in but nothing coherent. I'd put her GCS at seven. She was initially tachycardic at 120 but that's dropped in the last fifteen minutes to a rate of 90, respirations are shallow but air entry is equal and the oxygen saturation has been steady on 97 per cent on 10 litres.'

Standard monitoring equipment was being attached to the woman, like ECG leads, a blood-pressure cuff and an oxygen saturation monitor. Someone was hanging the fluids from a ceiling hook and another nurse was taking the woman's temperature.

'Thirty-five point six degrees centigrade,' she reported.

'Not hypothermic, then,' Emily commented.

'Blood pressure was initially one-twenty on eighty. Last measurement was one-thirty on seventy.'

'Widening pulse pressure,' Luke said. 'Rising intracranial pressure?'

'Quite possible. She has an abrasion and haematoma in the occipital area. No obvious skull fracture. Pupils were equal and reactive.'

'They're not now.' Emily was at the head end of the bed, shining a bright torch into the woman's eyes. 'Right pupil is two millimetres larger and sluggish.'

'Do we know her name?' Luke asked.

'No.' Hannah glanced at one of the nurses. 'Perhaps you could check her pockets? She may have some ID.'

'We need some radiography,' Luke said. 'Preferably a CT scan. And where's Alistair? If we've got a neurosurgeon available, this is where he should be.'

Charles pivoted his wheelchair. 'I'll find him.'

The movement of the woman on the bed was unexpected. Restrained, due to the straps still holding her to the backboard, but unmistakable.

'She's going to vomit,' Emily warned.

'Let's turn her side on,' Hannah ordered. 'I'll need suction.'

It was easy to turn the woman onto her side and keep her spine protected, thanks to the backboard, but it was another sign that the pressure could be building dangerously inside her head.

The nurse checking her pockets had easier access with the patient tipped to one side. 'I've found something,' she said. 'It's a passport. An Australian one.'

'Great. At least she'll understand the language. And we'll be able to use her name.' Hannah glanced up at the monitor, to see what was happening with the blood pressure. 'What is it?'

'Janey Stafford.'

'What?' The startled query came from Luke. 'Did you say *Janey Stafford*?'

'Do you know her?' Hannah asked. It could be helpful for an unconscious person to hear the voice of someone she knew.

'I… I'm not sure.' Luke was looking stunned. He reached over and lifted the oxygen mask the woman had on. Was he looking for a feature he might recognise? Hannah wondered. Like that small mole at the corner of her top lip?

Luke was backing away. Shaking his head.

'You don't know her, then?'

'Not really. It was her sister I knew.' The tone was dismissive. An 'I don't want to talk about this' sort of tone. 'It was a long time ago.'

Emily was staring at Luke. Then she blinked and refocussed. 'Do you want me to intubate?' she asked Hannah.

Alistair walked into the resus bay at that moment.

'I'll hand over to an expert,' Hannah said. Having given Alistair a rundown on their findings so far, she found herself stepping back. Luke did more than step back. He left the resus bay completely.

But then a new emergency was coming in. Luke hadn't pulled the curtain closed behind him and Hannah could see Ryan arriving with his multi-trauma case from the interior of the bus. They were still using a bag mask to ventilate this patient. There were two IV lines in place and Ryan looked worried.

'Bilateral fractured femurs,' Hannah heard him tell Charles. 'Rib fractures and a flail chest. GCS of nine.'

Charles directed them to resus 2 and Luke disappeared behind the curtain along with them.

The picture of Ryan's face was not so quick to disappear for Hannah. She had seen him work under duress before. Seen him tired and even not a hundred per cent well himself, but she had never seen an expression like the one he had walked in with.

So grim. Determined. So…lacking in humour.

Instinct told her that it wasn't just the grim situation that was making Ryan look like that. He was the one who always made an effort to defuse just such an atmosphere. He seemed like a different person. Gone completely was that sparkle. The laid-back, golden-boy aura that had always seemed to cling enough to be easily resurrected.

It didn't look like Ryan intended smiling for a long time to come and Hannah didn't like it. He was being professional and she knew he would have the skills to match anything he had to face, but something was wrong. Something big was missing. The real Ryan seemed shut off. Distant.

Was it sheer arrogance to wonder if his anger at her had something to do with his demeanour?

Hannah shivered and wasn't even surprised to hear Charles's voice from close by.

'Go and get out of those overalls. Get some dry scrubs on and get a hot drink. I don't want to see you back in here for at least ten minutes.'

It did feel better, being in dry clothes. And the hot chocolate and a sandwich she found in the staffroom were wonderful.

'At least you're getting a bit of the wedding breakfast.'

Hannah smiled back at the plump woman. Susie would be surprised to see that Dora had taken off her hat. 'It's delicious,' she said. 'Thank you so much.'

'You're all doing such a wonderful job. Those poor people out there. There are a lot that are badly hurt, aren't there?'

Hannah nodded, her mouth full of the first food she had eaten since a hurried lunch too many hours ago. She had taken a moment to check on Janey's progress, to find she'd gone for a CT scan and that Alistair was planning to take her to Theatre immediately afterwards, if necessary, to relieve any pressure building from a bleed inside her skull. Emily had gone to get ready to administer an anaesthetic.

Ryan was still busy stabilising his patient, ready for the surgery Luke would have to perform to deal with the major fractures sustained.

More cases were coming in, prearranged to arrive at a steady but not overwhelming rate. Susie had hopped past on her crutches, a sheaf of papers scrunched in one hand.

'I've got to locate a new supply of O-negative blood,' she told Hannah. 'And there's so many other things to do. We're still trying to discharge people to one of the rest homes and find accommodation for everyone from the bus. You OK?'

She was, surprisingly, more than OK, thanks to the food and hot drink.

In the corner of the staffroom sat two tired-looking children. Lily was still in her flower girl's dress and CJ hadn't changed out of his small suit.

'Can we go now?' CJ asked Dora.

'We're supposed to stay here,' she replied. 'You know what they said about my house. It's not fit to be in when the cyclone comes.'

'Is it definitely coming, then?' Hannah's appetite faded and she swallowed with difficulty.

'They reckon it's going to hit us by morning. Susie's arranged some beds for the children to stay in here overnight. Dr Wetherby and CJ's parents are going to be busy all night by the look of things.'

'But you said—' CJ's lip wobbled ominously '—you *said* we could go and see if the puppies have arrived before we have to go to bed.'

'My dog's due to whelp again,' Dora explained to Hannah. 'Goodness knows why Grubby keeps letting her get in pup. It's me who ends up doing all the work.'

'*Ple-ease?*' begged CJ.

Dora looked at the clock. 'I guess we've got a fair few hours before the weather gets dangerous. If we went home quick and then came back again, I guess Dr Wetherby won't notice we've gone.'

'Don't tell,' CJ ordered Hannah. 'Will you?'

'I'm sure nobody will ask me,' Hannah responded. She watched as Dora took a small hand in each of hers and led the children away. A very capable woman, Dora. Hannah was sure no harm would come to the children.

And that reminded her of the shoe.

Over the next hour, as Hannah assisted in the treatment of

several people, she had two things on her mind. One of them was watching for glimpses of Ryan, to see whether he was still looking so distant and miserable.

He was. More than once he passed Hannah with barely more than a glance. Never a smile. Or a comment that might have lifted her spirits. To imagine him telling a joke seemed ridiculous. He had changed into scrubs as well so he looked like the Ryan she had always known.

She just wished she could see a flash of him behaving the way he always had.

The other thing on her mind was the shoe. At every opportunity she asked different members of the staff whether they had come across a small child amongst the patients. Someone advised her to check with one of the clerks and, sure enough, when she did, she struck gold.

'There *was* a kid. A little blonde girl,' she was told. 'Chloe, I think her name was. She had a broken arm.'

'How old was she?'

'I can't remember. Four or five.'

The right sort of age to fit a shoe the size of the one Hannah had found.

'Where would she be now?'

'I have no idea, sorry. Maybe the plaster room? It was ages ago, though. She might have been sent home.'

Except that she had no home to go to, did she?

The thoughtful frown on Hannah's face must have looked like fatigue to Charles. He rolled towards her.

'You've been on duty for more than four hours,' he said. 'It's time you took a break. At least two hours' standdown before I see you back in here, please. It's going to be a long night and it might be just the beginning of what we need you for with the way Willie's decided to behave.'

Hannah nodded. A break was exactly what she needed right now, wasn't it?

* * *

The soaked pair of overalls lay where she had left them, in the corner of the women's locker room. Nobody had had time to tidy yet. Hannah fished the shoe out of the pocket and went looking for the child she now knew existed.

Jill Shaw, the nursing director, passed her in the corridor, with her arms full of a fresh supply of IV fluids.

'Have you seen a little girl?' Hannah asked. 'About five? With blonde hair?'

'You mean Lily? I think Mrs Grubb's looking after her. She should be in the hospital somewhere.'

'No, not Lily. A child from the bus crash. I need to know if this is her shoe.' Hannah showed Jill the worn sneaker with the faded fish picture on the toe.

Jill shook her head. 'Sorry.'

Ryan emerged from the door to the toilet just behind where Jill and Hannah stood.

He still looked grim. Distant. Lines of weariness were etched deeply into his face. He looked so...serious.

Too serious for Ryan Fisher under any circumstances. It just didn't fit. Hannah could feel her heart squeeze into a painful ball. She wanted to touch him. To say something that could raise just a hint of smile or bring back just a touch of life into those dark eyes.

But she couldn't. Partly because Jill was there and mostly because Ryan wasn't even looking at her. He was looking at the object in her hand.

'For God's sake, Hannah. There are more important things to be worrying about right now than a bloody *shoe!*'

Jill raised an eyebrow as she watched him stride away. 'It's time he had a break, I think.' She turned back to Hannah. 'They're collecting all the unclaimed property in Reception. Why don't you leave it there?'

Reception was crowded. People with minor injuries from the bus crash that had been treated were waiting for transport to the emergency shelters. Other accidents attributable to the awful weather conditions were coming in in a steady stream. And there were still the people that would normally present to Emergency with the kind of injuries and illnesses they could have taken to their GP in working hours. Many of these people had been bumped well down any waiting list. Some were giving up and going home. Others were still waiting—bored, miserable and increasingly impatient.

'I don't give a stuff about bloody tourists off a bus,' an irate man was shouting at the receptionist. 'I pay my bloody taxes and I want to be seen by a doctor. *Now!* I've been waiting hours. Is this a *hospital* or what?'

Hannah gave the receptionist a sympathetic smile. Near her desk was a sad-looking pile of wet luggage, some backpacks and other personal items like handbags, hats and sunglasses.

The angry man stormed back to his seat. Then he jumped to his feet. 'I've had enough of this,' he shouted. 'I'm bloody going home.'

Casting a glance around the waiting room, Hannah could tell nobody was sorry to see him go. She doubted there had been much wrong with him in the first place. He should see the kind of injuries that were having to wait for attention inside the department.

Hannah didn't really need a two-hour break. Maybe she should go back and help. She could leave the shoe on the pile because it probably did belong to the little girl and she might come looking for it.

Something made her turn back before she reached the pile, however. Something niggling at the back of her mind since her gaze had skimmed the more patient people still waiting for attention.

And there she was. A drowsy little blonde-headed girl, almost hidden with her mother's arms around her. She had a pink cast on her arm.

Hannah walked over to them, absurdly hopeful.

'Is this Chloe?'

The mother nodded, a worried frown creasing her forehead. 'Is there a problem? I thought we were all finished. We were just waiting for a ride to the shelter.'

'No problem,' Hannah assured her. 'I just wondered if this could be Chloe's shoe?' She held the small sneaker out but the hope that she might have solved this small mystery bothering her was fading rapidly.

Chloe was wearing some white Roman sandals. Two of them.

The little girl opened her eyes. 'That's not my shoe,' she said. 'It's the boy with the funny name's shoe.'

Hannah caught her breath. 'What boy?'

'The boy on the bus.'

'I didn't see a boy,' her mother said.

'That's because he was hiding in the back of the bus. With his friend.'

'A friend?' Hannah blinked. Surely the searchers couldn't have missed *two* children? And where were the parents? They would be frantic. Everybody would know by now if they had missing children.

'He had a dog called Scruffy,' Chloe added. 'They were hiding so the driver wouldn't see Scruffy.'

So the friend was a dog? There had been no reports of a dog at the accident site that Hannah was aware of and that would be something people would talk about, surely? Chloe's story was beginning to seem unlikely.

'Chloe has a very good imagination,' her mother said fondly. 'Don't you, darling?' Her smile at Hannah was apologetic. 'It was a pretty long, boring bus ride.'

'I can imagine.'

'I *did* see them,' Chloe insisted. 'I went down the back of the bus when you were asleep, Mummy. His name was F-F-*Felixx*,' she said triumphantly. 'Like the cat.'

'I don't think so, darling. I've never heard of a little boy being called Felixx.'

'But it's *true,* Mummy.' Chloe was indignant. She wriggled away from the supporting arm and twisted her head sharply up to glare at her mother.

And then the small girl's eyes widened in surprise.

A split second later she went completely limp, slumped against her mother.

For a stunned moment, Hannah couldn't move. This was unreal. Talking one moment and apparently unconscious the next? Automatically she reached out to feel for a pulse in Chloe's neck.

Chloe's mother was frozen. 'What's happening?' she whispered hoarsely.

Hannah's fingers pressed deeper on the tiny neck.

Moved and pressed again.

'I don't know,' Hannah said, 'but for some reason it seems that Chloe's heart might have stopped.'

Another split second of indecision. Start CPR here in the waiting room and yell for help or get Chloe to the kind of life-saving equipment, like a defibrillator, that she might desperately need? There was no question of what could give a better outcome.

She scooped the child into her arms. 'Come with me,' she told Chloe's mother as she ran towards the working end of the department.

'I need help,' she called as soon as she was through the door. *'Stat!'*

Ryan looked up from where he was squatting, talking to a man in a chair who had a bloodstained bandage on his hand. He took one look at Hannah's face and with a fluid movement he rose swiftly and came towards her.

'What's happened?'

'I have no idea. She just collapsed. I can't find a pulse.'

'Resus 2 is clear at the moment.' Charles was rolling beside them. 'I'll find help.'

Hannah laid Chloe on the bed. It had been well under a minute since the child had collapsed but, horribly, her instincts were screaming that they were too late. There had been something about the feel of the child in her arms.

Something completely empty.

Her fingers trembled as they reached for the ECG electrodes and stuck them in place on a tiny, frail-looking chest.

Ryan was reassessing her for a pulse and respirations. 'Nothing,' he said tersely. He reached for a bag-mask unit. 'What the hell is going on here?'

'Could it be a drug reaction? Anaphylaxis? What analgesia has she had for her arm?'

'Do you know if there were any prior symptoms?' Ryan had the mask over Chloe's face and was delivering enough air to make the small chest rise and then fall.

The normal-looking movement of breathing gave Hannah a ray of hope. Maybe they *weren't* too late. But then she looked up at the monitor screen to see a flat ECG trace. Not even a fibrillation they could have shocked back into a normal rhythm. She moved, automatically, to start chest compressions.

'She was fine,' she told Ryan. 'A bit drowsy but fine. She was talking to me. Telling me about the shoe and a boy who was on the bus.'

Any worries about a potentially missing child were simply not part of the picture right now.

More staff were crowding into the resus area to assist. One of the doctors, Cal, was inserting an IV line. One nurse was rolling the drugs trolley closer, the airway kit open on top of the trolley.

Charles was there. A solid presence. Beside him, Chloe's mother was standing, white faced, a nurse close by to look after her.

'An undiagnosed head injury?' Charles wondered aloud. 'A lucid period before total collapse?' He shook his head. 'Couldn't have been that dramatic.'

Ryan looked over to Chloe's mother. 'Does she have any medical conditions that you know of? Heart problems?'

'No-o-o.' The word was torn from the woman in the form

of a sob. The nurse put her arms around the distraught mother. As awful as this was, it was better for a parent to see that everything possible was being done, in case they had to deal with the worst possible outcome.

Hannah kept up the chest compressions. It wasn't physically hard on someone this small. One handed. Rapid. It didn't take much pressure at all.

'Stop for a second, Hannah.'

They all looked at the screen. The disruption to the trace that the movement of CPR was causing settled.

To a flat line.

'I'm going to intubate,' Ryan decided. 'Someone hold her head for me, please?'

'I'll take over compressions.' Cal stepped up to the bed and Hannah nodded. She moved to take hold of Chloe's head and keep it in the position Ryan required.

'Oh, my God,' she murmured a moment later.

'What?' Ryan snapped. His gaze caught hers as though challenging her to say something he didn't want to hear. She had never seen anyone that determined. Ever.

'It's her neck,' Hannah said quietly. 'The way it moved. It's...' She was feeling the top of Chole's spine now, her fingers pressing carefully. Moving and pressing again. 'There's something very wrong.'

It was hardly a professional evaluation but she couldn't bring herself to say what she thought.

It fitted. Chloe must have had a fracture that had been undisplaced. She might have had a sore neck but that could have been masked by the pain relief administered for her fractured arm.

A time bomb waiting to go off. That sharp, twisting movement when she'd looked up at her mother could have displaced the broken bones. Allowed a sharp edge to sever the spinal cord.

Death would have been instantaneous.

And there was absolutely nothing any of them could do about it.

In the end, she didn't have to say anything. Her face must have said it all. Cal's hand slowed and then stopped. He stepped back from the bed.

Chloe's mother let out an agonised cry and rushed from the room. The nurse followed swiftly.

Everybody else stood silent.

Shocked.

Except for Ryan. He moved to where Cal had been standing and started chest compressions again.

And Charles rolled silently to the head of the bed where he could reach out and feel Chloe's neck for himself.

'We don't *know* her neck's broken,' Ryan said between gritted teeth. 'Not without an X-ray or CT scan. We can't just give up on her. Cal, take over again. Hannah, I want an ET tube. Five millimetre. Uncuffed.'

Nobody moved. Only Ryan, his face a frozen mask, his movements quietly desperate.

Charles dropped his hand from Chloe's neck. 'Ryan?'

The word wasn't spoken loudly but it carried the weight of an authority it would be impossible to ignore. So did the next word. *'Stop!'*

For a few seconds it looked as though Ryan might ignore the command. Keep fighting to save a life when there was absolutely no chance of success. Hannah could feel his pain. She reached out to touch his shoulder.

Ryan jerked away as though he'd been burnt. Without a glance at anyone, he turned and strode away. Long, angry strides that didn't slow as he flicked the curtain aside.

'Everybody take a break,' Charles ordered. 'Jill and I will deal with what needs to be done here.'

The shock was dreadful. Hannah could understand why Ryan hadn't been prepared to give up. If there was anything that could have been done, she would have done it herself.

Anything.

They all faced terrible things like this, working in any emergency department. That it was part of the job didn't make it easy. Somehow they had to find a way to cope or they couldn't be doing this as a career.

What was making it worse than normal for Hannah was the feeling that Ryan *couldn't* cope with this particular case. There had been something in his body language as he virtually fled from the room that spoke of real desperation. Of reaching the end of a personal, if not professional, tether.

There was no way Hannah could leave him to deal with that on his own.

She had to try and help. Or at least *be* with him. To show him that she cared. That she understood.

An ironic smile vied with the tears she was holding back.

To wallow with him, even?

CHAPTER TEN

HE WAS DISAPPEARING through the doors to the ambulance bay.

Going outside into the storm.

As scary as that was, Hannah didn't hesitate to go after him. An ambulance was unloading another patient by the time she got there and Hannah had to wait a moment as the stretcher was wheeled through the doors. Mario had done the round trip again. He was holding a bag of IV fluid aloft with one hand, steering the stretcher with the other.

'How's it going, Hannah? OK?'

Hannah could only give him a tight smile and a brief nod, unable to think of anything but her personal and urgent mission. She skirted the end of the stretcher to dash outside before the automatic doors slid shut again.

The wind caught the baggy scrub suit she was wearing and made it billow. It teased her hair out of the band holding it back and whipped strands across her face. Her eyes stung and watered but Hannah barely registered any discomfort. It was too dark out here. The powerful hospital generators were being used for the vital power needed inside. Energy was not being wasted on outside lighting.

Where was Ryan?

Where would *she* go if she was in some kind of personal crisis and couldn't cope?

Just anywhere? Was Ryan even aware of the wild storm raging around him? Would he be thinking of his personal safety? Not likely. What if he went towards the beach? That surf had been wild and couldn't you get things like storm surges with an approaching cyclone? Like tidal waves?

If he had gone somewhere that dangerous, Hannah would still follow him. She *had* to. The bond she felt was simply too strong. If ever there was a case for following her heart, this was it.

Ryan *was* her heart.

Maybe he was heading for a safer personal space, Hannah thought as her gaze raked the swirl of leaves in the darkness and picked out the looming shapes of vehicles in the car park. He only had one space that could qualify in Crocodile Creek. His room in the doctors' house.

The room she had spent the most magical night of her life in.

Headlights from another incoming rescue vehicle sent a beam of light across the path Hannah was taking. Strong enough to show she was heading in the right direction to take her to either the beach or the house. The faded sign designating the area as the AGNES WETHERBY MEMORIAL GARDEN was tilted. Had it always been like that or was it giving up the struggle to stay upright under the duress of this storm?

Hannah wasn't about to give up.

She had to pause in the centre of the garden, just beside the sundial. She needed to catch her breath and gather her courage. The crack of a tree branch breaking free somewhere close was frightening. She would wait a few seconds in case the branch was about to fall on the path she intended to take.

It must have been instinct that alerted her to Ryan's presence in the garden. Why else would she have taken a second and much longer look at the dark shape in the corner which anyone could have taken as part of the thick hibiscus hedge behind it?

Or was it because that shadow was immobile whilst the hedge was in constant motion, fuelled by relentless wind gusts?

He was sitting on a bench seat, his hands on his knees, staring blankly into the dark space in front of him.

Hannah licked lips that were dry from more than the wind.

'Ryan?'

'Go away, Hannah. Leave me alone.'

'No. I can't *do* that.' With her heart hammering, Hannah sat down beside him. Close enough to touch but she knew not to. Not yet. Ryan was too fragile. Precious. A single touch might shatter him.

So she just sat.

Very still.

They were two frozen shapes as the storm surged and howled above them.

A minute went past.

And then another.

Hannah wanted to cry. She had no idea how to help. What would Ryan do if the situation were reversed? When had she ever been this upset over a bad case at work? The closest she could think of was that little boy, Brendon, with the head injury and the dead mother and the abusive father who hadn't given a damn.

And what had Ryan done?

Told a joke. A stupid blonde joke. His way of coping or helping others to cope. Trying to make them laugh and thereby defusing an atmosphere that could be destructive.

No atmosphere could be worse than this. The pain of loving someone and being totally unable to connect. To offer comfort.

Hannah chewed the inside of her cheek as she desperately searched her memory. Had she even *heard* a blonde joke that Ryan wouldn't already know?

Maybe.

'Hey...' Surprisingly, she didn't have to shout to be heard. The wind seemed to have dropped fractionally and the hedge was were offering a small amount of protection. 'Have...have you heard the one about the blonde who went to pick up her car from the mechanic who'd been fixing it?'

There was no response from Ryan. Not a flicker. But he'd never been put off by Hannah's deliberate indifference, had he? It took courage to continue, all the same. More courage than heading out into a potentially dangerous storm.

'She asked, "Was there much wrong with it?" and the mechanic said, "Nah, just crap in the carburettor."' Hannah had to swallow. This was so hard. How could anything be funny at a time like this? The punchline might fall like a lead balloon and she would seem shallow. Flippant. Uncaring. The things she had once accused Ryan of being. The *last* things she wanted to be seen as right now.

'And...and the blonde thought about that for a minute and then she nodded and she said, "OK...how often do I have to do that?"'

For a heartbeat, and then another, Hannah thought her fears were proving correct. The stone statue that was Ryan was still silent. Unmoving.

But then a sound escaped. A strangled kind of laughter. To Hannah's horror, however, it morphed into something else.

Ryan was *crying.*

Ghastly, racking sobs as though he had no idea *how* to cry but the sounds were being ripped from his soul.

Hannah felt tears sliding down her own face and there was no way she could prevent herself touching him now. She wrapped both her arms around him as tightly as she could, her face pressed against the back of his shoulder.

Holding him.

Trying to absorb some of the terrible grief that he seemed to be letting go.

Maybe it was Chloe's case that had caused it or maybe she'd been the straw to break the camel's back. The reason didn't matter. Ryan was hurting and if Hannah hadn't known before just how deep her love for this man went, there was no escaping that knowledge now.

She would never know how long they stayed like that. Time had no relevance. At some point, however, Ryan moved. He took Hannah's arm and pushed her away.

He couldn't bear it if Hannah felt *sorry* for him.

Adding weakness to the list of faults she already considered him to have.

He had to push her away. However comforting her touch had been, he didn't want her pity.

Searching her face in the darkness didn't reveal what he'd been afraid to find. The shine of tears on Hannah's face was unexpected.

'Why are *you* crying?'

'Because...' Hannah gulped. 'Because *you're* crying.'

Why would she do that? There was only one reason that occurred to Ryan. She cared about him. Cared enough to be moved by his grief, even if she didn't know where it was coming from.

A very new sensation was born for Ryan right then. Wonderment. He had revealed the rawest of emotions. Exposed a part of himself he'd never shared with another living soul and Hannah had not only witnessed it, she had accepted it.

Was *sharing* it even.

Oh, man! This was huge. As big as the storm currently raging over their heads.

Bigger even.

Ryan sniffed and scrubbed his nose with the palm of his hand. He made an embarrassed kind of sound.

'First time for everything, I guess.'

'You mean this is the *first* time you've ever cried?'

'Yeah.' Ryan sniffed again and almost managed a smile. The grief had drained away and left a curious sort of peace. Had the crying done that? Or Hannah's touch? A combination of both maybe. 'Well, since I was about five or six anyway.'

'Oh...' And Hannah was smiling back at him. A gentle smile that was totally without any kind of judgement. 'I'm glad I was here.'

'Yeah...' It was still difficult to swallow but the lump in his throat seemed different. A happy lump rather than an agonised one. How could that be? 'Me, too.'

They listened to the wind for a moment. Felt the fat drops of rain ping against their bare arms.

'I'm sorry, Ryan,' Hannah said.

'What for?'

'Lots of things.'

'Like what?'

'Like that we couldn't save Chloe.'

'We could have, if we'd only known.' Ryan felt the weight of sadness pulling him down again but he knew he wouldn't go as far as he had. Never again. Hannah had stopped his fall. Made something right in the world again. 'It shouldn't have happened.'

'No, of course it shouldn't, but I can see why it did. If there hadn't been so many injuries it would have been standard protocol to check her out a lot more carefully. To collar and backboard her until X-rays were done, given the mechanism of injury. But she was part of the walking wounded group. She only complained about her sore arm.'

'Tunnel vision.'

'Not entirely. With so many to care for, you don't have time to think outside the square. Tick the boxes that don't seem urgent. Anyway, it happened and it's dreadful and I know how you must feel.' A tentative smile curved Hannah's lips. 'I'm available for a spot of wallowing.'

Ryan shook his head. 'I don't do wallowing, you know that.' He snorted softly. 'Hell, if I went down that track with the kind of material I've got to keep me going, I'd end up like a character in some gloomy Russian novel. Chloe *did* get to me more than usual, though. Too close to home.'

'I don't understand.'

Of course she didn't. Why had Ryan thought that keeping his private life private would make things easier?

'I've got a niece,' he told her. 'Michaela. She's six and blonde and it could have been her in there instead of Chloe. Not that there's anything that could save Mikki so to have another little girl that didn't *have* to die and still did seemed just too unfair to be acceptable.'

'Mikki *has* to die?'

'It's inevitable. She's got neuroaxonal dystrophy. It's an auto-somal recessive genetic disease and it's incredibly cruel. They seem perfectly normal at birth and even for the first year or two, and then there's a steady deterioration until they die a few years later. Mikki can't move any more. She can't see or talk. She can still hear and she can smile. She's got the most gorgeous smile.'

When had Hannah's hand slipped into his like that? Ryan returned the squeeze.

'I love that kid,' he said quietly. 'She's got a couple of older brothers but she was special right from day one.'

'And she lives here, in Australia?'

'Brisbane. She's my older brother's child. He's taking it hard and it's putting a big strain on the marriage. He's a bit like me, I guess—not good at sharing the hard stuff in life. Easier to bottle it up and have a laugh about something meaningless.'

'Like a joke.' Hannah was nodding.

'Yeah. Shallow, isn't it?'

'You're not shallow, Ryan. You care more than anyone I've ever met. You've just been good at hiding it.' She cleared her throat. 'So Mikki's the reason you come back to Australia so often?'

'Yeah. I try to be there whenever things get really tough or when she has a hospital appointment. I can explain things again to her parents later.'

'It's a huge commitment.'

'I would have moved there to make it easier to be supportive but my parents live in Auckland. Dad had a stroke a couple of years ago. Quite a bad one and Mum's finding it harder to cope. So there I was in Sydney, commuting one way and then another. The travel time was playing havoc with my career so I had to choose one city and the job in Auckland happened to come up first. It doesn't seem to take any longer to get to Brisbane from Auckland than it did from Sydney and I'm only doing half the travelling I used to do.'

Hannah's smile was rueful. 'And I was thinking that Mi-chaela was a girlfriend. Or an ex-wife.'

Ryan snorted. 'For one thing, any wife of mine would never become an "ex". For another, I haven't had time in my life for a relationship for years. Who would, with the kind of family commitments I've got?'

'But you go out with everyone. You never miss a party.'

'I'm in a new city. I need to find friends. Sometimes I just need to escape and do normal, social things. I still feel lonely but if you can't find some fun somewhere in life, it takes all the sense out of struggling along with the bad bits.'

'I can't believe I accused you of being shallow, Ryan. I'm really, really sorry.'

'Don't be. I can see why you did. I've never told anyone at work what goes on in my private life. I had a feeling that if I started I'd never be able to stop and it would be too hard. I'd end up a mess and people would just feel sorry for me. I've got too much pride to take that on board.'

'*I* don't feel sorry for you.'

'You don't?'

'No.'

'What *do* you feel, Han?'

'I...feel a lot.' Hannah was looking down, avoiding his gaze. 'I'm...in love with you, Ryan.'

There.

She'd said it.

Opened her heart right up.

Made herself as vulnerable as it was possible to get, but what choice had she had? There was no escaping the truth and she couldn't live a lie.

And hadn't Ryan made himself just as vulnerable? He hadn't cried in front of anyone in his adult life. He could have hidden it from her. Stormed off and shut her out before he let himself go. He'd been exercising control over his emotions for year after year. He could have done the same for a minute or two longer.

But he hadn't. At some level he had trusted her enough to show her who he really was.

An utterly amazing, caring, committed man.

How could she have been so wrong about him?

Ryan deserved nothing less than the absolute truth from her, no matter how painful the repercussions.

She was too afraid to look at him. It was too dark to be able to interpret expressions accurately enough in any case.

She didn't need to be able to see, though. She could feel the touch under her chin as Ryan tilted her face up to meet his.

Could feel the touch of his lips on her own, the rain-slicked smoothness of her skin against the grating stubble of a jaw that hadn't been near a razor since what was now yesterday.

The kiss was as gentle as it was powerful.

It told Hannah she didn't need to be afraid. Ryan understood that vulnerability and he wasn't going to break her trust if he could help it.

The first words he spoke when he drew away had to be the most important Hannah would ever hear.

She wasn't disappointed.

'I love you, too, Hannah Jackson.'

The rain was pelting down now. Ryan smoothed damp strands of hair back from Hannah's forehead.

'We need to find somewhere dry,' he said.

Hannah laughed. Incredible as it seemed, in the wake of what they had just been through and with the prospect of more gruelling hours of work ahead, there was joy to be found in life. In each other.

'Where have I heard that before?'

'We're on a break. We've got two hours to escape. To forget about the world and be dry. And warm. And safe.' Ryan kissed her again. 'You'll always be safe with me, Hannah. I promise you that.'

She took his face between both her hands. 'And so will you be,' she vowed. 'With me.'

She let Ryan pull her to her feet and she smiled. 'I'd like to go somewhere dry with you. Very much.' Her smile broadened. 'Even though I already know how good our rapport is.'

'Yeah…' Ryan growled. 'I'm *fun*.'

'I didn't mean that, you know. It was so much more than that. I was just trying to protect myself.'

'From *me*?' Ryan sounded baffled.

'Yes. I thought it was far too dangerous to fall for someone like you.'

'Who, exactly, is someone like me?'

'Oh, you know. Someone fun. Clever. Exciting. Great looking. Too good to be true.'

'I'm someone like that?' Now he sounded very pleasantly surprised.

'Someone exactly like that. A bit too much like the man my mother fell head over heels in love with. And the one that Susie fell in love with. And they both got bored or hadn't been genuine in the first place, and it was me who had to pick up all the pieces. Do you know how many pieces you can get out of *two* broken hearts?'

'No. How many?'

'Heaps,' Hannah said firmly. 'Way *too* many.'

Ryan pulled her to a stop. Pulled her into his arms. 'Your heart's going to stay in one piece if I have anything to do with it,' he said seriously. 'I'm going to make it my mission in life.'

The promise was too big. Hannah didn't want anything to

make her cry again. She had to smile and try to lighten the emotional overload. 'Could be a full-time job.'

'I intend to make sure it is.'

'It might be a lifetime career.'

'I certainly hope so.'

'Of course, there's always the prospect of promotion.'

'Really? What kind of promotion?'

Why had she started this? Suddenly it didn't seem like a joke. 'Oh, maybe being an emergency department consultant?'

'I might not get that job. I've heard that I've got some pretty stiff competition.'

Hannah's heart was doing some curious flip-flops. 'I might not mind very much if I don't get that job.'

'Why not?'

'I might have more important things in my life than my career.'

Ryan was smiling. 'Such as?' He raised a hopeful eyebrow. 'You mean *me*?'

Hannah nodded shyly. 'Maybe even... How would you feel about a promotion to being a father?'

'Dr Jackson! Is that a proposal?'

'I don't know.' Hannah caught her bottom lip between her teeth. 'Would you like it to be?'

'No.'

Hannah's heart plummeted. But then she saw the gleam of Ryan's teeth.

'I'm old-fashioned,' he announced. 'If there's to be any proposing going on around here, *I'll* do it.'

And that's exactly what he did. In the heart of a tropical storm, in the middle of a garden, just beside a sundial, Ryan got down on one knee, holding both of Hannah's hands in his own.

'I love you.' He had to shout because the wind had risen again to snatch his words away and the rain was thundering down and the wail of a siren close by rose and fell.

'I love you, Hannah. You are the only person in existence

that I can really be myself with. The only time in my life I felt no hint of being alone was when I had you in my bed. You make me whole. I don't ever want to live without having you by my side. Will you—please—marry me?'

'Oh, I think so.' Hannah sank to her knees on the wet flagstones of the path. 'I love you, too, Ryan.' It was easier to hear now that their heads were close together again. 'You are the only person in existence that I've ever...had such a good rapport with.' They were grinning at each other now, at the absurdity of choosing this particular place and time to make such declarations. Then Hannah's smile faded. It had just happened this way and because it had, it was perfect. 'Yes,' she said slowly. 'I would love to marry you.'

Ryan shook the raindrops from his hair after giving Hannah a lingering, wonderful kiss.

'Can we go somewhere dry now?'

Hannah nodded but the wail of the siren was still going and she hesitated when Ryan helped her up and then tugged on her hand.

'What's up, babe?'

'I can't stop thinking about it.'

'The bus crash? The cyclone that's on its way that we'd better find some shelter from pretty damn quick?'

'No...the shoe.'

'Did Chloe really tell you there was a boy on the bus?'

'Yes.'

'And you believe her?'

'Yes.'

'We'd better find Harry or someone, then, and let them know.'

Hannah nodded. 'I'd feel a lot better if we did. Do you mind?'

'Why should I mind?'

'It'll take a bit longer to find somewhere dry. To have that break.'

'Babe, we've got all the time in the world to work on our rapport.' Ryan had his arm around Hannah, sheltering her from some of the wind and rain. They had to bend forward to move against the force of the elements and get themselves back towards Crocodile Creek Base Hospital's emergency department.

But it felt so different than when Hannah had been going in the opposite direction on her search for Ryan. With his strength added to her own, she knew there was nothing she wouldn't be prepared to face.

Ryan paused once more as they reached the relative shelter of the ambulance bay. 'It *is* real, isn't it?'

'What, the cyclone? Sure feels like it.'

'No, I mean, how we feel about each other. The love.'

'As real as this storm,' Hannah assured him. 'And just as powerful.'

'What happens when the sun comes out?'

'We'll be in a dry place.' Hannah smiled. 'Having fun.'

Ryan looked over her shoulder through the doors into the emergency department. 'I don't think fun's on the agenda for a while yet.'

'No.' Hannah followed the direction of his gaze. Chloe was still somewhere in there. So were a lot of other people who needed attention. And when the aftermath of the bus crash had been mopped up, they could be on standby for the first casualties from a cyclone.

'It's not going to be easy.'

'No.'

'Are you up for it?'

'With you here as well? Of course I am. We can do this, Ryan. We'll be doing it together.'

'Together is good. Oh, and, Han?'

'Yes?'

'Can I have that blonde joke? The one about the carburettor? It was great.'

'You can have anything and everything I have to give,' Hannah told him. 'Always.'

Ryan took hold of her hand once more and they both turned

towards the automatic doors. Ready to step back into a place that needed them both almost as much as they needed each other.

'Same,' Ryan said softly. 'For ever.'

* * * * *

The Nurse He's Been Waiting For

Meredith Webber

Dear Reader,

Writing is such a solitary pursuit that to be involved in a series with other people is really special. To be involved in a series with three good friends—Marion Lennox, Lilian Darcy and Alison Roberts—is extraordinarily special. More than that, it's tremendous fun. Although we live far apart, three of us in different states in Australia and Alison in New Zealand, we do manage to get together most years at the Australian Romance Writers' Conference.

It was at one of these conferences about four years ago that the idea for the Crocodile Creek series was born. The four of us spent more time in various hotel bedrooms plotting out our masterpiece than we did listening to conference speakers. Then we had to sell the idea to our editors, which took a little time and quite a lot of work on their part and on ours, but in the end we got the go-ahead, and suddenly Crocodile Creek became as real to us as our home suburbs, and the people who worked in the hospital and air rescue service became our friends.

I was very fond of Harry, the policeman, so I was delighted when I could match him up with Grace in this book. Grace's sunny nature and helpful personality make her the ideal woman for Harry. Unfortunately, she fears she is unlovable, and he just flat-out fears love. But as a cyclone whirls above their heads, things change.

And now? Well, while we might have sorted out the love lives of some of our friends in this second series, several new people have appeared who might also need some loving. I hope so, since being involved in the series has been special—almost as special as being in love.

Meredith Webber

PROLOGUE

AS A CYCLONE hovered off the coast of North Queensland, threatening destruction to any town in its path, several hundred miles away a small boy sneaked on board a bus. Terrified that his father, who was arguing with the bus driver, would discover the dog he'd threatened to drown, Max ducked between the two men and climbed the steps into the warm, fusty, dimly lit interior of the big vehicle. Mum would sort everything out when he got to Crocodile Creek—the fare, the dog, everything.

Mum would like a dog.

'Don't call her Mum—she's your flippin' sister! Or half-sister, if you really want to know.'

Echoes of his father's angry rant rang through Max's head, but Georgie hadn't ever minded him calling her Mum, and it stopped kids at school teasing him.

The kids that had mums, that was.

Mum would love Scruffy.

He shifted the backpack off his shoulder and hugged it to his chest, comforted by the squirming of the pup inside it, checking out the passengers as he made his way up the aisle. He'd been shunted back and forth across Queensland often enough to be able to pick out who was who among his fellow travellers.

The bus was nearly full and all the usual ones were there. A group of backpackers chattering away in a foreign language, a fat woman in the seat behind them—bet she'd been to visit her grandkids—bloke on the other side of the aisle—he'd be late back on the bus at all the rest stops—an old couple who looked like they'd been on the bus for all of their lives, and a tired, sad-looking woman with a little boy.

Max slipped into the seat behind them. He'd never told Mum and certainly wouldn't bother telling Dad, but scary things could happen on a bus, and he'd worked out it's always best to stick with someone with a kid, or to sit near a youngish couple, so he looked like part of a family.

Though with Scruffy to protect him...

He slid across the seat to the window, looking for his father, wondering if the argument was over—if his father had actually paid to get rid of him this time.

Wanting to wave goodbye.

The footpath was deserted, the bus driver now talking to someone in the doorway of the travel office. Twisting his head against the glass, Max could just make out a shambling figure moving through a pool of lamplight well behind the bus—walking away from it.

So much for waving goodbye.

'It doesn't matter!' Max told himself fiercely, scrunching up his eyes and blinking hard, turning his attention to the zip on his backpack before thrusting his hand inside, feeling Scruffy's rough hair, a warm tongue licking his fingers. 'It doesn't matter!'

But when you're only seven, it did matter...

CHAPTER ONE

MIDNIGHT, AND GRACE O'RIORDAN lay on one of the examination couches in the emergency department of the Crocodile Creek Hospital and stared at an amoeba-shaped stain on the ceiling as she contemplated clothes, love and the meaning of life.

In truth, the meaning of life wasn't overtaxing her brain cells right now, and she'd assured herself, for the forty-hundredth time, that the dress she'd bought for the wedding wasn't too over the top, which left love.

Love, as in unrequited.

One-sided.

Heavens to Betsy, as if she hadn't had enough one-sided love in her life.

Perhaps loving without being loved back made her unlovable. In the same way old furniture, polished often, developed a rich deep shiny patina, so loved people shone and attracted more love.

What *was* this? Sensible, practical, Grace O'Riordan indulging in wild flights of fancy? She'd be better off napping.

Although she was on duty, the A and E dept—in fact, the entire hospital—after a particularly hectic afternoon and early evening, was quiet. Quiet enough for her to have a sleep, which, given the frantic few days she'd just spent checking on cyclone preparations, she needed.

But she needed love, too, and was practical—there was that word again—enough to know that she had to get over her present love—the unrequited one—and start looking to the future. Start looking for someone who might love her back, someone who also wanted love and the things that went with it, like marriage and a family. Especially a family. She had been family-less for quite long enough...

This coming week would provide the perfect opportunity to begin the search, with people flying in from all over the globe for the weddings of Mike and Emily tomorrow and, a week later, Gina and Cal. Surely somewhere, among all the unattached male wedding guests, there'd be someone interested in a small-ish, slightly plump, sometimes pretty, Irish-Australian nurse.

She pressed her hand against her heart, sure she could feel pain just thinking about loving someone other than Harry.

But she'd got over love before, she could do it again.

'Move on, Grace!' she told herself, in her sternest voice.

'Isn't anyone on duty in this place?' a loud voice demanded. Harry's voice.

Grace slid off the table, pulled her uniform shirt straight, wondered, briefly, whether her short curls looked like a flattened bird's nest after lying down, and exited the room to greet the man she was trying to get over.

'If you'd come in through the emergency door, a bell would have rung and I'd have known you were here,' she greeted him, none too warmly. Then she saw the blood.

'Holy cow, Harry Blake, what have you done to yourself this time?'

She grabbed a clean towel from a pile on a trolley and hurried towards the chair where he'd collapsed, one bloody leg thrust out in front of him.

Wrapping the towel tightly around the wound to stem at least some of the bleeding, she looked up into his face. Boy, was it ever hard to get over love when her heart danced jigs every time she saw him.

Irish jigs.

She looked at his face again—as a nurse this time. It was grey with tiredness but not, as far as she could tell, pale from blood loss.

'Can you make it into an examination cubicle or will I ring for help?' she asked, knowing full well he was so stubborn he'd refuse help even if she called for it. But when he stood he wobbled slightly, so she tucked her shoulder into his armpit to take some of his weight, and with her arm around his back for added support she led him into the room.

He sat down on the couch she'd occupied only minutes earlier, then, as she pushed at his chest and lifted his legs, he lay down.

'What happened?' she asked, as she unwrapped the towel enough to know there was no arterial bleeding on his leg, then wrapped it up again so she could check his vital signs before she examined the wound.

'Carelessness,' he muttered at her. He closed his eyes, which made her wonder if his blood loss was more serious than she'd supposed. But his pulse was strong, his blood pressure excellent and his breathing steady. Just to be sure, she slid an oxygen saturation meter onto one of his fingers, and turned on the monitor.

'What kind of carelessness?' she asked as she once again unwrapped the towel and saw the torn, bloodstained trouser leg and the badly lacerated skin beneath the shredded fabric.

'Chainsaw! Does that stain on the ceiling look like a penguin to you?'

'No, it looks like an amoeba, which is to say a formless blob.' She was using scissors to cut away his trousers, so she could see the wound. Blood had run into his sock, making it hard to tell if the damage went down that far. Taking care not to brush against his wound, she took hold of his boot to ease it off.

'You can't do that,' he said, sitting up so quickly his shoulder brushed against her and his face was kissing close.

Kissing Harry? As if!

'Can't take your boot off?' she asked. 'Is there some regulation about not being a policeman if you're not wearing both boots?'

He turned towards her, a frown pleating his black eyebrows, his grey eyes perplexed. 'Of course not. You just wouldn't get it off.' He tugged and twisted at the same time and the elastic-sided boot slid off. 'I'll get the sock, too,' he added, pulling off the bloodstained wreck, but not before Grace had noticed the hole at the top of the big toe.

In a dream where Harry loved her back, she'd have mended that hole—she'd like doing things like that—the little caring things that said *I love you* without the words.

'Lie back,' she said, dream and reality coming too close for comfort with him sitting there. 'I'll flush this mess and see what's what.'

She pulled on clean gloves and set a bag of saline on a drip stand. She'd need tubing, a three-way tap, syringe and a nineteen-gauge needle to drip the liquid onto the wound while she probed for foreign particles.

Packing waterproof-backed absorbent pads beneath his leg, she started the saline dripping onto the wound, a nasty contusion running eight inches in length, starting on the tibia just below the knee and swerving off into his calf.

'The skin's so chewed up it's not viable enough to stitch,' she told him, probing a few pieces of what looked like mangled treetrunk, or possibly mangled trouser fabric, from the deepest part. Organic matter and clay were among the most likely things to cause infection in tissue injury. 'Ideally it should be left open, but I guess you're not willing to stay home and rest it for the next few days.'

'You *are* joking!' Harry said. 'I need it patched up now, and maybe in three days' time, when we know for sure Cyclone Willie has departed, I can rest it.'

'Harry, it's a mess. I'll dress it as best I can but if you don't look after it and come in to have it dressed every day, you're going to end up with ulceration and needing a skin graft on it.'

She left the saline dripping on the wound while she found the dressings she'd need and some antibiotic cream which she would spread beneath the non-adhesive dressing once she had all visible debris removed from it.

Harry watched her work, right up until she starting snipping away torn tatters of skin, when he turned his attention back to the penguin on the ceiling.

'Would you like me to give you a local anaesthetic while I do this? It could hurt.'

'It *is* hurting,' he said, gritting his teeth as a particularly stubborn piece of skin or grit defied Grace's efforts to be gentle. 'But, no, no needles. Just talk to me. And before you do, have another look—maybe the stain looks like the little engine on a cane train.'

Grace glanced towards the ceiling but shook her head as she turned back towards him.

'Since when do a penguin and a cane train engine share similarities in looks?'

'It's a shape thing,' he said, grabbing at her hand and drawing the shape on the back of it. 'Penguin, blob, train engine, see?'

'Not even vaguely,' she told him, rescuing her hand from his grasp then changing her gloves again before she continued with her job. 'And I can see right through you, Harry Blake. You're babbling on about penguins and cane trains to keep me from going back to the question you avoided earlier.'

She stopped talking while she spread cream across his leg. He didn't feel much like talking either.

Grace sealed the wound with a broad, long dressing, and bandaged over it with crêpe bandages, then pulled a long sleeve over the lot, giving it as much security and padding as she could because she knew he'd be putting himself in situations where he could bump it.

'That should give it some protection from physical damage, although, with the cyclone coming, who knows what you'll be called on to do? Just make sure you come in to have it checked and re-dressed every day.'

'You on duty tomorrow?'

Grace smiled sadly to herself. Would that he was asking because he was interested!

'You already know the answer to that one. I finish night duty in the morning and have three days off so I can cope with the wedding and the cyclone preparations without letting any one down here at the hospital.'

Harry sat up and swung his legs over the side of the bed, ready to leave.

'Not so fast,' she warned him. 'I need to check your tetanus status and give you some antibiotics just in case there's some infection already in there.'

She paused and her wide blue eyes met his.

'*And* you're not leaving here until you tell me how you did it.'

Harry studied her as he debated whether to tell her. Tousled curls, freckled nose—Grace, everyone's friend.

His friend, too. A friendship formed when he'd been in need of a friend in the months after Nikki's death. True, he'd had friends, good friends, among the townspeople and the hospital staff, but all the locals had known Nikki since she'd been a child while the hospital staff had all drawn close to her as they'd nursed her through the last weeks of her life.

And though these friends had all stood by him and had wanted to offer support, he'd avoided them, not wanting sympathy, needing to be left alone to sort out the morass of conflicting emotions warring within him.

Grace had arrived after Nikki's death, so there was no connection, no history, just a bright, bubbly, capable young woman who was willing to listen if he wanted to talk, to talk if he needed conversation, or just to share the silence when he didn't want to be alone.

A true friend...

'I'm waiting!'

She had her hands on her hips and a no-nonsense look on her face, but though she was trying to look serious a smile lurked in her blue eyes.

A smile nearly always lurked in Grace's eyes...

The thought startled him to the extent that confession seemed easier than considering what, if anything, noticing Grace's smiling eyes might mean.

'I hit my leg with the blade of a chainsaw.'

'And *what* were you doing, wielding a chainsaw, may I ask?'

'A tree had come down, out along the Wygera road, but part of the trunk must have been dead because the saw bounced off it when it hit it.' He waved his hand towards his now securely bandaged leg. 'One wounded leg.'

'That wasn't my question and you know it, Harry. It's one o'clock in the morning. You're a policeman, not a rescue worker. The fire service, the electricity workers and, or when requested, the SES crews clear roads. It's what they're trained to do. The SES manual has pages and pages on safe working with chainsaws.'

'I've been using chainsaws all my life,' Harry retorted, uncomfortably aware this conversation might not be about chainsaws but uncertain what it was about.

'That's not the point,' Grace snapped. 'What if the accident had been worse? What if you'd taken your leg off? Then who's in charge here? Who's left to co-ordinate services to a town that could be struck by one of the worst cyclones in history within the next twenty-four hours?'

'Give over, Grace,' he said, standing up on his good leg and carefully putting weight on the injured one to see how bad it felt.

Very bad. Bad enough to make him feel queasy.

'No, I won't give over.' No smile in the blue eyes now. In

fact, she was glaring at him. 'This is just typical of you, Harry Blake. Typical of the stupid risks you take. You mightn't care what happens to you, but you've got family and friends who do. There are people out there who'd be deeply hurt if you were killed or badly injured, but do you think about them when you pull on your superhero cape and go rushing blindly into danger? No, you don't! You don't think of anyone but yourself, and that's not noble or self-sacrificing or even brave—it's just plain selfishness, Harry.'

Harry heard her out, growing more annoyed every second. He'd had a shocking day, he was tired, his leg hurt and to accuse him of selfishness, well, that was just the last straw.

'And just what makes you think you have the right to sit in judgement on me?' he demanded, taking a careful stride towards the cubicle curtain so he could escape any further conversation. 'What makes you think you know me well enough to call me selfish, or to question my motives in helping people? You're not my mother or my wife, Grace, so butt out!'

He heard her gasp as he headed out of the cubicle, across the deserted A and E waiting room and out of the hospital, limping not entirely because of his leg but because he was only wearing one boot. The other he'd stupidly left behind, and that made him even angrier than Grace's accusation. He looked up at the cloud-massed sky and wanted to yell his frustration to the wind.

Perhaps it was just as well there was no one around, although if he'd happened on someone he knew he could have asked that person to go back in and retrieve the boot for him. The hospital was quieter than he'd ever seen it, with no one coming or going from the car park.

He was contemplating radioing the constable on duty to come over and collect it for him when he heard the footsteps behind him.

Grace!

Coming to apologise?

'Here's your boot, and some antibiotics, directions on when to take them on the packet. And in answer to your question about rights, I thought, for some obviously foolish reason, I had the right of a friend.'

And with that she spun on her heel and walked briskly back into the hospital.

Wonderful! Now Grace had joined the throng of people he'd somehow managed to upset, simply because they refused to let him get on with his life his way.

Alone! With no emotional involvement with anyone or anything.

Except Sport, the three-legged blue heeler cattle dog he'd rescued from the dump one day.

And his parents—he liked his parents. And they'd known him well enough to back off when Nikki had died...

He climbed into his vehicle and slumped back against the seat. Was the day over? Please, God, it might be. On top of all the damage and power disruptions caused by the gale-force winds stirred up by Cyclone Willie, he'd had to handle traffic chaos at the fishing competition, an assault on Georgie Turner, the local obstetrician, Sophia Poulos, mother of the groom at the next day's wedding, phoning every fifteen minutes to ask about the cyclone as if he was personally responsible for its course, and to top it all off, he'd had to visit Georgie again.

She was still shaken from the assault by a patient's relative earlier that day, and nursing a hairline fracture to her cheekbone. Now Harry had to tell her there was a summons out for her stepfather's arrest—her stepfather who currently had custody of her little brother Max.

Did Georgie know where he was?

She hadn't known where the pair were, and he'd hated himself for asking because now she'd be even more worried about Max, whom she'd loved and cared for since he'd been a baby, bringing him up herself—except for the times when the worthless scoundrel who'd fathered him swooped in and took him away, no doubt to provide a prop in some nefarious purpose.

Max was such a great kid, growing up around the hospital, loved and watched out for by everyone in the close-knit community.

So Harry had been driving away from the doctors' house, seething with frustration that he couldn't offer anything to help the white-faced, injured woman, when the call had come in about the tree coming down to block the Wygera road. His chainsaw had already been in the vehicle so he'd decided to take out some of his anger and frustration on a tree.

None of which was any excuse for being rude to Grace...

Not wanting to think about Harry or the crushing words he'd used, Grace retreated to cubicle one once again and climbed back onto the examination couch. She stared at the stain on the ceiling, trying to see a penguin or a cane train engine but seeing only an amoeba.

Was it because she lacked imagination?

Not that she couldn't see the penguin but that she couldn't let Harry alone to get on with his life his own way.

Did her lack of imagination mean she couldn't understand his grieving process?

Hurt enveloped her—that Harry could say what he had. And while she knew she should have welcomed his angry comment because now she knew for sure she had to move on, such rational reasoning didn't make the pain any less.

She studied the stain.

'Is this place totally deserted?'

Another male voice, this one deep and slightly husky. Grace sprang off the couch and was about to emerge from the treatment cubicle when the curtain opened.

Luke Bresciano, hunky, dark amber-eyed, black-haired, Italian-Australian orthopod, stood there, smiling at her.

'I always napped on examination couches when I was on duty in the ER, and for some reason it's always treatment room one,' he teased.

He had a lovely smile but it didn't reach his eyes—a tortured soul, Dr B. And although, this being Crocodile Creek, stories about his past abounded—a woman who'd left him, a child— no one really knew any more about him than they had the day he'd arrived. Age, marital status and qualifications.

'You're here late. Do you have a patient coming in?' Grace asked, being practical and professional while wondering if she remembered how to flirt and if there was any point in trying a little flirtation on Luke. Although was there any point in swapping one tortured soul for another?

'I find sleep comes when it wants to and it wasn't coming so I drove up to see a patient I'd admitted earlier. I looked in on Susie while I was here—'

'Susie? Our physio Susie? In hospital? But she can't be.' Grace was stumbling over her disbelief. 'She's Emily's bridesmaid tomorrow. Mrs Poulos will have a cow!'

Luke offered a kindly smile—much like the one Grace usually offered drunks or people coming out of anaesthetic who were totally confused.

'You obviously haven't heard the latest. Susie had a fall and sprained her ankle earlier today—or is it yesterday now? But the bridesmaid thing's been sorted out. Her twin sister Hannah is here—they're identical twins—and she's going to do bridesmaid duties so the photos won't—'

'Be totally spoilt by Susie's crutches,' Grace finished for him, shaking her head in bemusement that such a wonderful solution—from Mrs P.'s point of view—had been found. Grace was quite sure Emily wouldn't have minded in the least.

Nodding agreement to her ending of the story, Luke finished, 'Exactly! So after visiting Susie, who was sound asleep anyway, I was taking a short cut out through here when I realised how empty it seemed.'

He smiled at Grace but although it was a very charming smile, it did nothing to her heart. She'd really have to work on it if she wanted to move on from Harry. 'I thought I'd better check we did have someone on duty.'

'Yes, that's me. I can't believe how quiet it is. All I heard from the day staff was how busy they'd been and I was busy earlier but now...'

She waved her arms around to indicate the emptiness.

'Then I'll let you get back to sleep,' Luke said.

He turned to depart and she remembered the stain.

'Before you go, would you mind having a look at this stain?'

The words were out before she realised just how truly weird her request was, but Luke was looking enquiringly at her, so she pointed at the stain on the ceiling.

'Roof leaking? I'm not surprised given the rain we've been having, but Maintenance probably knows more about leaking roofs than I do. In fact, they'd have to.' Another charming smile. 'I know zilch.'

'It's not a leak. It's an old stain but I'd really like to know what you think about the shape. You have to lie down on the couch to see it properly. Would you mind checking it out and telling me what it looks like to you?'

'Ink-blot test, Grace?' Luke teased, but he lay obediently on the couch and turned his attention to the stain.

'It looks a bit like a penguin to me,' Luke said, and Grace was sorry she'd asked.

She walked out to the door with Luke, said goodbye, then returned to the cubicle.

It *must* be lack of imagination that she couldn't see it. She focussed on the stain, desperate to see the penguin and prove her imaginative abilities.

Hadn't she just imagined herself darning Harry's socks?

The stain remained a stain—amoeba-like in its lack of form. She clambered off the couch, chastising herself for behaving so pathetically.

For heaven's sake, Grace, get over it!

Get over Harry and get on with your life.

She stood and stared at the stain, trying for a cane train engine this time...

Trying not to think about Harry...

Failing...

It had come as a tumultuous shock to Grace, the realisation that she was love with Harry. She, who'd vowed never to risk one-sided love again, had fallen into the trap once more. She'd fallen in love with a man who'd been there and done that as far as love and marriage were concerned.

A man who had no intention of changing his single status.

They'd been at a State Emergency Service meeting, and had stayed behind, as they nearly always did, to chat. Grace was team leader of the Crocodile Creek SES and Harry, as the head of the local police force, was the co-ordinator for all rescue and emergency services in the area.

Harry had suggested coffee, as he nearly always did after their fortnightly meetings. Nothing noteworthy there—coffee was coffee and all Grace's defences had been securely in place. They'd locked the SES building and walked the short distance down the road to the Black Cockatoo, which, although a pub, also served the best coffee in the small community of Crocodile Creek.

The bar had been crowded, a group of young people celebrating someone's birthday, making a lot of noise and probably drinking a little too much, but Harry Blake, while he'd keep an eye on them, wasn't the kind of policeman who'd spoil anyone's innocent fun.

So he'd steered Grace around the corner where the bar angled, leaving a small, dimly lit area free from noise or intrusion.

The corner of the bar had been dark, but not too dark for her to see Harry's grey eyes glinting with a reflection of the smile on his mobile lips and Harry's black hair flopping forward on his forehead, so endearingly her fingers had ached to push it back.

'Quieter here,' he said, pulling out a barstool and taking Grace's elbow as she clambered onto it. Then he smiled—nothing more. Just a normal, Harry Blake kind of smile, the kind he offered to men, women, kids and dogs a million times a day. But the feeble defences Grace O'Riordan had built around her heart collapsed in the warmth of that smile, and while palpitations rattled her chest, and her brain tut-tutted helplessly, Grace realised she'd gone and done it again.

Fallen in love.

With Harry, of all people…

Harry, who was her friend…

CHAPTER TWO

GRACE FIDGETED WITH the ribbon in her hair. It was too much—
she knew it was too much. Yet the woman in the mirror looked
really pretty, the ribbon somehow enhancing her looks.

She took a deep breath, knowing it wasn't the ribbon worrying her but Harry, who was about to pick them all up to drive
them to the wedding.

The hurtful words he'd uttered very early that morning—
you're not my mother or my wife—still echoed in her head, made
worse by the knowledge that what he'd said was true. She *didn't*
have the right to be telling Harry what to do!

It was a good thing it had happened, she reminded herself.
She had to get past this love she felt for him. She'd had enough
one-sided love in her life, starting in her childhood—loving
a father who'd barely known she'd existed, loving stepbrothers who'd laughed at her accent and resented her intrusion into
their lives.

Then, of course, her relationship with James had confirmed
it. One-sided love was not enough. Love had to flow both ways
for it to work—or it did as far as she was concerned.

So here she was, like Cinderella heading for the ball, on the
lookout for a prince.

Harry's a prince, her heart whispered, but she wasn't having any of that. Harry was gone, done and dusted, out of her life, and whatever other clichés might fit this new determination.

And if her chest hurt, well, that was to be expected. Limbs hurt after parts of them were amputated and getting Harry out of her heart was the same thing—an amputation.

But having confirmed this decision, shouldn't she take her own car to the wedding? She could use the excuse that she needed to be with Mrs P. Keeping Mrs P. calm and rational—or as calm and rational as an over-excitable Greek woman could manage on the day her only son was married—was Grace's job for the day.

A shiver of uncertainty worse, right now, than her worry over Harry feathered down Grace's spine. Mike's mother had planned this wedding with the precision of a military exercise—or perhaps a better comparison would be a full-scale, no-holds-barred, Technicolor, wide-screen movie production.

Thinking now of Mrs Poulos, Grace glanced towards the window. Was the wind getting up again? It sounded wild out there, although at the moment it wasn't raining. When the previous day had dawned bright and sunny, the hospital staff had let out their collective breaths. At least, it had seemed, Mrs P. would get her way with the weather.

But now?

The cyclone that had teased the citizens of North Queensland for days, travelling first towards the coast then veering away from it, had turned out to sea a few days earlier, there, everyone hoped, to spend its fury without any further damage. Here in Crocodile Creek, the river was rising, the bridge barely visible above the water, while the strong winds and rain earlier in the week had brought tree branches crashing down on houses, and Grace's SES workers had been kept busy, spreading tarpaulins over the damage.

Not that tarps would keep out the rain if the cyclone turned back their way—they'd be ripped off by the wind within minutes, along with the torn roofing they were trying to protect—

'Aren't you ready yet?'

Christina was calling from the living room, although Grace had given her and Joe the main bedroom—the bedroom they'd shared for a long time before moving to New Zealand to be closer to Joe's family. Now Grace rented the little cottage from Christina, and was hoping to discuss buying it while the couple was here for the birth of their first child as well as the hospital weddings.

'Just about,' she answered, taking a last look at herself and wondering again if she'd gone overboard with the new dress and the matching ribbon threaded through her short fair curls.

Wondering again about driving herself but thinking perhaps she'd left that decision too late. Harry would be here any minute. Besides, her friends might think she was snubbing them.

She'd just have to pretend—she was good at that—only today, instead of pretending Harry was just a friend, she'd have to pretend that all was well between them. In a distant kind of way.

She certainly wasn't going to spoil Mike and Em's wedding by sulking over Harry all through it.

'Wow!'

Joe's slow smile told her he meant the word of praise, and Grace's doubts disappeared.

'Wow yourself,' she said, smiling at him. 'Christina's pregnant and you're the one that's glowing. You both look fantastic.'

She caught the private, joyous smile they shared and felt it pierce her heart like a shard of glass, but held her own smile firmly in place. She might know she'd lost her bounce—lost a little of her delight in life and all the wonders it had to offer—but she'd managed to keep it from being obvious to her friends. Still smiling, still laughing, still joking with her colleagues, hiding the pain of her pointless, unrequited love beneath her bubbly exterior.

Pretence!

'And you've lost weight,' Christina said, eyeing Grace more

carefully now. 'Not that it doesn't suit you, you look beautiful, but don't go losing any more.'

'Beautiful? Grace O'Riordan beautiful? Pregnancy affecting your vision?' Grace said, laughing at her friends—mocking the warmth of pleasure she was feeling deep inside.

Harry heard the laugh as he took the two steps up to the cottage veranda in one stride. No one laughed like Grace, not as often or as—was 'musically' the right word? Grace's laugh sounded like the notes of a beautiful bird, cascading through the air, bringing pleasure to all who heard it.

Beautiful bird? Was all this wedding business turning him fanciful?

Surely not!

While as for Grace...

He caught the groan that threatened to escape his lips. He was in the right—he had no doubt about that. What he did and didn't do wasn't Grace's business. Yet he was uneasily aware that he'd upset her and wasn't quite sure how to fix things between them.

Wasn't, for reasons he couldn't fathom, entirely sure he wanted to...

At least it sounded as if they were ready. He'd offered to drive the three of them, thinking his big four-by-four would be more comfortable for the very pregnant Christina than Grace's little VW, but now he was regretting the impulse. With the possibility that the cyclone would turn back towards the coast, he had an excuse to avoid the wedding altogether, which would also mean not having to face Grace.

Although Mike had been a friend for a long time...

A sudden gust of wind brought down a frond from a palm tree and, super-sensitive right now to any change in the atmospheric conditions, Harry stopped, turned and looked around at the trees and shrubs in the cottage's garden. The wind had definitely picked up again, stripping leaves off the frangipani and bruising the delicate flowers. He shook his head, certain now the cyclone must have swung back towards them again, yet knowing there was nothing he, or anyone else, could do to stop it if it continued towards the coast this time.

They would just have to check all their preparations then wait and see. Preparations were easy—it was the waiting that was hard.

'You look as if you're off to a funeral, not a wedding,' Christina teased as she came out the door, and though he found a smile for her, it must have been too late, for she reached out and touched his arm, adding quietly, 'Weddings must be hard for you.'

He shook his head, rejecting her empathy—not deserving it, although she wasn't to know that. Then he looked beyond her and had to look again.

Was that really Grace?

And if it was, why was his body stirring?

Grace it was, smiling at him, a strained smile certainly, but recognisable as a smile, and saying something. Unfortunately, with his blood thundering in his ears, he couldn't hear the words, neither could he lip-read because his eyes kept shifting from her hair—a ribbon twined through golden curls—to her face—was it the colour of the dress that made her eyes seem bluer?—to her cleavage—more stirring—to a slim leg that was showing through a slit in the dark blue piece of fabric she seemed to have draped rather insecurely around her body.

His first instinct was to take off his jacket and cover her with it, his second was to hit Joe, who was hovering proprietorially behind her, probably looking down that cleavage.

He did neither, simply nodding to the pair before turning and leading the way out to the car, trying hard not to limp—he hated sympathy—opening the front door for Christina, explaining she'd be more comfortable there, letting Joe open the rear door for Grace, then regretting a move that put the pair of them together in the back seat.

Mental head slap! What was *wrong* with him? These three

were his friends—good friends—Grace especially, even though, right now, he wasn't sure where he stood with Grace.

Very carefully, he tucked Christina's voluminous dress in around her, extended the seat belt so it would fit around her swollen belly, then shut the door, though not without a glance towards the back seat—towards Grace.

She was peering out the window, squinting upwards.

Avoiding looking at him?

He couldn't blame her.

But when she spoke he realised just how wrong he was. He was the last thing on Grace's mind.

'Look, there's a patch of blue sky. The sun *is* going to shine for Mike and Emily.'

Harry shook his head. That was a Grace he recognised, always thinking of others, willing the weather to be fine so her friends could be blessed with sunshine at their wedding.

Although that Grace usually wore big T-shirts and long shorts—that Grace, as far as he'd been aware, didn't have a cleavage...

Christina and Joe had both joined Grace in her study of the growing patch of blue sky, Christina sure having sunshine was a good omen for a happy marriage.

'Sunshine's good for the bride because her dress won't get all wet and her hair won't go floppy,' Joe declared, with all the authority of a man five months into marriage who now understood about women's hair and rain. 'But forget about omens— there's only one thing that will guarantee a happy marriage, and that's a willingness for both partners to work at it.'

He slid a hand onto Christina's shoulder then added, 'Harry here knows that.'

Grace saw the movement of Harry's shoulders as he winced, and another shard of glass pierced her vulnerable heart. She hadn't been working at the hospital when Harry's wife, Nikki, had died, but she'd heard enough to know of his devotion to her—of the endless hours he'd spent by her side—and of his heartbreak at her death.

You're not my wife!

The words intruded on her sympathy but she ignored them, determined to pretend that all was well between them—at least in front of other people.

'What's the latest from the weather bureau, Harry?' she asked, hoping to divert his mind from memories she was sure would be bad enough on someone else's wedding day. 'Does this wind mean Willie's turned again and is heading back our way, or is it the early warning of another storm?'

He glanced towards her in the rear-view vision mirror and nodded as if to say, I know what you're doing. But his spoken reply was crisply matter-of-fact. 'Willie's turned—he's running parallel to the coast again but at this stage the bureau has no indication of whether he'll turn west towards us or continue south. The winds are stronger because he's picked up strength—upgraded from a category three to a category four in the last hour.'

'I wouldn't like to think he'll swing around to the west,' Joe said anxiously, obviously worried about being caught in a cyclone with a very pregnant wife.

'He's been so unpredictable he could do anything,' Harry told him. 'And even if he doesn't head our way, we're in for floods as the run-off further upstream comes down the creek.'

'Well, at least we're in the right place—at a hospital,' Christina said. 'And look, isn't that sunshine peeking through the clouds?'

Harry had pulled up in the parking lot of the church, set in a curve of the bay in the main part of town. Christina was right. One ray of sunshine had found its way through a weakness in the massed, roiling clouds, reflecting its golden light off the angry grey-brown ocean that heaved and roared and crashed into the cove beneath the headland where Mike's parents' restaurant, the Athina, stood.

He watched the ray of light play on the thunderous waves and knew Joe was right—omens like that meant nothing as far as happiness was concerned. The sun had shone on his and Nikki's wedding day—for all the good it had done.

Grace felt her spirits lift with that single ray of light. Her friends were getting married, she was looking good, and so what if Harry Blake didn't want her worrying about him? This was her chance to look at other men and maybe find one who might, eventually, share her dreams of a family.

Unfortunately, just as she was reminding herself of her intention to look around at the single wedding guests, Harry opened the car door for her, and as she slid out a sudden wind gust ripped the door from his hands and only his good reflexes in grabbing her out of the way saved her from being hit by it.

It was hard to think about other men with Harry's strong arm wrapped around her, holding her close to his chest. Hard to think about anything when she was dealing with her own private storm—the emotional one—raging within *her* chest.

You're not my wife.

He's done and dusted.

She pulled away, annoyed with herself for reacting as she had, but determined to hide how she felt. He'd taken her elbow to guide her across the windswept parking lot outside the church and was acting as if nothing untoward had occurred between them. He was even pretending not to limp, which was just as well because she had no intention of asking him how his leg was. Because, Mr Policeman, two could play the pre-tend game.

She smiled up at him.

'Isn't this fun?'

Harry stared at her in disbelief.

Fun?

For a start, he was riven with guilt over his behaviour the previous night, and on top of that, the person he considered—or had considered up until last night—his best friend had turned into a sexpot.

That was fun?

Sexpot? Where on earth had he got that word?

He cast another glance towards his companion—golden hair gleaming in the sunlight, the freckles on her nose sparkling like gold dust, cleavage...

Yep. Sexpot.

'You OK?'

Even anxious, she looked good enough to eat.

Slowly...

Mouthful by sexy mouthful...

'Fine,' he managed to croak, denying the way his body was behaving, wondering if rain had the same effect cold showers were purported to have.

Although the rain appeared to have gone...

Bloody cyclones—never around when you needed them.

'Oh, dear, there's Mrs P. and she looks distraught.'

Grace's voice broke into this peculiar reverie.

'Did you expect her to be anything but?' he asked, as Grace left his side and hurried towards the woman who was wringing her hands and staring up towards the sky.

'I'm on mother-in-law watch,' Grace explained, smiling back over her shoulder at him. Maybe they *were* still friends. 'I promised Em I'd try to keep Mrs P. calm.'

Harry returned her smile just in case the damage done was not irreparable.

'About as easy as telling the cyclone not to change course,' he said, before hurrying after Christina and Joe.

Grace carried his smile with her as she walked towards Mrs Poulos, although she knew Harry's smiles, like the polite way Harry would take someone's elbow to cross a road, were part of the armour behind which he hid all his emotions.

And she was through with loving Harry anyway.

Mrs P. was standing beside the restaurant's big catering van, though what it was doing there when the reception was at the restaurant, Grace couldn't fathom.

'What's the problem, Mrs P.?' Grace asked as she approached, her sympathy for the woman whose plans had been thrown into chaos by the weather clear in her voice.

'Oh, Grace, it's the doves. I don't know what to do about the doves.'

'Doves?' Grace repeated helplessly, clasping the hyperventilating woman around the shoulders and patting her arm, telling her to breathe deeply.

'The doves—how can I let them fly?' Mrs P. wailed, lifting her arms to the heavens, as if doves might suddenly descend.

Grace looked around, seeking someone who might explain this apparent disaster. But although a figure in white was hunched behind the wheel of the delivery van, whoever it was had no intention of helping.

'The dove man phoned,' Mrs P. continued. 'He says they will blow away in all this wind. They will never get home. They will die.'

'Never get home' provided a slight clue. Grace had heard of homing pigeons—weren't doves just small pigeons?

Did they home?

'Just calm down and we'll think about it,' she told Mrs P. 'Breathe deeply, then tell me about the doves.'

But the mention of the birds sent Mrs Poulos back into paroxysms of despair, which stopped only when Grace reminded her they had a bare ten minutes until the ceremony began—ten minutes before she had to be ready in her special place as mother of the groom.

'But the doves?'

Mrs P. pushed past Grace, and opened the rear doors of the van. And there, in a large crate with a wire netting front, were, indeed, doves.

Snowy white, they strutted around behind the wire, heads tipping to one side as their bright, inquisitive eyes peered out at the daylight.

'They were to be my special surprise,' Mrs P. explained, poking a finger through the wire to stroke the feathers of the closest bird. 'I had it all arranged. Albert, who is our new trainee chef, he was going to release them just as Mike and Emily came out of the church. They are trained, you know, the doves. They know to circle the happy couple three times before they take off.'

And heaven only knows what they'll do as they circle three times, Grace thought, imagining the worst. But saving Em from bird droppings wasn't her job—keeping Mrs Poulos on an even keel was.

'It was a wonderful idea,' Grace told the older woman. 'And it would have looked magical, but you're right about the poor things not being able to fly home in this wind. We'll just have to tell Mike and Emily about it later.'

'But their happiness,' Mrs P. protested. 'We need to do the doves to bring them happiness.'

She was calmer now but so determined Grace understood why Emily had agreed to the plethora of attendants Mrs P. had arranged, and the fluffy tulle creations all the female members of the wedding party had been pressed into wearing. Mrs P. had simply worn Em down—ignoring any suggestions and refusing to countenance any ideas not her own.

'We could do it later,' Mrs P. suggested. 'Maybe when Mike and Emily cut the cake and kiss. Do you think we can catch the doves afterwards if we let them out inside the restaurant? All the doors and windows are shut because of the wind so they wouldn't get out. Then we could put them back in their box and everything will be all right.'

Grace flicked her attention back to the cage, and counted.

Ten!

Ten birds flying around inside a restaurant packed with more than one hundred guests? A dozen dinner-jacketed waiters chasing fluttering doves?

And Em was worried the sea of tulle might make a farce of things!

'No!' Grace said firmly. 'We can't have doves flying around inside the restaurant.'

She scrambled around in her head for a reason, knowing she'd need something forceful.

More than forceful...

'CJ, Cal and Gina's little boy—he's one of the pages, isn't he?' She crossed her fingers behind her back before she told her lie. 'Well, he's very allergic to bird feathers. Think how terrible it would be if we had to clear a table and use a steak knife to do an emergency tracheotomy on him—you know, one of those operations where you have to cut a hole in the throat so the person can breathe. Think how terrible that would be in the middle of the reception.'

Mrs Poulos paled, and though she opened her mouth to argue, she closed it again, finally nodding agreement.

'And we'd get feathers on the cake,' she added, and Grace smiled. Now it was Mrs P.'s idea not to have the doves cavorting inside the restaurant, one disaster had been averted.

Gently but firmly Grace guided her charge towards the church, finally settling her beside her husband in the front pew.

'Doves?' Mr Poulos whispered to Grace above his wife's head, and Grace nodded.

'No doves,' she whispered back, winning a warm smile of appreciation.

She backed out of the pew, her job done for now, and was making her way towards the back of the church, where she could see friends sitting, when Joe caught her arm.

'We've kept a seat for you,' he said, ushering her in front of him towards a spare place between Christina and Harry.

Sitting through a wedding ceremony beside Harry was hardly conducive to amputating him out of her heart.

Although the way things were between them, he might shift to another pew. Or, manlike, had he moved on from the little scene last night—the entire episode forgotten?

Grace slid into the seat, apprehension tightening ever sinew in her body, so when Harry shifted and his sleeve brushed her arm, she jerked away.

'Problems?' Harry whispered, misreading her reaction.

'All sorted,' she whispered back, but a flock of doves circling around inside the restaurant paled into insignificance beside the turmoil within her body. Remembering her own advice to Mrs P., Grace closed her eyes and breathed deeply.

Harry watched her breasts rise and fall, and wondered just how badly he'd hurt her with his angry words. Or was something else going on that he didn't know about? He glanced around, but apart from flowers and bows and a lot of pink and white frothy drapery everything appeared normal. Mike was ready by the altar, and a change in the background music suggested Emily was about to make an appearance.

So why was Grace as tense as fencing wire?

She'd seemed OK earlier, as if determined to pretend everything was all right between them—at least for the duration of the wedding.

So it had to be something else.

Did she not like weddings?

Had something terrible happened in her past, something connected with a wedding?

The thought of something terrible happening in Grace's past made him reach out and take her hand, thinking, at the same time, how little he knew of her.

Her fingers were cold and they trembled slightly, making him want to hug her reassuringly, but things were starting, people standing up, kids in shiny dresses and suits were scattering rose petals, and a confusion of young women in the same pink frothy stuff that adorned the church were parading down the aisle. Emily, he assumed, was somewhere behind them, because Mike's face had lit up with a smile so soppy Harry felt a momentary pang of compassion for him.

Poor guy had it bad!

Beside him Grace sighed—or maybe sniffed—and he turned away from the wedding party, sorting itself with some difficulty into the confined space in front of the altar, and looked at the woman by his side.

'Are you crying?' he demanded, his voice harsher than he'd intended because anxiety had joined the stirring thing that was happening again in his body.

Grace smiled up at him, easing the anxiety but exacerbating the stirring.

'No way,' she said. 'I was thinking of the last wedding I was at.'

'Bad?'

She glanced his way and gave a nod.

'My father's fourth. He introduced me to the latest Mrs O'Riordan as Maree's daughter. My mother's name was Kirstie.'

No wonder Grace looked grim.

And how it must have hurt.

But her father's fourth marriage?

Did that explain why Grace had never married?

'His fourth? Has his example put you off marriage for life?'

No smile, but she did turn towards him, studying him for a moment before replying, this time with a very definite shake of her head.

'No way, but I do feel a trifle cynical about the cele-bratory part. If ever I get married, I'll elope.'

'No pink and white frothy dresses?' he teased, hoping, in spite of the stirring, she'd smile again.

Hoping smiles might signal all was well between them once again.

'Not a froth in sight! And I think it's peach, not pink,' she said, and did smile.

But the smile was sad somehow, and a little part of him wondered just how badly having a marriage-addicted father might have hurt her.

He didn't like the idea of Grace hurting…

Handling this well, Grace congratulated herself. Strangely enough, the impersonal way Harry had taken her hand had helped her settle down. But just in case this settling effect turned to something else, she gently detached her hand from his as they stood up. And although he'd put his arm around her shoulders and given her a hug, it was definitely a friend kind of a hug and had reminded her that's what she was to him.

Now all she had to do was close her mind to the words being spoken at the front, pretend that Harry was nothing more to her than the friend she was to him, and keep an eye on Mrs P. in case she thought of some new reason for panic.

Fun!

It *was* fun, Grace decided, some hours later.

True, Harry had excused himself and left the church not long after the ceremony began, but whether because he couldn't bear to sit through it or to check on the latest weather report and weather-related incidents, she didn't know. Something had certainly happened—tiles or something coming off the roof— because there'd been loud crashing noises then the minister had insisted everyone leave through the vestry, disrupting the wedding party to the extent Grace had to calm Mrs P. down once again, persuading her the wedding was still legal even if the happy couple hadn't left as man and wife through the front door of the church.

Grace had driven to the restaurant with Mr and Mrs Poulos so hadn't caught up with Christina and Joe until the reception.

People milled around, sipping champagne, talking and even dancing. Luke Bresciano came up to her, took the champagne glass out of her hand, set it down on a handy table, and swept her onto the dance floor.

'I was looking for you,' he said, guiding her carefully around the floor. 'Have you heard the ink-blot joke? I remembered it after we looked at the stain last night.'

Grace shook her head, and Luke launched into the story of the psychologist showing ink-blot pictures to a patient.

'So the fellow looks at the first one, and says that's two rabbits having sex. The psychologist turns the page and the fellow says, that's an elephant and a rhino having sex. The psychologist is a bit shocked but he offers a third. That's three people and a dog having sex. Floored by this reaction, the psychologist loses his cool. "You've got a dirty mind," he tells his patient. "Me?" the patient says. "You're the one showing filthy pictures."'

Grace laughed, looking more closely at this man she barely knew. The lines around his eyes suggested he was older than she knew he was. Signs of the unhappiness she'd heard was in his background?

She asked about his early life but somehow the questions ended up coming from him, so by the end of the dance she knew no more than she had at the beginning.

Except that he had a sense of humour, which was a big point in his favour.

But when she glimpsed Harry across the room, bending down to speak to Charles, the excited beating of her heart told her she had a long way to go in the getting over him stakes. Fortunately the best man—some friend of Mike's who'd come across from New Zealand—appeared and asked her to dance, so Harry was not forgotten but tucked away behind her determination to move on.

The dance ended, and she noticed Harry heading in her direction. Dancing with Harry was *not* part of the plan, so she picked up her glass of now flat champagne and pressed into an alcove of pot plants, hoping to hide in this corner of the greenery festooning the restaurant.

Could one hide from a policeman?

'You know I can't dance with my leg!'

It wasn't exactly the greeting she'd expected. In fact, the slightly petulant statement made no sense whatsoever.

'What are you talking about? What do you mean?' she demanded, looking up into Harry's face, which seemed to be flushed with the same anger she'd heard in his voice.

'That I can't dance with you,' he said, his words as cross as his first statement had been.

'Then it's just as well I'm not your mother or your wife,' Grace retorted, unable to keep up the 'friends' pretence another second. 'Because if I was, you'd be expected to dance with me.'

She tried to turn away but the greenery defeated her—the greenery and Harry's hand on her shoulder.

'I shouldn't have said that to you,' he said, tightening his grip when she tried to shrug it off. 'I'm sorry.'

Grace looked at him for a long moment. The flush had faded, leaving his face pale and so tired-looking she had to sternly stem the flash of sympathy she felt towards him.

'No,' she told him, knowing this was the perfect time to begin to distance herself from Harry. 'I think it needed to be said. You were right, it's not my place to tell you what to do or what not to do. I overstepped the boundaries of friendship but it won't happen again, I promise you.'

Harry stared at her, totally befuddled by what had just occurred. Hadn't he apologised? Said what had to be said to make things right again between himself and Grace? So why was she rejecting his apology? Or, if not rejecting it, turning things so it had been her fault, not his?

He opened him mouth but what could he say? *Please, keep telling me stuff like that? Please, stay concerned for me?*

Ridiculous!

He should let it go—walk away—and hope everything would come right between them in time.

Hope they could go back to being friends.

But if he walked away she'd dance with someone else, and seeing Grace in that Italian doctor's arms, laughing up at some funny thing he'd said, had made Harry's gut churn.

'I can shuffle if you don't mind a shuffling kind of dance,' he heard himself say, and saw astonishment similar to what he was feeling reflected on Grace's face.

Her 'OK' wasn't overwhelmingly enthusiastic, but he was

happy to settle for even grudging acceptance. He put his arms around her, tucked her body close to his, and felt her curls tickle the skin beneath his chin.

Grace knew this wouldn't do much for her distancing-Harry plans, but surely a woman was allowed a little bit of bliss. She slid into his arms and put her arms around his back—allowable, she was sure, because it was going to be a shuffling kind of dance.

You are stupid, the sensible voice in her head muttered at her.

It's just pretence, she told her head. Everything else seemed to be about pretence these days so why not pretend, just for a short while, that they were a couple? After all, she could go back to distancing tomorrow.

It was heaven.

The band was playing a slow waltz, or maybe a slow two-step. Dancing was something she did naturally but had little knowledge about, and she and Harry were at the edge of the dance floor, barely moving to the music, content, as far as Grace was concerned, just to be in each other's arms.

What Harry was thinking was a mystery but, then, Harry in a social setting—apart from coffee at the pub— was something of a mystery as well.

No matter—he had his arms around her and that was enough.

Well, nearly enough. Outside the wind had gathered strength again and rain lashed the garden beyond the restaurant and flung itself against the windows. It was definitely 'snuggling closer' weather. If she moved just slightly she could rest her head against his chest, and for a little while she could dream.

Later, she couldn't remember whether she'd actually made this daring move or not, but what she did remember was that the lights went out, then Harry spun her around, into even denser blackness in a corner of the restaurant.

And bent his head.

And kissed her.

Harry kissed her...

Folded in his arms, her curls tickling at his chin, Harry had ignored the cleavage as much as possible as he'd shuffled back and forth with this different Grace on the corner of the dance floor. But when the lights went out, he lost the slim reins of control he'd been clinging to and whisked her into the shadows of one of the palms that dotted the restaurant.

He bent his head, and kissed her, curls first, then her forehead, finding the salt of perspiration on her skin and a sweetness he knew by instinct was pure Grace.

His lips moved to her temples, felt the throb of a vein, then claimed her mouth, more sweetness, but this time mingled with heat as Grace responded with a fire that lit his own smouldering desire, so need and hunger fought common sense and a determination to not get involved.

A losing battle—as useless as trying to stop the wind that now raged again outside—as useless as trying to stop a cyclone...

He clamped Grace's curvy body hard against his leanness, and drank in the taste of her as his mouth explored and challenged hers. She met his challenge and responded with her own, so he was lost in the wonder and sweetness and fire that was this new Grace.

Gripped in the toils of physical attraction, a voice whispered in his head, but he ignored it and kept kissing the woman in his arms.

Lamplight. Flickering candles. Maybe the voice wasn't in his head. Someone was calling his name.

Urgently.

'Harry Blake.'

CHAPTER THREE

CHARLES WETHERBY, the wheelchair-bound head of the hospital, was illuminated by candelabrum, held aloft by a young policeman, Troy Newton, the newest member of Harry's staff.

'Charles?'

Harry eased Grace gently away, tucking her, he hoped, into deeper shadows, and took the two long strides needed to bring him close to Charles.

'Bus accident up on the mountain road—road's subsided and the bus has slid down the mountain. Dan Macker called it in.'

'Do we know exactly where, and who's on the way?' Harry asked, looking towards the windows and know-ing there was no way the rescue helicopter, based at the hospital, could fly in this wind.

'Where? This side of Dan's place. He saw the bus go past, then later heard a noise, and when he investigated he saw the landslide. Who's on the way? The fire truck, two ambulances each with two crew and the hospital's four-wheel-drive is on its way here to pick up whatever hospital staff you think you might need on site. Have you seen Grace? If we've got to set up a triage post and then get people off the side of the mountain, we'll probably need an SES crew up there as well—she can organise that.'

'I'll tell her,' Harry said, 'and head out there myself.'

Charles made an announcement aimed mainly at the hospital staff, telling them the hospital would go to the code black disaster plan, then Harry spoke, reminding people who would be taking part in the rescue on the mountain that there were open diggings and mine shafts on the slopes, legacy of the gold rush that had led to the birth of the township that had become Crocodile Creek.

He looked around the room, wondering who he'd take, picking out hospital staff he knew were fit and active, telling them to take the hospital vehicle while he'd check on his other staff and be right behind them.

He turned back towards the shadows but Grace had gone, no doubt because she'd heard the news. More candles had been lit, but it was impossible to pick her out in the milling crowd. Joe touched his arm.

'You go, I'll organise a lift back to the cottage for Grace and Christina then go up to the hospital to see if I can help.'

Harry nodded to Joe but his eyes still searched for Grace, although common sense told him she'd be in a corner somewhere, on her mobile, starting a phone relay to gather a crew at SES headquarters in the shortest possible time. Then she'd head to the headquarters herself to organise the equipment they'd need.

As he left the restaurant, striding towards his vehicle, that thought brought with it a sense of relief he didn't quite understand. Was it tied up with the fact that Grace was safer at headquarters, organising things, than on the side of a slippery mountain riddled with old mineshafts, fighting cyclonic winds in pitch darkness?

Surely not!

Although, as a friend, he was entitled to feel some concern for her safety, so it had nothing to do with the aberration in his feelings towards her—which was purely physical.

The wind was now so strong he had to struggle to open the car door—memories of a soft body held against his chest...

Get your mind focussed on the job!

He started the car and turned out of the car park, concentrating on driving through the lashing wind and rain.

Ignoring the physical aberration? That was the voice in his head again.

Of course he was ignoring it. What else could he do? Physical attraction had led him into a terrible mistake once before and had caused pain and unhappiness, not only to himself but to Nikki as well. It had flung him into an emotional swamp so deep and damaging he'd blocked emotion out of his life ever since.

So there was no way he could allow whatever physical attraction he might be feeling towards her to touch his friendship with Grace.

If he still had a friendship with Grace. Her words before the dance had indicated she was backing away from whatever it was they'd had.

Yet she'd kissed him back—he was sure of that.

He'd have to put it aside—forget about the kiss and definitely forget about the lust he'd felt towards his friend.

Determinedly setting these thoughts aside, Harry drove cautiously down towards the town, automatically noting the level of the water beneath the bridge, forcing himself to think rescue not Grace.

He had to go, of course he did, Grace told herself as she watched Harry leave. She was on the phone to Paul Gibson, still the nominal head of the local SES, although since he'd been undergoing treatment for prostate cancer, Grace, as senior team leader, had taken over a lot of his responsibilities. But Paul's knowledge and experience were still invaluable, so Grace forgot about Harry and listened, mentally repeating all Paul had said so she'd remember.

Rolls of netting—she'd seen them in the big shed and often wondered about them—were useful in landslides. You could anchor them on the level ground and unroll them down the slope to make it easier for rescuers to clamber up and down.

'Belongings,' Paul continued. 'Gather up what you can of people's belongings. They're going to be disoriented enough, ending up in a strange hospital—if we can return things to them, it helps. And remember to search for a hundred yards all around the bus—people can wander off. As soon as my wife gets back from checking on the family, I'll get her to drive me up to Headquarters. I mightn't be much use out in the field, but I'll handle the radio calls and relays up there, which will leave you free to be out in the field.'

Through the window Grace saw Harry's big vehicle leave the car park.

'Thanks, Paul,' she said, staring out the window at the vehicle, hope sneaking in where wonder and amazement had been.

Harry had kissed her.

Surely he wouldn't have done that if he wasn't interested in her?

The sneaky scrap of hope swelled like a balloon to fill her chest.

Maybe, just maybe, she wouldn't have to get over Harry after all.

Or was she being stupid? The way she'd been with James? Thinking flowers and dinners out and a physical relationship meant love?

Not that she'd had any of that with Harry. Only one interrupted kiss.

The balloon deflated as fast as it had filled, leaving her feeling empty and flat.

One thing she knew for sure—she'd been stupid for kissing him back, for letting her lips tell him things her head knew she couldn't tell him.

She tucked her phone back into her beaded handbag and looked around the room, checking who was leaving, who might give her a lift home so she could change before going to Headquarters. Charles was leading the way out the door, Jill Shaw, director of nursing, moving more slowly to guide Susie, who was swinging along on crutches, thanks to her accident the previous day.

'Would you lot drop me home?' Grace asked, coming up to them. 'I can hardly organise my crew dressed like this.'

'No problem,' Charles told her, while Jill, who must have been running through the nursing roster in her head, added, 'You're off duty until Tuesday, aren't you, Grace?'

Grace nodded. Her month on night duty had finished at seven that morning and the change in shift meant she had three days off.

'But I grabbed a few hours' sleep this morning so I'm happy to be called in. If Willie's really heading back towards us, we'll need all available staff standing by.'

'We might need all staff back on duty, not standing by, if the bus that's come off the mountain had a full load of passengers,' Charles said, as the women ducked behind his wheelchair to escape some of the wind that was ripping across the car park, grabbing at Charles's words and flinging them into the air. 'With this weather, we can't fly people out, and at last report the coast road was flooding. We could have a very full hospital.'

Jill confirmed this with a quiet 'I'll be in touch' as she dropped Grace at the cottage, but nursing was forgotten as Grace stripped off her dress and clambered into her bright orange SES overalls, fitted on the belt that held her torch, pocket knife and radio then grabbed her keys and headed for Head-quarters. The crews would be gathering. She'd send one support vehicle straight up the mountain, and hold the second one back until she heard from Harry in case some special equipment not on the main rescue vehicle was needed.

Or...

She went herself, with the first crew, partly because Paul had arrived to handle the office but also because she knew an extra person with nursing skills would be useful in the rescue mission. This truck held the inflatable tent they'd use for triage and the generator that kept it inflated. They'd have to make sure the tent was anchored securely in this wind.

The men and women chatted casually, but Grace, huddled in a corner, mentally rehearsed the jobs that lay ahead as she watched the wind slice rain across the windscreen and cause the vehicle to sway from side to side. Willie had turned and was heading their way—the cyclone warnings on the radio had confirmed what increased velocity in the wind had already told most locals.

How much time did they have to get ready?

Who would need to be moved from their homes? An evacuation list would have been drawn up but before she, or anyone else, could start moving people to safety, they had to get the accident victims off the mountain…

'Your crews finished?'

Grace was kneeling by a young woman, the last person to be pulled from the bus after the jaws of life had been used to free her. Unconscious and with probable head injuries, she lay on an undamaged part of the road, her neck in a collar, her body strapped to the cradle stretcher on which she'd been pulled up the muddy slope. Now, as the wind howled around them, they awaited the return of one of the ambulances that had been shuttling back and forth to the hospital for hours.

About half an hour earlier, once most of the accident victims had been moved out of it and ferried down the mountain, Harry had deemed the inflatable tent too dangerous. So Grace's crew had packed it and the generator back into the SES truck prior to departure.

A makeshift shelter remained to protect this final patient, but the wind was getting stronger every minute and now blew rain and forest debris beneath the sodden tarpaulin. Grace had angled her body so it shielded the young woman's face. She smoothed the woman's hair and removed leaves that blew onto her skin, but there was little else she could do for her—just watch and wait, holding her hand and talking quietly to her, because Grace was certain even unconscious people had some awareness.

'Are your crews finished?'

As Harry repeated his question, Grace turned to look at him. She'd heard him the first time but her mind had been too busy adjusting to his abrupt tone—and trying to work out what it meant—for her to answer.

'Just about,' she said, searching his face, lit by the last emergency light, for some hint of his mood. Disappointment because they'd failed to save the bus driver? No, deep down Harry might be gutted, but he would set it aside until the job was done.

Was his leg hurting?

It had to be, though if she offered sympathy it was sure to be rejected.

She stopped guessing about his mood, and explained, 'One of the team is already on its way back to base and the other is packing up the gear and should be leaving shortly. Why?'

'Because I want everyone off the mountain, that's why,' Harry said, his voice straining against the wind, but Grace's attention was back on her patient.

'She's stopped breathing.'

Grace leant forward over the young woman, tilted her head backwards then lifted her chin upward with one hand to make sure her airway was clear, and felt for a pulse with the other. Her fingers pushed beneath the woman's chin, and found a flutter of movement in the carotid artery.

She stripped off the oxygen mask and gave the woman two breaths, then checked the pulse again. Looked at Harry, who was now squatting by her side.

'You monitor her pulse—I'll breathe.'

They'd practised so often as a team, it seemed effortless now, Grace breathing, Harry monitoring the young woman's vital signs. Yet it was taking too long—were their efforts in vain?

'We'll get her,' Harry said, and the conviction in his voice comforted Grace, although she knew he couldn't be as certain as he sounded.

Or could he?

Grace stopped, and held her breath. The rise and fall of the young woman's chest told them she'd resumed breathing on her own.

'Yes!' Grace said, lifting her hand for a high-five of triumph, but Harry's hands were by his side, and the bleak unhappiness on his face was far from triumph.

Whatever pretence at friendship they'd managed during the wedding was gone.

Burnt away by the heat of that kiss?

Though why would *he* be upset over the kiss? Because it had broken some rule he'd set himself when his wife died?

Thou shalt kiss no other after her?

That was weird because Harry wasn't stupid and he must know that eventually nature would reassert itself and he'd want a sexual relationship with some woman—sometime.

Although as far as she knew, monks didn't...

'I want you off the mountain,' he said.

'I want us all off the mountain,' Grace retorted, battling to understand his mood. OK, he was worried about the cyclone, but they all were, and it certainly hadn't made the other rescuers go all brisk and formal. In fact, the others had made an effort to smile even as they'd struggled up the steepest parts of the slope—everyone encouraging each other.

All but Harry, who'd frowned at Grace whenever they'd passed, as if he couldn't understand who she was or perhaps what she was doing there.

'But that's hardly possible,' she continued crisply, 'without magic carpets to whisk us all away. The second SES crew will be leaving soon. The rest of the hospital personnel have gone back to deal with the patients as they arrive. I'm staying with this patient and I'll go back in the ambulance when it gets here.'

'This place is dangerous. The wind's increasing all the time. More of the road could slip, trees could come down.'

He was worrying about her safety. That was the only explanation for Harry's strange behaviour. The thought brought such warmth to Grace's body she forgot about distancing herself. She forgot about the cruel words he'd flung at her, and reached out to touch his arm.

'This is my job,' she said softly. 'We've had the risk-taking conversation, Harry, and while you mightn't like me talking about it you have to admit, as part of your job, you do it all the time. So you should understand I can't just get in the truck and go back to town, leaving this young woman with no one.'

'*I'm* here!' Harry said, moving his arm so her hand slid off—squelching the warmth.

It had been such a stupid thing to say Grace didn't bother with a reply. She checked the oxygen flowing into the mask that was once again covering the young woman's mouth and nose, and kept a hand on the pulse at her wrist.

Harry stood up and walked away, no doubt to grump at someone else. But who else was still here? Grace had no idea, having seen the last of the SES crew heading down the road towards their truck. The first truck had taken a lot of the less badly injured passengers back to the hospital to be checked under more ideal conditions than an inflatable tent and arclamps in lashing wind and rain. The team leader of that truck would then assist in finding accommodation for those not admitted to hospital, while the other members would begin preparations for the arrival of Willie, now on course to cross the coast at Crocodile Creek.

'That you, Grace?'

She turned at the shout and saw two overalled figures jogging towards her.

'Mike! Not on your honeymoon, then?'

Mike Poulos, newly married helicopter pilot and paramedic, reached her first and knelt beside her patient.

'Could hardly leave without Em, who's in Theatre as we

speak, so I decided I might as well make myself useful. I can't fly in this weather but I still remember how to drive an ambulance. Who's this?'

'We don't know,' Grace told him, watching the gentle way he touched the young woman's cheek. 'Maybe a young backpacker—there were quite a few young people among the passengers. No one seems to know for certain who was on the bus.'

'Mainly because the driver was killed and we can't find a manifest in the wreckage.' Harry was back, nodding to the two paramedics as he explained. 'This patient's the last, but we need to take the driver's body back to the hospital.'

'She's unconscious?' Mike asked Grace, who nodded.

'And though there are no obvious injuries, she's very unstable. She stopped breathing after she was brought up from the bus,' Grace told him.

'I hate transporting a dead person with a live one, but the bus driver deserves the dignity of an ambulance,' Mike said. He looked towards Harry.

'If we take the bus driver, can you take Grace?'

Harry looked doubtful.

'As against leaving me up here all night? Taking two patients means I won't fit in the ambulance,' Grace snapped at him, aggravated beyond reason by this stranger in Harry's body.

'I'll take Grace,' he conceded, then he led the two men away to collect the driver's body, before returning for Grace's patient.

Grace walked beside the young woman as the men carried her to the ambulance, then watched as she was loaded, the doors shut, and the big four-by-four vehicle took off down the road.

'My car's this way,' Harry said, and strode off into the darkness. He was carrying the last of the lights and the tarpaulin they'd used as a shelter, and though he looked overladen he'd shaken his head when had Grace asked if she could carry something.

Still puzzling over his strange behaviour, she followed him down the road to where it widened enough for a helicopter to land—*when* weather permitted. His was the only vehicle still there.

She waited while he stacked the gear he'd carried into the back, then she made her way to the passenger side, opened the door—no chivalry now—and climbed in.

'What is with you?' she demanded, as soon as he was settled into the driver's seat. 'Is your leg hurting? Should I have a look at it?'

He glanced towards her, his face carefully blank, then looked away to turn the key in the ignition, release the brake and start driving cautiously down the wind- and rain-lashed road.

'My leg's fine.'

Grace knew that was a lie—it couldn't possibly be fine—but she wasn't his mother or his wife so she kept her mouth shut.

Between them the radio chattered—the ambulance giving the hospital an ETA, a squad car reporting on more power lines down. Yet the noise barely intruded into the taut, chilly atmosphere that lay between the two of them as they crawled at a snail's pace down the mountain road.

'Is it the bus driver? I know there's nothing worse than losing a life at an accident, but he'd have been dead the moment the bus rolled on him, poor guy. There was nothing anyone could have done, and from what the rescuers were saying, he did all he could to save the bus from being more badly damaged—all he could to save more lives.'

'So he dies a hero. Do you think that makes it better for his kids? His name was Peter. He had two kids. Photo in his wallet.'

Making him a person in Harry's eyes. No wonder he was upset.

'Someone's father,' Grace whispered, feeling the rush of pity such information always brought, but at the same time she wondered about Harry's reaction. She'd seen him bring in dead kids from car accidents without this much emotional involvement. 'No, I'm sure, at the beginning at least, the hero stuff won't make a scrap of difference to two kids growing up without a father. But all we can do is help the living, Harry. We can't change what's past.'

Harry sighed.

'You're right, and if I think rationally about it, the simple fact of having a father is no guarantee of happiness,' he said glumly. 'Georgie's Max—his father's just a nasty waste of space—and yours doesn't sound as if he brought you much joy.'

'It might not have been all his fault. I kind of got dumped on him,' Grace told him, defending blood ties automatically. 'I didn't ever know him as a small child, then, when I was seven, my mother died and my aunt got in touch with my father, who'd emigrated from Ireland to Australia, and I was sent out here.'

She paused, remembering the small sad child who'd set off on that long journey, scared but somehow, beyond the fear, full of hope. She'd lost her mother, but ahead had lain a father and a new family, a father who'd surely love her or why else had he sent the money for her ticket?

'What number wife was he on at that stage?' Harry asked, and Grace smiled.

'Only number two, but, looking back, I think the marriage was probably teetering at the time and my stepmother had only agreed to take me because she thought it might keep my father with her. Poor woman, she was kind, but she was stuck with me when he took off again, so to her I always represented a terrible time of her life. And the little boys, my stepbrothers, well, I can't blame them for hating me—I arrive and their father leaves. In their young minds there had to be a connection.'

'No one could have hated you, Grace,' Harry said, but although the words were kind his harsh voice suggested that there was more than the dead bus driver bothering him.

She listened to the radio calls, not knowing what to guess at next, but certain she needed things sorted out between them because the success of both the preparations for, and the work after, Willie's arrival depended on them working harmoniously together.

With a sigh nearly as strong as one of the wind gusts outside, she tried again.

'Is that all that's bothering you? The bus driver? His kids?'

He turned to look at her and even in the dimly lit cabin she could read incredulity.

'We're in a serious situation here,' Harry said, spacing the words as if he'd had to test each one in his head before letting it out.

'We've been in serious situations before, Harry,' Grace reminded him, ducking instinctively as a tree-fern frond careened towards her side of the car. 'Remember the time we went out to the reef in a thunderstorm to rescue the diver with the bends? That wasn't serious?'

No comment.

Grace sighed again.

Was she becoming a sigher?

Surely not. And if she considered it, being at odds with Harry could only help her getting-over-him decision. A sensible woman would welcome this new attitude of his and get on with her life. But this was, as Harry had just pointed out, a serious situation and Grace knew she wouldn't give of her best if there was added tension between the two of them.

She knew too that they'd be in some dangerous situations in the future, and if they didn't have one hundred per cent attention on the job, a dangerous situation could become a disaster.

She had to sort it out.

But how?

Bluntly!

There was only one other thing that had happened this evening that could explain his attitude.

Or maybe two things.

'Are you still annoyed about me nagging you to be careful?' she asked, thinking it was easier to bring this up than to mention the kiss.

'I apologised for that.'

More silence.

That left the kiss.

Grace's last remnant of hope that the kiss might have meant something to Harry died.

For sure, he'd started it, but the worst of it was, she'd kissed him back.

She knew it had been a mistake from her side of things, but had it also worried Harry? Had she revealed too much of how she felt?

Was that what was bothering him?

If so, she had to get around it somehow. Act as if it had meant nothing to her—pretend it had been nothing more than a casual smooch in the darkness.

More pretence!

She took a deep breath, and launched into the delicate conversation.

'Is this because we kissed? Has one kiss turned you into some kind of cold robot? If so, that's ridiculous. It was a mistake so let's get past it. We've been friends for more than two years, Harry, and friends talk to one another. We can talk about this. Isn't that easier than carrying on as if we've broken some immutable law of nature? I mean, it was a nice kiss as kisses go, but it's not likely that we'll ever do it again.'

As the flippant words spun around the cabin of the vehicle, mingling with the radio's chatter and the wind that whirled outside, Grace felt her heart break.

But this was how it had to be. She didn't want Harry thinking the kiss meant any more to her than it had to him.

He glanced her way, his face still betraying nothing.

'*Do* we talk to one another?' he asked, delving so far back into Grace's conversation it took her a moment to remember she'd made the comment.

'Yes,' she said, although doubts were now popping up in her head.

They did talk, but about their work, their friends, the hospital, the town, the price of sugar cane—Harry's father being the owner of the local mill—the weather, and just about everything under the sun.

'Not about ourselves,' Harry said, still staring resolutely through the windscreen, although, given the debris flying through the air, that was a very good idea. 'Today's the first time I've heard you mention a father.'

'Everyone has one,' Grace said glibly, but the look Harry gave her told her flippancy wasn't going to work.

'OK, you're right. We don't talk much about ourselves,' Grace admitted, though she wasn't sure what this had to do with the kiss, or with Harry's mood. 'But talking's a two-way street, Harry. Talking—really talking—means sharing small parts of yourself with another person, and it's hard to do that if the other person isn't willing to share as well. Sharing that kind of talk leads to intimacy in a friendship and intimacy leaves people vulnerable. You treat everyone the same way probably because you don't want that intimacy—don't want anyone coming that close to you. The last thing in the world you'd want to seem is vulnerable.'

Harry glanced her way, frowned, then turned his attention back to the road, slowing down as the branch of a blue fig tree crashed onto the road right in front of them. He manoeuvred the car carefully around it.

'So you start the talking,' he finally said, totally ignoring her comments about his behaviour. 'Is it just because of your father you don't like weddings?'

It was the very last conversational gambit Grace had expected.

'Who said I don't like weddings?'

'You were so tense you could have snapped in half in there this afternoon.'

Because it *was* a wedding and I was sitting next to you, and it was hard not to indulge, for just a wee while, in a pointless daydream.

Grace was tempted to say it—to tell him of her feelings. The way the wind was blowing, literally, and sending tree limbs onto the road, they could both be killed any minute.

Would it be better or worse if Harry died knowing she loved him?

The thought of Harry dying made her heart squeeze into a tight little ball, while memories of the one time she *had* told a man she loved him made her cringe back into the seat.

She could still hear James's voice—his snide 'Love, Gracie? How quaint! What a sweet thing you are! Next you'll be telling me you're thinking of babies.'

Which she had been.

No wonder she could still feel the hurt…

'Well?' Harry persisted, and Grace had to think back to his question.

'It wasn't the wedding,' she managed to say, as Harry slammed on the brakes and his left arm shot out to stop her forward momentum.

'Thank heaven for traction control,' he muttered as the car skidded sideways towards the edge of the road then stopped before plunging off the side of the mountain. 'What was it, then?'

Grace shook her head.

'I can't believe we're having this conversation,' she said. 'Any minute now a tree's going to land across us and you're worried about why I was tense at the wedding.'

She paused, then added crossly, 'Anyway, this conversation isn't about me—it's about you. I didn't change from a friend to a frozen robot in the time it took to drive from town up the mountain.' She peered out through the windscreen. 'Why have we stopped?'

'I don't like the look of that tree.'

Harry pointed ahead and, as Grace followed the line of his finger, the huge forest red gum that had been leaning at a crazy angle across the road slid slowly downwards, the soaked soil on the mountainside releasing its tangle of roots so carefully it was only in the last few feet the massive trunk actually crashed to the ground.

'Oh!'

The nearest branches of the tree were right in front of the bonnet of Harry's vehicle, so close some of their smaller limbs were resting on it.

'We'll never clear it by hand. I'll radio for a car to come and get us on the other side, but we'll have to climb around the tree. For the moment, we'll just sit here until we're sure it's settled.'

Even as he said the words Harry regretted them. Of course they were safer in the vehicle than out there in the maelstrom of wind, rain and flying debris, but out there, talk would be impossible. In the car—in the dry warm cocoon it provided— even with the radio going, there was a false sense of—what?

He shuddered—Grace's word 'intimacy' seemed to fit.

What's more, there was no excuse to not talk…

He finished his call, telling base not to send someone to clear the tree as the conditions were too dangerous and the exercise pointless because the road was cut further up at the landslide. He glanced at Grace, who was still staring at the tree that hadn't collapsed on top of them, and he felt the stirring her blue dress had triggered earlier. She'd changed into her bulky but protective SES overalls, but hadn't removed the ribbon from her hair, so it now snaked through her wet curls, slightly askew so a bit of it crossed the top of her delicate pink ear.

He'd never looked at Grace's ears before, he realised as he reached over and used his forefinger to lift the ribbon from the ear then tease it gently out of her sodden hair. He had, of course, intended giving it back to her, but when she eyed the tatty wet object and muttered, 'What a fun way to end a wedding,' he decided she didn't want it, so he dropped it into his shirt pocket, did up the button and patted it into place.

He wasn't going to accept Grace's 'frozen robot' description, but he couldn't deny anger had been churning around inside him for the last few hours. Why *was* he so cranky?

Because he was worried, sure, but if he was honest with himself it was more than that. He could only suppose it was because Grace had added to his worries. From the moment she'd appeared at the accident site, he'd felt a new anxiety gnawing at his gut, and every time he saw her, each time wetter and paler than the time before, anxiety had taken another vicious bite.

That it was related to the kiss and the new attraction he felt towards her he had no doubt, but on a treacherous mountain road as a cyclone roared towards them and trees came crashing down, this was neither the time nor the place for introspection.

Or distraction.

Although maybe if he kissed her again, it would sort itself out. He could spend the waiting time kissing her, which would also make talking impossible. His body liked the idea, but his head knew that was the worst possible way to pass the time.

However appealing it might seem.

'You didn't answer about the kiss.'

Her statement startled him. There she was, still staring at the tree, yet picking up on some vibe he didn't know he was giving out.

But this was Grace—she deserved an honest answer.

'It was physical attraction, Grace,' he began, and waited to see if she'd turn towards him. Perhaps speak and save him the necessity of saying more.

She didn't, although she did glance his way momentarily.

'Strong physical attraction—we both felt it—but physical, that's all.'

Another glance, then all he got was her profile, although he fancied now she might be frowning, so he waited some more.

'And that's bad?' she finally queried.

'I believe it is. Well, not necessarily bad in a right and wrong sense, but dangerous, Grace. Misleading. Troublesome.' There, it had been said. Now they could get back to being friends.

Or as close to friends as they'd be able to get after his comments earlier.

CHAPTER FOUR

GRACE STARED OUT through the windscreen at the fallen tree as she ran the explanation through her head, suspecting it might be Harry's way of saying that physical attraction was all he could feel for a woman these days. Putting it like that was less blunt that telling her he was still in love with his dead wife and always would be.

And although she'd always kind of suspected this, the confirmation of the idea caused Grace pain—physical pain, like a cramp around her heart.

The hateful, hurtful words, *you're not my wife*, took on a whole new meaning.

Perhaps she was wrong, and he wasn't saying that at all. One last gulp of hope remained in the balloon. Forgetting she was supposed to be distancing herself, she turned back towards him, determined to sort this out once and for all.

'Why is it dangerous? Misleading?'

Harry was staring at her, frowning slightly as if he wasn't certain who she was, and showed no sign of understanding her questions, let alone answering them.

'You must have a reason for believing it's bad,' she persisted.

Harry, who'd been thinking how pretty her eyes were and wondering why he'd never considered Grace's eyes before any more than he'd considered her ears, shrugged off the remark, although he suspected she wasn't going to let this go. But how could he explain the still bruised part of his heart that was Nikki? Explain the magnitude of their mistake?

'We should start walking.'

'No way!' She nodded towards the radio which had just advised them the car was forty-five minutes away. 'Even if it takes us half an hour to get over or around the tree, we'd still be waiting in the rain for fifteen minutes, and that's if the road's not blocked further down.'

He nodded, conceding her point, but said nothing, pretending fascination with the babble on the radio—trying to forget where physical attraction had led once before *and* trying to block out the insidious desire creeping through his body every time he looked at Grace.

He patted his pocket.

One more kiss won't hurt, his physical self tempted, but a glance at Grace, wet curls plastered to a face that was pinched with tiredness, told him that it would hurt.

If not him, then definitely her.

And he hated the idea of hurting Grace any more than he had already.

Hated it!

Another glance her way told him she was still waiting for an answer.

Would wait all night...

'It confuses things,' he said. 'I mean, look at us, good friends, and suddenly we're all hung up over a kiss.'

'We weren't exactly good friends when it happened,' she reminded him. 'And *I'm* not hung up over it.'

'Maybe not, but you're only pushing this kiss business because you don't want to talk about why you were so uptight at the wedding.' Good thinking, Harry, turn defence into attack. 'That, if you remember, Grace, was where this conversation started. With the fact that we don't really talk to each other.

And now I know about your father, I would think you'd be as wary of physical attraction as I am. Or did he fall madly and totally in love with all four of his wives?'

It was a low blow, and he sensed she'd cringed a little from it, making him feel a bastard for hurting her. But it would be better this way—with the kiss passed off as the aberration he was sure it was and the two of them getting on with the friendship they'd always shared.

Not totally convinced by this seemingly sensible plan, he checked the weather, acknowledged an ETA call from the car coming to collect them, waited until the wail of the three hourly cyclone warning coming from the radio stopped, then pushed his companion a little further.

'Do you know what I know about you, Grace? Really know about you?' He didn't wait for her to answer, but held up two fingers. 'Two personal things—that's all. You hate being called Gracie, and you think you're too short.'

'I think I'm too short?' Grace repeated, confused by that accusation and disturbed by the 'Gracie' echo of her own thoughts earlier. 'What makes you think I think I'm too short?'

He had the hide to smile at her! Smug smile of a man who thought he'd scored a point.

'Because of the way you throw yourself into things—especially the SES. You told me you joined the equivalent operation down there in Victoria the moment you were old enough—why? I bet it was because people had always seen you as small and cuddly and cute but in need of protection, and you had to prove to them and to yourself that you could hold your own both with bigger, taller women and with men. I see it every time we're on calls together and even when we're doing exercises—you have to go first and go highest, or deepest, or whatever. You're proving you're not only equal to other team members but better than most of them.'

'And you think that's because I'm short?' Grace demanded, hoping she sounded incredulous, not upset because he'd read her so well—although she'd got past proving her stuff a long time ago.

'I know it was, but now it's probably because you are the best—or one of the best—that you do the things you do.'

Conceding her point was definitely a low blow but, unable to refute this statement, she went back to the original bit of the 'short' conversation.

'You can add a third thing to what you know of me—I hate being thought cute!'

Harry smiled again, causing chaos in Grace's body—palpitations, tingling nerves, butterflies swarming in her stomach. Not good things to feel towards a man who'd more or less admitted he'd never love again. Not good things to feel when she was in her getting-over-him phase.

'You're especially cute when you're angry,' he teased, sounding like her friend Harry once again, although the palpitations persisted, accompanied by a twinge of sadness for what couldn't be.

Attack—that would be a good distraction for both her heart and her head.

'Well, I don't know how you can talk about always going highest or deepest—at least I don't take risks,' she told him. 'You're the one who plunges into situations the rest of us feel are too dangerous.'

'I'm not a volunteer like you guys. It's my job.'

No smile, and he'd turned away so all she could see was his profile. Hard to read, Harry's profile, although it was very nice to look at. Very well defined with its straight nose and black brow shadowing a deep-set eye. High cheekbones with shadows underneath, and lips—

She had to stop this! She had to push her feelings for Harry back where they belonged—deeply hidden in her heart.

For the moment.

Just till she got rid of them altogether.

Returning to the attack might help…

'Oh, yes? Like every policeman in Australia would have gone down in those shark-infested waters, with a storm raging, to rescue that diver?'

'Every policeman who can swim,' he said, smiling to lessen the lie in the ridiculous statement.

'Rubbish!' Grace dismissed both smile and lie with a wave of her hand. 'If your guess—and I'm not admitting it's right, Harry—is that I went into the SES because I was short, then my guess is you do all this dangerous stuff because you don't give a damn about what happens to you. That's understandable to a certain extent, given the loss of your wife. Taking risks might have helped dull the pain at first but now it's become a habit.'

Sheesh! Was she really doing this? Talking to Harry about his wife, and his attraction to danger? The very subject he'd warned her off last night?

And how was he reacting now?

He'd turned away, the profile gone, and all she had was a good view of slightly over-long hair.

Silky hair—she'd felt it when her fingers had somehow made their way to the back of his head as they'd kissed.

Her fingers were remembering the slide of his hair against her skin when he turned back to face her.

Half smiling...

'I asked for that,' he said quietly, reaching out and touching her face, perhaps pushing a wet curl off her forehead. 'Saying that we never talked.'

Then he leaned towards her and very gently pressed a kiss against her lips.

'Time to move, my tall, brave SES friend. Where's your hard hat?'

The tender kiss and Harry's softly teasing voice caught at Grace's heart and made her vision blur for an instant. But Harry was right—they had to move, and she had to get her mind off kisses and tenderness and concentrate on getting around the tree.

She felt around her feet for the hard hat then remembered

she'd given it to the volunteer who'd climbed into the bus to tend that final passenger while others had cut her free. The helmet had a lamp on it that meant he'd been able to see what he'd been doing.

She explained this to Harry who made a huffing noise as if such an action had been stupid.

'Not that it matters now,' she told him. 'They never do much to keep off the rain.'

But Harry had other ideas, reaching behind him for the wide-brimmed felt hat issued to all police officers up here in the tropics and plonking it down on her head.

'There, it suits you,' he said, and she had to smile.

'Because it's so big it covers all my face?'

The hat had dropped to eyebrow level, but she could still see Harry's face, and caught the frown that replaced the smile he'd offered with the hat.

'That's another thing I know about you,' he said crossly. 'You're always putting yourself down. Not like some women do when they're looking for compliments, but it's as if you genuinely believe you're not smart, and pretty, and...'

Grace had her hand on the catch of the door, ready to open it and brave the wild weather outside, but Harry's pronouncement stopped her.

'And?' she asked, half wanting to know, half uncertain.

'And tonight in that blue thing you looked beautiful,' he said. 'Bloody beautiful!'

He was out the door before Grace could react. Actually, if he hadn't opened her door for her he could have been halfway to Crocodile Creek before she reacted, so lost was she in a warm little cloud of happiness.

Harry thought she'd looked beautiful...

Bloody beautiful...

Harry shut the car door, took Grace's hand and drew her close to his body. Since Grace had forced him to think about it, he'd realised his problem was physical attraction mixed with angry concern. The combination was so unsettling it was muddling both his mind and his body at a time when his brain needed to be crystal clear and all his senses needed to be on full alert.

On top of that, his inability to do anything about their current precarious situation—to protect Grace from this fury Nature was flinging at them—had his jaw clenched and his muscles knotted in frustration.

And his leg hurt…

He tried to tuck Grace closer as they followed the beam of light from his torch, clambering over the lesser boughs and branches, heads bent against the wind and rain. She was so slight—had she lost weight lately and he hadn't noticed?—she could blow away.

He gripped her more tightly.

'Harry!'

Had she said his name earlier that this time she pressed her lips against his ear and yelled it?

'What?'

'I think that way's clearer,' she yelled, pointing towards the base of the tree. 'There's a branch there we can use to climb onto the trunk, and even if we have to jump off the other side, it might be better than scrambling through the tangle of branches up this way.'

She was right and he should have worked it out himself, but the mess on the road was nothing to the mess in his head. He had to get past it—to rid his mind of all extraneous thoughts. Tonight, more than ever before, he'd need to be clear-headed in order to protect the people of his town.

She'd moved away though still held his hand, leading him in the direction she'd indicated, picking her way over the fallen branches. A sudden whistling noise made him look up and he dived forward, seizing Grace in a flying tackle, landing with her against the protective bulk of the huge treetrunk.

The branch that had whistled its warning crashed to the ground in front of them.

'This is ridiculous. I want you to go back and wait in the car,' he said, holding her—too tightly—in his arms, desperate to keep her safe.

'Are you going back to sit in the car?' she asked, snuggling up against his chest, which didn't help the mess in his head.

'Of course not. There's a cyclone coming. I have to get back to town.'

She reached up and patted his cheek.

'So do I,' she said softly. 'So maybe we'd better get moving again.'

'No thank-you kiss for saving your life?'

Oh, no! Had he really said that? What was wrong with him? The very last thing he needed to be doing was kissing Grace.

'I think kissing has caused enough problems tonight, don't you?' she replied, but the hand that was resting on his cheek moved and one fingertip traced the outline of his lips, reminding him of the heat the kiss had generated earlier—stirring the glowing coals of it back to life.

He stood up, still holding her, controlling breathing that was suddenly erratic, while looking around for any new source of danger. But though the wind still blew, it seemed relatively safe.

'I'm going to boost you up onto the trunk. Get over the top and into the shelter of it on the other side as quickly as you can.'

He lifted her—so light—and set her on the trunk, then heaved himself up, his leg objecting yet again to the rough treatment it was getting. Then he followed her as she dropped swiftly down to road level again. There were fewer branches to trip or slow them down on this side, so he took her hand again and hurried her along the road, sure the car would meet them before long, although driving through the storm had its own problems.

'Lights!'

Grace pointed as she yelled the word at Harry. Even if he

didn't hear her, he'd surely see the lights. She couldn't wait to get to the car, not because the wind and rain and flying leaves and branches bothered her unduly but to get away from Harry—out of touching distance, where it was impossible to make sense of all that had happened during the course of this weird evening.

The thought that Harry might be physically attracted to her had filled her with joy, but his evident distrust of such attraction could only mean he still had feelings for his wife. In his mind, physical attraction to another woman must seem like betrayal—a form of infidelity—although Nikki had been dead for nearly three years.

Then there was the question of whether they were still friends.

And her determination to move on from Harry—now made harder than ever because of the kiss.

Grace sighed. If she wanted a husband and family, she *had* to move on. She may have looked beautiful in her blue dress earlier today, but what chance did she have against the memory of a woman who'd not only been tall and slim and elegant, but a former local beauty queen—the Millennium Miss Caneland— and a popular television personality?

Even when she was dying, Nikki Blake had been beautiful. Grace had seen enough photos of her to know that much.

And nice with it, according to the staff who'd nursed her.

Grace sighed again.

'Not right. The lights aren't getting closer.'

She caught the end of Harry's sentence and peered ahead through the worsening deluge. Not only weren't the lights moving, but they appeared to be pointing upwards.

'He's slid off the road.'

Harry's words confirmed her thoughts and she broke into a jog, running behind him as he dropped her hand and raced towards the lights.

Hairpin bends around the mountain—they rounded one, then two, and were on the outward curve of a third when they saw the vehicle, which had come to rest against a pillar-shaped rock, its headlights pointing uselessly into the blackness of the forest.

'Stay here,' Harry ordered, but Grace was already picking her way carefully down the slope, testing each foothold before shifting her weight.

The torch beam cut through the useless illumination provided by the vehicle's headlights, but revealed nothing more than a cloud of white behind the windscreen. The air bags had obviously worked.

Then, as the torch beam played across the vehicle, Grace saw a movement, a hand, pushing at the cloud of white, fighting against it.

'It's Troy!'

Harry's voice held all the anxiety and pain she knew he'd feel about this, the youngest of the men on his staff.

'Sit still,' he yelled, scrambling faster down the slope, cursing his bad leg, and unheeding of the danger to himself as he plummeted towards the young policeman. 'The less you move, the less risk there is of the vehicle moving.'

Grace followed more cautiously, aware, as Harry was, that Troy wouldn't hear the warnings over the wind and through windows wound up tightly against the weather.

Harry reached the car, more careful now, not touching it—not touching anything—but circling, motioning with both hands for Troy, whose face was now visible, to be still. Grace stopped a little further up the hill, then turned to look back the way they'd come.

'Would you trust that red gum to hold the car if we wind the winch cable around it?'

She pointed towards a tree not unlike the one that had fallen close to them earlier, but this one was on the far side of the road.

'We'll have to,' Harry said. 'For a start, we'll just use it to anchor the vehicle while we get Troy out. I won't risk using the winch with him in the cabin. You stay clear of everything while I take the cable up to the tree.'

He made his way to the front of the vehicle where the winch was sited and bent to release the cable.

Grace watched the careful way he touched the winch and understood his caution. The vehicle might seem secure enough, resting as it was against a massive rock, but with all the rain they'd had, the rock could have been undermined and any change in the dynamics of the vehicle could send it and Troy plummeting into the gully.

'Damn! I can't get in the back to get a bag,' Harry muttered, looking helplessly around then focussing on Grace. 'I don't suppose you're wearing something—no, of course you're not. It'll have to be my jacket.'

He handed the hook of the winch cable to Grace to hold and for the first time she realised he was still in his dinner suit. The bow-tie was gone but, yes, that was definitely a filthy, sodden dinner jacket he was removing.

'What do you need it for?' Grace asked as he took the cable hook from her and turned towards the road.

He looked back at her and smiled.

'To wrap around the tree. We all keep bags in the back of our vehicles to use as tree protection but as I can't get at a bag, the jacket will have to do. If there's no protection the steel cable can ringbark the tree and possibly kill it.'

Grace shook her head. Here they were in the rainforest, with gale-force winds and torrential rain whipping the vegetation to ribbons, and Harry was protecting a gum tree?

She watched him clamber and limp his way back up to the road, seeing the way his wet shirt clung to his skin, defining the muscles and bones as well as if he'd been naked.

She shut her eyes, trying to blot images of a naked Harry from her mind, then turned back to Troy, using her hands as Harry had, to motion him to stillness, smiling encouragement. And something worked because although all his instincts must be screaming at him to escape the confines of the vehicle, he stayed where he was—statue still.

'I'll just hook this up—doubling the cable back to the vehicle halves the weight on the winch, although the vehicle's only a couple of tons and the winch's weight capacity is five tons.' Harry explained, returning with the hook end of the cable, which he attached to a towing point at the front of the vehicle. 'Now, I'll take up any slack in the cable then get in the cab to check the lad.'

'*I'll* get in the cab to check him,' Grace said. 'And don't bother arguing because you know it makes sense. I weigh half as much as you do so, like with the cable, we're halving the risk of the vehicle moving.'

Even in the torchlight she saw Harry's lips tighten, going white with the pressure of not arguing, but in the end he gave a nod.

This wasn't anything to do with the new physical attraction, Harry assured himself as he very carefully opened the passenger door of the cambered vehicle—the door not jammed against the rock. His anxiety was for Grace, his friend.

'You OK?' he asked, peering through the maze of white towards the young constable.

'I think I've hurt my leg.'

Troy's voice wavered slightly and Harry understood. Barely more than a kid, he'd had to drive out through the wind and rain and flying missiles, then the car had skidded and he'd thought he'd had it.

'Grace will check you out,' Harry told him, turning towards Grace so he could help her into the cabin.

Beneath his wide-brimmed hat, her face was pale and streaked with dirt, and the embattled smile she gave him tweaked at something in his heart.

Concern, that's what it was. The same concern that was making his stomach knot as she slid across the seat, cutting at the air bags with the penknife off her belt, talking all the time to Troy about where he hurt and how he felt.

'There'll be a torch snapped in grips underneath the dash,'

he told Grace when she'd collapsed the air bags and pulled them out of the way.

'Thanks!'

She found the torch and turned it on, setting it down so its light shone on her patient. Then, as her small but capable hands slid across Troy's head, feeling for any evident damage, Harry remembered this was only the beginning of the salvage operation. Unless they wanted to walk the forty-odd kilometres back to Crocodile Creek, he had to get this vehicle back up onto the road.

He prowled around it, checking the tyres—all intact—and damage to the body that might inhibit movement of the wheels. The mudguard, which had taken the brunt of the collision with the rock, was pushed in, but he found a strong branch and levered it off the rubber of the tyre. Everything else looked OK, which wasn't surprising as his reading of the accident had the vehicle going into a slow slide, first across the road, then down the slope to where it had come to rest against the rock.

'Where do you keep the first-aid kit in these new vehicles?' Grace called to him, and he turned to see she'd clambered over the back of the front seat and was now searching around behind the back seats.

'It should be strapped against the back of that seat you're on,' he told her, managing to answer although his lungs didn't want to breathe while she was moving in the cabin.

'Got it. I think Troy's right leg might be broken. I'll give him a painkiller before I try to move him, then splint it as best I can.'

She turned back to her patient, the small medical kit already open on her lap.

'Actually, Troy, it might be best if you fainted when we move you. That way you mightn't feel the pain so much.'

The lad grinned at Grace and Harry shook his head. They were like two kids playing doctors, seemingly unaware that a twisted metal cable was all that held them from the very real possibility of death.

'Do we really need to get him out?'

Grace had skidded across the seat to speak quietly to Harry, while Troy's eyelids were closing, no doubt in response to the drug she'd given him.

'I don't want to try winching it with anyone inside,' Harry told her once again. 'In ordinary circumstances it's better for have someone steering, but not in this situation where we don't know if the anchoring tree will hold the weight. The winch will pull the front around this way, then drag the vehicle up the slope.'

'We hope,' Grace said, and for the first time since their adventure together had begun she sounded tired.

'The cable's holding—let me in there!' Harry said, his stomach knotting with more anxiety.

'No, I'll manage and I need you there to help Troy out and lift him down to the ground. Would there be something in the back we can wrap him in? He's already shocky from the accident and his leg. I don't want that getting worse.'

Harry pictured the gear they all carried in the back of the big police vehicles.

'There'll be a small waterproof tarp folded in the pocket behind the driver's seat and a space blanket in a pouch beside it. Get them both out and we'll wrap him in the space blanket then the tarp. It will make moving him easier as well.'

Grace found them both and wriggled across the seat to drop them out the door to Harry, then, satisfied the painkiller had had time to work, she turned her attention back to her patient.

Her first examination of him had told her he was holding up well. His pulse and breathing were steady, his pupils responding evenly to light, and he was able to move all his limbs so the front and side air bags seemed to have done their jobs, protecting his head and holding his body firmly in the seat belt so his spine wasn't compromised.

But even with a painkiller circulating in his blood and blocking messages to and from his brain, he was going to be in agony when he moved his leg.

'Troy, I need to get you over onto this passenger seat before we can get you out. The best way I can see to do it would be for you to lie sideways across the centre console so your head and shoulders are on the passenger seat behind me, then if you can bring your good leg up onto your seat and use it to help you inch your way towards the door until your butt's on this side. Can you do that?'

Troy looked at her, his eyes glazed by the medication, but he nodded and turned so he could wiggle across the seat. His groan as he moved confirmed her thoughts, but she had to get him out of the vehicle before she could splint his leg and stabilise him properly.

She was squatting in the footwell on the passenger side, her body canted across the gear lever as she reached out to take a firm grip on his injured leg. She had to get it up onto the seat of the car before she could examine the damage and was concentrating on doing this is carefully as possible, trying not to hurt him, when the vehicle moved.

Troy let out a yelp, and Harry roared, 'Keep still!'

'As if I needed to be told that!' Grace muttered to herself, frozen in place with Troy's calf held gingerly in her hands.

'It's my weight coming onto this side,' Troy said.

But it was Harry's 'I need to get you both out now!' that caught Grace's attention.

She couldn't see anything from where she was so she continued with her job, lifting Troy's injured leg up onto the seat.

He gave a whistling sigh then slumped against the seat, the pain making him pass out.

Swelling around his ankle suggested the problem was there, or at the base of his tib and fib, but there was no time to do anything but get him out, preferably while he was still unconscious.

'How are we going to do this?' she called to Harry, who now had the door propped or tied open in some way.

'You push his shoulders down towards me, and I'll ease him out. Do what you can to protect his leg as we move him.'

Back in the footwell on the passenger side, she eased Troy's body around so his shoulders slid out the door. Harry's hands caught him, then lifted him as Grace grasped the injured limb to lift it over the centre console and gently out the door.

Harry cradled the young man in his arms, holding him as easily as she'd have held a baby, then he knelt and rested his burden on the spread-out covers on the ground, so carefully Grace shook her head in wonder at his gentle strength.

'The space blanket's a bit wet but it will still keep his body warmth in,' he said, wrapping first it and then the tarp around Troy's upper body, leaving his legs unwrapped so Grace could see to his injury.

Again using her knife, she cut through the leather of his boot, wanting to ease the constriction on his blood vessels that the swelling would be causing.

'Does he need this to order a new pair?' she asked Harry, tossing the wrecked boot to one side, cutting off Troy's sock now so she could put a half-splint around his foot to hold it steady while allowing for more swelling.

The police car's first-aid kit didn't run to splints, but there were plenty of sticks which she could pad with torn strips of sock before binding them into place around his foot and ankle.

Harry watched her work—small, capable hands moving so steadily she might have been in A and E, not on a dangerous, slippery slope with wind and rain raging about her.

She was good!

'OK?'

Had she said something that he'd missed while thinking about her, that now she was standing beside him, waiting for a response?

'He's done?'

Harry looked down at the young policeman who was now fully wrapped in the space blanket and tarp.

'We just need to get him up the hill,' Grace said, nodding up the slope. 'I'll take his legs.'

For a moment Harry considered arguing but although he'd been able to lift Troy free, he knew he couldn't carry him all the way up the slippery hill when he was healthy, let alone with a bung leg. Between them they lifted the injured man and carried him up the slope, slipping and sliding, Troy groaning from time to time, but eventually they had him safely on the road.

Grace took off Harry's hat and placed it, carefully tilted, on Troy's head to keep the worst of the rain from his face, then she watched as Harry made his way back down the slope and, using a hand-held remote control, started the winch.

She heard the winch motor whirr and held her breath then, oh, so slowly, the front of the big police vehicle swung around and, with wheels churning the surface of the slope to mud, it began to move, inch by inch, towards the tree that held its weight.

Harry had placed Troy well away from where the car would reach the road, and out of danger should the tree fall, but still Grace felt her nerves tighten, fear for all of them should the tree come down, or the vehicle not make the road, clutching at her stomach.

It was nearly up, front wheels on the verge, the winch whining complaints all the way, when the back wheels skidded, sending a final flurry of slush into the air before ploughing forward onto the bitumen.

'You did it!' Grace yelled, abandoning her patient to jump up in the air in excitement. She'd have hugged Harry if their earlier conversation hadn't suggested even friendly hugs should be avoided. 'You got it up!'

'But will it go?'

Harry's question tempered her delight, but she sensed satisfaction in his voice and knew he was fairly confident the vehicle would be drivable. He was unhooking the towing cable, then using the winch to wind it up, while Grace walked over to the tree to retrieve his dinner jacket.

'Beyond repair?' Harry asked, seeing the muddy, crumpled garment in her hands.

'We'll see,' she said, clutching the jacket to her chest, holding onto something that was Harry's, barely restraining an urge to sniff at it in the hope of picking up something of his scent.

'You're so tired you've gone loopy!' she muttered to herself, returning to her patient, who was peering out from underneath the hat, no doubt wondering if there was any chance he could be moved out of the rain.

Harry started the car then drove slowly towards them, checking the vehicle was safe to drive. He stopped beside Troy and Grace, leaping out to open the back door and lift Troy inside.

'See if you can strap him in there so he's comfortable,' he said to Grace, who scrambled in beside her patient. 'Then you hop in the front and put on your seat belt. We don't want any more patients delivered to the hospital today.'

Grace obeyed, making Troy as comfortable as she could, checking his pulse again before abandoning him to climb over into the front seat and strap on her seat belt.

'OK?' Harry turned towards her as he asked, and the smile he offered was so kind Grace felt tears prickle behind her eyelids. She knew it was relief that they were all safe, and tiredness as it had been a very long day, but try as she may she couldn't answer him, making do with a very watery smile instead.

She was exhausted, Harry realised, remembering something she'd said that morning when they'd been called out to an accident at Wygera—something about just coming off night duty.

'When did you last sleep?' he demanded, anxiety making his voice more abrupt than he'd intended.

But Grace didn't answer. She was already asleep.

At least he'd got everyone off the mountain…

'Scruffy!'

Max slid and scrambled down the hill, stumbling over rocks,

ducking around the ferns, yelling until he thought his chest would burst.

The bus had been on its side, that's all he remembered. The bus being on its side and no windows where the windows should have been.

No Scruffy either.

His dog was gone.

'Scruffy! Come on, boy. Scruffy!'

He listened for the yelp that Scruffy always gave in answer to his name, but how to hear a small dog's yelp when the wind was howling and stuff was crashing in the bush all around him?

'Scruffy!'

CHAPTER FIVE

HARRY DROVE CAREFULLY down the road, one hand fiddling with the radio, which seemed to be the only thing not working in the vehicle. Had a wire come loose? He twirled knobs and banged his hand against it, but couldn't pick up even a burst of static.

No distraction there…

He checked the rear-view mirror. Troy appeared to be asleep as well. So he looked back at Grace, at her pale face and almost translucent eyelids, at the shadows under her eyes and the spread of freckles now dark against her skin.

Grace!

He shook his head, unable to deny the attraction that still stirred within his body.

What was happening to him? Why had his body chosen this of all times to remind him of his physical needs?

And chosen Grace of all women?

He guessed a psychologist would tell him it was because the grieving process was finally over, but he knew what had kept him celibate since Nikki's death had been as much guilt as grief. Guilt for the pain he'd caused her. Yes, there'd been grief as well, grief that someone as young and lovely as Nikki should have to die. Grief for the child he'd lost. And grief for the friendship he'd damaged somewhere along the way in his relationship with Nikki.

He looked at Grace, knowing a similar close friendship was at risk here.

Grace! Every now and then, in the past, he'd caught a fleeting glimpse of another Grace behind the laughing, bubbly exterior most people saw—a glimpse of a Grace that disturbed him in some way.

Tonight, learning about her father—thinking about a small child flying all the way from Ireland to Australia in search of the love she hadn't found—he'd found a clue to the hidden Grace and understood a little of the pain and tears behind the laughter.

So now, more than ever, he didn't want to hurt her...

'Did I sleep?'

Grace peered blearily around her. They were in the emergency entrance at the hospital and, outside the car, Harry was holding the rear door while a couple of orderlies lifted Troy onto a stretcher.

'Like a log,' Harry told her, his smile lifting the lines tiredness had drawn on his face.

'No, stay right where you are,' he added, as she began to unbuckle her seat belt. 'I'm taking you home. Quite apart from the fact you're exhausted, you're so filthy you're the last thing anyone would want in a hospital.'

'You're not so sprucy clean yourself,' Grace retorted, taking in the mud streaks on the wet shirt that clung to Harry's chest.

Then, remembering, she clutched his dinner jacket more tightly.

Pathetic, that's what she was, but the filthy, ragged garment in her hands had become some kind of talisman.

Though it would hardly have the power to ward off a cyclone.

'Willie?' she asked, looking beyond the well-lit area to where the wind still lashed the trees and threw rain horizontally against the building.

'Definitely heading our way.' Harry watched the orderlies wheel Troy towards the hospital, obviously torn between wanting to follow and getting Grace home. 'We're down to hourly warnings.'

'Then I've got work to do,' Grace said, unbuckling her seat belt once again. 'You go with Troy, I'll grab a hospital car, go home and change, then see what's happening on the evacuation front. I assume the SES crews started with the nursing home down by the river, so most of those people should be in the civic centre hall by now. I'll get the list and organise for all the others to be collected or chivvied into shifting under their own steam.'

She'd opened the car door while she'd proposed this eminently sensible plan, but Harry took the door from her grasp, used one firm hand to push her back into the seat and shut the door again.

'I'll take you home,' he repeated. 'Two minutes to see someone's attending to Troy and I'll be right back. We need to do the individual evacuations on our list together. We discussed this in the contingency meetings. You'll need police presence to get some of those stubborn elderly die-hards in the most flimsy of old houses to move.'

Grace acknowledged his point with a pathetically weak smile. Battling wind and rain and an approaching cyclone was bad enough, but battling all the conflicting emotions the evening had stirred up at the same time was making the job doubly— no, a hundred times—more difficult.

Harry followed Troy's stretcher into A and E, where the scene resembled something from the film set of a disaster movie.

Only this wasn't a movie, it was real.

'How's it going?' he asked Charles, who had rolled towards him as Troy was taken into a treatment cubicle.

'It looks worse than it is. I think we've got things under control, although we've some badly injured people here in the hospital. There's one young woman with head injuries. Thank heavens Alistair—you know Alistair? Gina's cousin?—was here. He's a neurosurgeon with skills far beyond anyone we have on staff. He's put her into an induced coma for the moment—who knows how she'll wake up? We lost one young girl, and that last patient…' Charles paused and shook his head. 'She died before she got here.'

He seemed to have aged, but Harry understood that—he felt about a hundred years old himself.

'How's everything out there? Did you get everyone off the mountain?'

Harry nodded then looked around again, looking ahead, not thinking back. He'd done enough of that lately.

'You've obviously cleared the walking wounded. Where are they?'

'If they weren't locals with homes to go to, they were sent to the civic centre hall. Volunteers there are providing food and hot drinks.'

Charles paused then added, 'Actually, if you're going that way and I'm sure you will be some time, you might take the belongings we haven't matched to patients with you and see if you can find owners for them at the hall. The gear's in Reception.'

Someone called to Charles, who wheeled away, while Harry strode through to Reception, aware he'd been longer than the two minutes he'd promised Grace. Perhaps she'd fallen asleep again.

Wet, squashed, some muddy, the belongings rescued from the bus formed a sorry-looking heap on the floor in one corner of the usually immaculate reception area. How was he going to ferry this lot out to the car? He'd walked through from the corridor, thinking about the belongings, and now saw the two people who stood beside it.

Georgie Turner and Alistair—the doctor Charles had mentioned. They would have been working flat out since the casualties had begun coming in, but they weren't thinking medicine now. Georgie was staring down at the small, muddy backpack in her hands. She'd emptied it—a pathetic bundle of child's clothing and a ragged teddy bear had tumbled out and were lying at her feet.

While he watched, she knelt and lifted the teddy bear. The face she raised to him was terror-stricken.

'Max was on that bus,' she whispered.

'Your Max?'

Harry found himself staring helplessly at her. Georgie's beloved Max—hell's teeth, they all loved Max.

'Harry, have you found any kids?' Georgie demanded. And then the remaining colour drained out of her face. 'He's not... he's not one of the bodies, is he? Oh, God, please...'

'He's not,' Harry said, crossing swiftly to her, kneeling and gripping her hands. 'Georgie, I've been up there. We searched the surrounding area. We found no kids.'

'His dad... Ron's on the run. They might both...'

'I know Ron, Georgie. He wasn't on the bus.'

'But he might be hiding. He might—'

'Georgie, any person in that bus would be far too battered to be thinking about hiding. And the wind's unbelievable. Ron might be afraid of jail but there are worse things than jail, and staying out in the rainforest tonight would be one of them.'

'But Max is definitely there,' Georgie faltered. She looked up at Harry. 'He is,' she said dully, hugging the bear tighter. 'This is Spike. Max has just stopped carrying Spike round but Spike's never far from him.'

Behind them the phone rang, but the pile of child-size clothes on the floor reminded Harry of something.

'There's a shoe,' he told her, looking through the mass of wet belongings and not finding it. 'I'll just ask someone.'

He left the reception area, remembering the bridesmaid, Hannah, had found the shoe. Where was it now? He tracked it down at the desk of the children's ward.

The shoe was small and very muddy, with an orange fish painted on it, the eye of the fish camouflaging a small hole.

Harry held it in his hand and hurried back to Georgie, showing her the shoe then seeing a quick shake of her head.

'That's not Max's.'

Her dismissal of it was so definite, Harry shoved the shoe into his pocket to think about later.

'We've got to go back out there,' Georgie added.

Images of young Max, a kid who'd had enough problems in his life thanks to his wastrel, drug-running father, alone in the bush, maybe injured, definitely wet, and probably terrified, flashed through Harry's mind. His gut knotted as he realised the impossibility of doing what she'd suggested.

'There's a tree across the road—we can't get through. I'd go myself and walk in, Georgie, but I can't leave town right now.'

He could feel her anguish—felt his own tearing him apart—but his duty had to be to the town, not to one small boy lost in the bush while a cyclone ripped the forest to shreds above his head.

'Of course you can't, go but I can. I'm going out there now.'

He saw the determination in her eyes, but could he stop her? He had to try…

'Georgie, there's a cyclone hitting within hours. There's no way I can let you go, even if you could get through, which you can't. The tree's crashed down across the road not far from the landslide. We were lucky to get the last of the injured out.'

'I'll take my dirt bike,' she snapped. She tried to shove Harry aside but he wouldn't move.

Harry ignored the fists beating at his chest, trying desperately to think through this dilemma. Georgie could throw her bikes around as competently as she wore the four-inch heels she fancied as her footwear. She'd be wearing a helmet—

As if that would help!

'Georgie, he might not even be out there. You said yourself it's not his shoe.'

'Then there are two kids. Let me past.'

Georgie shoved at him but Harry held her, and made one last attempt to persuade her not to go.

'We've got no proof he's there. It's suicide.'

'We do have proof,' Alistair said from behind them. 'We've had confirmation Max was on the bus. Suicide or not, there's a child's life at stake. I'll go with her.'

Harry's mind processed what he knew of Alistair. Gina's cousin—Harry had met him at a fire party on the beach some months ago when the American had come to visit Gina—or more to check out Gina's fiancé Cal, the locals had thought.

Stuffed shirt had been Harry's immediate reaction.

Stuffed shirt who could ride a bike?

The pushing stopped. Georgie whirled to face Alistair, her face a mixture of anguish and fear. 'You can't.'

'Don't you start saying can't,' Alistair said. 'Harry, the tree's blocking the road, right? Who else in town has a dirt bike?'

'I've got one,' Harry told him, thinking it through. If Max *was* out there...

Maybe he had no choice but to let them go. 'It's in the shed, Georgie, fuelled up, key above the door. And be careful, keep in mind at all times that there are open mineshafts on that mountain.'

But Georgie wasn't listening. She was staring at Alistair.

'You really can ride?'

'I can ride.'

'You'd better not hold me back,' she snapped.

'Stop arguing and get going—you don't have long,' Harry told them. 'You've got a radio, Georg? Of course not. Here, take mine and I'll pick up a spare at the station. Your cellphone might or might not work. And take a torch, it's black as pitch out there. Rev your bikes, he might hear the noise.'

Harry watched them go then pulled the shoe out of his pocket, grasping it in his hand, feeling how small and insubstantial it was.

Were there two children lost in the bush?

Surely not.

But his heart clenched with worry, while his hands fondled the little painted shoe. Georgie had said it was too small for Max. Max was seven, so the shoe would fit...

A two-and-a-half-year-old?

Harry shook his head. Why did thoughts like that creep up on him at the most inopportune times?

And wasn't he over thinking back?

He tucked the shoe back into his pocket, gathered up a bundle of backpacks and suitcases and headed out to his vehicle, thanking someone who'd come out from behind the reception desk and offered to help carry things.

It wasn't until he'd packed them into the back of the big vehicle that he realised he'd lost his passenger.

'If you're looking for Grace, she went into A and E,' a nurse standing outside in the wind and rain, trying hard to smoke a cigarette, told him.

Harry was about to walk back inside when Grace emerged from the side door, head bowed and shoulders bent, looking so tired and defeated Harry hurried towards her, anxiety again gnawing at his intestines.

He reached her side and put his arms around her, pulling her into an embrace, holding her tightly as the wind and rain swirled around them.

'What's happened?' he asked as she burrowed her head into his chest as if trying to escape herself.

'She died.' The whispered words failed to register for a moment, then Grace lifted her head and looked up into his face. 'Our woman, Harry. The last one out of the bus. I've just seen Mike. She died before they reached the hospital. Massive brain injuries, nothing anyone could do.'

'Oh, Grace!' he said, and rocked her in his arms, knowing exhaustion was adding to the regret and hurt of the woman's death. He'd felt the same extreme reaction when Charles had given him that news.

'She had a boyfriend on the bus,' Grace continued. 'He was seated with her and got out uninjured, but she had to use the bathroom and was in there when it happened. They're from Germany and now he has to phone her parents.'

'I'll do that, it's my job,' Harry said, but Grace shook her head.

'Charles is phoning now—he speaks German so he'll support the boy. But fancy someone phoning, Harry, to say your daughter's dead.'

She began to shiver and Harry led her to the car, helping her in, wanting to get her home and dry—and safe.

Safe? Where was safe tonight? Nowhere in Crocodile Creek, that was for sure.

Grace fell asleep again on the short drive to her cottage and this time, when he stopped the car, Harry sat and looked at her for a minute. He had the list and could do the evacuations himself, although that would be pretty stupid as he was likely to be needed other places or would be taking calls that would distract him.

And on top of that, she'd be furious.

He sighed, reached out to push a wet curl off her temple, then got out of the car, walked, with difficulty as the wind was far stronger here on the coast, around the bonnet, then carefully opened the passenger door, slipping his hand inside to hold Grace's weight so she didn't slide out.

Her lips opened in a small mew of protest at this disruption, but she didn't push him away so he reached across her and undid the catch on her seat belt, conscious all the time of the softness of her body and the steady rise and fall of her breasts.

She stirred again as he lifted her out, then she rested her head against his shoulder and drifted back to sleep.

But once inside he had to wake her—had to get her out of her sodden garments for a start.

'Grace!'

He said her name so softly he was surprised when she opened

her eyes immediately. Was it her nursing training kicking in that she could come so instantly awake?

And frowning.

'Harry? Oh, damn, I fell asleep again. You should have woken me. You've carried more than your share of people tonight, and your leg must be killing you.'

'You don't weigh much. I'll set you down and as you still have power, I'll put the kettle on. I want you to get dry, have a hot drink then gather some things together for yourself. I'll drop you at the civic centre and you can sleep for a couple of hours.'

He eased her onto her feet just inside the door of her cottage.

'Sleep?' She looked so astounded he had to smile.

'What you've been doing in the car. Remember sleep?'

The feeble joke fell flat.

'I can't sleep now!' she muttered at him, then added a glare for good measure. 'Unless you're going to sleep as well,' she dared him. 'Then I might consider it.'

'You know I can't—not right now—but I'll be only too happy to grab a nap whenever I can. You should be, too, and now's as good a time as any.'

'So you can run around on your own, doing all the evacuations I'm supposed to be doing, fielding phone calls and giving orders and generally doing your superhero thing. Well, not on my watch,' she finished, her usually soft pink lips set in a mutinous line.

He was about to deny the superhero accusation when he realised that was exactly what she wanted. She was turning the argument back on him.

'Well, fine,' he grumbled. 'But you're not going anywhere until you've had a hot drink.'

He stalked towards her kitchen.

Joe had obviously remembered the cyclone preparations from his time working in the town because the windows were all taped with broad adhesive tape, and a note on the kitchen table told them he'd taken Christina to the hospital because he was working there and hadn't wanted to leave her at the cottage on her own.

'Also large as she is,' he'd added, 'she swears she can still be useful.'

Harry filled the kettle, banging it against the tap because his frustration with Grace's behaviour still simmered.

'Stubborn woman!' he muttered to himself, finding the instant coffee and spooning a generous amount into two cups, adding an equal amount of sugar. It wasn't sleep but maybe a caffeine and sugar boost would help them tackle what still lay ahead of them this night.

Still grumpy, though not certain if it was because of Grace's refusal to obey his orders or her repetition of the superhero crack, he was carrying the filled cups and some biscuits he'd found in the pantry through to the living room when a small mumble of frustration made him turn. Grace was slumped on the sofa. She had managed to remove her boots but was now fumbling with the press studs that held her overalls together down the front.

Grumpiness was swallowed by concern so strong he felt shaken by the power of it.

'Here, let me,' Harry said, setting down the coffee and stepping towards her, telling her at the same time about the note and the preparations Joe had made, hoping the conversation might mask the trembling of his fingers.

He undid the studs then the Velcro strips and eased the heavy, wet fabric off Grace's shoulders. His voice—in the midst of explaining that Joe had left the water bottles, bedding, radio and batteries in the bathroom—faltered and his fingers shook a little more as he saw the swell of Grace's breasts, clad only in some scraps of dark blue lace—the colour making her ivory skin seem even paler.

Reminding himself that this was Grace, his friend, he helped her stand so he could drag the clammy, all-concealing garment off her body, trying desperately to ignore his body's reaction to the matching scrap of blue lace lower down, and the surprisingly shapely legs the stripping off of the garment revealed.

'You'll have to do the rest yourself,' he told her, his voice coming out as a throaty kind of growl.

'I had better,' she said, a teasing smile illuminating her tired face. 'Although,' she added wistfully, 'I'm not so certain physical attraction is all bad.'

'Right now any distraction at all is bad, Grace, and you know it. Now, scat, and take your coffee with you. Get into the shower and into some dry clothes—I'll slip home and change, check that everything's organised at the station and come back for you in ten or fifteen minutes.'

Getting away from her—doing things that needed doing—would surely distract him from...

From what?

He couldn't find an answer, and she didn't scat. She just stood there for a few seconds with her blue lace and white skin and exhausted face, seemingly about to say something, then she shook her head and turned away, revealing the fact that the blue lace was a thong so the pert roundness of her butt had him almost agreeing that physical attraction couldn't be all bad.

Except that he knew it was...

Grace stepped over the pile of emergency supplies Joe had deposited in her bathroom, and reached in to turn the shower on. She stripped off the sexy underwear she'd bought to go with the dress, sighing as she did so. She may as well have been wearing a nursing bra and bloomers for all the effect it had had on Harry. Although if she'd been too tired to argue as he'd stripped off her gear, he'd probably been too tired to think about attraction.

She showered, cringing as noises from above suggested half the forest was landing on the roof. Joe had been right to put the emergency gear in here—bathrooms were usually the safest room in the house, but if the roof blew off, or if a large branch caused damage, anyone sheltering in the bathroom would still get very wet.

'Better wet than dead,' she reminded herself, and a wave of sadness for a woman she didn't know engulfed her so suddenly she had to rest her head against the wall of the shower for a few minutes, hoping the hot water would sluice away the pain for those they hadn't saved.

Another crashing noise outside reminded her she had work to do, so she turned off the shower, dried herself and dressed hurriedly, pulling on a light pair of cargo pants with a multitude of pockets, and a T-shirt. Both would eventually be soaked even underneath a heavy raincoat but at least they'd dry faster when she was indoors. Boots next—only an idiot would be outside on a night like this without solid boots.

They were wet and didn't want to go on, and within minutes her dry socks had absorbed water from them. She shrugged off the discomfort, knowing it would soon be forgotten once she was involved in her work.

She unhooked her two-way radio and pocket knife from her belt and tucked them into the big pockets on her trousers, then added some spare batteries for the radio to another pocket. In the kitchen she found a packet of health bars and put four and a small bottle of water into the pockets down near her knees. Finally the list, carefully sealed inside a waterproof plastic bag, completed her preparations. She had another hard hat from her days in Victoria, and with that on her head and her bright yellow rain jacket around her shoulders, she headed out to the veranda to wait for Harry.

She'd taken down the hanging baskets from their hooks beneath the veranda roof before she'd dressed for the wedding, but although she'd packed them under other plants in the garden, one look at the already stripped stems told her how damaged they were going to get.

'Plants are replaceable,' she reminded herself, leaning against the wall as all the veranda chairs were stacked inside, but now, as she waited, her mind turned to Harry. Had it been the sense of imminent danger that had prompted them to speak of things that had always been unsaid between them?

She had no doubt that her friendship with Harry had developed, in part, because she *hadn't* been on the staff at the hospital when Nikki had died. Harry was the kind of man who would have shunned the sympathy on offer from all those who knew him—the kind of man who'd have pulled away from friends to work his grief out on his own.

But everyone needed someone and Grace had filled the void, providing a friendship not linked to either of their pasts and not going beyond the bounds of good but casual acquaintances.

If anything, since her discovery that she loved Harry, she'd pulled further back from anything approaching intimacy, so they'd laughed and joked and shared coffee and discussed ideas connected with the bits of their lives that touched—work and the SES.

She was still mulling over the shift in their relationship— if one kiss and some personal conversation could be called a shift—when Harry pulled into the drive. Pleased to be diverted from thoughts that were going nowhere—she was putting Harry out of her life, remember—she dashed towards the car, ducking as a plastic chair went flying by.

'Some stupid person hasn't tied down his outside furniture,' Harry muttered as she did up her seat belt.

'It looked like one of the chairs from beside the pool at the doctors' house,' Grace said. 'I guess with the wedding and then the emergencies coming in from the bus accident, no one's had time to secure that furniture.'

Harry was already turning the car that way.

'We'll do it before we start on our evacuations,' he said. 'Imagine some poor person seeking help at the hospital and being knocked out by flying furniture before he even gets there.'

He drove up the circular drive in front of the old house that had originally been built as the Crocodile Creek hospital, and which now housed an assortment of hospital staff, parked at the bottom of the front steps and told Grace to stay where she was.

She took as much notice of this order as she had of his earlier orders to do this or that, and followed him through the downstairs area of the big building and out to where the garden furniture was indeed still around the pool.

'Just throw it in the pool,' Harry told her. 'It's safest in there and it'll get a good clean at the same time.'

He picked up a plastic table as he spoke and heaved it into the pool, following it with a sun lounge, while Grace took the smaller chairs and tossed them in.

'This is fun!' she said, grabbing the last chair and tossing it high so it made a satisfying splash.

'You find the weirdest things fun!' Harry grumbled at her, then he took her hand. 'Come on, let's have more fun—getting Mr and Mrs Aldrich to move out of their house.'

OK, so it was a protective gesture and meant nothing, especially in the context of getting over Harry, but holding hands with Harry felt so good Grace couldn't help but smile.

They ran back through the big recreation room under the doctors' house, out to the car. In the cove below the headland, the sea roared and tumbled, sending spray higher than the cliffs.

Willie was flexing his muscles.

CHAPTER SIX

'WHAT TIME'S HIGH TIDE?' Grace asked as they strapped themselves back into the vehicle.

'It was midnight, so it's going out now,' Harry said. 'I suppose we can be thankful for small mercies. The storm surge from the cyclone will be bad enough at low tide, but if it had coincided with a high tide, who knows how many places might have been washed away?'

They were driving past the pub as Harry spoke and Grace shivered, imagining a wave of water sweeping over the row of businesses beside it. The police station was directly behind the shops, although on a slight rise.

'Are you free to be doing evacuations?' Grace asked, thinking of the enormous task of co-ordination that must be going on, with the station at its hub.

'There's no room for me over there,' Harry replied, nodding towards the station. 'One of the benefits of getting a new building last year is that it's built to the stringent category five building regulations so all the staff who live in less well-constructed flats or houses have shifted their families in. It was part of our contingency plans and it works because it means I now have five trained staff there ready for emergencies and on standby for clean-up later, and also have enough people to cut down shifts on the radio to two-hourly.'

'Two-hourly shifts? Is that all they can take? Is it so tense?' Grace asked, wondering why she'd never thought about this aspect of an emergency. With the SES, all the members on duty had radios tuned to the police emergency frequency and although she and other team leaders radioed their members, they relied mainly on the police radio operator to co-ordinate their efforts.

'It's the radio operator who's under the most stress at the moment,' Harry explained. 'Taking emergency calls and relaying them to wherever they need to go, so being able to run two-hour shifts cuts down on tension and the possibility of mistakes. But having staff in the station also means I've got someone there whose sole task is to plot the cyclone's course, taking all the direction, speed and intensity readings from the Met and marking them on the map. He'll give me a call when Willie's an hour from crossing the coast and also get the radio operator to order any emergency crews off the streets. Once Willie's that close, anyone outside is in danger.'

Grace nodded her understanding. All her people had orders to return to their homes as soon as they'd evacuated the people on their lists. In times like this their families had to be their prime concern.

They were driving past the Grubbs' house and Grace nodded towards it.

'Good thing the hospital preparations included orders for all staff in older housing to take shelter there. The Grubbs' house always looks as if it will blow down in a strong wind or slide the rest of the way down the slope into the creek. Heaven knows what Willie will do to it.'

Harry looked towards the house where the hospital yardman lived with his wife, who was in charge of the housekeeping side of the hospital. The old place had been added onto so often it was starting to resemble a shed on an intensive chicken farm.

The oldest part, nearest the creek, stood on timber stumps so old they'd shrunk so the veranda on that side and the small room they'd enclosed on it were cantilevered out from the rest of the house—the stumps taking none of the weight.

'Charles has been trying to talk them into letting him build them a new house for years, but the Grubbs refuse, saying the place suits them as it is.'

'Or until it blows down,' Grace commented, then, as Harry slowed down at an even older house further along the street, she wondered how it would feel to be so attached to a dwelling you wouldn't want to change it—or leave it in a cyclone.

Was that what 'home' was all about?

Although her stepmother had always been kind, the concept of home had eluded Grace. Sometimes in her dreams she saw it as a whitewashed cottage set amid green fields, but that was wrong. She knew she'd lived in Belfast and had seen enough pictures of the city to know there was nary a field nor a cottage in sight.

'You're too tired to be doing this!'

Harry's cross exclamation brought her back to the present. He was frowning anxiously at her, and his hand was warming the skin on her forearm.

'Not tired, just thinking,' she told him, pressing her hand over his. 'Thinking about homes.'

Harry shook his head and got out of the car. Why would such a simple remark—thinking about homes—get under his skin?

Because he now knew Grace had never really had a home?

But should that make him want to wrap his arms around her and hold her tight against his body?

He couldn't blame physical attraction for this urge, because it wasn't part of the equation. Not this time...

He'd parked so the passenger door was away from the wind, making it easier for Grace to get out, although walking to the front door of the old weatherboard house was a struggle, so he kept an arm protectively around her shoulders.

Mrs Aldrich greeted them with a battery-powered lantern held at shoulder height, the light good enough to show a tear-stained face *and* the attitude of belligerence written across it.

'I've got this lantern and torches and water and biscuits in the bathroom and Karen from next door has taped my windows and I'm not going,' she said, and Harry heard Grace sigh as if she understood the older woman's feelings and didn't want to argue.

'You have to, Mrs Aldrich.' Harry used his firm policeman voice. 'Your house just isn't safe. We need to move you and Bill down to the civic centre.'

'Bill's dead.'

Harry's stomach clenched. Another look at Mrs Aldrich's face told him this was true.

Floored by this unexpected development, Harry could only stare at her. Fortunately Grace had more presence of mind.

'What happened?' she asked gently, stepping past Harry and putting her arm around the elderly woman, carefully guiding her further into the house.

'He just died,' Mrs Aldrich replied, her resolute voice abandoning her so the words quavered out. 'We knew it was close. I was sitting by him and he touched my hand like he was saying goodbye then that rattly breathing he'd had earlier just stopped.'

'Oh, Mrs Aldrich, I'm so sorry,' Grace said, completely ignoring the little hurry-up motions Harry was making with his hands. 'Have you had a cup of tea? Can I get you something? I should have a look at Bill, just to be sure. Do you mind?'

She hesitated, perhaps aware she was asking too many questions, then, as Harry wondered just how she'd handle this, she added another one.

'What if Harry makes you a cup of tea while you show me where Bill is?'

Harry wondered if she'd gone mad. OK, so Mrs Aldrich was in her nineties and she and Bill had been married for more than seventy years. Was Grace thinking they had to do this carefully if they didn't want another death on her hands?

'Strong, sweet tea,' she said to Harry, as she guided the older woman towards the rear of the house where the bedrooms were.

'Cyclone warnings are now hourly, Willie's due to hit us in two to three hours and instead of evacuating people I'm making tea,' Harry muttered to himself, but he'd known Bill and Daisy Aldrich all his life and his heart ached for Daisy and the sadness she must be feeling right now.

He made the tea, still muttering to himself, knowing in his gut that this wasn't the end of the Aldrich saga for the night.

'We've got to get her to the civic centre,' he whispered to Grace, who was sitting next to Daisy, beside the bed where Bill indeed lay dead.

'I heard that, Harry Blake,' Daisy countered. 'Seventy years Bill and I have shared this house, our kids were born here, the roof's blown off in other cyclones, but it's survived. So if you think I'm leaving Bill alone here tonight then you're very much mis-taken.'

For one wild moment Harry considered the possibility of taking a dead body to the safe haven of the civic centre, then he saw Grace shake her head and wondered if she'd read his thoughts.

Of course they couldn't. All their attention had to be on the living, but he knew he'd have a battle on his hands moving Daisy.

Grace was holding the cup to Daisy's lips, encouraging her to drink, while Harry stood helplessly beside her, anxious to keep moving, knowing there was so much still to do.

'Harry, would you get a thick bedcover from one of the other beds? I'll wrap it around Mrs Aldrich's shoulders so she's got some protection should a window go. And one for Bill as well.'

Glad to have something to do, Harry went through to another bedroom where both the single beds had thick coverlets.

He brought them back and watched as Grace placed one carefully over Bill, folding down the top of it so they could still see his face.

'If the window breaks or the roof goes, you can pull it up,' she said to Daisy, now wrapping the second bedcover around the frail old woman. 'Harry and I will try to get back—or one of us will—to sit with you. But if we don't, use the cover to protect yourself, and if things get really wild, get under the bed.'

Daisy smiled through the tears that seeped down her face.

'Bill always said he'd protect me, no matter what,' she said, then she touched Grace's cheek. 'You're a good girl. If that Harry had a scrap of sense he'd have snapped you up a long time ago.'

Grace bent and touched her lips to the lined cheek.

'You take care,' she said, then she led a bemused Harry out of the room.

'You're going to leave her there? Not even argue about it? We can't just give in like that?'

'Can't we?' Grace said softly. 'Think about it, Harry. How important is her life to her right now? I know in a month or so, when the worst pain of her grief has passed, she'll find things she wants to live for, but at the moment she has no fear of death—in fact, she'd probably welcome it. And look at it from her point of view—Bill's been her whole life, how could she possibly go off and leave him now?'

Harry began to reply but Grace had turned back towards the bedroom, fishing her mobile phone out of her pocket as she went.

'Here,' she said, offering it to Mrs Aldrich. 'The phone lines are all down but the cellphones will still work. This one is programmed to reach Harry's cellphone, the one he's carrying today. Just press the number 8 and it will ring through to Harry.'

'Won't you need the phone?' Harry demanded, although what he wanted to know was who had the number one to seven positions on Grace's cellphone.

He knew she didn't have a mother...

'I've got my radio,' she reminded him, 'and just about everyone at the civic centre will be clutching their mobiles so they can report on conditions to their relatives in far-flung places or sell their phone pictures to television stations. I think I'll manage without one.'

'Because you've no relatives in far-flung places?' Harry asked, disturbed that the question of family and Grace had never occurred to him before tonight's revelations.

'Because I'll be far too busy to be phoning anyone,' Grace replied. 'Come on, we've people to evacuate.'

They ran from the house to the car, and he struggled to open the door and let her in, but even if conversation had been possible he wouldn't have known what to say. In some vague way he sensed that Grace was right about leaving Daisy where she was, but for so long his practical self had ruled his emotional self that it took a little bit of adjusting to accept emotion might have a place even in emergency situations.

Fortunately the next four couples were more easily moved, and by the time they had the last of them settled in the civic centre, everyone had been checked off the evacuation list.

Harry looked around the crowded area. Babies cried, and small children, excited by the different location and the thrill of being awake in the early hours of the morning, ran around excitedly. Somewhere a dog barked, and a cockatoo let out a loud squawk of complaint, but most of the refugee pets were as well behaved as their human owners.

'At least the majority took note of what we said, about making sure they had animal carriers for their pets as part of their cyclone preparations.'

Grace was by his side and he nodded, acknowledging it had been a good idea. The circular dropped in the letterbox of every dwelling in town had not only been an initiative of the SES, but had been delivered by the volunteers.

'Where's Sport?' she asked, looking at a small kelpie cross who was protesting loudly about his accommodation.

'He's at my parents' place. I couldn't risk leaving him in the house when I knew I wouldn't be there.'

'Bet he's furious he's missing all the fuss,' Grace said, and

Harry smiled. He'd rescued the small kelpie pup from the local rubbish dump after a wild thunderstorm. Whether he'd been abandoned because of an injury to one leg, or the injury had happened during the storm, Harry didn't know. He'd paid to have the leg treated, and when that hadn't worked, the leg had been amputated. He'd intended giving the dog away, but the fiercely loyal animal had had other ideas, finding his way back to Harry's no matter where he'd been taken.

In the end, his sheer determination had persuaded Harry to keep him.

'I need to check on a few people,' Grace said, and moved into the small corridor between sleeping bags, mattresses and assorted padding brought along by the evacuees.

He watched her bend to speak to a heavily pregnant woman who should probably have been at the hospital rather than here, then, mindful that watching Grace was not his job right now, he walked through to the kitchen area where volunteers were making sandwiches and handing out tea or coffee to anyone who wanted it. He grabbed a cup of coffee and a sandwich, thinking Grace was probably in need of sustenance as well.

She was at the far end of the hall, talking to one of her SES crew, her arms waving in the air as she explained some detail. And although she was wearing plain cargo trousers and a T-shirt, all Harry could see was a curvy figure in two scraps of blue lace.

Muttering to himself once again, he took his coffee into one of the meeting rooms so he could concentrate on the messages coming through on his radio. Reports told him where power lines were down and where the emergency crews on duty were handling problems. The hour when the radio operator would order every-one into safe shelters, whether at their homes, at the police station or here at the civic centre, was fast approaching. Another report told him the hospital had been switched over to generator power, and even as that message came through the lights went out in the civic centre.

There was a momentary darkness, which caused the kids to scream with pretend fear, then the generators kicked in and the lights flickered back to life, but that instant of darkness had reminded Harry of the blackout earlier.

Had reminded him of kissing Grace...

'Boy, this food is good! It's the roast lamb from the wedding. Apparently, after we left, Mrs P. set the remaining guests to making sandwiches with the leftover food. Some was delivered to the hospital and the rest here.'

Grace was munching on a sandwich as she came up behind Harry. Everything had been OK between them—maybe a trifle strained but still OK—while they'd been caught up in rescuing Troy and getting off the mountain. Then, apart from a slight altercation over sleep, while they'd organised the evacuations. But now, in this lull before the storm—literally—she wasn't sure just where she stood with Harry.

Knew where she should stand—far, far away.

'We've got about ten of the less injured people from the bus here,' she said, taking another bite of sandwich and chewing it before getting back to the conversation. 'Apparently all the belongings we gathered up at the accident site were taken to Reception at the hospital. By now most of the stuff belonging to the hospitalised people will have been matched up to them, so I wondered if we could go over and collect the rest—it must belong to those who are here and I'm sure they'll all feel better if they have their own belongings with them.'

Harry shook his head, unable to believe he'd forgotten about the stuff he'd packed into the back of his vehicle.

'It's not at the hospital, it's here. I'll grab an able-bodied male and go get it from the car.'

'Get two able-bodied men and let them do it. Take a break,' Grace suggested, but Harry wasn't listening, already talking to one of the locals who then followed him out of the hall.

Grace followed him to the door, waiting until the two men

brought in the luggage and handbags, then she spread it out so people could identify their belongings. The bus passengers, recognising what was going on, moved through the crowded room, then one by one they swooped on personal possessions, every one of them clutching the piece of luggage to their chests, as if they'd found lost treasure.

'It's a security thing,' Grace murmured, thinking how she'd clutched Harry's dinner jacket—remembering she'd left it in a sodden heap on her living-room floor.

Slowly the pile diminished until all that remained was a new-looking backpack.

'I wonder if the shoe belongs to that one,' Harry said, and knelt beside it, opening the fastening at the top and spilling out the contents.

'Damn it to hell!' Grace heard him whisper, as he pushed small shorts and T-shirts into one pile and some women's clothing into another. 'There *is* another child!'

'That's my dog!'

Max knew he should be pleased he'd finally found Scruffy, but the kid from the bus was clutching the dog against his chest and looked as if he'd never let him go.

All eyes, the kid. Huge eyes Max could see even though it was as dark as dark could be.

The kid was crouched under a tree fern—stupid place to shelter 'cos the water came straight through the leaves of tree ferns.

'Come on,' he told the kid. 'We've got to find the road. Or get back to the bus so we can get out of the rain.'

The kid shook his head and must have squeezed Scruffy tighter because Scruffy gave a yelp.

'You can hold the dog,' Max offered, and watched while the kid considered this. Then he stood up and Max saw his feet. One foot—bare—the other in a sneaker, the bare one cut and scratched and probably bleeding, although it was too dark to see the red of blood.

Everything was black.

'Hang on,' he told the kid and he sat down and took off his sneakers, then his socks, then he pulled his sneakers back on over his bare feet. Hard 'cos they were wet.

'You have the socks,' he told the kid. 'Put both on your foot that's lost its shoe. I'd give you my shoe but it'd be too big. Go on, sit down and do it. I'll hold the dog.'

The kid sat and reluctantly gave up his hold on Scruffy, though when Max hugged his pup against his chest Scruffy gave a different yelp.

'He's hurt,' Max whispered, holding the dog more carefully now.

The kid nodded, but he was doing as he was told, pulling on one sock then the other over it.

The dog was shivering so Max tucked him inside his T-shirt, then he reached out and took the kid's hand.

He'd walked downhill from the bus, so it and the road must be uphill.

'Let's go, kid,' he said, hoping he sounded brave and sensible. Sensible was good, he knew, because Mum always kissed him when she said he'd been sensible.

And brave was good. All the knights he read about were brave.

He didn't feel brave. What he felt was wet and cold and scared...

CHAPTER SEVEN

GRACE WATCHED AS Harry reached for his cellphone and dialled a number, then shook his head in disgust and slammed the offending machine back into his pocket.

Whoever he was phoning must be out of range.

Now he pulled his radio out and began speaking into it, calling to someone, waiting for a reply, calling some-one to come in.

Urgently!

Harry put the radio away and began repacking the clothing into the backpack, folding small T-shirts with extraordinary care. Grace watched him work, but as he pulled the cord tight and did up the catch on the top, she could no longer ignore the anguish on his face.

She knelt beside him and took the capable hands, which had trembled as he'd folded clothes, into hers.

'Are there kids out there? Do you know that for sure?'

He nodded.

'Georgie's Max we know for sure, and now this.'

He pulled the little sneaker from his pocket, poking the tip of his finger in and out of the hole that made up the eye of the fish painted on it.

'Two kids.'

Despair broke both the words.

'We can go back,' Grace suggested, urgency heating her voice. 'Go and look for them.'

'I *can't* go, and logically nor can you. You're a team captain—this cyclone will pass and we'll both be flat out sorting the damage and running rescue missions.'

He took a deep breath, then eased his captured hand away from hers.

'Georgie's gone to look—she and Alistair. We'll just have to hope they're in time.'

In time—what a dreadful phrase.

But the second child?

'If there's a second child unaccounted for, why has no one mentioned it? Why has no one said my child's missing?'

One possible answer struck her with the force of a blow.

'The woman who died? Oh, Harry, what if it's her child?'

'That's what I've been thinking,' Harry said bleakly, 'although there's a woman at the hospital who's in an induced coma at the moment, so maybe the child belongs to her. And the woman who died had a boyfriend—surely he'd have mentioned a child.'

Grace tried to replay the rescue scene in her mind—a badly injured woman *had* been rescued early in the proceedings. Susie's sister, who'd acted as a bridesmaid at the wedding, had been looking after her.

'Let's hope it's her and that she lives and that Georgie finds both kids,' Grace said, although this seemed to be asking an awful lot.

Worry niggled at her mind—two children lost in the bush in a cyclone?

Worry was pointless, especially now with Willie so close. There were things she had to do. She looked around at the people settling down to sleep, at the two paramedics and four SES volunteers, not sleeping, watchful.

'Everything's under control here. If you wouldn't mind giving me a lift, I'll go back to Mrs Aldrich's place and sit out the blow with her.'

'Sit out the blow?' Harry echoed. 'It's obvious you've never been in a cyclone. The whole house could go, Grace.'

'So I can give her a hand to get under the bed. I had a look at that bed. It's an old-fashioned one, with solid timber posts on the corners and solid beams joining them. Safe as houses—safer, in fact, than some of the houses in this town.'

'And you talk about me taking risks?' Harry muttered, but as he, too, had been worried about Daisy Aldrich—in between worrying about two children—maybe it wasn't such a bad idea. Only...

'You stay here, I'll go and sit with her,' he said and knew it was a mistake the moment the words were out of his mouth.

'We've already been through the hero thing a couple of times tonight! But not this time, Harry. Mrs Aldrich is my responsibility—'

The ringing was barely audible in the general hubbub of the room. Harry pulled his cellphone out of his pocket and checked the screen.

'Your number,' he said to Grace as he lifted the little phone to his ear and said a tentative hello.

'Harry, Daisy Aldrich. Karen from next door is here and she's having her baby and it's early and she can't get hold of Georgie who's not at the hospital or at home so can Grace come?'

'We'll be right there,' Harry promised, closing his phone and motioning to Grace.

'You win,' he said. 'We need a nurse. Daisy's next-door neighbour is having a baby.'

'Karen? I saw her last week when she came for a check-up. She's not due for three or four weeks.'

'Tell the baby that,' Harry said, leading the way out of the hall.

Daisy was in her kitchen, boiling water on a small gas burner when Grace and Harry arrived.

'I don't know why people boil water,' she said, waving her hand towards the simmering liquid. 'No one ever did anything with boiling water when I was having my babies.'

A cry from the back of the house reminded them of why they were there.

'We dragged a mattress into the bathroom and she's lying on that. She'd never have got under the bed, the size she is.'

Grace was already hurrying in the direction of the cry. Another battery lantern was barely bright enough to light the room, but Grace could see the shadowy shape that was Karen, hunched up on the mattress which had been placed between the wall and an old-fashioned, claw-footed bath.

Fluid made dark smears across the mattress, but before Grace could check if it was water from the birth sac or blood, Karen cried out again, helplessly clutching the edge of the bath, her body contorting with pain.

'It hurts too much,' she said. 'Make it stop. Please, make it stop.'

Grace knelt beside her, sliding her hand around to rest on Karen's stomach, feeling the rigidity there.

'How long have you been having contractions?' she asked Karen as the stomach muscles relaxed.

'This morning,' the girl sobbed, 'but I thought they were those pretend ones with the silly name. The baby's not due for three weeks. And everyone was telling me first babies are always late so they had to be the pretend contractions.'

'Have you timed them at all?' Grace asked, trying to unlock Karen's death grip on the bath so she could lay the young woman down to examine her.

'No!' Karen roared, crunching over in pain again. 'You time them!'

She puffed and panted, occasionally throwing out combinations of swear words Grace had never heard before.

Grace pulled a towel off the towel rail, then looked around to see Harry and Mrs Aldrich peering in through the door.

'Could you find something soft to wrap the baby in? And some spare towels would be good. And scissors, if you have them,' she said, then looked at Harry.

'How long do we have before Willie arrives?'

'Three quarters of an hour, according to the latest alert. He's also been upgraded—definitely a category five now.'

He looked around at the walls and ceiling of the bathroom.

'This room's too big for safety—the load-bearing walls are too far apart—although the bath looks solid enough.'

But Grace's attention was back on Karen, who with a final shriek of pain had delivered a tiny baby boy.

He was blue, but as Grace cleared mucous from his mouth and nose, he gave a cry and soon the bluish skin turned a beautiful rosy pink.

'You little beauty,' Grace whispered to him, holding him gently in the towel.

Mrs Aldrich returned with the scissors, more towels and a soft, well-worn but spotlessly clean teatowel.

'That's the softest I've got,' she said, peering into the room then giving a cry of surprise when she saw the baby. 'It's the way of the world—one dies and another takes his place,' she said quietly, then she padded away, no doubt to sit beside her Bill.

'I'll call him William Harry,' Karen said, as Grace wrapped the baby in the teatowel and handed him to Karen, suggesting she hold him to her breast. But Karen didn't hear, her eyes feasting on the little mortal in her arms, her attention so focussed on his tiny form Grace had to blink away a tear. 'William after Bill, who was always kind to me, and Harry after Harry because he was here.'

Grace looked up at Harry who was pale and tense, shaking his head as if he didn't want a baby named after him. But even as Grace wondered about this reaction she became aware of the roaring noise outside the house and understood his lack of emotion. Another William—Willie—was nearly on them.

She turned her attention back to Karen, massaging her stomach to help her through the final stage of labour, then cutting and knotting the cord and cleaning both mother and child.

Harry returned as she tucked a towel around the pair of them. He was carrying one of the bedcovers he'd found earlier, a pillow and a couple of blankets.

'I'm going to put these in the bath, Karen, then I want you and the baby to get in there. We'll put the mattress over the top to keep you both safe from falling debris. You'll still be able to breathe and it's not heavy, so if you feel claustrophobic you can lift it up a bit.'

Karen and Grace both stared at him, Karen finding her voice first.

'In the bath?'

Harry, who was making a nest of the blankets and bedcover, nodded.

'It's an old cast-iron bath—far too heavy to move even in a cyclone. Its high sides will protect you both and support the mattress. I wouldn't do it but the house has already lost a bit of roof and the walls are moving.'

Karen stopped arguing, handing the baby to Harry to hold while she stood up and clambered into the bath. Grace helped her, leaning over to make sure she was comfortable. She turned to Harry to take the baby and the look of pain and despair on his face made her breath catch in her lungs.

'I'll give him to Karen,' Grace said gently, moving closer so she could take the little bundle. Harry's eyes lifted from the baby to settle on Grace's face, but she knew he wasn't seeing her—wasn't seeing anything in the present.

Had there been a baby? she wondered as he stepped forward and leant over, very gently settling the baby in his mother's arms.

Then he straightened up and strode out of the room, returning seconds later with a light blanket, which he tucked around the pair of them.

Karen smiled at him then tucked the baby against her breast, murmuring reassuringly to the little boy, although Grace knew the young woman must be terrified herself.

'Here,' Grace said, fishing in her pocket for the bottle of water and a couple of health bars. 'Something to eat and drink while Willie blows over.'

Karen smiled and took the offerings, setting them down on her stomach, but her attention was all on the baby at her breast.

With Grace's help Harry lifted the mattress onto the top of the bath, leaving a little space where Karen's head was so she could see out.

'Put your hand up and move the mattress so I know you can,' he said, and Karen moved the mattress first further back then up again so only the tiny space was visible.

'You OK?' Grace asked, sliding her fingers into the space and touching Karen's fingers.

'I think so,' the young woman whispered, her voice choked with fear.

'We'll just be next door, under Daisy's bed,' Harry told her, then he put his arm around Grace's shoulders and drew her out of the room.

'I hate leaving her like that. Surely we should all be together,' Grace said, looking back over her shoulder at the mattress-covered bath.

'Better not to be,' Harry said, and Grace shivered as she worked out the implications of that statement.

Daisy met them as they entered her bedroom, and handed Grace the cellphone.

'Give it to Karen. And this torch. Tell her about pressing 8 to talk to Harry. It might make her feel less lonely.'

Grace turned, but Harry stopped her, taking both the cellphone and the torch.

'You help Daisy down onto the floor. If she lies on the mat I can pull her under the bed if we need the extra protection. And turn off your radio. I'm turning mine off as well. There's nothing anyone can do out there, so we might as well save batteries.'

He walked away, leaving Grace to put a pillow on the mat, then help the frail old woman down onto the floor.

'Cover Bill so things don't fall on him,' she whispered to Grace, and Grace did as she asked, drawing the bedcover over the peaceful face of the man on the bed. Then she sat on the floor and held Mrs Aldrich's hand while outside the house the world went mad.

'We're going under the bed,' Harry announced, returning with the second mattress from the spare bedroom. 'I'm putting this on top as extra padding.'

He arranged the mattress so it rested from the bed to the floor, making a makeshift tent, then pulled the mat to slide Mrs Aldrich under the big bed.

'Your turn,' he said to Grace, who slid beneath the bed, leaving room for Harry between herself and the older woman.

Harry eased himself into the small space, wondering what on earth he was doing there when he could be in a nice safe police station or civic centre hall.

That it had to do with Grace he had no doubt, but he couldn't think about it right now. Right now he had to get these women—and the baby—through the cyclone.

He put his arm protectively around Daisy, but she shrugged him off.

'For shame, Harry Blake, and with Bill in the room. If you want to cuddle someone, cuddle Grace. She looks as if she could do with an arm around her, and you certainly need a bit of loving.'

Mrs Aldrich's voice was loud enough for Harry to hear above the roar of the approaching force, but would Grace have heard?

And if she had and he didn't put his arm around her, would she think—?

He had no idea what she'd think. Somehow this wild, erratic force of nature had blown the two of them into totally new territory.

Territory where he *did* need a bit of loving?

Surely not.

But just in case Grace had heard—or maybe just in case he did need loving—he turned so he could put his arm around Grace, and when she didn't object he drew her closer, tucking her body against his and once again feeling her curls feathering the skin beneath his chin.

'Cuddling me, Harry?' she said, her light, teasing voice defeating the noise outside because her lips were so close to his ear. 'Aren't you afraid? I mean, if a shuffling dance provoked the deadly physical attraction, what might a cyclone cuddle do?'

She was making fun of him, but still it hurt, and somehow, because this was Grace and maybe because Bill and Daisy had loved one another for seventy years or maybe even because within minutes they could all be dead, he started telling her.

'We'd known each other for ever, Nikki and I, our parents friends enough for me to call hers Aunt and Uncle. She left town to go to university in Townsville while I went to Brisbane for my training. Then, about three and a half years ago, her parents were killed in a car accident. She came home to see to everything, I helped her—well, my parents arranged everything for her, but I was there for comfort.'

Grace felt his arms tighten around her, and kept as still as she could. She wasn't sure if she really wanted to hear about him loving Nikki, but listening to Harry was definitely better than listening to the raging fury of the cyclone and wondering if any of them would survive.

And maybe he needed the catharsis...

'Comfort is physical, as you know, and suddenly we both felt the attraction that being close had stirred. Wild attraction, heightened most probably on Nikki's side by grief.'

He paused then added in an undertone, 'I didn't have that excuse.

'We thought it love, Grace, and married, caught in a whirl of physical delight that left no room for plans or practicality, then, as suddenly as it had come, it seemed to leave. Not the physical attraction—that was always there—but when we weren't in bed there was—I can only describe it as an emptiness. Nikki was still grieving for her parents and she also missed her job, while I spent more time than was necessary at mine.'

Grace turned in his arms so she could hold him. She told herself it was because the noise of the cyclone was as loud as an express train roaring through a tunnel, but really it was so she could rub her hands across his back, offering silent sympathy he might or might not want.

Her heart ached for him—for the pain she heard in his voice and in the silence that now lay between them. But she couldn't prompt him, knowing he had to get through this story his own way.

'We didn't talk about it—in fact, I didn't know if Nikki felt it—but I was gutted, Grace, to think I'd mucked up so badly. Then I thought about it—really thought about it—and decided it would all be OK—that we could work it out. We'd always loved each other as friends, so surely that would remain as a solid foundation, and we had compatibility, so that had to count in building a future...'

He paused again and she felt his chest fill with air then empty on a sigh. She tightened her arms around him, offering the only comfort available.

'Eventually she told me she'd been offered a new television job in Brisbane. She'd been with the same station in Townsville but this was a promotion. Would I transfer to the city to be with her?'

Somewhere outside a tortured screeching noise suggested a roof was being torn apart. Mrs Aldrich's roof?

Grace snuggled closer, fear moving her this time.

'Go on,' she prompted, knowing Harry's story was probably the only thing holding at bay the terror that was coiled within her.

'I said I would, wanting so much to make it work, although all my life all I'd ever wanted was to be a policeman here where

I belonged. We made arrangements, looked at housing on the internet, then she went to Townsville to see her old boss.'

The story stopped, and with it the noise.

'It's over?' Grace whispered, then heard how loud her voice sounded in the silence and realised she hadn't whispered at all.

'It's the eye passing over,' Harry told her as he slid out from under the bed and cautiously lifted the mattress aside. 'You two stay right where you are. I'll check on Karen and the baby and be straight back.'

Grace reached out to stop him, but it was too late, so she had to wait, fearful for his safety, having heard enough of cyclones to know that the eye was only the calm before the storm returned, only this time the wind would blow the other way.

'Both sound asleep, would you believe,' Harry reported as the howling, roaring noise drew close again. 'I guess having a baby and being born are both tiring experiences.'

He slid beneath the bed, lying between the two women, reporting to Mrs Aldrich that her kitchen roof had gone and a part of the bathroom wall had been damaged, but generally things looked OK. Radio calls to the station had assured him everything was OK there and at the civic centre.

'It's the second blow, once everything is loosened, that knocks houses about,' Mrs Aldrich told him, as they all squiggled around to relieve cramped muscles and tired bones. 'Will you go on talking, Harry?' she added. 'I can't hear the words but I like to hear your voice—it's very soothing and it makes the cyclone noise easier to bear.'

Horrified that Daisy had even heard his voice, Harry hesitated, but the cyclone was roaring again, and Grace had snuggled close, so it was easy to finish the tale he'd carried inside him for so long, locked away but probably festering because it hadn't ever been told.

He tucked Grace closer, held her tightly, and blurted out the words.

'She went to Townsville to have an abortion.'

There, it was said.

For the first time he'd actually told someone about the almost routine operation that had led to the discovery of Nikki's inoperable cancer.

He felt Grace stiffen, then her hand crept up to touch his face, cupping his cheek in her palm.

'No wonder seeing that new baby hurt you,' she whispered, her voice choked with tears.

He shook his head although he knew neither woman would see the gesture, frustrated at this situation. What was he thinking, lying under a bed—a bed with a dead body in it—in a category five cyclone, playing out his past like a series of episodes in a soap opera?

Fortunately—for his sanity—at that moment the roar grew louder and above the wild fury of the wind they heard the scream of metal sheets being torn from their anchors, nails screeching in protest as the rest of Daisy's roof peeled away.

'The weight of rain could bring the ceiling down so we stay here until we know the wind has eased,' Harry warned the two women, reaching out and drawing both of them closer, knowing they all needed human contact at the moment. 'Now Willie's crossed the coast, he'll lose his power.'

But what had that power done as it passed over the town? What havoc had it caused?

Anxiety tightened all the sinews in his body—anxiety for all the townsfolk but most of all for two small children out there on the mountain.

Had Georgie and Alistair reached them in time?

Were all four safe?

Max watched the light creep into the blackness of the hole in which they huddled, turning the dark shadows that had frightened him in the night into harmless posts and odds and ends of timber.

The kid was sleeping, curled up in a puddle of muddy-looking water, Scruffy in his arms. The kid had needed Scruffy, not because he'd said anything but because the way his face had looked when Max had heard Georgie calling to them and he'd answered her.

Instead of being happy they'd been found, the kid had started crying. Not bawling loudly, like CJ sometimes did when he was hurt, but silent crying, the light from the torch Mum was shining on them picking out the tears running down his face.

Max had thought at first he was crying because Mum had said she couldn't get them out straight away because it was too dangerous and that they'd have to wait until the cyclone stopped blowing trees over. But the kid had kept crying even after Mum had thrown down her leather jacket and some chocolate bars, and Max had figured out he was crying because his Mum wasn't there.

So Max gave him Scruffy to hold because earlier, when Max had had a little cry because Mum wasn't there, holding Scruffy had made him feel really, really brave.

Max pushed the leather jacket over the sleeping kid and waited for more light to come.

CHAPTER EIGHT

IT WAS ANOTHER hour before the noise abated sufficiently for Harry to slide out from under the bed. The roof had indeed gone and the ceiling had collapsed in the far corner of the room, pouring water onto the floor, but thankfully the rest of the room was, for the moment, dry.

Grace joined him, staring about her at the devastation, then heading for the door.

'Don't go,' he said, catching her hand. 'You stay here with Daisy while I check out what's solid and what isn't.'

She turned, anxious eyes scanning his face in the murky dawn light.

'Be careful,' she said, touching her hand to his cheek, so many things unspoken in the gesture that Harry felt a hitch in his breathing.

The house was a mess. One of the bathroom walls had collapsed across the bath, so Harry had to toss boards and beams aside to get to the mattress-covered bath. Fortunately the ceiling had held so the room was relatively dry. He could hear Karen and the baby both crying, Karen hysterical when he lifted the mattress.

'Come on, I'll help you out. You can shelter in the bedroom with Daisy until it's safe enough to drive you to the hospital.'

'With Daisy and dead Bill? I can't do that. I can't take my baby into the room with a dead person.'

Harry sighed but he kind of understood. There'd been ghosts beneath that bed with him.

'All right, but I'll have to put the mattress back on top of you.'

'That's OK,' Karen said, stifling her sobs and settling back down in her nest of blankets. 'Now it's getting lighter and I know you're not all dead and that noise has stopped, it's not nearly as scary.'

He replaced the mattress—if the ceiling did come down he didn't want wet plasterboard smothering the pair of them—then did a recce through the rest of the house. To his surprise, the dining room, a square room to one side of the kitchen, was apparently unscathed, and from the kitchen he could see that the roof in that area remained intact.

Once they had tarpaulins over the rest of it, Daisy might be able to move back into her home as soon as services like electricity, sewerage and water were restored, although that could be weeks away.

Sure his charges were safe, he ducked into the dining room, sat down on a chair and pulled out his cellphone. Time to check on the damage in the rest of the town.

Unbelievable damage from all accounts, the policeman on duty at the station told him, but no reports of casualties. Harry breathed a sigh of relief.

'Just let me sort out a few problems here,' he said, 'and then I'll do a run through town to see what's what. Expect me back at base in about an hour. In the meantime I'll be on air on the radio or you can get me on the cellphone.'

He rang the hospital. No word from Georgie but they'd despatch an ambulance to pick up Karen, the baby and Daisy Aldrich. They'd also contact the funeral home to send a car for Bill.

Grace was standing in the doorway as he ended the call.

'*Did* she have the abortion because of her career?' she asked, and the question was so unexpected he answered without thinking.

Answered honestly.

'No,' he said bleakly, remembering the terrible day he'd stared in disbelief at Nikki while she'd told him this—and then, disbelief turning to denial, added that she was dying of cancer. 'At least, she said not, but it might have had something to do with it. She said she had it because we didn't love each other. She said she knew that almost as soon as we were married— knew it was just lust between us, lust and her grief, and that I was there. She said she didn't want to bring a baby into that situation because without love we'd probably split up.'

Grace came closer and put her arms around him, holding him tightly.

'Then she told me about the cancer—that when she had the operation they found inoperable cancer.'

'She was dying of cancer?'

Harry nodded.

'Which made my anger at her—my fury that she'd gone ahead and aborted my child without discussing it with me— totally absurd. The baby wouldn't have lived anyway, but that fact couldn't penetrate the anger. I said things then that should never have been said—hard, hot, angry things, and through all that followed—her time at home and then in hospital—that was the guilt I had to carry. To have reacted with anger towards Nikki who'd been my friend for ever, to have hurt her at any time, let alone when she was dying...'

His shoulders hunched and he bent his head as if the weight of the emotional baggage he'd carried since that time still bur- dened his body.

'Physical attraction, Grace, do you wonder I'm suspicious of it?'

'But anger is a natural reaction to bad news,' Grace whis- pered to him. 'Your anger might have found an outlet in yell- ing about the abortion but it would have been far deeper than that—it would have been about the death sentence Nikki, your friend and lover, had just received.' She held him more tightly. 'It was natural, not cruel or unfair, Harry, and I'm sure Nikki would have understood that.'

'Would she?' he whispered hoarsely, the headshake accompanying the words telling Grace he didn't believe her.

The wailing cry of a siren told them the ambulance was close by. Grace let him go and headed for the door, wanting to help Karen and the baby out of the bath.

She heard the vehicle pull up, the sound of doors opening, the wheels on a stretcher dropping down.

'So now you know why he feels the way he does,' she muttered helplessly to herself, 'but what if it isn't just physical attraction?'

She understood so much more now—understood it was guilt and anger at himself that prompted not only Harry's risk-taking but also the emotional armour he'd drawn around himself.

Grace mulled it over as she led the paramedics first into the bathroom to collect Karen and baby William, then, once they were safely loaded, she walked with Daisy to the ambulance.

'Yes, I'll stay with Bill until the people from the funeral home arrive,' she promised Daisy, and was surprised at Daisy's protest.

'You'll do no such thing—you stay with Harry. Cyclone Willie shook a lot of things loose in that boy's heart. He's hurting and he needs someone with him.'

'As if Harry would ever admit to needing someone,' Grace said, but fortunately the funeral car arrived at that moment so she didn't have to make a choice.

Harry had returned to the dry refuge of the dining room while she'd been seeing the two vehicles depart. He looked grey with fatigue—or was it more than that? He looked...

Despairing?

'Georgie? You've heard from Georgie?'

He shook his head, then muttered, 'I'm thinking no news is

good news out there. I told Alistair we'd left the vehicle beyond the fallen tree—they could have sheltered in that.'

But this not good but not precisely bad news did nothing to ease the knots of worry in his features.

'What's wrong?' Grace asked, walking towards him and reaching out to take his hands. Watching his face carefully, ready to read a too-easy lie.

But he didn't lie, saying only, 'It's Sport,' in a tone of such flat despair Grace thought her heart would break.

'Dead?' she whispered, then remembered where the dog had been. 'Your parents? They're OK?'

'Sport's not dead but gone. My parents are fine. Very little damage to the house, although the sheds have been destroyed and the sugar crop's flattened. But Sport's disappeared. Mum said he grew more and more agitated as Willie passed over, then, when Dad opened the door to look at the damage during the calm of the eye, Sport took off, last seen heading back towards the town.'

Grace pictured Harry's parents' place, not far from the sugar mill on the outskirts of town.

She could imagine the dog, hip-hopping his way through the fury of the cyclone.

Sport, a ragged, crippled mutt that had somehow wormed his way through the emotional barriers Harry had built around himself.

Wormed his way into Harry's heart.

She wrapped her arms around him and held him tightly.

'I love you, Harry,' she said, although it was the last thing she'd meant to say.

Bloody dog!

She was resting her head against Harry's chest so couldn't see his reaction, although she felt his chest move with a sharp intake of air.

'I know you don't want to hear that,' she added, anxious to get it all smoothed over and things back to normal between them again. 'But we've been through so much—touched by death then welcoming new life, our physical world destroyed around us—I had to say it, and it's OK because I don't expect you to love me back. I've got over love before and I'll get over this, but it needed to be said.'

One of his arms tightened around her and he used his free hand to tilt her chin, so in the rain-dimmed morning light she saw his face.

Saw compassion, which she hated, but something else.

Surprise?

Natural enough, but was it surprise?

Before she could make another guess, Harry bent his head and kissed her, his lips crushing hers with hot, hard insistence. She melted into the embrace and returned the kiss, letting her lips tell him, over and over again, just how she felt.

One corner of her mind was aware of the futility of it all, but this was Harry and right now he needed whatever physical comfort she could give him.

And *she* needed something that at least felt like love...

Perhaps a minute passed, perhaps an hour, although, looking at her watch as she pushed out of Harry's arms, Grace knew it hadn't been an hour.

Two, three minutes maybe—a short time out from all the chaos that lay both behind and ahead of them.

And if her heart cringed with shame that she'd told Harry how she felt—a confession prompted by pity that he'd lost his dog, for heaven's sake—then she was good enough at pretence by now to carry on as if the words had not been spoken.

Which, she knew, was what Harry would do...

'We've got to go. Sport will be looking for you,' she said, and Harry nodded.

'Damn stupid dog!'

'We'll look at your place first,' Grace said.

Harry turned towards her, frowning now.

Grace loved him?

'We can't go out looking for a dog,' he growled. 'I need to see the damage, talk to people, get arrangements going.'

Talk about coming out of left field! Grace, his friend, suddenly declaring love for him?

'You need to drive through town to see the damage,' this friend he suddenly didn't know reminded him, then she repeated what she'd said earlier. 'We'll go past your place first.'

And now carrying on as if she hadn't just dropped a bombshell on him.

As if love had never been mentioned.

He had to put it right out of his mind. The town and its people needed him—and needed him to have a fully functioning brain, not some twitchy mess of grey matter puzzling over love and Grace.

Grace first—he'd deal with Grace the friend and that way might not keep thinking about the Grace he'd kissed.

Twice...

'What's this *we*? I'll drop you home, that's if your cottage is still standing. Or at the hospital. You need to sleep.'

'No, Harry, we'll do a drive around town then you can drop me at SES Headquarters so I can start sorting out what's needed and who we've got to help.'

Unable to think of a single argument against this—well, not one that she would listen to—he led the way out to where he'd left the police vehicle, tucked in under the Aldrichs' high-set house. It seemed to have survived the onslaught with only minor damage.

Sadness filled her heart as Grace snapped her seat belt into place. She sent a sidelong glance at the object of her thoughts, who was talking seriously to someone on his cellphone. Now those fatal words had been said, they could never be unsaid, so things could never really be the same between them again.

That was probably just as well, because although she'd spoken lightly about getting over love, she knew this was going to take a huge effort, and not seeing much of Harry would certainly help.

Although, comparing what she'd felt for James with what she felt for Harry, maybe he was right about physical attraction giving an illusion of love.

Certainly the love she'd felt for James had never hurt like this...

It was at this stage of her cogitations that she became aware of the world around her—or what was left of it.

'I don't believe it,' she whispered, trying desperately to make some sense of the devastation that lay around them. Harry was driving very slowly and carefully, picking a path along a road strewn with corrugated iron, fibro sheeting, furniture and bedding, not to mention trees, branches and telegraph poles, the latter flung about as if they'd weighed no more than matches.

The rain poured down with unrelenting insistence, as if Nature hadn't yet done enough to bring the town of Crocodile Creek and its inhabitants to their knees.

'We'll need the army. The mayor phoned earlier. He's already asked the premier for help,' Harry said as he pulled into his driveway.

'But today?' Grace asked, staring helplessly around. 'What can we do today? Where do we start? How can we help people?'

'Food and water. I'll check Sport's not here, then drive around town. We'll stop at the civic centre first, although I've had a report that everyone's OK there. We're broadcasting messages asking anyone who needs help to get out of their house to phone the dedicated line at the police station—the number we gave out at the end of all the cyclone warnings.'

'Four, zero, six, six, eight, eight, nine, nine,' Grace repeated, remembering the trouble Harry had had getting a number so easy to remember.

The radio was chattering at them. All downed power poles and torn lines would have to be removed before the authorities would consider turning power back on. No reports of casualties

so far, apart from those lost in the bus crash. Banana plantations and cane fields had been flattened. The farmers were in
for a grim year, but Willie, his violence spent, had continued
moving westward and was now dumping much-needed rain on
the cattle country beyond the mountains.

'So Willie moves on,' Grace whispered as she heard this report. 'But how do people here move on? How can anyone move
on from something like this?'

Harry glanced towards her, and she knew he was thinking
of her stupid declaration.

Well, so what if he was? Like Willie, she was moving on.

Moving on…

CHAPTER NINE

THEY STOPPED AT the house just long enough for Harry to satisfy himself Sport wasn't there. Neither was his dirt bike, which meant Georgie and Alistair were still out in the bush.

They were both sensible people, they had his vehicle out there to shelter in—or the bus—they'd be OK.

But had they found the kids?

Worry knotted inside him and he sent a silent prayer heavenward, a plea that they and the two children were all right. Then he looked around at the havoc and wondered if heaven had given up answering prayers, because plenty of people had prayed the town would be spared a cyclone.

'Do you think the old bridge will hold?' Grace asked as they approached the bridge across the creek that separated the hospital part of the town from the main commercial and residential areas.

'The council engineers looked at it when it was forecast Willie might head this way and declared it would probably outlast the new bridge across the river, but the problem is, because it's low and water is already lapping at the underside, all the debris coming down the creek will dam up behind it, causing pressure that could eventually push it off its pylons.'

'Debris piling up is also causing flooding,' Grace said, pointing to where the creek had already broken its banks and was swirling beneath and around houses on the hospital side.

'Which will get worse,' Harry agreed, concern and gloom darkening his voice.

They were driving towards the civic centre now, Grace looking out for Sport, although the streets were still largely deserted.

Except for teenagers, paddling through floodwater on their surf-skis here and there, revelling in the aftermath of the disaster.

'I'll be in meetings for the rest of the morning,' Harry said, turning towards Grace and reaching out to run a finger down her cheek. 'You do what you have to do then get someone to run you home, OK? You need to sleep.'

'And you don't, Harry?' she teased, discomfited by the tenderness of his touch—by his concern.

'I can't just yet,' he reminded her, then he leant across the centre console and kissed her on the lips, murmuring, 'I'm sorry, Grace,' and breaking her heart one last time because the apology had nothing to do with not sleeping.

One of her fellow SES volunteers drove her home to check the cottage was all right. She'd lost a window and the living room was awash with water, her garden was wrecked, but apart from that she'd got off lightly. They drove on to SES Headquarters, passing people wandering through the wreckage of countless homes, oblivious of the rain still pelting down, looking dazed as they picked an object from the rubble, gazed at it for a moment then dropped it back.

Some were already stacking rubbish in a pile, hurling boards that had once made up the walls of their houses into a heap on the footpath. It would take forever to clear some of the lots, but these people were at least doing something. They were looking to bring some order back into their lives.

Once at Headquarters, she set up a first-aid station. Volunteers would be injured in the clean-up and would also know to bring anyone with minor injuries to the building.

What she hadn't expected was a snakebite.

'Bloody snake decided it wanted to share our bathroom with us. I had the kids in there,' the ashen-faced man told her. 'I picked it up to throw it out, and the damn thing bit me on the arm.'

He showed the wound, which Grace bandaged with pressure bandages, down towards the man's fingers then back up to his armpit.

But it was really too late for bandages. The wound had been oozing blood, and snake venom stopped blood clotting properly.

'Did you drive here?' she asked, and the man nodded, his breathing thickening as they stood there.

'Good. We'll take your car.'

She called two of the volunteers who'd come in looking for orders to carry the man out to the car.

'The less effort you make, the less chance of poison spreading.'

'It didn't look like a brown or taipan,' the man said, but Grace had already taken the car keys from his hand and was hurrying towards the door. Even so-called experts couldn't always identify snakes by their looks.

The volunteers settled her patient into the car, and she took off, making her way as fast as she could through the hazardous streets. At the hospital she drove straight into the emergency entrance, leaping out of the car and calling for a stretcher.

'Bringing your own patients, Grace?' someone called to her as she walked beside the stretcher.

'Snakebite,' she snapped, pushing the stretcher in the direction of a trauma room. 'We need a VDK.'

Inside the trauma room she started with the basics, knowing a doctor would get there when he or she could. She slipped an oxygen mask over her patient's head, opened his shirt and set the pads for electrocardiogram monitoring, and fitted an oxygen saturation monitor to one finger.

IV access next—they'd need blood for a full blood count and for a coag profile, urea, creatinine and electrolytes, creatine kinase and blood grouping and cross-matching. Urine, too—the venom detection kit worked on urine.

She talked to the man, Peter Wellings, as she worked, hoping a doctor would arrive before she got to the catheterisation stage.

A doctor did arrive, Cal Jamieson, looking as grey and tired as Grace was feeling.

She explained the situation as briefly as she could, then was surprised when Cal picked up a scalpel and turned to her.

'Where exactly was the bite?'

Grace pointed to the spot on the bandaged arm.

'And it was definitely bleeding freely?'

She nodded.

'OK, we can take a swab from there for venom detection, rather than wait for a urine sample. I'll cut a small window in the bandages, and in the meantime let's get some adrenaline for him in case there's a reaction to the antivenin—0.25 milligrams please, Grace. And get some antivenins ready—the polyvalent in case we can't identify the snake, and some brown, tiger and taipan, which are the most likely up here.'

Cal was working swiftly, cutting through the bandages, swabbing, talking to Peter as well as telling Grace what he required next. He took the swab and left the room, returning minutes later to go through the antivenins Grace had set out on a trolley.

'Tiger,' he said briefly, more to Grace than to Peter, who looked as if he no longer cared what kind of snake had bitten him. 'I'm going in strong because of the delay. The Commonwealth Serum Laboratories recommend one ampoule but we're going two. I've actually given three to someone who had multiple wounds. But he'll need careful monitoring—straight to the ICU once I've got the antivenin going in his drip.'

He glanced towards Grace as he worked.

'You've obviously been outside. How bad is it?'

Grace thought of the devastation she'd seen and shook her head.

'I can't describe it,' she said. 'I can't even take in what I've seen. All the photos of floods and hurricanes and even bombsites you've ever seen mixed into one. I don't know how people will begin to recover. And the rain hasn't let up one bit. That's making things worse.'

Cal nodded.

'We'll see plenty of post-traumatic stress,' he said. 'Hopefully we'll be able to get the staff we need to handle it—it's such a specialist area.'

He was adjusting the flow of the saline and antivenin mix, ten times the amount of saline to antivenin, and calibrating the flow so Peter would receive the mixture over thirty minutes.

Grace wrote up the notes, and the latest observations, wanting everything to be in order as Peter was transferred.

'He'll need to be on prednisolone for five days after it to prevent serum sickness,' Cal said, adding his notes. 'And watched for paralysis, which with tigers starts with muscles and tendons in the head.'

He was silent for a minute then added, 'And renal failure.'

Grace knew he was talking to himself, adding reminders as he would be the person caring for Peter in the ICU. Mistakes happened and were more likely when people were exhausted by extra shifts, and only by constant checking and rechecking would they be avoided.

'You staying?' he asked Grace.

'Am I needed?'

He shook his head.

'I think we've got things pretty well under control. The worst of the accident victims, a young woman called Janey, is coming out of her induced coma, and everyone else is stable so, no, if you're not on duty, buzz off home. You look as if you could do with about three days' sleep.'

'Couldn't we all?' Grace said, but she was grateful for Cal's dismissal. She could walk home and look for Sport on the way. Later she'd return to SES Headquarters for another shift, but she'd be a far more effective participant in the clean-up operation if she slept first.

She tapped on Jill's office door before she left, wanting to be one hundred per cent sure she wasn't needed.

'Go home and sleep,' Jill ordered in answer to Grace's query. 'You look as if you need about a week to catch up. Go!'

She waved her hands in a shooing motion.

'We've all been able to grab a few hours—mainly thanks to all the extra staff available because of the weddings. Joe's been marvellous, and even Christina has put in a couple of shifts on the monitors in ICU. They're both safe and sleeping at my place at the moment, in case you were worrying about them.'

Grace shook her head in amazement that she hadn't given her friends a thought for the last few hours, although she *had* known they were at the hospital and so had assumed they'd be safe.

'Some friend I am,' she muttered to herself as she left Jill's office, then her weary brain remembered Georgie and the children. She poked her head back around the door.

'Georgie?'

Jill frowned in reply.

'We think she's OK. A truckie out west picked up a message that would have been sent about the time the eye was passing over. Something about finding two children, but the signal kept breaking up so he didn't catch it all.'

Jill looked worried but Grace realised there was little they could do until they heard more.

The wind had eased off, but not the rain, so she took an

umbrella from one of the stands at the entrance to Reception. She'd return it when she came back on duty, although so many umbrellas were left at the hospital no one would ever notice one was missing.

The scene outside hadn't improved. The Agnes Wetherby Memorial Garden between the hospital and the doctors' house had been flattened, but the old house stood, apparently having come through the violent cyclone unscathed. Grace didn't pause to check it thoroughly—her own home was calling to her.

But as she passed the big house on the headland, she looked down into the cove, staring stupidly at the waves crashing on the shore. It was low tide, there should be beach, but, no, the storm surge had pushed the water right up to the park that ran along the foreshore so the beautifully ugly breadfruit trees and the delicate casuarinas that grew there now stood in water.

Every shop in the small shopping mall had lost its roof, while the Black Cockatoo looked as if it had lost most of its upper storey, although, from the sounds of revelry within, it was still open for business.

Grace turned down a side street, wanting to walk closer to the police station and Harry's house, hoping she'd see Sport.

Had the dog sensed Harry was in danger that it had taken off?

It seemed possible—

The scream was so loud and so fear-filled all thoughts of Harry and his dog fled. Grace turned in the direction it had come from and began to run, though to where she had no idea, until she turned a corner and saw the floodwaters. Filthy brown water swirling angrily along the street, washing under high-set homes and straight through those set lower.

Treetrunks, furniture, books and toys all rode the water, and further out something that looked like a garden shed sailed on the waters.

Another scream and this time Grace could pinpoint it. The Grubbs' house, Dora standing on her front veranda, water all around her, lapping at her feet, but seemingly safe, although she screamed and pointed and screamed again.

Grace pushed her way through shallow water towards the house, feeling how stupid it was to be carrying an umbrella with floodwaters up to her waist.

'No, no!' Dora cried, waving her arms when she saw Grace approaching. 'It's not me, it's the kids,' she yelled, pointing out into the maelstrom, towards the garden shed. 'The pantry broke off the house. I had the kids in there because it was safe and, look.'

'What kids?' Grace yelled, wondering if the cyclone had affected Dora's rationality. From what Grace had learned, Dora's 'kids' were in their thirties and living far from Crocodile Creek.

'CJ and Lily. I was minding them then Molly had the pups and the kids wanted to be there, and they're all in that room.'

Peering through the falling rain, Grace could almost imagine white, scared faces in the doorway of what she'd taken to be a shed.

'It will stop at the bridge,' she said to Dora. 'Have you got a cellphone?'

Dora shook her head.

'No matter, I've got a radio. Hopefully it's waterproof. I'll swim out to the kids and radio from there, but in the meantime, if anyone comes by, tell them to get onto the police and let them know to meet us at the bridge.'

Meet us at the bridge? she thought as she waded deeper and deeper into the murky water. As if they were going for a pleasure jaunt on the river.

Tourists went out on the river, but that was to look for and photograph crocodiles.

This was the creek, not the river, she reminded herself, but she still felt fear shiver up her spine.

'No,' she said firmly. 'Crocodiles have enough sense to stay out of flooded rivers *and* creeks.'

She bent into the filthy water to pull off her boots, then began to swim, setting her eyes on the floating bit of house, praying it would stay afloat at least until she got there.

The water fought her, pushing her one way and then another, making her task seem almost impossible. But then she looked up and saw the children. Cal's son, CJ, and Lily, Charles's ward, clinging to each other in the doorway of the floating room. Then CJ left the safety of the room, venturing out onto what must have been a bit more veranda, bending over as if to reach into the water.

'Stay back,' she yelled at him. 'Get back inside.'

He looked up as if surprised to see her, then pointed down to the water beside him.

'It's Sport!' he called, and Grace sighed as she splashed towards them. Now she had a dog to rescue as well.

'I'll get him,' she called to CJ, then she put her head down and ploughed through the last twenty metres separating her from the children.

Sport was struggling to get his one front foot onto the decking, and Grace grabbed him and boosted him up, then, fearful that her weight might unbalance the makeshift boat and bring them all into the water, she called to the kids to stay back as far as they could and eased her body up until she could sit on the wooden boards. Then, with caution, she got on to her hands and knees so she could crawl towards them.

She looked around, realising the pantry must once have been part of the veranda because a bit of veranda was still attached, working like an outrigger to keep the structure afloat.

For how long?

With legs and arms trembling either from the swim or fear, she hesitated, breathing deeply, trying to work out what might lie ahead.

She guessed they were maybe three hundred yards from the

bridge, and she was reasonably sure the bridge would stop them, but whether it would also sink them was the question.

Kids first.

She crawled forward, wondering where Sport had gone, then entered the small room, where preserves and cereal and sauce bottles were jumbled in with two small children, two dogs, and too many newborn puppies for Grace to count.

'It's like being on a boat, isn't it, Grace?' CJ said as Grace knelt and wrapped her arms around the children.

'It is indeed,' she said, realising he'd been boosting Lily's confidence with talk of boats and adventure. CJ had never lacked imagination. 'And soon it's going to dock down at the bridge and we can all get off. I'm going to radio for someone to meet us there, OK?'

She detached the children, patted the wet Sport and the only slightly drier Molly—was Sport the father of this brood that he'd come through a cyclone to be with their mother? Did dog love work that way? Like human love?—and walked outside to radio SES Headquarters and explain the situation.

'Dora Grubb's been in touch,' Paul told her, 'and we've notified the police to be ready at the bridge. Have you any idea how you're going to get them off?'

'If all goes well and we don't sink, I'll pass the two kids over to rescuers then the pups and then the dogs.'

'Dogs?' Paul echoed weakly. 'Dora mentioned her dog Molly and some pups, but dogs?'

'Harry's Sport has joined the party,' Grace told him. 'Though what a policeman is doing with an un-neutered dog I'd like to know.'

'I guess Harry thought Sport had already lost a leg so didn't deserve to lose anything else,' Paul suggested.

Grace huffed, 'Men,' and stopped transmission.

Time to see to the kids and try to work out how to keep them all alive if their fragile craft sank.

* * *

Harry was in a meeting with local councillors, electricity officials and city engineers when he heard something different over the radio he had chattering quietly on the table beside him.

He'd been paying little attention to it, but had known he had to keep it on, half listening for any situation where he might be needed. Half listening for a report that Georgie and Alistair had returned with two kids.

But nothing so far.

Flood reports had begun to come in, but nothing serious as yet, until he heard a combination of words—flood, house, bridge, kids, and nurse from the hospital with them.

Instinct told him it was Grace and he turned the volume up a little, then, when he realised the transmission had finished, he excused himself to walk to a corner of the room and use his phone to call the station.

'No worries, Harry,' the constable who answered said. 'We've got it all under control. A bit of the Grubbs' house came adrift with a couple of kids inside, but Grace swam out to the kids and she's radioed in and reckons the room will stop when it hits the bridge. We'll have people there—'

'I'm on my way,' Harry said, anger and concern churning inside him. Grace accused him of taking risks and here she was, swimming through floodwaters filled with debris, snakes and crocodiles.

Stupid, stupid, stupid woman!

'Small crisis,' he said to the people gathered in the room as he strode out the door. Contingency plans could wait, or could be sorted without him—he needed to be on that bridge.

Which, please God, would hold.

How detailed had the engineer's inspection been? How minutely had he checked the structure?

He drove towards the bridge, passing more and more people on the rain-drenched streets, all with the bewildered expressions of disaster survivors. Rebuilding houses was one thing—could you rebuild people?

Maybe…

Maybe the anger he felt towards Grace was something to do with his own rebuilding process…

He swore at himself for such inane philosophising when his thoughts should be centred on rescue.

Swore at the Grubbs for their ridiculous habit of adding bits and pieces to their house—bits and pieces that could break off and be swept away by floodwaters. Damn it all, he'd seen that bit of the house—it had been ready to slide into the creek without the flood.

Then he was at the bridge and one look at the people gathered there made him shake his head. It was like a party—the fishing competition all over again. How word had got around he had no idea, but there must be fifteen people on the bridge with more arriving on foot and on surf-skis. And, far off, he could hear an outboard engine.

A boat! He should have thought of that first, but then he shook his head. With the debris in the water, whoever was running their outboard was also running the risk of hitting a submerged log and being tipped into the water.

Someone else to rescue.

He stopped the car and climbed out, looking upstream. One of his men came to stand beside him, explaining they'd stopped all traffic on the bridge and were getting the volunteers to spread out across it. Beyond his car an ambulance pulled up, then the hospital four-wheel-drive, a woman tumbling out.

The constable was saying something about ropes being in place and more equipment coming, but Harry barely heard, his eyes on the bobbing, slewing apparition riding the water towards them.

The craft looked for all the world like a Chinese junk floating on some exotic harbour, but then an eddy caught it and twirled it round and round, and above the raging noise of the water Harry heard a child's shrill scream.

His stomach was clenched so tightly it was like a boulder in his abdomen, and he wanted to plunge into the waters and swim towards the now teetering room.

'It's going to hit hard—let's get some tyres ready to give it some protection.'

Harry turned towards the man who'd spoken, recognising a member of Grace's SES team, then he saw Paul Gibson, looking grey and ill but there because a member of his service was in danger.

'There are tyres and rubber mooring buffers on the way,' Paul said, then pointed to an SES truck pulling up on the road at the end of the bridge. 'Or just arriving.'

More volunteers poured out of the truck, opening hatches to collect their booty. Soon they were walking across the bridge, mooring tyres and buffers in their arms.

'We'll wait until she gets closer,' Paul said, 'then work out where it's going to hit and use the protection there.'

Harry was glad to let him take charge. He was far too emotionally involved to be making cool decisions, and rescuing Grace and the children would need the coolest of heads.

Why he was so emotionally involved he'd think about later.

The wobbly room came closer, moving faster as the main current of the creek caught it and swirled it onward towards the bridge. He could see Grace now. She appeared to have wedged herself in the doorway of the room, and she had the two children clasped in her arms.

It made sense. All around town there were doorways still standing, the frames holding firm while the walls around them were blown to smithereens.

It looked like she was wearing a bikini, which, to Harry's dazed and frantic mind, seemed strange but still acceptable.

Once he'd accepted a room floating on the creek, he could accept just about anything.

He moved across the bridge, trying to guess where they'd hit, needing to be right there to help her off.

And to rescue the children, of course.

A dog was barking.

Sport?

Harry peered towards the voyagers.

Grace couldn't have been stupid enough to swim out there for Sport?

Love me, love my dog?

His mind was going. It was the waiting. The room was barely moving now, pulled out of the main channel into an eddy. If he got a boat, they could row out to it.

The thought was turning practical when a child screamed again and the structure tipped, taking in water as it met the current once again, and this time hurtling towards the bridge.

Harry was there when it hit with such a sick crunching noise he couldn't believe it had stayed afloat. Now anger mixed with relief and his mind was rehearsing the lecture he was going to give Grace about taking risks.

He took a child, Lily, and passed her on to someone, took the other child, CJ, chattering away about his adventure but far paler than he should have been.

'I've got him,' someone said, and CJ was reefed out of his arms. He turned to see Gina, CJ's mother, clasping her son to her body, tears streaming down her face.

CJ kept talking but it was background noise. Harry's attention was on the rapidly sinking room.

'Here,' Grace said, coming out of the small room and passing a squirming sack to one of the SES men.

Not a bikini at all. It was a bra, but white, not blue.

Harry reached out to grab her but she disappeared inside again, returning with Sport, who saw Harry and leapt onto his chest. He fell beneath the weight of the dog's sudden assault, and was sitting on the bridge, comforting Sport, when Grace passed the Grubbs' dog Molly, a strange Dalmatian cross and no lightweight, across to rescuers.

Harry pushed Sport off him, and stepped around the crowd who'd emptied the sack—Grace's T-shirt—of puppies onto the bridge and were now oohing and aahing over them.

He was at the railing, reaching out for her, when the timbers groaned and shrieked, then something gave way and the little room was sucked beneath the water and the bridge.

'Grace!'

He saw her body flying through the air, registered a rope, and stood up on the railing, ready to dive in.

Paul stopped him.

'We slipped the loop of a lasso over her before she started passing the kids and dogs. She jumped clear as the timber gave way, so we'll just wait until she surfaces then haul her in.'

Haul her in?

As if she were a bag of sugar-cane mulch?

More anger, this time joining with the crippling concern he was feeling as he and all the watchers on the bridge searched the waters for a sight of her.

He grabbed the rope from the volunteer who was holding it and began to pull, feeling the dragging weight on the end of it, wondering if he was drowning Grace by pulling on it but needing to get her out of the water.

Others joined him, then her body, limply unconscious, surfaced by the bridge. Eager hands reached out to grab her, but as she was lifted from the water, Harry grasped her in his arms, vaguely hearing one of the paramedics giving orders, telling him to put her down, turn her on her side, check her pulse, her breathing.

But this was Grace and he hugged her to him, although he

knew he had to do as the man had said—had to put her down to save her life.

He dropped to his knees and gently laid her on the tarred surface of the road, seeing sharp gravel from the recent resurfacing—little stones that would dig into her skin.

That's when he knew, with gut-wrenching certainty, that it wasn't physical attraction—right then when he was thinking about sharp gravel pressing into Grace's skin...

CHAPTER TEN

THE TWO PARAMEDICS took over, moving him aside with kind firm hands, clearing her airway, forcing air into her lungs, breathing for her, then waiting, then breathing again.

No chest compressions, which meant her heart was beating, but somehow registering this information failed to make Harry feel any better.

He loved her?

The concept was so mind-blowing he had to keep repeating it to himself in the hope the three words would eventually become a statement, not an incredulous question.

Was it too late?

He watched the two men work, saw oxygen delivered through bag pressure and a needle being inserted into the back of her hand. But mostly he just watched her face, the skin so pale it took on a bluish hue, her freckles dark against it.

One day he'd kiss each freckle, and with each kiss repeat, 'I love you.' He'd make up for all the time they'd lost, he'd—

Sport abandoned his paramour and puppies and came to press against him. Harry dug his fingers into the dog's rough coat, despair crowding his senses as he looked into the animal's liquid brown eyes and made silent promises he hoped he'd have the opportunity to keep.

'We're moving her now,' one of the paramedics said, and together they lifted Grace onto a stretcher, raised it to wheeling height, then ran with it towards their ambulance.

Running? Did running mean the situation was even more disastrous than he imagined?

Harry followed at a jog, cursing himself now that he'd sat communing with his dog, now loping unsteadily beside him, when he should have been asking questions about Grace's condition.

'What do you think?' he demanded, arriving at the ambulance as the driver was shutting the back door.

'She's breathing on her own—although we're still assisting her—and her heart rate's OK, but she's unconscious so obviously she hit her head somewhere underwater. There'll be water in her lungs, and she'll have swallowed it as well, so all we can do is get her into hospital and pump antibiotics into her and hope the concussion resolves itself.'

Totally unsatisfactory, especially that last bit, Harry thought as he drove to the hospital behind the ambulance. His radio was chattering non-stop and he really should return to the meeting, but he had to see Grace first—wanted her conscious—wanted to tell her...

But seeing Grace was one thing—speaking to her impossible.

'You're needed other places, Harry. I'll contact you if there's any change at all.'

Harry wanted to shrug off the hand Charles was resting on his arm and tell the man to go to hell, but he knew Charles was right. There was nothing he could do here, except glare at the nursing staff and grunt when the doctors told him all they could do was wait and see.

Wait and see what, for heaven's sake?

Frustration grumbled within him, and tiredness, so heavy he

could barely keep upright, blurred his senses. He left the hospital, pausing in the car park to call the station and tell them he was going home to sleep for an hour then back to the civic centre to hear the latest in the evacuation and services restoration plans.

Power had to come first—without it water and sewerage systems failed to work. It would be reconnected first in the area this side of the creek, the original settlement, where the hospital and police station were. But with the flooding...

On top of that, there was still no word from Georgie—not since the one radio transmission that might or might not have come from her. She had his radio—why *hadn't* she called in?

It was the inactivity on that front that ate at him. Until the road was cleared they couldn't get vehicles in, while the heavy rain made an air search impossible. It was still too wet and windy for one of the light helicopters to fly searchers in—if they had searchers available.

Which they didn't! Sending sleep-depleted volunteers into the mountains was asking for trouble.

So all he could do was wait. Wait for the army, with its fresh and experienced manpower, and heavy-duty helicopters that could cope with wind and rain.

Or wait to hear.

And keep believing that she and Alistair were sensible people and would stay safe...

At midnight, when exhausted city officials and the first wave of army brass had headed for whatever beds they could find, Harry returned to the hospital. Grace, he was told, was in the ICU.

'Intensive Care? What's she doing in there?' he demanded, and a bemused nurse who'd probably only ever seen nice-guy Harry, looked startled.

'She's unconscious and running a low-grade fever and has fluid in her lungs so it's likely she's hatching pneumonia, in which case the fever could get worse. And on top of that there's the chance it's something nastier than pneumonia. Who knows what germs were lurking in that water?'

And having set him back on his heels, almost literally, with this information, the nurse gave a concerned smile.

'We're *all* very worried about her, Harry,' she added, just in case he thought he was the only one concerned.

Harry nodded, and even tried to smile, but that was too damn difficult when Grace was lying in Intensive Care, incubating who knew what disease.

He strode towards the isolated unit, determined to see her, but no one blocked his path or muttered about family only.

She was lying in the bed, beneath a sheet, wires and tubes snaking from her body.

So small and fragile-looking—still as death.

Gina sat beside her, holding her hand and talking to her. She looked up at Harry and, although wobbly, at least *her* smile was working.

'She always talks to coma patients when she's nursing them,' Gina said, her eyes bright with unshed tears. 'I thought it was the least I could do.'

Then the tears spilled over and slipped down her cheeks.

'She saved my son. She plunged into that filthy, stinking water and swam out to save him. She can't die, Harry, she just can't.'

'She won't,' Harry promised, although he knew it was a promise he couldn't make come true. Gina stood up and he slipped into the chair and took the warm, pale hand she passed to him.

Grace's hand, so small and slight, Grace's fingers, nails neatly trimmed.

'Does she know?' Gina asked, and Harry, puzzled by the question, turned towards her. 'That you love her?' Gina expanded, with a much better smile this time.

'No,' he said, the word cutting deep inside his chest as he thought of Grace dying without knowing. Then he, too, smiled. 'But I'm here to tell her and I'll keep on telling her. You're right, she does believe unconscious patients hear things, so surely she'll be listening.'

He paused, then said awkwardly to Gina, 'She loves me, you know. She told me earlier today.'

It must have been the wonder in his voice that made Gina chuckle. She leant forward and hugged him.

'That's not exactly news, you know, Harry. The entire hospital's known how Grace felt for the past six months.'

'She told you?' Harry muttered. 'Told everyone but me?'

Gina smiled again, a kindly smile.

'Would you have listened?' she said softly, then she gave him another hug. 'And she didn't tell us all in words, you know. We just saw it in the way she lit up whenever you were around and the way she said your name and the way she glowed on meeting nights. There are a thousand ways to say "I love you", Harry, and I think your Grace knows most of them.'

'*My* Grace,' Harry muttered, unable to believe he hadn't seen what everyone else had. Hadn't seen the thousand ways Grace had said 'I love you'. But Gina was already gone, pausing in the doorway to tell him Cal would be by later and to promise that Grace would have someone sitting with her all the time, talking to her and holding her hand so she could find her way back from wherever she was right now.

Again it was Charles who told Harry to leave.

'I don't ever sleep late—growing up on a cattle property in the tropics, where the best work was done before the heat of midday, instils the habit of early waking.'

He'd wheeled into the room while Harry had been dozing in the chair, his body bent forward so his head rested on Grace's bed, her hand still clasped in his.

'So I'm doing the early shift with Grace,' Charles continued, manoeuvring his chair into position. 'If you want some technicalities, her breathing and pulse rate suggest she's regaining consciousness but the infection's taking hold and her temperature is fluctuating rather alarmingly.'

Harry knew he had to go. He had to get some sleep then return to the planning room. Evacuation of people who had family or friends to go to close by had begun yesterday and today they were hoping to begin mass evacuation of up to a thousand women and children. Defence force transport planes would bring in water, tents, food and building supplies and fly people out to Townsville or Cairns. Power would come on in stages, and it could be months before all services were fully operational. Getting people out of the crippled town would ease the pressure on the limited services.

He left the hospital reluctantly, and was in a meeting when Cal phoned to say Grace had regained consciousness but was feverish and disoriented, mostly sleeping, which was good.

Harry raged against the constraints that held him in the meeting, knowing he couldn't go rushing to Grace's side when he was needed right where he was. But later...

Later she was sleeping, so he slipped into the chair vacated this time for him by her friend Marcia, and took her hand, talking quietly to her, telling her he was there.

Grace turned her head and opened her eyes, gazing at him with a puzzled frown. Then the frown cleared, as if she'd worked out who he was, and she said, 'Go away Harry,' as clear as day.

Nothing else, just, 'Go away Harry.' Then she shut her eyes again as if not seeing him would make him vanish.

She was feverish, he told himself, and didn't know what she was saying, but when she woke an hour later and saw him there, her eyes filled with tears and this time the knife she used to stab right into his heart was phrased differently.

'I don't want you here, Harry,' she said, her voice piteously weak, the single tear sliding down her cheek doing further damage to his already lacerated heart.

Cal was there, and his quiet 'I don't want her getting upset' got Harry to his feet.

But go?

How could he walk away and leave her lying there, so still and pale beneath the sheet?

'There's work for you to do elsewhere,' Cal reminded him, following him out of the ICU and stopping beside the wide window where Cal had propped himself. 'I'll keep you posted about her condition.'

So Harry worked and listened to Cal telling him Grace was as well as could be expected, not exactly improving but the new antibiotics they were trying seemed to be keeping the infection stable.

It was in her lungs and now he had to worry if pulling her through the water had made things worse, but there were no answers to that kind of question so he worked some more, and went home to sleep from time to time, to feed Sport and talk to him of love.

On the third day after Willie had blown the town apart, Grace was moved out of the ICU and two days later released from hospital, but only as far as the doctors' house, where resident medical staff could fuss over her and keep an eye on her continuing improvement at the same time.

So it was there that Harry went, late one afternoon, when the urgency had left the restoration programme and he could take time off without feeling guilty.

She was on the veranda, Gina told him. On the old couch. As he walked through the house he sensed Gina tactfully making sure all the other residents had vamoosed.

He came out onto the veranda and there was Grace, pale but pretty, her golden curls shining in the sun that had finally blessed them with its presence and what looked like a dirty black rag draped across her knees.

'Grace?' he said, hating the fact he sounded so tentative, yet fearful she'd once again send him away.

'Harry?'

The word echoed with surprise, as if he was the last person she expected to be calling on her.

A thought that added to his tension!

'Come and sit down. I'm not supposed to move about much. One lung collapsed during all the fuss and it's not quite better yet, so I'm stuck in bed or on the couch, but at least from here I can see the sea. It's qui-etened down a lot, hasn't it?'

Harry stared at her. This was the Grace he used to know. Actually, it was a much frailer and quieter and less bubbly version of her, but still that Grace, the one who was his friend. Chatting to him, easing over difficult moments—showing love?

He had no idea—totally confused by what he'd come to realise after that terrible moment when Grace had disappeared beneath the murky floodwaters and then by the 'go away' order she'd issued from the hospital bed.

Stepping tentatively, although the old house had withstood Willie's fury better than most of the houses in town, he moved towards the couch, then sat where Grace was patting the space beside her on the couch.

'I thought I'd lost you,' he began, then wondered if she was well enough for him to be dumping his emotions on her. 'You disappeared beneath the waters and I realised what a fool I'd been, Grace. Stupid, stupid fool, hiding away from any emotion all this time, letting the mess I'd made of my marriage to Nikki overshadow my life, then, worst of all, blaming physical attraction for the kiss. I know it's too late to be telling you all this—that somehow with the bump on your head you got some common sense and decided you could do far better than me—but, like you had to say it when I thought I'd lost Sport, so I have to say it now. I love you, Grace.'

Having bumbled his way this far through the conversation, Harry paused and looked at the recipient of all this information. She was staring at him as if he'd spoken in tongues, so he tried again.

'I love you, Grace,' he said, and wondered if he should perhaps propose right now and make a total fool of himself all at once, or leave the foolish proposal part for some other time.

'You love me?' she finally whispered, and he waited for the punch-line, the 'Oh, Harry, it's too late' or however she might word it.

But nothing followed so he took her hands in his and nodded, then as tension gripped so hard it hurt, he rushed into speech again.

'I know you don't feel the same way but you did love me once, so maybe that love is only hidden, not completely gone.'

'Loved you once?' she said, and this time the repetition was stronger, and now her blue eyes were fixed on his. 'What makes you think I'd ever stop loving you, Harry?'

He stared at her, trying to work out what this question meant—trying to equate it with the 'go away, Harry' scenarios.

Couldn't do it, so he had to ask.

'You sent me away,' he reminded her. 'At the hospital, you said to go away and that you didn't want me there.'

'Oh, Harry,' she whispered, and rested her head against his chest. 'You silly man, thinking I'd stopped loving you. As soon stop the sun from rising as me stop loving you.'

This definitely made him happy, happy enough to press a kiss to her soft curls, but he was still confused. Maybe more confused than ever.

'But you sent me away when all I wanted was to be with you.'

She turned towards him and lifted one hand to rest it on his cheek.

'I didn't want you sitting by my bedside—not at that hospital—not again. I didn't want you remembering all that pain and anguish, and suffering for things that happened in the past through no real fault of yours.'

She pressed her lips to his, a present of a kiss.

'The fact that you talked about Nikki and your marriage suggested you were ready to move on, so I didn't want you being pulled back into the past because of me.'

'You'd have liked me there?' Harry asked, unable to believe that, sick as she had been, she'd still found this one way of the thousand to say 'I love you'.

'Of course,' she whispered, nestling her head on his chest. 'Loving you the way I do, I always want you near.'

She smiled up at him, then added, 'Look how pathetic I am—look at this.'

She lifted the black rag from her knee and it took a moment for him to recognise it as his dinner jacket.

'I brushed off most of the mud and when Gina said I had to keep something over my knees when I sit out in the breeze, it seemed the best knee cover any woman could have. Gina wanted to have it dry-cleaned but it would have come back smelling of dry-cleaning fluid, not Harry, so there you are.'

Her smile mocked her sentimentality but it went straight to Harry's heart, because it wobbled a bit as if she felt she'd made a fool of herself.

'Snap!' he said softly, and reached into his shirt pocket, pulling out a very tattered blue ribbon he'd kept with him since that fateful night.

Then he closed his arms around her and pulled her close, pressing kisses on her head and telling her things he hadn't realised he knew, about how much he loved her, but more, that he admired her and thought her wonderful, and how soon would she be his wife?

They'd reached the kissing stage when a voice interrupted

them, a voice filled with the disgust that only a five-year-old could muster when faced with demonstrations of love.

'You're kissing, Grace,' CJ said, coming close enough for them to see he held a squirming puppy in his hands. 'I didn't think policemen did that kind of thing.'

'Well, now you know they do,' Harry said, tucking Grace tightly against his body, never wanting to let her go.

CJ sighed.

'Then I guess I'll have to be a fireman instead,' he said, passing the puppy to Harry. 'Mum said you were here, and this is the one Lily and I decided should be yours because it looks more like Sport than all the others, although it's got four legs.'

Harry took the squirming bundle of fur and peered into its face. He failed to see any resemblance at all to Sport, but knew once CJ and Lily had decided something, it was futile to argue.

'Do you mind if we have two dogs?' he asked Grace, who smiled at him so lovingly he had to kiss her again, further disgusting CJ, who rescued the pup and departed, making fire-siren noises as he raced away.

'Two dogs and lots of kids,' Grace said, returning his kisses with enthusiasm. 'Is that OK with you?'

Harry thought of all he now knew about Grace's background. Loving without being loved must have been so hard for someone with her warm and caring nature.

'Of course we'll have lots of kids,' he promised, and was about to suggest they start on the project right now when he remembered she was just out of hospital and very frail.

But not too frail to kiss him as she whispered, 'Thank you.' Then added, 'I love you, Harry Blake,' and made his day complete.

* * * * *

Their Lost-And-Found Family

Marion Lennox

Marion Lennox was born on an Australian dairy farm. She moved on—mostly because the cows weren't interested in her stories! Marion writes Medical™ Romance as well as Mills & Boon® Romance. Initially she used different names, so if you're looking for past books search also for author Trisha David. In her non-writing life Marion cares (haphazardly) for her husband, kids, dogs, cats, chickens and anyone else who lines up at her dinner table. She fights her rampant garden (she's losing) and her house dust (she's lost!). She also travels, which she finds seriously addictive. As a teenager Marion was told she'd never get anywhere reading romance. Now romance is the basis of her stories, her stories allow her to travel, and if ever there was one advertisement for following your dream, she'd be it! You can contact Marion at www.marionlennox.com

Recent titles by the same author:

HIS MIRACLE BRIDE*
THE PRINCE'S OUTBACK BRIDE
THE SURGEON'S FAMILY MIRACLE
RESCUE AT CRADLE LAKE
THE HEIR'S CHOSEN BRIDE
  (Castle at Dolphin Bay)
THE DOCTOR'S PROPOSAL
  (Castle at Dolphin Bay)
HIS SECRET LOVE-CHILD
  (Crocodile Creek)

Dear Reader

For the *Crocodile Creek* series I've been working with three wonderful friends: authors Lilian Darcy, Meredith Webber and Alison Roberts. Our stories are based in a tropical paradise, and we've filled our linked hospital and doctors' residence with dedicated—and very sexy—medics from all over the world. Each of these medics has their own romance as the dramas of the wider Crocodile Creek community unfold around them.

In our first series my co-writers introduced the Crocodile Creek obstetrician, a leather-clad, Harley-riding, stiletto-shod redhead, who has sole responsibility for seven-year-old Max. Georgie jumped off the pages as a heroine needing her own story, and my friends gave her to me. They set up a tropical storm like no other, placed Georgie in the middle of it, and said, 'Go for it.'

So I went for it. It needed a truly spectacular hero to get my heroine out of the havoc my fellow writers created. If you love Georgie and Alistair's story then you need to thank my writing mates. They gave me Georgie and my drama. All I've done is lift Alistair out of his very comfortable career as an eminent US neurosurgeon and send him off to Georgie's rescue.

Have fun. I surely did.

Marion Lennox
www.marionlennox.com

PROLOGUE

THE BUS TRIP took a day—thirteen hours with occasional stops for refuelling. All that time Max sat in the far corner of the bus's rear seat, trying to make himself invisible. He stroked Scruffy—Scruffy should be in the cargo hold but the driver had relented—and sang a tiny song into the dog's lopsided ears.

'We're going to Georgie. We're going to Georgie.'

There was another kid on the bus, younger than Max's seven years. He didn't seem to speak, not to the lady he was with or to anyone else. Every now and then, as if drawn, the kid would slip away from the lady and come up to Max's hidey-hole to share in the Scruffy stroking.

'What's your name?' Max asked once, but the kid didn't answer. No matter. It was enough that he was cuddling Scruffy.

Was the kid going to Crocodile Creek, too? Maybe he and the lady he was with knew Georgie. The lady seemed nice, Max decided. She'd bought Max a sandwich and a drink at the last stop, and an extra sandwich and water for Scruffy. Dad hadn't left him with any money for food. The more Max thought about it, the more he thought he'd been lucky Dad had paid his bus fare.

Maybe he'd had to. Dad was on the run and if Max had been left alone on the streets of Mt Isa, Georgie might have got on her Harley and come and murdered Dad. Georgie's anger was great. She'd never yelled at him, but she'd yelled at Dad. Dad had punched her once and Georgie had punched him right back.

He was going to Georgie.

How much longer?

'Soon we'll be there,' he told Scruffy and the silent kid. 'Soon we'll be with Georgie and she'll punch anyone who's mean to us. If Dad comes and gets us, she'll punch him again.'

But she'd never been able to stop Dad taking him away every time he'd wanted to.

'Dad won't want me any more,' he told his disreputable little dog and his silent friend. 'We'll be safe. Georgie can be our mum.'

The little dog nuzzled into Max's windcheater, infinitely comforting.

'Yeah, Georgie can be your mum, too,' he whispered to the little dog. 'There'll be you and me, and Georgie can be Mum to both of us. She's waiting.'

CHAPTER ONE

'GINA, YOU CAN have Alistair Carmichael or you can have me. But not both.'

Gina chuckled.

'I mean it.'

'No, you don't.' Dr Georgie Turner's reputation was that of drama queen—wild girl of Crocodile Creek Hospital. Georgie's favourite party gear consisted of close-fitting leather pants, which showed every curve of her neat, trim body, and low-cut tops displaying an excellent cleavage. Her cropped curls were jet black and shining, and her lips were always glossed dramatic crimson. Her beloved Harley Davidson for normal travel and an off-road bike for the rough stuff completed the picture.

Georgie. Ready for anything.

Georgiana Turner, obstetrician extraordinaire.

Georgie was Gina's best friend. Gina loved her to bits. Underneath that admittedly really brash exterior Georgie had a heart as soft as putty.

'To know you is to love you,' Gina said simply. 'I love you. All your patients love you. Let Alistair know you and he'll love you, too.'

'Right. Like he got to know me last time. He'll use the occasion to lecture me on morals while you guys are signing the register.' Georgie took a deep breath and glowered for added emphasis. 'No. There are some things up with which I will not put.'

Gina sighed. She and Georgie were doctors at Crocodile Creek, base for Air Sea Rescue and the Flying Doctor for most of far north Queensland. Gina was engaged to Cal, another Croc Creek doctor. Six months ago Alistair, Gina's only cousin, had flown in from America to see what sort of set-up his baby cousin was getting herself into.

Unfortunately his visit had coincided with a ghastly patch in Georgie's life. Georgie's stepfather had just dragged her small half-brother away to join him in the seedy life Georgie knew he led. Max was seven years old. Their mother had disappeared into the limbo of drug addiction soon after giving birth to him and Georgie had become Max's surrogate mum. She loved him so fiercely it was as if he was hers.

But he wasn't hers. Half-sisters had fewer rights than fathers, no matter how creepy Georgie's stepfather was. She'd had to let him go.

So Georgie had waved Max off, and then she'd gone to Gina's engagement party. She had been off duty. She'd been trying desperately not to cry. She'd hit the bar, and then Alistair-Stuffed-Shirt Carmichael had asked her to dance.

Which had been...unfortunate.

Alistair had a great body. He was big and warm and strong, and she'd had too much to drink, too fast. She'd seen him earlier in the day and had thought—vaguely—that he was gorgeous. Now, at the party, battered with shock and grief, she'd let her hormones hold sway. She'd let him hold her as she'd needed to be held. She'd flirted unashamedly, and then...

He'd half carried her from the hall and they'd both known what his intentions had been. She hadn't cared. Why the hell should she care when her life was going down the drain?

Only Gina had intercepted them at the door. 'Georgie,' she'd said in that soft voice, the one that said she cared, and suddenly

Georgie had pushed away from Alistair, then sat down on the hall steps and sobbed her heart out, while the rest of Crocodile Creek had streamed in and out around her.

'What the hell...?' Alistair had demanded.

And Georgie had looked up at him and said, through tears, 'I'm sorry, mate. It's not that I don't fancy you. I'm just drunk.'

He'd turned, just like that. From the big, gentle man he'd seemed to the prissy, disapproving toad he really was.

'This is your best friend, Gina?' He'd said it incredulously.

'Yes. She's just—'

'I've just had too much to drink,' Georgie had said, cutting across his question and glaring daggers at Gina, sending visual refusal for Gina to tell him more. 'Gina's right. I gotta go to bed.'

'I'll take you,' Gina had said.

'But it's your engagement party,' Alistair had objected, staring at Georgie as if she'd been some sort of pond scum.

'That's OK,' Gina had said. 'I'll come back soon, but I'm taking my friend home first.'

'You don't need to take me. I have wheels. Hey, you want a ride on my bike?' Georgie had asked, veering off on a tangent and motioning to her beloved Harley parked nearby.

'I think we might leave your bike where it is, don't you?' Gina had said, and had smiled and tugged the decidedly wobbly Georgie to her feet. 'I know you take risks on that thing but we don't want to push it.'

So that had been Georgie's introduction to Alistair. The next day Gina had taken him for a tour of the hospital and he'd been flabbergasted to find Georgie was an obstetrician.

'She's a really good one,' Georgie had heard Gina tell Alistair as they'd disappeared from sight. They'd thought she'd left the ward but she'd forgotten something and returned just in time to hear them talk about her. 'We're lucky to have her.'

'I know you're desperate for doctors,' Alistair had said. 'But I sure as hell wouldn't let her within a mile of any patient of mine.'

So that had been that. Alistair had left the day after, flying back to his very important career as paediatric neurosurgeon in a prestigious US hospital. Georgie had been delighted to see the end of him. But now…

'He's giving you away,' she moaned to Gina. 'We'll have to be in the same church as each other.'

'It's not like he's best man. You won't have to partner him.'

'He thinks I'm a slut.'

'Hey, he was taking you to bed. His behaviour wasn't exactly above reproach.'

'He was taking me to bed because he thought I was a slut.'

'Exactly.'

'So two sets of appalling behaviour cancel each other out?' She flopped onto the bed and groaned theatrically. 'Agh, agh, agh.'

'You could always turn over a new leaf,' Gina said cautiously. 'Greet him in twin set and pearls.'

Georgie choked. 'Yeah. I could.'

'That's what his fiancée wears.'

Georgie lifted her head from the pillows and gazed at Gina in astonishment. 'He has a fiancée?'

'Eloise. He's been engaged for years.'

'So he was engaged when he carted me off the dance floor?'

'See what I mean? Two sets of bad behaviour, and yours is the lesser.'

'Twinset, eh?' Georgie said, and looked thoughtfully at her reflection in the mirror. Her soft black top had crept up a little. She tugged it down to make it more revealing. Which was very revealing.

'Don't you dare,' Gina said nervously. 'Behave.'

'I don't have to wear twinset and pearls as bridesmaid?'

'I was thinking you might like to wear purple tulle.' And then, as Georgie stared at her in horror, Gina giggled and threw a pillow at her friend. 'Gotcha.'

'Cow. Purple tulle?'

'Wear what you want,' Gina said. 'You're my only brides-maid so the choice is yours. Leathers if you want.'

'Sleek black,' Georgie said, and grinned. 'Not trashy.'

'Trashy if you want.'

'I only do that—'

'I know. When you're angry. But, Georgie...' She hesitated. 'Do you know where Max is now?'

Georgie's smile faded. She picked up the pillow Gina had just tossed at her and hugged it, like it was a baby.

'I have no idea. I had a phone call five months ago, saying he was in Western Australia, but they were moving on that day. My stepfather's always one step in front of the law.'

'Oh, Georg...'

'I wish he'd get caught,' Georgie said fiercely. 'I know he's involved up to his neck in drugs. I want him to go to prison.'

'Because then you'd get Max back?'

'I'm all he's got.'

'Your stepfather must love him to keep him with him.'

'Don't you believe it,' Georgie said fiercely. 'He's just using him. Last time he was here—last time Ron spent time inside—Max told me he does the running. He acts as lookout. Max shops for them when Ron doesn't want to get recognised. Ron even used him for drops. When he was six years old!'

'Oh, Georg...'

'Ron's rotten,' Georgie muttered. 'My whole family's rotten. That's why I'm here in Crocodile Creek—I'm as far as I can get from any of them. Except Max. My one true thing. Max—and I can't do a thing about him.'

There was a long silence. Gina stared at her friend in real concern. Georgie, who'd hauled herself up the hard way, who'd fought her way through medical school, who'd come from the school of hard knocks and was tough on the exterior, but under-neath...

'If you really don't want to be my bridesmaid...' she said tentatively, and Georgie's eyes flew up to meet hers.

'Who said I didn't want to be your bridesmaid?'

'But Alistair...'

'I can cope with Alistair Carmichael,' she said grimly. 'He's the least of my worries. Engaged, huh? I can cope with Alistair Carmichael with my hands behind my back.'

'Georgie...'

'Nothing outrageous,' she said, and threw up her hands as if in surrender. 'I agree.'

And then she added, under her breath, 'Or nothing outrageous that you're going to know about.'

It had been some flight. Alistair emerged into the brilliant sunshine of Crocodile Creek feeling almost shell-shocked. He'd been coping with sleepless nights before he'd left. They were setting up a new streamlined process to move patients from Theatre to Intensive Care—not such a difficult process when you said it like that, but in reality, with paediatric problems the transfer was too often a time of drama. He'd orchestrated a whole new method of processing transfers, and he'd hoped to have it securely in place before he'd left, but there'd been last-minute glitches. He'd spent the days before he'd left going through the procedures over and over, supervising mock transfers, timing, making sure the team knew exactly who was doing what.

In the end he'd been satisfied but Eloise had driven him to the airport and even she had been concerned.

'You're pushing yourself too far.'

'Says the youngest ever professor of entomology.'

'I know my limits, Alistair.'

'I know mine, too. I can sleep on the plane.'

But as it had turned out, he hadn't. There'd been turbulence and the plane had been diverted to New Zealand. There he'd endured eight hours in an airport lounge and finally clearance to fly on. More turbulence—this time so severe that some passengers had been injured. Apparently there was a cyclone east of Northern Australia.

Luckily it was southeast of Crocodile Creek and the last short leg had been drama free. Thank God. He descended the plane steps, looking forward to seeing Gina. Trying not to look exhausted. Trying to look as if he was eager for this visit to begin.

Gina wasn't in the small bunch of waiting people. Instead...

His heart sank. Georgie. Dr Georgiana Turner.

He'd hoped she'd have left town by now. What Gina saw in this...tramp, he didn't know.

'Hey, Alistair.' She waved and yelled as he crossed the tarmac.

She was chewing gum. She was wearing tight leather pants and bright red stilettos. She had on a really tight top—so tight it was almost indecent. She was all in black. The only colour about her was the slash of crimson of her lips, her outrageous shoes and two spots of colour on her cheeks.

'How's it going, Al?' she said, and chewed a bit more gum.

'Fine,' he said, trying to be polite and not quite succeeding. 'Where's Gina?'

'See, she was expecting you yesterday. So today she and Cal are running a clinic out on Wallaby Island. The weather's getting up so they thought they ought to go when they could.'

'You couldn't have taken her place?'

'Hey, I deliver babies. Gina's the heart lady. There's not a lot of crossover. You got bags?'

'One. Yes.'

She sniffed, in a way that said real men didn't need baggage. She turned and headed for the baggage hall, her very cute butt wiggling as he walked behind her.

It was some butt.

OK, that's what he couldn't allow himself to think. That was what had landed him into trouble in the first place. She was a tart. Somehow she'd gained a medical degree but, no matter, she was still a tart.

But even so, he shouldn't have tried to pick her up.

Now they stood side by side at the luggage carousel, wait-

ing for his bag. It took for ever. There were other doctors there
from the plane.

'There's some other wedding happening here,' he ventured
for something to say, and Georgie nodded, looking at the baggage carousel as if it was she who'd recognise his bag.

'Yep. One this Saturday, one next. Planned so those going to
both needn't make two trips. We were starting to think there'd
be no guests for the first one.'

'It's some storm down south,' he said reflectively. 'That's
how I met these guys. The trip from New Zealand should have
been cancelled. We hit an air pocket and dropped what felt like
a few thousand feet. Anyone who wasn't belted in was injured.'

'You got called on as a doctor?'

'A bit. I was asleep at first.'

'Off duty,' she said blankly, and he winced. There was no
criticism in her voice. It was a simple statement of fact, but she
knew how to hurt. When he'd woken to discover the chaos he'd
felt dreadful. He'd helped, but other doctors had been more pro-
active than him.

'Look, I—'

'Is this your bag? It must be. Everyone else has theirs.'

'It's mine,' he said, and she strode forward and lugged it off
the conveyor belt before he could stop her. She set it up on its
wheels and tugged out the handle, then set it before him. Making him feel even more wimpish.

'Right,' she said. 'My wheels are in the car park.'

'Your car?'

'My wheels.' She was striding through the terminal, talking
to him over her shoulder. He was struggling to keep up.

He was feeling about six years old.

'Hey, Georg.' People were acknowledging her, waving to her,
but she wasn't stopping. She was wearing really high stilettos
but still walking at a pace that made him hurry. She looked like
something out of a biker magazine. A biker's moll?

Not quite, for her hair was closely cropped and cute—almost classy. The gold hoop earrings actually looked great. She was just…different.

'Doc Turner.' An overweight girl—much more your vision of a biker's moll than Georgie—was yelling to get her attention. 'Georgie!'

Georgie stopped, spinning on her stilettos to see who was calling.

The girl was about eighteen, bottle-blonde, wearing jeans that were a couple of sizes too small for her very chubby figure and a top that didn't cover a stomach that wobbled. She was pushing a pram. A chubby, big-eyed toddler clung to a fistful of her crop top, and a youth came behind, lugging two overstuffed bags. The youth looked about eighteen, too, as skinny as his partner was chubby.

They were obviously friends of Georgie. 'Lola,' Georgie said with evident pleasure. 'Eric. How goes it?'

'Eric's mum's paid for us to go to Hobart,' Lola said with evident pride. 'She's gonna look after us for a coupla weeks till all me bits get back together.'

'Lola had a lovely little girl last week,' Georgie told Alistair, looking into the pram with expected admiration. 'It was a pretty dramatic birth.'

'Had her on the laundry floor,' Lola said proudly. 'Eric had gone to ring the ambos and there she was. Pretty near wet himself when he came back.'

'Lola, Eric, this is Dr Carmichael,' Georgie said. The rest of the passengers from the plane were passing them on the way out to the car park. Nice ordinary people with nice ordinary people meeting them. Not a tattoo in sight.

Lola had six tattoos that he could see. Eric… Eric was just one huge tattoo.

'Doc Carmichael is Gina's surrogate father, here to give her away at the wedding,' Georgie said.

'He's Gina's surrogate father?' Lola checked him out. 'What's surrogate?' Then she shrugged, clearly not interested in extending her education. 'Well, he's older than my old man so I guess he'll do.' She surveyed him critically. 'That silver in your hair. Natural?'

'Um…yes,' Alistair said, discomfited.

'Looks great. Love a bit of silver. Looks real distinguished. Eric, you oughta get some put in. Next time I get me tips done you come, too.' She moved forward a bit to get a closer look and smoothed Alistair's lapel in admiration. 'Cool suit. Real classy. Anyone ever told you we don't do suits in this town?'

'You taking him into town?' Eric asked.

'Yeah,' Georgie said.

'You got a spare helmet?' Lola demanded. 'He's gonna look real dorky in that suit on the back of your bike. And what about his bag?'

'I've got a spare helmet and I hooked up the trailer.'

'Sheesh,' Eric said. 'Rather you than me, mate. She rides like the clappers.'

'I'm not going on a motorbike,' Alistair said, feeling it was time he put his foot down. 'Georgia, I'll get a cab.'

'Ooh, listen to him,' Lola said, admiring. 'Georgia. Is that your real name?'

'Georgiana Marilyn Kimberly Turner,' Georgie said, grinning.

'Sheesh,' said Lola.

'We gotta go,' Eric said, looking ahead at the security gates with a certain amount of trepidation. 'Lola, you sure about the—?'

'The baby stuff,' Lola corrected him, far too fast, and reached over and gave her beloved a wifely cuff. 'Yeah, it's packed. Shut up.'

Georgie chuckled. It was a good chuckle, Alistair thought, low and throaty and real.

'They're in for a rough flight,' he said, watching the little family head off toward Security. By mutual unspoken agreement they stayed watching. Lola picked the baby up out of her pram, handed her to Eric, lifted the pram and dumped the whole thing sideways on the conveyor belt. Then she grabbed all the bags they were carrying and loaded them on top. Bags, bags and more bags.

A security officer from the far end of the hall had strolled down to where they were tugging their gear off the belt. The officer had a beagle hound on a leash.

The beagle walked up to Lola, looked up at her and sat firmly at her feet.

'Hey, great dog,' Lola said, and fished in her nappy bag. 'You want a peanut-butter sandwich?'

'Don't feed the dog, ma'am,' the officer said curtly, and Lola swelled in indignation.

'Why the hell not? He's too skinny.'

'Can we check the contents of the bag you're carrying, please?'

'Sure,' Lola said, amenable. She walked back to the conveyor belt with her nappy bag, lifted it high and emptied it. She put the baby on top for good measure.

'She's carrying the contents of a small house,' Alistair said, awed, and Georgie grinned.

'That's our Lola. She's one of my favourite patients.'

'I can see that,' he said morosely, and she shrugged, starting to walk away.

'Yeah, it's a long way from the keep-yourself-nice brigade I'd imagine you'd prefer to treat. But we need to be flexible up here, mate. Non-judgmental. Doctors like you wouldn't have a chance in this place.'

He bit his lip. She was being deliberately provocative, he thought. Dammit, he wasn't going to react. But...

'About the bike...'

'Yeah?' she said over her shoulder as she headed outside.

'I'll get a cab.'

'Someone's already taken the cab. I saw it drive off.'

'There must be more than one cab.'

'Not today there isn't. It's the northern waters flyfishing meet in Croc Creek. The prize this year is a week in Fiji and every man and his dog is fishing his heart out. And everyone else from the plane left while we were talking to Lola. You're stuck with me.'

They were outside now, trekking through to the far reaches of the car park. To an enormous Harley Davidson with an incongruous little trailer on the back.

'I can usually park at the front,' Georgie said. 'But I had to bring the trailer.' Once again that unspoken assumption that he was a wuss for bringing more than a toothbrush.

'I'd rather not go on the bike,' he said stiffly.

She turned and stared. 'Why not?'

'I don't—'

'Like the feel of the wind in your hair? It's not a toupee, is it?' She kicked off her stilettos and reached into her saddle bag for a pair of trainers that had seen better days. 'Go on. Live dangerously. I'll even try to stay under the speed limit.'

'I'd rather not.'

'I brought you a helmet. Even the toupee's protected.'

'No.'

There was a moment's silence. Then she shrugged. Before he knew what she was about she'd hauled his suitcase up and tossed it onto her trailer. Then she shoved her helmet over her curls, clipped it tight and climbed astride her bike. The motor was roaring into life before he had time to say a word.

'Fair enough,' she yelled over the noise. 'It's your toupee after all, and maybe I'd worry myself. You can't take too much care of those little critters. I'll drop the case off at the hospital. It's three miles directly north and over the bridge.'

'You can't—'

'See ya,' she yelled, and flicked off the brake.

And she was gone, leaving a cloud of dust and petrol fumes behind her.

* * *

'You dumped him.'

'I didn't dump him. I went to collect him and he declined my very kind offer to be my pillion passenger.'

'Georgie, it's hot out there. Stinking hot.' On the end of the phone Gina was starting to sound agitated.

'That's why I couldn't understand why he didn't accept my offer. He's wearing a suit. A gorgeous Italian suit, Gina. With that lovely hair, his height, those gorgeous brogues... Ooh, he looks the real big city specialist. You wouldn't think someone like that would want to walk.'

'He won't have realised... He'll have thought there were taxis.'

'I told him there weren't.'

'Georgie, I want you to go back and get him.'

'No way.'

'In a car. You could have taken a hospital car.'

'What's wrong with my bike?'

'Georgie Turner, are you my very best friend and my brides-maid or what?'

'I might be,' she said cautiously.

'Then your job as my bridesmaid is to make sure that the man who's going to give me away doesn't turn into a grease spot while hiking into Crocodile Creek.'

'He shouldn't—'

'Georgie.'

'He thinks I'm some species below bedbug.'

'You wore your leathers?'

'So what?'

'And your stilettos?'

'I dressed up. I thought it was important to make a good im-pression.'

'Georgie, go fetch him.'

'Won't,' Georgie said, but she grinned. OK, she'd made her point. She supposed the toad could be fetched. 'Oh, all right.'

'In the car,' Gina added.

'If I have to.'

'You have to. Tell him Cal and I will be back at dinnertime.'

'Sure,' Georgie said, and grimaced. 'He'll be really relieved to hear that higher civilisation is on its way.'

The kid was sitting in the middle of the bridge. He'd be blocking traffic if there was any traffic, but Crocodile Creek must hunker down for a midday siesta. Alistair hadn't passed so much as a pushbike for the last mile.

He'd abandoned his jacket, slinging it over his shoulder and considering losing it altogether. It was so hot if he'd really been wearing a toupee he'd have left it behind a mile ago. He was thirsty. He was jet-lagged to hell and he was angry.

There was a kid in the middle of the bridge. A little boy.

'Hi,' he said as he approached, but the child didn't respond. He was staring down at the river, his face devoid of expression. It was a dreadful look, Alistair thought. It wasn't bored. It wasn't sad. It was simply…empty.

He was about six years old. Indigenous Australian? Maybe, but mixed with something else.

'Are you OK?' Alistair asked, doing a fast scan of the riverbank, searching for someone who might belong to this waif.

There was no one else in sight. There was no answer.

'Where's Mum or Dad?'

'Dad's fishing,' the child said, breaking his silence to speak in little more than a quavering whisper. Alistair's impression of hopelessness intensified.

'And you're waiting for him to come home?'

'Yeah.'

'Maybe you could wait somewhere cooler,' Alistair suggested. The middle of the bridge was so hot there was shimmer rising from the timbers.

'I'm OK here.'

Alistair hesitated. This kid had dark skin. Maybe he wouldn't burn like Alistair was starting to. If his dad was coming soon…

No. The child was square in the middle of the bridge and his face said he was expecting the wait to be a long one.

He squatted down beside the boy. 'What's your name?'

'I'm not allowed to talk to people I don't know.'

'I'm a doctor,' Alistair said. 'I'm here to visit the doctors at the Crocodile Creek Hospital. I know them all. Dr Gina Lopez. Dr Charles Wetherby. Dr Georgie Turner.'

The kid's eyes flew to meet his.

'Georgie?'

'You know Georgie?'

'She helps my mum.'

'She's a friend of mine,' Alistair said gently, knowing he had to stretch the truth to gain trust. 'She'll be at the hospital now and that's where I'm going. If I take you there, maybe she could take you home on the back of her motorbike.'

The child's eyes fixed on his, unwavering.

'You're a doctor?'

'I am.'

'You fix people?'

'Yes.'

'Will you fix my mum?'

His heart sank. This was getting trickier. The sun was searing the back of his neck. He could feel beads of sweat trickling downward. 'What's wrong with your mother?'

The child's expression had changed to one of wary hope. 'She's sick. She's in bed.'

What was he getting himself into? But he had no choice. 'Can you take me to your mum?'

'Yes,' the little boy said, defeat turning to determination. He climbed to his feet, grabbed Alistair's hand and tugged. 'It's along the river.'

'Right,' Alistair said. He definitely had no choice. 'Let's go.'

CHAPTER TWO

SHE NEARLY MISSED HIM. She drove slowly back toward the airport, starting to feel really guilty. It was unseasonably hot even for here, she thought. The wind was starting to feel like they were in for a major storm, even though the sky was clear.

There was a cyclone out to sea—Cyclone Willie—but it was so far out it should never come near them. The weather guys on the radio were saying the winds they were feeling now were from the edge of the cyclone.

Just don't rain for Mike and Em's wedding tomorrow, she told the weather gods. Or for Gina's the Saturday after.

Right. Back to worrying about Alistair. She'd gone two miles now and was starting to be concerned. Surely he should have walked further than this. But it was so hot. She should never have let her temper hold sway. He wouldn't have realised how hot it was.

Maybe he'd left the road to find some shade. She slowed down and started studying the verges. Here was the bridge...

She nearly didn't see them. A path ran by the river, meandering down to a shanty town further on. Here were huts built by itinerant fishermen, or squatters who spent a few months camping here and then moved on. Periodically the council cleared them but they came back again and again.

There was a man in the distance, just as the track disappeared into trees. Holding a child's hand.

Even from this distance she could pick the neat business suit and jacket slung over his shoulder. Not Crocodile Creek wear. Alistair.

What the hell was he doing? She pulled onto the verge and hit the horn. Loudly. Then she climbed out and waved.

In the distance Alistair paused and turned. And waved back.

Who was he with?

She stood and waited. He'd have talked one of the local kids into taking him to shelter, she thought, expecting him to leave the child and come back to the road. He didn't. He simply stood there, holding the child's hand, as if he expected her to come to him.

Really! It was hot. She was wearing leather pants. OK, maybe they weren't the most practical gear in this heat. She'd put them on to make a statement.

She'd also put her stilettos back on before bringing the car out. Her nice sensible trainers were back at the hospital.

He expected her to walk?

He wasn't moving. He simply stood by the riverbank and waited.

Didn't he know you didn't stand near the river? Not for long. There were crocs in this river. It was safe enough to walk on the bank as long as you walked briskly, but to stand in the one spot for a while was asking for trouble.

OK. She gave a mental snort and stalked down the path toward them. Dratted stilettos…

Davy Price.

She recognised the child before she'd reached the riverbank. Immediately her personal discomfort was forgotten. What the hell was Alistair doing, holding Davy's hand? Davy was six years old. He was the eldest of four children, the last of whom she'd delivered four days earlier. They lived in the worst of this motley collection of shacks.

While Lizzie, Davy's mum, had been in hospital, she'd tried to persuade her to move to council housing. But...

'My old man wants to live by the river. He won't move.'

Georgie fretted about the family. Lizzie's 'old man' was Smiley, an indolent layabout, drunk more often than not. Lizzie tried desperately to keep the kids healthy but she was almost beaten. To let her go home to this mosquito-ridden slum had gone against every piece of logic Georgie possessed. But you can't make people do what they don't want—who knew that better than Georgie?

But now... She slipped on her way down the grassy verge and she kicked her stilettos off. By the time she reached them she was almost running.

'What's wrong, Davy?' she asked as she reached them. She ignored Alistair for the moment. It'd take something really dire to prise this shy six-year-old from his mum. There had to be something badly amiss. How had Alistair become involved? She had him twigged as the sort of guy who didn't get involved.

He was still holding Davy's hand. He was obviously very involved.

'Mum said to go and get Dad,' Davy whispered. 'But Dad's gone fishing.'

'He went out this morning?'

'He was going to win some prize,' Davy said, and swiped a grimy fist over an even more grimy face. 'But Mum can't get out of bed and the baby keeps crying and crying and there's nothing for Dottie and Megan to eat. I don't know what to do.'

'So Alistair's taking you home,' she said, casting Alistair an almost approving glance before stooping and tugging the little boy close.

'He said he was your friend,' Davy whispered.

'Of course he's my friend.' She hugged the little boy hard and then put him away from her, holding him at arm's length. She glanced up at Alistair and surprised a look of concern on his face. Well, well. The guy had a human side.

'OK, let's go find your mum and see if we can help until your dad comes back,' she said.

'That's just what we were doing,' Alistair said. 'But you're very welcome to join us.'

The hut was one of the most poverty-stricken dwellings Alistair had ever seen. The smell hit him first—an almost unbelievable stench. Then they rounded a stand of palms and reached the hut itself. Consisting of sheets of rusty corrugated iron propped up by stakes with a roof of the same iron weighted down by rocks, it looked more a kid's cubby hut than a real house.

'My God,' he whispered, and Georgie cast him a warning look.

'Most of these houses are better,' she said. 'But they're mostly used by itinerant fishermen, not by full-time residents. Even so... This hut is a long way from any other for a reason. Davy's dad is...not very friendly.'

He was starting to get a clear idea of Davy's dad and it wasn't a flattering picture. What sort of man left a wife who'd just given birth while he joined a fishing competition?

'You don't know the half of it,' Georgie said grimly, watching his face and guessing his thoughts. 'Stay out here for a moment and I'll see what's happening.'

She ducked inside the lean-to shed, leaving him outside, trying to ignore the smell.

Her inspection lasted only seconds. 'Come in,' she called, and something in her voice prepared him for what was inside.

The hut consisted of a rough chimney at one end with a dead fire at the base, a table and an assortment of camping chairs in various stages of disrepair. There were two double-bed mattresses on the floor and that was the extent of the furnishings. There was a baby lying in the middle of one mattress, wrapped neatly enough in a faded blue blanket. On the other bed were two little girls, four and two maybe. They were huddled as closely as they could get to a woman lying in the middle of the bed. The woman looked like she was sleeping. But...

'She's almost unconscious,' Georgie said, stopping his deepest dread before it took hold. 'The pulse is really thready and she's hot as hell. Damn. I need an ambulance. There's no cellphone reception down here but I'm driving the hospital car. It's parked up on the bridge and there's a radio in that. Right. The mum's Lizzie. The little girls are Dottie and Megan—Megan's the littlest—and this is baby Thomas. Take care of them. I'm fetching help.'

She left before he could answer.

Help.

This wasn't exactly familiar territory. He was a neurosurgeon. He was accustomed to a hospital with every facility he could possibly want. He'd reached the stage in his career where he was starting to train younger doctors. He'd almost forgotten this sort of hands-on medicine.

'Is she dead?' Davy whispered, appalled.

'No.' He hauled himself together. He was the doctor in charge.

'She's not.'

Move. Back to basics. Triage. He did a fast check on the baby—asleep but seemingly OK. He loosened the blanket and left him sleeping. Then he crossed to the mattress, stooped and felt the woman's pulse. It was faint and thready. The two little girls were huddled hard against her, big-eyed with terror.

'Davy, I need you to take your sisters onto the other bed while I look after your mother,' he told the little boy. He made to lift the first girl but she sobbed and pulled away from him.

'He's going to make our mum better,' Davy said fiercely. He grabbed her and pulled. 'Dottie, get off. Now.'

'I promise I'm here to help,' Alistair told them, and smiled. One of the little girls—the littlest—had an ugly bruise on her arm. And a burn on her knuckles. He winced. He remembered this pattern of burn mark from his training. Once seen, never forgotten.

'I'm here to help you,' he said softly. 'I promise. Dottie, Megan, will you let me see what's wrong with your mum?'

'He's Georgie's friend,' Davy said stoutly, and it was like he'd given a password. They shifted immediately so he could work. But they watched his every move.

Alistair smiled at them, then turned his attention to their mother. He didn't know how long it would be before help came. With a pulse like this...

The woman's eyelids flickered, just a little.

'Lizzie,' he said softly, and then more urgently, 'Lizzie.'

Her lids lifted, just a fraction.

On a makeshift bench there was a jug of water, none too clean, but he wasn't bothering about hygiene now. The woman had puckered skin, and she was dry and hot to the touch. A severe infection, he thought. The bedclothes around her were clammy, as if she'd been sweating for days.

He poured water into a dirty cup—there were no clean ones—swished it and tossed it out, then refilled the cup. In seconds he was lifting her a little so he was supporting her shoulders and holding the mug to her lips.

She shook her head, so fractionally he might have imagined it.

'Yes,' he said fiercely. 'Lizzie, I'm Dr Georgie's friend. Georgie's gone for help but I'm a doctor, too. You're dangerously dehydrated. You have to drink.'

Nothing.

'Lizzie, drink.'

'Drink, Mum,' Davy said, and Alistair could have blessed him. The woman's eyes moved past him and found her son.

'You have to do what the doctor says,' Davy quavered. 'He's Georgie's friend. Drink.'

She closed her eyes. He held her mug hard against her lips and tilted.

She took a sip.

'More,' he said, and she took another.

'Great, you're doing great. Come on, Lizzie, this is for Davy.'

He pushed her to drink the whole mug. Sip by tiny sip. She was so close to unconsciousness that it seemed to be taking her an almost superhuman effort.

These children were solely dependent on her, Alistair thought grimly. And she was so young. Mid-twenties? Maybe even less. She looked like a kid, a kid who was fighting for her life.

He could help. He poured more water into a bowl, stripped back her bedding and started sponging her. 'Can you help?' he asked Davy. 'We need to get her cool.' As Davy hesitated, Alistair lifted Lizzie's top sheet and ripped. OK, this family looked as if they could ill afford new sheets, but he'd buy them himself if he had to. He handed a handful of linen to each of the children.

'We need to keep your mum wet,' he said. 'We have to cool her down.' He left the woman's flimsy nightgown on and simply sponged through the fabric.

It was the right thing to do, on all sorts of fronts. It helped Lizzie, but it also gave the children direction. Megan seemed a bit dazed—lethargic? Maybe she was dehydrated as well. But Dottie and Davy started working, wetting their makeshift washcloths, wiping their mum's face, arms, legs, and then starting again. It kept the terror from their faces and he could see by the slight relaxing of the tension on Lizzie's face that it was doing her good. Cooling or not, the fact that there was another adult taking charge must be immeasurably reassuring.

He poured another drink for the little girl—Megan—and tried to persuade her to drink. She drank a little, gave a shy smile and started sponging as well.

Brave kid.

Then, faster than he'd thought possible, Georgie was back. She'd run in her bare feet, and she'd hauled an oversized bag back with her.

'This stuff is always in the hospital car,' she said briefly as his eyes widened. 'Emergency essentials.' When she saw what he'd been doing, she stopped short. 'Fever?'

'I'm guessing way above normal. But she's drunk a whole mug of water.'

'Oh, Lizzie, that's great.'

But Lizzie was no longer with them. She'd slipped back into a sleep that seemed to border on unconsciousness.

No matter. Her pulse was already steadying.

'Great work, kids,' Georgie said, setting her bag down on the floor and hauling it open. 'With workers like you guys, you hardly need me, but now I've brought my bag...let's see if what I have here might help her get better faster.'

They worked as a team. The bag was magnificently equipped. Within minutes they had a drip set up and intravenous antibiotics and rehydration were started. Georgie had lugged an oxygen cylinder with her and they started that as well. Covering all bases.

'Oh, God, if we hadn't come...' Georgie whispered.

It didn't bear thinking about. They both knew just how close to disaster the woman had been.

'Check the baby,' he said. He hadn't had time to give the children more than a cursory check, but while they were setting up the drip Davy had lifted the baby onto his knees and was cuddling his little brother. Davy—all of six years old with the responsibility of this entire family on his shoulders.

'Will you let me see him?' Georgie said softly to Davy, and Davy glanced up at her as if he was still uncertain who to trust. She smiled down at him—a tender smile that Alistair hadn't seen before. Another side of Georgie?

Davy relinquished his bundle and Alistair thought, Yeah, I would too if she smiled at me like that.

Crazy thought. Concentrate on work.

Georgie lifted the bundle into her arms, wrinkling her nose

at the stench. She laid the baby on the end of Lizzie's bed, removed his nappy and started cleaning.

Was this the sort of thing doctors did here? Alistair wondered. Medicine at its most basic.

'Has Thomas been drinking?' she was asking Davy.

'I dripped water into his mouth when he cried.'

'Good boy,' Georgie said in a voice that was suddenly un-
steady. 'You've done magnificently, Davy.' She glanced across
at Alistair. 'I'll leave the nappy off. He's hot as well, and probably dehydrated, like his mum. We need a drip here, too, I
reckon.'

Alistair checked the bag, and found what he needed. He
swabbed the tiny arm, preparing to insert a drip.

'You can do this on newborns?' Georgie queried. Veins in
neonates were notoriously difficult to find.

'I'm a neurosurgeon,' he told her. 'Paediatrics is my specialty.'

'We don't want brain surgery here,' she whispered. 'We just
need the ability to find a vein.'

Which he did. The syringe slid home with ease and he sensed
rather than saw the tension leave Georgie.

She cared about these people, he thought with something
akin to shock. He wouldn't have thought it of her. But, then,
she was an obstetrician. She just hadn't acted like one the first
time he'd met her.

There was the sound of a siren, from far away but moving
closer.

'Davy, can you go up to the road and show them where to
come?' Georgie asked, but as Davy rose Alistair gripped his
hand and held it.

'I'll come with you,' he said. 'Dr Georgie has done everything we need to do here. Davy, your mum's going to be OK, and
so is the baby. You found help. You've done everything right.'

The little boy's eyes filled with tears.

'Go and get the ambulance officers with Dr Alistair,' Georgie said to him. 'And that's the last thing we'll to ask you to do. We're taking you all to hospital where we can give you all a great big meal, pop you all into a lovely comfy bed near your mum and let you all have a long sleep until your mum is better.'

There was one last complication. They wouldn't all fit into the ambulance.

Megan was definitely dehydrated. Thomas hadn't been fed properly, maybe for twenty-four hours. He needed a humidicrib and intensive care. And Lizzie was waking a little more now, emerging from her semi-conscious state but moving to uncomprehending panic.

She was gripping Georgie's hand as if it was her lifeline. Every time she opened her eyes she searched in panic for Georgie. So Georgie had to go with her. Which made four in the ambulance. Lizzie, Megan, Thomas and Georgie.

'I can't go to hospital,' Lizzie murmured as the ambulance officers shifted her to a stretcher. 'Smiley'll kill me.'

'Yeah, well, maybe I'll kill him first,' Georgie said fiercely. 'So it should be quite a battle. Lizzie, you're moving out of here. I told you last time and now I'm insisting. And you needn't be afraid of Smiley. If you agree, I'll swing it so he never comes near you again. We'll organise you safe housing. I swear I'll fix it.'

Alistair blinked. These weren't calming, reassuring words to a desperately ill woman. But it seemed to work. Lizzie slumped back onto the stretcher and the tension seeped out of her.

'You're one of us,' she whispered. 'Thank God. Oh, Georgie, thank God.'

'Right to go?' the senior ambulance officer asked. These two may be ambulance officers but they didn't look like ambulance officers. They looked like fishermen.

'I stopped you fishing,' Lizzie whispered, becoming more aware of her surroundings.

'Nah,' the man said. 'The competition got called off half an hour ago 'cos the wind's getting up. Phyllis Dunn won. She wins every bloody year. Mind, she always ends up raffling her prize in aid of the hospital. Going to Fiji isn't Phyllis's style.'

What sort of town was this, where the ambulance officers went fishing while they were on duty? Alistair wondered. The younger officer looked at Alistair and grinned, guessing his thoughts.

'Hey, you needn't worry, mate,' he said. 'We had the ambulance parked right behind us while we were fishing, and most dramas were going to happen on the river anyway. Right?' he queried his partner, and they lifted the stretcher. They'd have to carry it—there was no car access here.'

'I'm coming with you,' Georgie said. She was cradling the baby in one arm and cuddling tiny Megan in the other.

'Let me carry them,' Alistair said, but as Megan buried her face in Georgie's neck, Georgie shook her head. She gave a rueful smile. 'Megan knows me,' she said. 'And Lizzie trusts me. It's easier if I sweat a bit. But we need Dottie and Davy to go with you. Davy, you know that Dr Carmichael is my friend?'

Davy knew what was coming. He gulped but then he looked up at Alistair and what he read in his face seemed to satisfy him. 'Y-yeah.'

'I want you to help Dr Carmichael drive my car,' Georgie said. 'He's an American and they don't even know what side of the road to drive on. And, Davy, I want you to hold Dottie's hand and take her with you. Will you do that? Dottie, will you do that? We won't all fit in the ambulance and Dr Carmichael will bring you straight to the hospital to be with your mum.'

There was a moment's hesitation.

'It's OK,' Davy whispered to Dottie, and once more he repeated his mantra. 'He's Georgie's friend.'

Dottie stared up at him dubiously, but then seemed to come to a decision. She tucked her hand into Alistair's and held on.

'The key's in my pocket,' Georgie said.

Really? In her pocket? There was a distracting thought coming from left field. He wouldn't have thought there was room for anything at all in those tight-fitting leathers.

She had no hand free to get them out. And he had one hand free.

'Front left,' she said patiently.

Front left. Right. Surgical removal of car keys. But, hell, those pants were tight. Hell, those pants were...

Maybe he'd better concentrate on other things. Dottie was holding his hand, waiting for him to get on with it. The younger ambo officer was looking at him and grinning, and he just knew what the guy was thinking.

What the hell. He grinned back and retrieved the keys, almost managing to keep his thoughts on the job at hand. Almost.

But as the keys came free he had room for another thought. What Georgie had said.

'Australians drive on the left.'

'We do,' Georgie said patiently. 'Problem?'

'You want me to drive Davy and Dottie to the hospital in your car?'

'In the hospital car. That's the idea, Einstein.' She was back to being tough. Any minute she'd start with the gum chewing again. The ambo boys were looking at her in surprise but he didn't have time to think about why she was being like she was.

'Look, this'll be the first time I've driven on the left... I'm not covered. Insurance-wise, I mean. If anything happens to the kids...'

'Here we go,' Georgie said, and sighed. 'American insurance paranoia.' The ambos had already started carrying the stretcher to the door and she was moving with them. 'Firstly, there's no one around to crash into,' she said over her shoulder. 'It's midday, and only mad dogs and Englishmen go out in the midday sun. Or Yankee neurosurgeons. So the roads will be deserted and there's no one to hit. Second, it's a straight line from here to the hospital. You can follow the ambulance. If you're nervous then move over and tell Davy to drive. He's probably as competent as you are.'

And with that she left, leaving him to follow.

The hospital was just as he remembered it. Long and low and cool, open to the ocean breeze. Actually, the ocean breeze was more than a breeze at the moment. The surrounding palms were tossing wildly, and the sea was covered in whitecaps. But the place still looked lovely. If you had to be sick this was one of the best places in the world to be.

Alistair pulled up in the car park and took the two children inside.

The children hadn't complained as their mother had left. Now they took a hand apiece, infinitely trusting. He felt really off balance, walking into Crocodile Creek Hospital Emergency with a child on each hand.

The ambulance was in the unloading bay, already unloaded. He hadn't followed it closely, preferring to travel slowly and safely. For all Georgie's reassurance, the left-hand-drive thing was a challenge, and having two small passengers made him careful.

There was no sign of Lizzie or Megan, but Georgie was in the emergency department, carrying Thomas. She was still in bare feet. He'd picked up her abandoned stilettos from the pathway—they were still in the car—a monument to stupidity. But she didn't look stupid now.

There was a nurse beside her. He recognised this woman from his last visit, too. Grace?

Grace gave him a smile of welcome but Georgie ignored him, bending down to greet the kids.

'Dottie. Davy. Dr Alistair got you here safely, then? That's great. Well done, both of you. And well done, Davy, for getting help so fast. Now, we're just giving your mum a proper wash and getting her really cool. She hasn't been drinking—that's why she's been sick. You know we popped a needle into her arm, and into Thomas's, to get water in faster? We've done the same to Megan. Megan's having a little sleep. But you guys will be thirsty as well, and probably hungry. So do you want to come and find your mum and Megan straight away or can Grace take you to the kitchen and give you some chocolate ice cream?'

It was exactly the right thing to say, Alistair thought. By the look of that hut, these kids must be starving. But Georgie wasn't sending them away with Grace without their consent. They were being given the choice. Your mum is safe. You can see her now, or there's ice cream on offer. The choice is yours.

'How about you have the ice cream and then come back and see your mum?' Grace said, tipping the scales. 'You know Mrs Grubb, don't you? She gave you ice cream when your mum was having the baby. She's in the kitchen right now, getting out bowls. And I think she has lemonade, too.'

'I really like ice cream,' Dottie whispered, and she even smiled. It was a great little smile, the first Alistair had seen from the children. He released their hands and watched them go, but as he did so he was aware of a sharp stab of something that almost seemed like…loss? Which was crazy.

The door through to the hospital kitchens swung closed behind them, and he became aware that Georgie was watching him. She had the saline drip looped over her shoulder, holding Thomas low so it was gravity feeding. She needed a drip stand.

'Do you want help with Thomas?' he asked.

'I'll take him through to the nursery in a minute, but apart from horrible nappy rash he seems OK. You know Davy's been dripping water into his mouth? What a hero.'

'He is,' Alistair said, and he thought back to the frail child sitting in the middle of the bridge and felt stunned. Awed.

'You remember Charles Wetherby—our director? Charles has Lizzie in his charge,' Georgie continued. She'd walked over to a drip stand and he moved with her, taking the saline bag from her shoulder and hanging it on its wheeled hook. 'It looks like severe infection. Charles is continuing the IV antibiotics and the nurses are cleaning her up. She's a mess.'

'When did she have the baby?'

'Four days ago.'

The image of Davy was still in the forefront of his mind. Lizzie, going home to the care of a six-year-old. 'You let her go home to that?' he demanded incredulously. 'Did you know her circumstances?'

It wasn't implied criticism. It was a direct attack.

Back home Alistair was head of a specialist neurosurgery unit. He had hiring and firing capabilities and he used them. The voice he had used then was the one that had any single subordinate—and many who weren't subordinate—shaking in their shoes. At least cringing a little.

Georgie didn't cringe. She met his gaze directly, as if she had nothing to search her conscience over.

'Yes.'

'What were you thinking?'

'I wasn't thinking anything. I was making the best of a bad situation. I spent the whole of Lizzie's pregnancy convincing her to come to the hospital for the birth. She's had the last three children at home. But this time I succeeded. She came in. I was hugely relieved, but when her partner insisted she go straight home I sent her with everything she needed. Including a course of antibiotics. No, at that stage she didn't need it, but I knew the hut.'

'It was criminal to let her go back there. You know the little girl's been burned. That's a cigarette burn.'

'I know. That's new. Up until now Lizzie would have stood up to him if he'd hurt the children. It's a sign of how sick she is.'

'But you let her go back.'

'You think I should have chained her up?'

'Surely a woman with sense—'

'Lizzie is a woman of sense,' she said, practically spitting.

'She's had a lousy childhood, she has a dreadful self-image and her partner...'

She broke off. Someone was coming into Emergency—no, two men, a uniformed police officer with a younger man in front of him. The young man was dark, but not the dark of the Australian indigenous people, as Lizzie was. He looked European. Mediterranean? He was dressed in filthy fishing clothes, he looked as if he hadn't shaved for a week, and the smell of him reached them before he did.

He didn't look like he wanted to be there, but the policeman was behind him, prodding him forward, giving him no choice. 'Hi, Georgie,' he said, but he didn't smile. 'You wanted to talk to Smiley?'

'Smiley,' Georgie said, and Alistair stared. Georgie was tiny, five feet two in her bare feet. She looked like you could pick her up and put her wherever you wanted. Not with that tongue, though. What she unleashed on the man before her was pure ice.

'Thanks, Harry,' she said, and nodded to the policeman with what was to be the last of her pleasantries. 'Alistair, can you take Thomas for a minute?' Before he could answer she'd handed over the sleeping baby, forcing Alistair to move closer to the drip stand. Then she poked her finger into the middle of Smiley's chest and pushed him backward.

'What the hell did you do with Lizzie's antibiotics?' she demanded, and although she spoke softly her words were razors. 'And the supplies we gave her. The nappies. The canned food.'

'I...'

'You sold them, didn't you?' she snarled. 'I don't even have to guess. I know. You took them down to the pub because someone might give you a buck for them. You thieving, filthy piece of pond scum. You nearly killed Lizzie. If Alistair here hadn't found her today, she'd be dead. She'd be dead because you stole her medicine. There's no food in your house. The kids are starving. You spent today on the river and Harry's just pulled you

out of the pub. And Megan's bruised arm and burned hand...
You did that, didn't you? You stinking, bottom-feeding low-life.'

'Hey—'

'Enough,' Georgie snarled. 'That's enough. Lizzie's conscious—only just, but she's conscious enough to agree to press
charges. You stole her medicines and you hit your kids and you
burned Megan.'

'I didn't hit anyone. If she says I did then she's lying. And
can I help it if the kid plays with matches? I didn't touch her.'
The man's reply was scornfully vituperative.

'Oh, yes, you did.' Georgie was still prodding the man in the
chest, poking with her finger to emphasise every word. The policeman appeared watchful but he was standing back, letting
Georgie have her say.

Alistair was stuck by the drip attached to the baby in his
arms. He didn't like this. The man looked...evil?

Georgie obviously thought he was. 'You hit Lizzie all the
time, don't you, Smiley? You keep her starving. You thump
her around and when she's not looking, you thump your kids.
You're nothing but a cowardly—'

'There's no way she'll press charges.'

'Because you'll hit her again if she does? Of course you will.
But you never hit anyone bigger than you, do you, Smiley?
You're a snivelling coward.'

'Shut up, bitch,' he snarled, but she wouldn't shut up. It was
as if she was driving him.

'So what happened on the river today, Smiley?' she spat,
continuing to prod him. 'Did you catch any fish? Or did you
come last as usual? You play the big man but you're nothing but
a loser. The whole town thinks you're a loser and the only way
you can big-note yourself is to hit women and kids.'

'Georg,' Harry said urgently, and the policeman took a
step forward. So did Alistair but he was holding Thomas, and
Thomas was attached to the drip.

'Don't push me,' Smiley yelled.

She pushed him. Hard.

No, Alistair thought. He moved—but he was caught by the drip stand.

'Georg, no,' Harry yelled, and lunged forward.

He was too late.

Smiley hit her. Just like that, Smiley's fist came up and smashed into the side of her face with a sickening crunch. Georgie fell sideways. She'd barely hit the floor before Harry had Smiley, hauling him away, and Alistair was just as fast. In one swift movement he'd hauled the drip stand over so it was lying on the floor and baby Thomas was lying safely beside it. Alistair had Smiley's arms, tugging them behind him. Smiley struggled but he was no match for the two of them.

Georgie lay prone for a moment, but before they could reach her she'd staggered upright, her hand to her cheek, clutching the trolley for support.

They had him secured. Harry was clipping handcuffs on Smiley's wrists, but Alistair was no longer with him. He'd moved to Georgie's side to see the damage. He felt sick. Oh, God, why hadn't he stopped it? Why had she pushed him? She had her hand to her eyes. 'Georgie...'

'He hit me,' she muttered.

'Let me see.'

'No.' She sounded close to tears. Where a moment ago she had been a tight knot of pure aggression, she now sounded limp and defeated. 'He hit me,' she whispered.

'What's he done?' Harry sounded anxious.

'I'll need X-rays,' she whispered, and Harry's face darkened as he turned back to the man he held.

'Smiley Price, I'm arresting you for assault,' Harry said. 'You do not have to say anything but anything you say may be—'

'I know my rights,' Smiley yelled. 'This is a set-up.

'I didn't see a set-up,' Harry said grimly. 'I saw you assaulting a doctor when she was discussing your wife's medical treatment.' He glanced across at Georgie. 'Georg, let Alistair see your face.'

'Take care of Thomas,' Georgie whispered to Alistair. On the floor Thomas was considering his options. He'd been unceremoniously dumped. Until how he'd been silent, sleeping, mostly because he was badly dehydrated. But fluid had been flowing for maybe an hour now and he was starting to feel more like expressing himself.

He did. He opened his mouth and he roared.

'That's great,' Georgie said, giving a weak smile. 'Alistair, pick him up.'

He didn't. He took Georgie's hand and tugged it away from her face.

The punch hadn't hit her eye, for which he was profoundly thankful. Instead, it had smashed into her cheekbone. The soft tissue was swelling while he watched, and the skin had split a little. A trickle of blood was inching down toward her neck.

'You bastard,' Harry said, twisting Smiley's arm and dragging him toward the door. He nodded to Alistair. 'I'll need a witness statement from you. Get photographs. Not that we'll need them.' He was gripping Smiley's arm in a hold that said he wasn't going anywhere. 'If you remember, mate, you're already on a two-year suspended sentence for theft. With what you've done today they'll throw away the key.'

'Get him out of my sight,' Georgie whispered, as Harry prodded him through the door, and then she roused. 'And if I can find anything at all to charge you with, I will,' she yelled after him. 'Two years is just the beginning.'

The door closed after them.

They were left alone. Except for one screaming baby.

Georgie picked Thomas up before Alistair could stop her. She hugged him tight. The baby's sobs stopped, just like that. Alistair lifted the drip stand and turned back to her. She was hugging the baby as if it was she who needed comfort.

Involuntarily his hands came out to take her shoulders. It

was an instinctive gesture of comfort but she drew back as if his touch burned.

'No.'

'I'm sorry…'

'No.' She held her spare hand to her eyes for a moment as if things were more than she could face. Then she took a deep breath and another.

'OK,' she said, moving on. 'Your bag's over in the doctors' quarters. You have the same room as you had last time you were here. Gina will be home about five. There's food and drink in the kitchen. Have a swim. Make yourself at home.'

'Your face needs attention.'

'I'll give it a wash later.' She took a deep breath and tried to smile. 'But wasn't it fantastic? He's been hitting Lizzie and the kids for years and she won't press charges. She's said she will now, and she might when she knows he's going to jail anyway, but it's no longer up to her. I'll be doing the pressing of charges.'

'You planned it,' he said, stunned.

'I knew about the suspended sentence,' she admitted.

'Are you mad? He could have blinded you.'

'He didn't. I've learned how to take a hit over the years. I was moving away as he struck. But I had to let him make contact.'

'You're crazy.'

'And Smiley's in jail. A good afternoon's work, I reckon. Now… I need to sort out a carer for the kids. I need to contact welfare officers and the housing people. I'm moving so fast here Smiley won't know what's hit him. If you can—'

'You let him hit you.'

'Get over it.'

'Of all the…' Before she could stop him he'd lifted Thomas from her arms. He tugged the drip stand with him over to an examination trolley. Gently he laid the little one down. Thomas accepted the move with equanimity. Strange things were happening in his world, and he was learning early that fussing didn't necessarily get him anywhere.

'I don't want him down,' Georgie said, moving to pick him up again, but Alistair intercepted her.

'I've done the triage, Dr Turner. Not before I've checked that eye.'

'It's fine.'

For answer he picked her up and sat her on the trolley next to Thomas. She opened her mouth to squeak a protest but he was already gently probing, checking bone structure, peering intently at her eye, looking for internal bleeding.

She was so slight. A diminutive woman with courage that would put men twice her size to shame. She submitted to his ministrations but he had the feeling she was simply humouring him.

'No brain injury,' she said, gently mocking. 'Nothing here you're interested in.'

Maybe not. But he was suddenly aware of what he'd felt six months ago. The feeling that had surfaced as he'd danced with her.

He'd thought she was a woman with morals somewhere below that of a guttersnipe.

Maybe he'd misjudged her...

'What's happening?'

It was Grace, bursting in to see what was happening. Appalled. 'Georgie, you're hurt. I just saw Harry taking Smiley away. He said—'

'I'm fine,' Georgie said.

'But Harry said Smiley hit you.' Grace sounded incredulous. 'You let him hit you?'

'I had to.'

'She does karate,' Grace said to Alistair. 'She's black belt. No man can get near her. Harry knew that or he'd never...' She'd moved closer to Georgie as she'd spoken, edging in on Alistair's space. 'Harry's feeling dreadful and sent me to check. Let me see.'

'I'm fine.'

'You're shaking.'

'I am not. Leave me be.' Georgie jumped down from the trolley before Alistair could stop her. 'If you want to be useful, take Thomas.'

'That's another reason I'm here,' Grace admitted. 'Lizzie's asking for him and Charles wants to check him. But, Georgie, come through and let Charles see the damage.'

'I'm fine,' Georgie snapped again.

'I'll take care of it,' Alistair said, and Grace looked at him dubiously. Then her face cleared as she obviously remembered stuff she'd been told about him. 'Of course. You're Gina's Alistair. You're a neurosurgeon.'

'That's right,'

'Then I guess you can cope. If you think she needs an X-ray, give a yell.'

'He won't do any medicine,' Georgie said, sounding contemptuous. 'I know US doctors. They think treating people messes with their insurance.'

'Now, that,' Grace said roundly, 'is just plain rude. And wrong. The ambo boys said Alistair's already put in a drip. And I'm sure he'll help any way he can. Won't you, Alistair?'

'Of course.' Black belt in karate, huh? He eyed Georgie with increasing respect.

'I only pick on people my own size,' Georgie said.

'I wasn't thinking—'

'Yeah, you were. Wimp.'

'Georgie, behave,' Grace said severely. Thomas opened his mouth again, a preliminary to wailing. Ready, set, yell. She smiled ruefully down at him. 'OK, sweetheart, I'll take you to your mum. Alistair, there's a digital camera in the desk drawer. Use it. Please. Harry says we need photographs. I'm sorry to leave you like this but this place has gone crazy. I'll be back as soon as I can. Georgie, behave,' she repeated.

And she was gone.

CHAPTER THREE

THERE WAS A moment's silence. Georgie's hand had crept to her cheek again, hiding the damage.

'I do need to clean and dress it,' he said gently, but she shook her head and started following Grace.

She was limping.

'Georgie?'

'I'm fine.'

'You're not.'

Alistair moved then, fast, catching her by the shoulders and turning her around. Gently. Aware of her black belt.

But her black belt had been punched right out of her.

'Leave me be.' She sounded suddenly…drained.

'Let me see your face. And your foot.'

'No.'

She was like a little wildcat, he thought. Tough as nails, all claws and hiss. But she was shaking. He could feel the tremors in her shoulders.

To hell with the black belt. He lifted her up again and dumped her on the nearest examination trolley. 'Stay where you're put.'

'Do you mind?' She seemed practically speechless. 'I need to—'

'Nothing's more urgent than your face. You should have

stayed put in the first place.' He pulled her fingers away. 'Hell, Georgie...'

'Don't swear. You make me feel like it's worse than it is.'

'It's bad.'

'It's not. I've learned how to ride a punch. I can feel my cheekbone. He didn't break anything.'

She'd learned how to ride a punch? In karate? He didn't think so. Everything about this woman spoke of a tough background.

Except that she was an obstetrician.

First things first. If she'd gone to this much effort, it wasn't about to be wasted for want of effort on his part. He wheeled across to the desk by the door and found the camera. 'Let's do this before we do any cleaning.'

'Oh, very good,' she said, and managed a smile. 'OK, I submit.'

'Lie down.'

'No, I—'

'You'll look more pallid and wan against the pillows.'

'I don't want to look like a victim.'

'I'm very sure you do.' He fiddled with the camera. 'If you could manage a few tears...'

She thought about that, and then she managed a smile. It was a great smile, despite the bruising. Like the sun had just come out.

'Right,' she said, and she lay back on the pillows, moving into her role of victim with gusto. He adjusted the camera, turned to focus on her cheek—and to his astonishment her eyes were brimming.

He stared.

'Neat trick, huh?' she said. 'Don't interrupt. I'm thinking sad thoughts.'

Sad thoughts. He couldn't make her out. He focused and shot. The photograph would be damning, he thought. Her dark curls accentuated the pallor of her skin. The knuckle marks of

Smiley's hand were clearly visible and the splitting of the skin before it was cleaned looked worse than it actually was.

And she was playing it for all it was worth. Her eyes were brimming, seemingly pain-filled. There were tears coursing down her cheeks.

He wanted to… He wanted to…

'Enough,' she declared as the camera clicked for the fourth time. She swung herself upright.

He put the camera aside and pushed her down again.

'Do you mind?'

'Not at all. Let's do a bit more triage. Foot first.' He'd moved before she knew what he intended. He had her left foot in his hand, lifting it high. 'Ouch.'

'It's fine,' she snapped. 'I can't use that against Smiley.'

'It'd be good if we could,' he agreed, examining her heel with care. 'Hell, woman, were you out of your mind, running in bare feet?'

'I scarcely had a choice.'

'You had a choice as to what to put on this morning.' He hauled a nearby trolley closer and stared dubiously at its contents. 'Stilettos?'

'You're criticising my footwear?'

'I am. There's a splinter in here. A deep one.'

'I'll get it out myself.'

'Shut up and lie back,' he told her, and then, as she struggled to sit up and opened her mouth to argue, he took her by the shoulders and propelled her back onto the pillows. 'Not a word.'

'You're not an emergency doctor,' she said resentfully, and he tugged on gloves, located a pile of antiseptic swabs and ripped one open.

'No. I'm a neurosurgeon. You want a little brain surgery on the side?'

'Look, honest—'

'Lie still and think of England,' he told her. 'This might sting.'

* * *

It did sting. But for a big man he had really gentle hands, she thought as she did what she was told and lay back and thought... well, not of England but of what this man represented.

He'd almost taken her to bed. Six months ago she'd been out of her mind with grief and worry, and Alistair had taken advantage of it.

He hadn't known she'd been out of her mind with grief and worry. Maybe he'd thought she was always a tart.

Well, he was hardly stain-free. Propositioning her when he'd been engaged to another woman...

Was he still engaged? Maybe he was married. She hadn't asked Gina.

What was she doing, wondering what his marital status was? He was a stuffed shirt. An eminent US neurosurgeon. He was about as far from her world as it was possible to get.

'Ouch!' Her exclamation was involuntary. Alistair had positioned the light directly above her foot and was operating with a scalpel and a pair of tweezers. She glanced down at what he was doing and winced.

'A scalpel! You don't think that's a bit of overkill?'

'I promise I'm not amputating.'

'Oh, very good. I'm reassured, I don't think. Yike!'

'I'm sorry, but I'm being quick. Local anaesthetics in the heel will hurt a lot more than I need to hurt you now. So stay still.'

'But a scalpel?'

'If you wiggle, I might be forced to amputate.'

'I want a second opinion.'

He grinned. Which took her aback somewhat. It was a really great grin.

She'd never seen him smile, she thought. Or maybe she had that night six months ago but she'd hardly been in a state where she could remember anything.

She could remember that she'd decided to sleep with him. So there must have been something...

'Got it,' he said in satisfaction, and then, as she made to sit up, he lifted both feet, which had the effect of propelling her down again.

'There's cleaning yet to be done.'

'Fussy…'

'Yeah, and I don't wear stilettos either. But I'm still a qualified doctor.'

He was…gorgeous? Just like last time.

No matter. There was no way she intended to be attracted by this man again. She'd made a fool of herself six months ago and that was the end of it.

She lay back and concentrated on not concentrating on anything at all for a bit. Finally he adjusted a neat dressing on her foot and moved to her end of the bed.

'Now, let's see to your face,' he said. 'Your foot's OK. Just don't walk on it for a bit. It'll bleed.'

'Then your dressing's not good enough.'

'Georgie…'

'I know.' She sighed and glowered, and then submitted as he cleaned her face. He was so gentle. He'd hurt her a bit, getting the splinter out—that had been unavoidable—but he wasn't hurting her now.

'Steristrips will do it,' he said as he worked. 'It doesn't need stitching. But the bruise is extensive. We'll take an X-ray to make sure.'

'I don't need an X-ray. There's nothing displaced. Even if there's a hairline fracture, there's nothing to be done about it.'

'But think of the damage you could do with a broken bone,' he coaxed. 'It's bound to put another year or so on the sentence.'

She stared up at him. And then she choked on an unexpected bubble of laughter.

'That's better,' he said, and smiled down at her, and suddenly they were smiling into each other's eyes like…

Fools?

'I need to put a dressing on,' he said unevenly, and she gave a shaky little nod.

'Yes.'

What the hell was happening? Why did this man have the power to move her?

Hell, hadn't he caused enough trouble in her life?

'Georg!' For some reason—or maybe she knew the reason but she wasn't all that happy to admit it—she hadn't heard the doors opening behind them. Now Alistair turned with what seemed almost a guilty start. Which was crazy. He'd just been...

Looking?

No. He'd been examining a patient. Nothing more. She dragged her eyes away from his face and turned to see who'd entered.

It was Gina—Dr Gina Lopez—walking swiftly into the room and across to Georgie's trolley. She looked frightened. 'I just met Harry,' she said, ignoring Alistair for the moment and concentrating on Georgie. 'He said you made Smiley hit you.'

'I did no such thing.'

She bent to hug her. 'You dope.'

'He'll get put away for ages,' Georgie said, but suddenly her voice was trembling again. 'Gina, don't hug me.'

'She doesn't let people hug her,' Gina told Alistair, pulling back and sounding emotional. She swallowed and turned to her cousin. 'Hi,' she said, and she gave Alistair the hug she'd certainly wanted to give Georgie. 'It's lovely to see you. I'm so sorry Cal and I weren't here to meet you. In the end we couldn't get all our work done on the island anyway—the pilot started to get concerned about the weather and brought us back early. But I gather you've arrived to excitement.'

'You asked Georgie to meet me. Of course I arrived to excitement.'

'She's not always...' Gina paused, turned to her friend sitting up defiantly on the examination trolley, barefoot, leather-clad, dressings on her foot and on her face, her lipstick still defiantly crimson… 'Yeah, OK, she is always exciting,' Gina said. 'But we love her anyway.'

Alistair was starting to look confused. As if he wasn't quite understanding what was going on. Good, Georgie thought, because that was how she was feeling.

'Don't let her stand on her foot,' he managed.

'I'll take her over to the doctors' house,' Gina told him, looking around. She located what she was looking for, darted over and hauled back a wheelchair. 'Can you help her into this, please, Alistair?'

'I'm not getting in that thing,' Georgie said, revolted.

'I want you off that foot for a few hours,' Alistair said. 'Pressure will make it bleed. I also want an X-ray. Get into the chair and we'll take you.'

'Do what the doctor says,' Gina said, and grinned.

'No way,' Georgie snapped, and suddenly Alistair smiled as well.

'You know, you're sounding like me at the airport,' he said. 'Get on my bike or suffer the consequences. I didn't get on your bike and I suffered the consequences, so now I'm expecting you to be wiser. Right.' He stepped forward and lifted her into his arms in one swift movement. 'Lead the way, Gina. I'm taking this lady to X-Ray and then I'm taking her to bed.'

Maybe it had been the wrong thing to say. Georgie's face turned crimson suddenly.

'To your sickbed,' he amended. 'Don't look like that. OK, I know we were introduced in very different circumstances six months ago, but we're adults. Let's get a bit of professional detachment here. I'm sure we can handle it.'

He might be able to handle it. She couldn't. Safely tucked up in bed—Gina had ignored her protests, helped her off with her clothes and insisted she stay where she was—Georgie had the rest of the afternoon to think about the events of the day.

She wasn't all that upset about being in bed, she conceded.

She'd been shaken more than she cared to admit. The punch to her face had done more than bruise her. It had brought back sweeping memories of the way she'd once lived—memories she'd spent her entire life fighting to get away from.

She was still feeling shaky. The X-rays were showing a hair-line cheek fracture. She was getting slow in her old age, she thought bitterly, but it was still worth it. Smiley would definitely be going to jail. Gina had given her analgesics—'Humour me in this, OK, Georg?'—and she was grateful for them. They made her sleepy. She closed her eyes and let herself sink into her cool pillows, but sleep didn't come.

What came was the image of Alistair. A big man with gentle hands. The image of the way he'd held Thomas sprang to mind. He'd held the baby just as a baby needed to be held. Most men would be afraid of such a newborn, but not Alistair.

'He's still a prig,' she told her pillow. 'And he's still engaged.'

But she could see why Gina had asked him to give her away. He was a real father figure.

Um…actually not. There was nothing fatherly about the way she was feeling about him. He wasn't as old as she remembered. Mid-thirties? Young to be an eminent neurosurgeon.

The guy had to be seriously good.

But all the same…

'Stay away from him,' she told herself. 'He's only here for a week. I don't know why he upsets your equilibrium, but he does. Just keep clear.'

She finally did sleep, and when she woke it was dark. She was hungry, she decided. That had to be a good sign.

Her jaw ached. That wasn't such a good sign. She tried opening and closing her mouth a few times. She'd live, but she was in for an uncomfortable few hours.

The house was deathly quiet, apart from the whistling of the wind round the corners of the building. She lay still and tried to remember what day it was. Friday. The day before Em and Mike's wedding. There were celebrations taking place that night. Hens' night and bucks' night. Or a mixture of both, because there'd been hassles with the bridesmaids. Everyone who wasn't working would be down at the Athina.

They hadn't woken her. They'd have figured she wouldn't want to go.

She rose, flicked on her light and caught her reflection in the mirror. Wow. The bruising looked even worse than it had before she'd slept.

She needed Alistair and his camera.

Despite the discomfort, she grinned. This should really go down well in court. Hopefully by the time Smiley was released Lizzie would have her life together and would have found the strength to tell Smiley where to go.

A bruise in a good cause.

She got up and went to the bathroom, swallowed a couple of painkillers and returned to bed.

She was hungry.

As the painkillers dulled the ache, she grew hungrier.

They'd all be down at the tavern.

She didn't want to be at the tavern. She could do without noise and crowds tonight. But...

She had the fridge to herself, she thought, cheering up. Mrs Grubb, the hospital cook, kept their fridge laden and, as far as she knew, she was all by herself. Anyone who wasn't working would be at the party.

She pushed on a pair of scuffs as a concession to her sore foot—which wasn't all that sore—Alistair had done a decent job. Then she padded through the house, her stomach leading the way.

The place was in darkness. She flicked on the kitchen light and loaded a plate. Cold chicken. Quiche. Some sort of noodly salad. Apple slice—hoorah for Mrs Grubb. A glass of milk and she was set.

It was hot inside. Outside there was wind—an abundance of

wind by the sound of it—but the veranda was usually sheltered. Clutching her plate, she pushed the screen door wide.

'Hi,' Alistair said, and she almost dropped her plate.

She wasn't dressed for company. She was wearing a very skimpy nightgown. Pink scuffs. Nothing else.

She retreated a bit but he'd pushed himself out of the ancient settee and was taking her plate from her.

He'd taken off his stupid suit. He was wearing shorts, a khaki, open-necked shirt and nothing on his legs and feet. He looked... amazing.

'I'll pull up a table.'

'There's no need.'

'There is a need,' he said gently. 'Hey, I'm not going to jump you, Georgie. If you want, I'll even go away. You've earned the right to eat where you like tonight.'

'I didn't think you were going to jump me,' she said a trifle breathlessly, and he smiled.

'That's good, then. Sit.'

She sat.

'Are you hurting?'

'Gina gave me something. I'm fine.'

He nodded and went back to staring over the sea. Which gave her space to eat. It didn't hurt too much to eat. She still had space in her thoughts to watch him covertly. And think about him.

He wasn't a father type at all, she thought. Why Gina thought he could give her away....

She shouldn't be thinking like that. She tried really hard to concentrate on her food. Which was hard. It's the painkillers, she thought. They were making her fuzzy.

'Georg?' There was a yell from inside the house.

'We're out here,' Alistair called back.

It was Harry. He was still in his police uniform. Still on duty.

'I rang the bell and no one answered,' he said apologetically.

'Sorry, Georg. Your bedroom door was open so I knew you were up somewhere.'

'People come and go as they please in this house,' Georgie told Alistair, as he looked confused. 'And Harry's one of us.'

'One of you?'

'The host of young professionals who run the Croc Creek rescue base,' she said. 'Medics. Policemen. Pilots. We're a huge team. Why aren't you at the party?'

'Duty,' Harry said bitterly. 'Plus this storm. I've been on the radio for the past hour, trying to persuade stupid bloody fishermen that they need to get into port right now. This cyclone's supposed to be blowing out to sea, instead of which it's lurking off the coast like a great black time bomb.' He sighed. 'Anyway, how's the face?' He flicked the porch light on. Then he flicked it off again. 'Ugh.'

'Hey, I have to be a beautiful bridesmaid in eight days,' Georgie protested. 'Say something bracing like, "Naught but a scratch, lass."'

'Naught but a scratch, lass,' Harry said, but he didn't sound convincing. He glanced at Alistair in indecision. 'Um… Georg, I need to talk to you.'

'I'm here.'

'About your old man,' he said, and Georgie stilled.

'What's he done now?' she whispered.

Harry hesitated. He glanced at Alistair, and Alistair obviously got the message. 'I'll leave you two alone,' he said.

But Georgie shook her head. For some dumb reason she suddenly wanted him to stick around. Strength in numbers? Something like that.

'Just tell me, Harry,' she said wearily, and both men looked at her in concern. 'I don't care who else knows.'

'He's wanted for a bank job in Mt Isa.'

She flinched.

'You didn't know?' Harry asked, watching her closely.

'No,' she whispered.

'He hasn't been in contact with you?'

'No.'

'But Max...'

She felt sick. 'Oh, God, Harry, I haven't heard from Max for months. I've been going out of my mind with worry.'

'Who's Max?' Alistair asked, and she flashed him a butt-out glance.

'He's mine!'

'Max is seven,' Harry explained. 'He usually lives here with Georgie but Ron took him away six months ago.'

'Which is why I drank too much at Gina's engagement party.' Georgie stood up, then leaned forward and grabbed the veranda rail for support. Alistair was by her side before she reached the rail, holding her steady.

'I'm fine,' she muttered. She bit her lip and looked up at Harry, meeting his gaze head on. 'What do you want me to do?'

'Nothing,' Harry told her. 'I was pretty sure you hadn't heard but the big boys are telling me to ask you. Maybe they'll tap your phone.'

'If anyone phones me, it'll be Max. Not Ron. And they're more than welcome to listen to any conversation I have with Max. Where the hell is he?'

Harry shook his head. 'That's what I'm asking you.'

'Ron knows I'll kill him if any harm comes to Max.'

It was a flat statement of intent. She meant it. She shivered and Alistair was suddenly holding her close, hugging her against him.

'She's had enough,' he said, and Harry nodded.

'Yeah. I know that. I didn't want to ask. But you'll let me know, Georg.'

'If I hear, I'll yell it to the rooftops.'

'Even if it means jail for Ron?'

'You think I want him outside? Messing with Max? I want sole custody but they won't give it to me.'

'So you want him in jail,' Harry said, with a lopsided grin.

'You're putting them all away tonight. I'll do my best to get him where you want him to be. Can I put out a missing person bulletin for Max?'

'Ron won't have deserted him. He wouldn't dare.'

'It can't hurt to broadcast that he's missing. People are more likely to respond to a plea for a missing kid rather than information wanted about Ron.'

'OK,' she said wearily. 'If it'll help… Please, Harry.'

'Leave it with me,' he told her, and then, with a last curious look from one to the other, he left them, striding down through the garden to the beach path below.

There was a long silence. The wind was rising to storm level now, bending the palms between them and the beach, whistling around the old house, making their sheltered veranda seem even more isolated. Even more of a refuge.

He should go in and leave her to her thoughts, but Alistair didn't want to. She'd pulled away from him. Now she was leaning on the veranda rail, staring at nothing.

He shouldn't get involved.

He was involved, like it or not.

'Your… Max left six months ago?' he said softly, and she didn't respond.

'Georgie?'

'Yeah,' she said flatly, at last. 'The night of Gina and Cal's engagement party. Ron just arrived and demanded Max go with him. He had the right. He took Max, even though Max was desperate to stay. Max is almost the same age as Gina's CJ. They'd just started to be friends. It was…' She broke off. 'Sorry. It's boring. Ron has the right and I don't.'

'So your behaviour the night of the engagement party….'

She rounded on him then, angry. 'I was drunk. I was out of my mind with worry. You don't think I really fancied you, do you?'

'I…'

'I was dumb, right?' she snapped. 'Get over it.'

'But you'll get Max back,' he said, thinking maybe he ought to leave it, but, regardless, he was compelled to keep going.

'If Ron's caught.'

'How the hell did you get caught up with a man like Ron?'

Silence.

'Georgie—'

'Leave it.'

'No,' he said, stupidly maybe, but, hell, he couldn't leave it like this. 'Georgie, I'm no expert but it seems to me the courts usually give custody to the mother. That's the way it is in the States at least, and I can't see why it's different here. If they granted Ron custody...well, maybe you were wild in the past. But there's enough people here who'd vouch for you now. You've got a great job in a terrific little community. If Ron goes to jail you could apply again...'

There was a deathly silence. He'd messed it up, he thought. He shouldn't have said it.

'You think I might have been a bad mother in the past,' she whispered.

'Hell, I don't know...'

'Just because I wear leathers.'

'They're great leathers.'

'But they put me in the right socio-economic class to be a bad mum.'

'Georg...'

'I'd slap you,' she said wearily, 'but I'm all slapped out. You stand there with your righteous answer-to-all solution. Prove to the courts that I'm respectable and... Hell, you think I should wear a twinset?'

She was close to hysteria, he thought.

'I think it'd be a damned shame if you wore a twinset.'

She stared—and then she choked, half with laughter, half with tears. 'You don't know what you're talking about,' she whispered.

'I do know you look fantastic.'

'In leathers. Every man's fantasy.'

'Actually, I was thinking you look fantastic in nightie, scuffs and bandages.'

'Cut it out.'

'Right.'

'You propositioned me last time you were here,' she whispered. 'Behind... What's her name? Eloise or something's back. Slime-ball.'

'You're talking about my fiancée?'

'Yeah, isn't that presumptuous of me? Low-life talking of her betters.'

'Where the hell did you get that chip on your shoulder?'

'If you give crazy compliments when you're engaged to another woman...'

'I'm not engaged.'

She blinked. 'Not...'

'There were...repercussions after the last time we met,' he told her.

'She found out? Someone told her? We didn't get past the hall door,' she said. 'Was that enough to make her call it off?'

'I called it off,' he said gently. Maybe it wasn't the time or the place to be saying this, but it suddenly seemed important that Georgie know. 'Eloise and I are solid professional colleagues who enjoy working together. We work long hours and it seemed an extension of that that we ate together and spent spare time together and finally moved in together. We just sort of drifted toward marriage. Only then... I came out here.'

'And you fell head over heels for me?' she mocked in incredulous disbelief. He shook his head.

'I hardly fell in love with you.'

'Well, you wouldn't.'

'Let me finish,' he said. 'Georgie, I was attracted to you. It was a crazy aberration and we have Gina to thank that it went no further, especially now I know what state you were in. But it did make me see that what I had with Eloise wasn't enough.'

'So I caused you to break off your engagement,' she whispered. 'Well, well. But you didn't say...'

'It was hardly appropriate to get off a plane shouting that I'd broken off my engagement. I didn't want to burden you with it.'

She blinked at that. 'Excuse me?'

'Yeah, that's presumptuous, too,' he agreed. Hell, he wasn't getting it right here. 'Look, I just want to tell you that I wasn't as big a slime-ball as you thought. Or maybe I was, but it was a big deal and what happened made me think through where I was going.'

She stared at him for a long moment. She raked her curls with her fingers and shuddered. The shudder made him move instinctively toward her, but she held up a hand as if to ward him off.

'No.'

'I'm not—'

'I know you're not,' she whispered. 'And I'm not either. But I am really, really tired.'

'I'll help you to bed.'

'No,' she said. 'Thank you. I'll go on my own.'

'Is there anything I can do?'

'I don't think so.'

'If you think of any place you want searched,' he offered, 'I have a week before Gina's wedding. I was going to do some sightseeing but if you'd like me to help search for your son...'

'My son.'

'Max.'

She bit her lip. Then she whispered. 'No. Thank you. I don't know where to start looking and if Ron doesn't want to be found then he won't be. Even if I found them... I couldn't turn Ron in. I just...couldn't.'

'You still have feelings...'

'I don't have any feelings at all,' she whispered. 'Not for Ron. You're thinking he's my ex-husband. Well, that fits. Leathers, stilettos, bike, an ex-husband who's a criminal. Sorry to disappoint you but no.'

'Then…'

'Ron's my stepfather,' she whispered. 'He's the man who taught me to ride a punch. He's the reason I left home at fourteen and have never been back. And he's Max's father. My lovely Max. My kid brother. He calls me Mum because I'm the only mother figure he's known. He's the only male I've ever loved and ever will. Now, if you'll excuse me, I'm going back to bed.'

Out to sea, Hurricane Willie paused. For no good reason. The massive front of bad weather had been inching eastward. It had been expected to blow out to sea but now it seemed indecisive. It stilled, building strength. Building fury.

Even now the force from its epicentre was being felt by the mainland, from Brisbane to Cooktown. The mainlanders checked their weather charts and listened to the forecasts.

No one knew…

CHAPTER FOUR

'I'm not sure where she is,' Gina told Alistair. 'She could even be sleeping in. This is an odd day. Georgie normally does an antenatal clinic out on Wallaby Island on Saturday morning but it'd be curtailed anyway because the wedding's at four. And now...this weather's so awful there's no way anyone's going out there.'

It certainly was awful. Alistair had been planning to take a diving trip to the Great Barrier Reef. Now he was trapped in Crocodile Creek, surrounded by wedding preparations for a couple he hardly knew.

'Maybe I should check on her,' he said, and Gina paused in what she was doing—was she really tying silver-painted chicken wishbones to baskets of sugared almonds?—and looked at him. Thoughtfully.

'Don't. She doesn't want you to. You upset her last night.'

'I didn't mean to,' he said, taken aback.

'She said you treated her like a tramp.'

'I didn't mean to do that either.'

'You suggested it was no wonder she didn't get custody of Max.'

'Hey.' He sighed and sat down at the kitchen table in front of

Gina. And tried to think what to say. And couldn't. 'How many of these do you have to tie?' he said at last, which was pathetic but small talk had never been his forte.

'A hundred and twenty.'

'How many have you done?'

'Thirty.'

'And they're for?'

'Fertility. Mrs Poulos says.'

'Silly me for asking,' he said, and picked up a wishbone. 'Tell me about Georgiana.'

Gina kept on tying. 'She says you have her summed up.'

'I did have her summed up,' he said ruefully. 'I may have got it wrong.'

'She doesn't always wear stilettos,' Gina conceded.

'You mean she only did it for my benefit?'

'I suspect she was horrified about the way she behaved when you were here last.'

'I was pretty horrified at myself, too.'

'So have you apologised?'

'I... No.'

'She had a reason for behaving appallingly. What was yours?'

'I thought she was...'

There was a lengthy pause. Four more chicken wishbones got attached to baskets.

'You thought she was cheap?' Gina suggested.

'I thought she was gorgeous,' Alistair admitted. 'Cheap, yeah. But still gorgeous. When she threw herself at me, I couldn't resist.'

'Men!'

'She was...gorgeous. Trashy but great. You don't feel like that when you look at Cal?'

'Hey, we're talking about my future husband here,' Gina said with asperity. 'My husband in a week. Someone I respect. You're talking about someone you're describing as trashy.'

He winced. 'Are these wishbones for your wedding or for the one this afternoon?'

'This afternoon. Mike's mum read it in *Vogue* about a hundred years ago and she's had her heart set on them ever since. Every chicken that's gone through this kitchen has died for the greater good of Mike's wedding.' She tied another. 'So...' She looked at him dubiously across the table. 'You saw Georgie and you got the hots for her.'

'I'm sure there are better ways of framing it.'

'I don't have to watch my mouth with my cousin. Do you still have the hots?'

'No!'

'But six months ago...you felt so strongly that you went home and broke it off with Eloise'

'How do you know that?'

'Just because our mothers are dead, it doesn't mean I don't know your intimate secrets, Alistair Carmichael. Not that breaking off an engagement is an intimate secret. Why didn't you tell me?'

'It wasn't important.' He glowered. 'We're still friends and professional colleagues. So how exactly did you find out?'

'Georgie told me. She said you told her last night.'

She and Georgie had talked about him. That was...interesting.

'So why didn't you tell me?' Gina asked again.

'I didn't want you to—'

'To get the wrong impression,' she finished for him, suddenly thoughtful. 'You know, I'm starting to think there might be some other purpose in you agreeing to come here and give me away.'

'There's not,' he said shortly.

'No?'

'No.'

'But if Eloise is out of the picture...'

'Don't even go there.'

They went back to tying ribbons. Great intellectual exercise. It left Alistair's mind free to wander in places he didn't particularly want to wander. Finally they were interrupted. It was Gina's fiancé, Dr Cal Jamieson. He saw what they were doing and grinned. 'Hey, you've got another suck—I mean helper,' he told Gina. 'Well done, mate. Gina asked me to help but I was really busy. Lawns to watch grow. Imperative stuff like that.'

He got two wishbones thrown at him simultaneously. Followed by two baskets of almonds.

'Hey, don't both of you shoot,' he said, wounded.

'We're cousins,' Gina said briefly. 'It's called family support.'

'Why isn't CJ doing this?' Cal asked.

'He said it was boring.'

'Which it is—mate,' Alistair said, and rose. 'I've done twelve. That's my quota.'

'Actually, I have a job for you,' Cal said, turning serious. 'If you don't mind.'

'Anything that doesn't involve chicken wishbones and painted almonds. And I'm not even going to this wedding...'

'It's Georgie,' Cal said. 'She's over in the nursery. She and Charles are fretting about Megan. We want your advice.'

'I'm a neurosurgeon,' Alistair said, frowning. 'Advice?'

'She's hoping she doesn't need it,' Cal said, suddenly grim. 'But she's afraid that she might.'

Hell, this weather was wild. The moment they stepped out the door Alistair reeled back against the strength of the wind. Cal, who'd come out behind him, shoved his hands in the small of his back and pushed.

'Just a nice, gentle, ocean breeze, kiddo,' he said, grinning as both men put their heads down and battled the short distance to the hospital.

'My God... This is cyclone stuff.'

'Edge of a cyclone,' Cal agreed. 'Willie. But the weather guys are still saying it'll turn out to sea. They're predicting strong winds for this afternoon's wedding, but not as strong as this. It'll settle soon.'

'Do you often get cyclones?'

'Not bad ones. Or not often. Tracy took out Darwin on Christmas Day twenty years ago and one came through south of here last year and flattened the nation's banana crop.' He was yelling, but as he spoke they reached the hospital and walked inside. Cal's last couple of words echoed round the silence of the hospital.

'Why does Georgie want me?' Alistair asked. He knew this wasn't a social call. He knew she'd be avoiding him. So what now?

'She's worried,' Cal said. 'And Charles and I concur, but there's not a lot we can do about it. If this wind wasn't grounding all planes, we'd do an evacuation but...well, let's see what you think.' And he pushed open the doors to the nursery.

Charles was there, in his wheelchair. It hadn't taken long for Alistair to discover that Crocodile Creek's medical director was a really astute doctor. Charles had lost the use of his legs through an accident in his youth, but what he lacked in mobility he more than compensated for with the sheer breadth of his intellect.

Charles was a big man with a commanding presence, but right now Alistair hardly noticed Charles. For Georgie was beside him. The bruise across her cheek had darkened overnight and swelled still more. She'd removed the dressing he'd put over the split, and the cut looked...vicious.

They could throw away Smiley's key as far as he was concerned, Alistair thought darkly. Hitting a woman...

Hitting Georgia...

But they were standing by a cot, looking worried. He needed to focus on their problem.

'Cal said I might be able to help,' he said softly, and Georgie turned.

'Dr Carmichael,' she said.

They were obviously on professional ground here. OK, he could do that. He nodded. 'Dr Turner.' He nodded to Charles. 'Dr Wetherby.'

He looked down into the cot. Megan was lying on her side, one thumb pressed hard into her mouth. She wasn't asleep. But...

She was quiet. She was oddly still. First rule for care of children. Worry about the quiet ones.

And she looked so small. Malnourished? Probably. The cigarette burn on her hand looked stark and raw, and once again his gut clenched in anger.

No. Put emotion away. He was there for a reason.

'How's her mother?' he asked, still watching the little girl. They'd called him for something and he needed to figure out what. He was switching into professional mode, checking visually with care. Yesterday Megan had seemed lethargic. This morning he'd have expected her to be brighter. But she seemed apathetic. When he put his hand down in front of her eyes she blinked but didn't otherwise respond.

Hell.

'Lizzie's good,' Georgie said softly into the stillness. She was watching Megan's reactions as well. 'She's even managed a little breakfast. We've put Davy and Dottie into the ward beside her so they can see her as she sleeps, and she's a hundred per cent better than yesterday. Certainly she's out of danger. And so is Thomas.'

This was the benefit of a country hospital, Alistair thought. To combine medicine with family... It'd be great to be able to do these things.

'But you're worried about this little one,' he said.

'We are.'

'Tell me all you know.'

'It's not a lot but it's more than yesterday. Damn, we should have picked this up on admission.' Charles' words were almost a growl as he wheeled away from the cot to bring an X-ray back from the desk. He handed it to Alistair without a word.

Silence.

The X-ray showed the little girl's skull. With damage. The fracture was only hairline—no worse than the fracture of Georgie's cheek. But under Georgie's fracture lay muscle which could bear damage. Under Megan's skull fracture lay her fragile brain. Internal bleeding would be a catastrophe.

Internal bleeding may well be causing the symptoms they were worried about.

'Can I check?' he asked at last, and got three sharp nods for assent.

He crossed to the sinks and washed, carefully. Megan had survived the squalid circumstances of the hut. There was no way Alistair was risking infection now.

What infections did chicken bones carry? He washed twice as diligently as he normally did, and then he washed again.

Then he examined her. Cal left them, obviously needing to be elsewhere, but Georgie and Charles stayed. He ignored them. Instead, he talked to Megan, explaining gently that he was looking at her head, trying to find what was hurting her, trying to find a way to make her feel better. He wasn't sure that she was taking in anything.

He could see no retinal haemorrhage. That had to be a good sign. There was no obvious swelling.

'No fever?' he asked.

'No,' Georgie whispered. 'But… Charles didn't like the look of her. It was more on a hunch than anything that we did the X-ray.'

'Good hunch.'

'Which is when we bailed out and called you,' Charles said.

'Do we have the facility to do a CT scan?'

'Our radiotherapist is on his way in,' Charles told him. 'He's boarding up his mother's windows or he'd be here now.'

'Send someone else to board windows. I want him here now,'

Alistair snapped. He closed his eyes, thinking things through. But his decision was inevitable. 'This little one was talking and responding normally last night. The provisional diagnosis is that she's bleeding internally, but slowly. If I'm right then we get in there now to try to stop lasting damage. There's no choice.'

We? Him.

He was under no illusion as to why Georgie had called him. He was a neurosurgeon.

But here…

He wanted a major city hospital. He wanted MRI scans. He wanted…

'We can't fly her out,' Charles said, sounding apologetic. 'Even by road we're starting to get worried. We've had a couple of big trees come down already, and the road's getting dangerous. They're saying it's worse down south—not better. With this level of wind it might be a few days before we can evacuate.'

'But we can't wait,' Georgie said. She looked terrified, he thought. She looked a far cry from the cocky, gum-chewing, bike-riding Georgie who'd greeted him at the airport yesterday. This morning she was wearing a professional white coat over jeans, T-shirt and sandals. Her sandals were crimson, matching her toenails. There were little gold crescent moons on each toenail. Despite her bruising, she'd gone to some trouble with her make-up—her lips matched her toenails.

There were traces of yesterday's Georgie left, but she looked young, vulnerable and afraid.

How could he ever have thought she was a tart?

'I don't want her brain damaged,' she said fiercely. 'I'll operate myself if I have to.'

She knew what the score was. Internal bleeding could cause—would cause—irreparable damage. The only option was to operate to relieve pressure, a tricky operation at the best of times, but here…

'You're not doing anything while we have Alistair. Gina says you're good,' Charles said grimly.

'Let's run a CAT scan first,' he said. 'I'm not doing anything on the basis of one X-ray. I don't have a clue where the bleeding is. We need to get a definitive diagnosis and I'm not moving without it. And then I need the equipment.'

'I suspect we have most of what you need,' Charles told him. 'Many of our indigenous people refuse to go elsewhere for treatment so if someone's available, we fly in specialists and they operate here. We've had a couple of neurosurgeons who've done locum work here, and they've set up a store of surgical equipment. If you weren't here, I'd have to ask Cal to do it. But he's a general surgeon. He doesn't have your level of expertise.'

'He'd still do it,' Georgie said bluntly. 'Will you?'

And the thing was decided. 'Of course,' he said. 'OK, get this radiologist here now. I'll check the scans, the equipment and the personnel available, and then we go. Let's move.'

If anything could take Georgie's mind off Max, this was it. Urgent, lifesaving surgery.

It had to be done. The CT—computerised tomography—scan showed very clearly a build-up of fluid, and when they shaved Megan's hair they could see swelling. Not huge swelling, but it was there.

Then there was a swift family conference. Lizzie was exhausted, but fully conscious and aware. She was appalled at what was happening to her daughter—but at first she couldn't believe Smiley would have done such a thing.

But the evidence was irrefutable. The white-faced woman held Davy's hand and trembled while Davy answered Georgie's questions.

'It was when Megan was hungry and Mummy was asleep,' Davy said, faltering. 'Megan started crying. Dad burned her with his cigarette and then when she wouldn't stop he hit her hard against the wall.'

For a moment Lizzie looked like she was about to pass out, but then anger took over and by the time Georgie explained exactly what the problem was, it was just as well Smiley was safely locked up.

'Just save her for me,' Lizzie said, close to tears. 'I swear he'll never lay a finger on her again but, please, Georgie, make her well.'

'We have Alistair,' Georgie said, and felt an almost over-whelming relief that this skilled surgeon was right here, right now.

She returned to Theatre to find everything was in place. Alistair examined Megan once more and then he nodded.

'We have no choice. We go in now or brain damage's inevi-table. As it is...'

'I should have picked it up yesterday,' Georgie repeated, im-measurably distressed.

'There were no signs yesterday. All her symptoms could be explained by dehydration. They probably were caused by de-hydration. I'm thinking this bleeding's gradual and slow, so we might be in time. There's no need to punish yourself over it.'

'So stop blaming yourself,' Charles told her. 'That's Geor-gie's specialty,' he told Alistair. 'She takes on the problems of the world and makes them her own.'

'Well, you're not on your own here,' Alistair said. 'Lizzie's OK'd the operation? If she approves, we go in.'

'We shouldn't ask you. You're not covered by insurance or medical indemnity,' Charles reminded him.

'But you are asking, right?'

'I guess we are,' Charles said, and managed a smile.

'But Lizzie wouldn't sue,' Georgie said, horrified.

'Smiley might,' Charles said.

'Alistair won't care,' Georgie said roundly, and Alistair met her look and held it.

'God knows, I have no taste for heroic surgery,' he said bluntly. 'I'd like a skilled paediatric surgical team on this one, but we make do with what we've got.'

'Maybe you'd better put your suit on first,' Georgie said faintly.

'Suit?'

'It makes you look clever,' she told him. 'Shorts and sandals don't cut it in the clever stakes and I want you to be clever.'

'So no stilettos, Dr Turner?'

She managed a shaky smile. 'No stilettos. Megan is too important.'

And after that there was no time to think of anything. There was certainly no time for Alistair to don his suit—he put on operating gear over his shorts and left it at that. Emily was called away from her hair appointment to perform the anaesthetic. Yes, this afternoon she planned to be a bride but 'I've got hours and hours and how long does it take to put on a dress?' Cal assisted Alistair and Georgie assisted Cal. Four doctors, three nurses and they were all needed.

That they all knew what to do was a testament to Alistair's skill. 'He does a lot of teaching,' Gina had told Georgie, and she believed her. For not only did Alistair's fingers move with skill and precision, knowing exactly what he was doing, improvising for any equipment he couldn't find with a dexterity that left her awed, he also seemed to know exactly what everyone else in Theatre was doing—where every person needed to be moments before they needed to be there.

His soft orders filled the room, and under his commands they worked as a team that a major teaching hospital could be proud of.

The procedure sounded straightforward enough, but what looked straightforward in textbooks was technical surgery of the most challenging kind. First he needed to lift a piece of Megan's small skull, working with infinite precision, aware that any false movement would aggravate the bleed. Then he worked carefully through the dura mater—the tough membrane around the brain—carefully separating the dura to locate the subdural clot causing the swelling.

After that he had to evacuate the haematoma and make sure there was no further bleeding from ruptured blood vessels. The skill lay in causing no more damage. This tiny brain was still developing. Any fractional miscalculation could have consequences for life.

Alistair worked as if this were a normal, everyday procedure. His demeanour was calm and methodical, as if this was nothing more serious than an inflamed appendix. But so much hung on his skill. OK, Cal would have tried to do this alone if Alistair hadn't been there, but as a general surgeon Georgie knew his chances at succeeding would have been much less. If all the bleeding vessels weren't located, the damage would continue.

Georgie knew instinctively that neither of these things would happen after Alistair had operated. This man was just too competent.

Too competent for his own good? Ego driven? Maybe, she thought, but now wasn't the time to quibble about egos. He could be as egocentric as he liked, as long as he saved Megan.

And gradually it seemed that the combined skill of Alistair and Cal might do it. Hopefully they'd caught it in time. Hopefully there'd be no damage and Megan would grow up to be a normal, healthy kid like her brothers and sister.

Thanks mostly to Alistair. Georgie worked on with quiet competence, but inside she felt like weeping. They were so lucky this man was there. And to think she'd nearly abandoned him in the heat.

'Yeah, you still owe me for that,' Alistair said, as Cal carefully suctioned the wound, and she jerked her head up to meet his eyes.

The toad was smiling.

'You didn't want—'

'And you figured that was exactly what I'd do.'

'What are you guys talking about?' Emily queried, and to

her fury Georgie felt herself blushing. She turned back to her tray of equipment, thinking, Dammit, did the man have a mind-reader on board?

He scared her witless.

But he was saving Megan.

Maybe he'd already saved her. The worst of the damage had been cleared. Now he waited patiently, taking his time, watching carefully for any ongoing haemorrhage. Then, satisfied that the area was dry, he began the laborious task of suturing the dura and reattaching the bone.

He left nothing to chance. His fingers were so skilful Georgie could only watch in awe. Hand him equipment as it was needed. Try to anticipate his needs. Marvel at the skill of the procedure she was watching.

Finally he moved on to the superficial sutures. Even that wasn't straightforward. For such surgery a specialist unit would have ready-made staples, but here Alistair could only suture, and the results of his suturing now would mean the difference between major scarring or whether Megan could wear her hair any way she liked as she grew up. Maybe such scarring didn't matter so much in the greater scheme of things—he was well within his rights to hand over to Cal for this last step—but Georgie could tell by Alistair's fierce concentration that he knew what scars could mean to a young woman. He was thinking forward to Megan's life after this surgery.

He cared.

There would be minimal scarring from this man's work today, she thought as he worked on. For a surgeon already weary from such an intense procedure, his sutures were flawless.

And then, finally, he could relax. They could all relax. Finally Georgie could hand over dressings, he could fit them over the child's neat wound and he and Cal could step back from the table.

'We'll need a further CT scan in a few days but it's looking good,' he breathed.

Only then did Georgie notice a trickle of sweat running down his face. The release of pressure... He'd held himself contained, until now.

There were advantages to being a control freak, she thought, but suddenly she was far from being in control herself. She was suddenly shaking. She stepped back from the table and leaned hard against the wall.

'Cal,' Alistair said urgently, and Cal was by her side, pressing her onto a nearby stool, pushing her head between her knees.

'I'm not fainting,' she protested weakly, for that was exactly what her body felt like doing. 'I never faint. Go back.'

'You've excuse enough to faint if you feel like it,' Alistair growled. 'Take her out, Cal. We're done here.'

'But we've succeeded,' Georgie whispered, and Alistair allowed himself the luxury of a smile.

'Yeah. We've succeeded. With a little luck—but not much, because this is as fine a job as any I've seen in major US teaching hospitals, and you picked it up so early that it's my guess she'll end up with nothing to show for this morning's dramas but a tiny scar.'

Georgie didn't answer. She couldn't. Why was she shaking now?

It was the bruised cheek and the drama of yesterday, she told herself, though she knew it was no such thing. It was a mixture of all sorts of stuff, not the least the way she was feeling about the man at the operating table.

He was way out of her league, but he was so...

'Go,' he said gruffly, and she looked up and her eyes met his. A silent message passed between them. Unmistakable. Go on. You've done well here. Look after yourself.

It wasn't said out loud but it may as well have been.

Why it made her eyes well with tears...

She didn't cry. She never cried. She wiped her eyes with an angry swipe and stood up. Once more she had to grab for the wall for support.

'Take her, Cal.'

Alistair sounded as if he wanted to take her himself, she thought, but maybe that was just wishful thinking on her part.

She glanced at him again. Once more that look…

She had to get out of there.

She went.

He found her twenty minutes later. Transferring a small child from the operating table to a bed in Intensive Care sounded on the surface an easy thing to do, but the attached tubing, monitors and assorted medical paraphernalia were complex. At this stage nothing was to be left to chance. Alistair had supervised it all. Finally free, with Cal doing the first shift of ICU watch, he went to do what every surgeon must. He went to tell the family.

Lizzie.

This woman had been living a nightmare. Hopefully now the nightmare would lift.

He pushed open the door to her ward and Georgie was there. Of course. And Davy. The six-year-old was sitting on the bed with his mother while Georgie was talking to them both.

'I thought I told you to go to bed,' he growled, and Georgie smiled at him.

'No. You just told me to go away.'

'I meant you to go to bed.'

'You're not my doctor—sir.' She was still smiling.

'My Megan is going to be all right?' Lizzie whispered. 'Georgie says she should…'

'She's not completely out of danger yet,' Alistair said, knowing there was no point in being less than honest. 'But the outlook is good.'

'Georgie's explained it to me,' Lizzie said. 'So I know.'

'It's great,' he said softly, smiling at Georgie, and she smiled back. The shaking had stopped. She'd regained a bit of colour. Basically back to normal?

Except for one smashed cheek and one missing kid brother.

'And I know what happened to Georgie's face,' Lizzie continued. Lizzie's strength was returning as the antibiotics took hold. Antibiotics had been flowing for twenty-four hours now, knocking the infection, and the difference was amazing. 'I hardly noticed her face this morning but now I have, and the police have been in to get my statement. But they said Smiley's going to jail, no matter what I say, so I may as well be truthful. It didn't make sense but then I saw Georgie's face. I really saw...'

'I ran into a door,' Georgie muttered, and put a hand to her cheek.

'Called Smiley. I know his punches. I can practically recognise his knuckle marks.'

'It doesn't—'

'He had it in for you,' Lizzie said, and the woman looked shyly up at Alistair, trying to explain. 'My last birth...with Megan, I bled and bled. I was OK in the end but this time Georgie told Smiley that if he didn't bring me into hospital when I went into labour she was going to use his testicles for fish bait. She said it real casual-like, and when he laughed she got quiet and said, "Don't push it, mate, 'cos I've got the entire Hell's Riders bikers' gang behind me and they don't like you any more than I do." So when I had pains he brought me in, just like it was his idea, but I know he hated it.'

'You need to leave him behind,' Georgie said softly, and Lizzie's eyes filled with tears.

'Yeah, but when he gets out of jail...'

'He won't be back for a while. With his suspended sentence, plus what he gets for this, it'll be at least a couple of years.'

'Even then...'

'Then you need to refocus,' Alistair said, watching Georgie thoughtfully. Maybe some things needed to be faced. 'You know that Georgie had it tough when she was a kid?'

'Hey,' Georgie said, astounded.

'You told me people used to punch you,' he said softly. 'So it seems you went out and got a black belt in karate.'

'I did,' she said, and she managed a smile.

'But Smiley still punched you,' Lizzie whispered.

'Only because you wanted him to punch you,' Alistair said.

There was absolute silence in the room at that. Davy was big-eyed, unsure of what was going on but smart enough to keep his mouth shut and listen.

And Lizzie figured it out, just like that. 'You did that for me?' Lizzie whispered.

'She did it to give you another chance,' Alistair said. 'Do you think you might take it?'

'Lizzie's tired,' Georgie interjected, embarrassed. 'We shouldn't be pushing it now.'

'There's never a better time to take a stand,' Alistair said. 'A line in the sand. Lizzie, yesterday Smiley was your dog-ugly, violent partner. Today he can be your ex-partner, a bad memory you can use the law to protect yourself from.'

'You reckon I could learn karate?' Lizzie asked, half-joking, but Alistair didn't smile and neither did Georgie.

'You can have your first lesson before you get out of here,' Georgie promised. 'As soon as you're up to it.'

'I'd... I'd like that.'

'Then it's a deal,' Georgie said, and rose and nudged Alistair. Her message was clear. Lizzie had had enough.

'You've made my mummy better,' Davy said suddenly, snuggling down against his mother and smiling up at them.

'Would you like to learn karate, too?' Georgie asked, and the little boy's face lit up.

'I've seen karate on telly. Pyjamas and kicking. It looks cool.'

'It's also fun. You and your mum could have fun together.'

'Fun,' Lizzie whispered, as if it was a foreign word, and Georgie smiled and turned and left the room, leaving Alistair to follow.

He caught her before she reached the outer doors. She was sagging again, her shoulders slumping a little as she pushed against the glass doors. He caught her and pulled her inside again. What he wanted to say couldn't be said in the fierce wind.

'How much did you sleep last night?' he demanded, tugging her back and letting the doors swing closed again.

'Enough.'

'Not enough,' he growled. 'You're grey around the edges.'

'I am not.'

'Not outwardly but inside...'

'Oh, cut it out. You sound like Charles. Trying to make me stay in bed.'

'If Dr Wetherby was saying you need the day in bed, I concur.'

'I can't,' she said.

'Why not? Is anyone in labour?'

'No, but—'

'There you go, then. The entire medical staff of Croc Creek is stuck indoors, waiting for this weather to clear. Plus there are at least half a dozen spare doctors here for the wedding. Before Megan's drama Gina was so bored she resorted to putting ribbons around chicken bones.'

Georgie smiled at that. Albeit weakly. 'I should help her. And the wedding's at four.'

'No,' he said, gently but firmly. 'You need to sleep. No one's going to be upset if you miss the wedding.'

'I need to phone—'

'Who do you need to phone?'

'Anyone who might know where Max is.'

'Do you have a list?'

'I... Yes.' She gave a shamefaced smile. 'I sort of...found it last time Ron was here. When I knew he was taking Max away. He stayed overnight at the pub. I suggested to the publican that he might let me into his bedroom. I borrowed an address book he had.'

'You borrowed...'

'I copied out every phone number,' she said. 'Just 'cos I knew he was taking Max and I thought...'

'It was a great idea. You've been ringing the numbers?'

'Yes.'

'So how far through the list are you?'

'About a third.'

'No response?'

'No.' She bit her lip. 'Some of them recognise me. They know my stepfather hates me.'

'So I might get further?' he said thoughtfully.

'But you don't want—'

'I do want. I can contact people and say I'm a doctor who's deeply concerned about Max's welfare. I can say there are medical imperatives that make contacting him urgent.'

'Medical imperatives...'

'It'll make you sleep at night,' he said. 'Definitely medical imperatives.'

She choked, half with laughter, half with tears. Then she took a deep breath, squared her shoulders and met his gaze head on. And came to a decision.

'It might work,' she said.

'I might get a better reception. A doctor saying there's an urgent medical need to contact a kid is bound to get a better reception than you looking for your father for a reason they don't know.'

'I... You're sure you don't mind?'

'I'll come and get the list. I'm not invited to this wedding. The weather's keeping me indoors. I have all the time in the world.'

They walked back slowly to the doctors' quarters. The wind was still howling. It seemed the most natural thing in the world for Alistair's arm to come around her waist and support her against its force.

They walked back inside the house—and stopped dead.

The house had been taken over by chaos.

There were bridesmaids everywhere—four or five at least—

and a couple of flowergirls for good measure. There were three little boys in pale pink trousers and white shirts. There were women—lots of women. In the middle enveloped in white tulle was…

'Emily,' Georgie said, awed. 'Look at you.'

'I look like a toilet brush,' Emily wailed.

'Toilet brush?'

'Have you seen the toilet brushes Mrs Poulos uses? They're all white tulle. Just like me. Why did I agree to a Greek wedding?'

''Cos you fell in love with a Greek?' Georgie suggested, and grinned. Then her smile faded. 'Em, would you mind very much if I missed a bit of your wedding?'

'Not at all,' Emily said promptly. 'I'm with you. Shall we do a Thelma and Louise—fast car to Texas?'

'Not with Mike chasing us,' Georgie said. 'He'd catch us before the edge of town. You're committed now, girl. You need to face the music.'

'But your face is hurting,' Emily said, her expression softening as she took in the strain in her friend's eyes. 'And you're terrified about Max. Harry told us how worried you are.' She looked thoughtfully at Alistair. 'But you have Alistair to look after you.'

'I don't need looking after.'

'Hey, she does,' Emily said, pushing through assorted bridesmaids and flower girls to hug Georgie with affection. 'She's prickly as a hedgehog on the outside but inside she's just marshmallow,' she told Alistair. 'Georgie, go to bed. That's where you should be.'

'I need to make phone calls.'

'No, I'm making phone calls,' Alistair reminded her, 'while you rest.'

'That sounds like a great idea,' Emily said, but then she was distracted. A middle-aged lady in flowery Crimplene was hovering in the background with what looked like a crimping wand.

The woman was practically vibrating with anxiety. 'No, Sophia, I don't want any more curls. I look like Shirley Temple as it is.'

'Hey, you need to get on with Operation Wedding,' Georgie said, and kissed her friend and pushed her away. 'I'll pop into church and see you tie the actual knot. But I might give the reception a miss.'

'If you decide you can make it, Alistair can bring you.' Emily looked ruefully around at the chaos. 'With this mob no one will notice an extra. Or a hundred extras.'

'I think we both might give it a miss,' Alistair said faintly, taking charge, putting his arm around Georgie and steering her through the sea of bridesmaids as he'd steered her into the blasting wind. 'Georgie's beat.'

'But we'll be there in spirit,' Georgie called over her shoulder. 'Make sure you save me an almond basket with wishbone.'

'They're for fertility,' Emily said, as the crimping machine descended. 'You sure you want one?'

'We've changed our minds,' Alistair and Georgie said in unison. 'No fertility baskets.'

CHAPTER FIVE

ALISTAIR INSISTED THAT Georgie go to bed, but she refused. She wanted to listen to his phone calls. They compromised by using the hands-free phone, with him sitting in her bedside chair, gradually working his way through her list of names. The sounds of the impending wedding were all through the house—mass hysteria was a good description—and the rising wind made the sounds almost surreal. Inside Georgie's bedroom was an oasis of calm. Intimate even.

Which was the wrong way to look at it, Georgie decided as she lay back and watched Alistair work. She shouldn't be doing this, but there seemed little choice.

The painkillers Alistair had insisted she take were making her woozy. The panic of the last few hours was settling. Crazy or not, this man seemed a calming influence. 'Leave it to me, I'll take care of it,' he'd said. There was something to be said for big men. There was something to be said for men with gorgeous, prematurely silver hair and tanned skin and smiley eyes and…

And she'd had too many painkillers. Alistair was running through number after number and she needed to concentrate on what he was saying.

He made no mention of her. Alistair presented himself as Dr Alistair Carmichael, paediatric consultant at the Centre for

Rural Medical Services in North Queensland. He obviously saw no need to mention that he wasn't actually employed here. He obviously saw no need to mention the name Crocodile Creek which, if her father had shot his mouth off about her, would be instantly recognisable to his mates.

What he said was truly impressive. Almost scary.

'We have urgent medical concerns regarding seven-year-old Max.'

That was about her, Georgie thought dreamily. Alistair's medical concern was that not knowing Max's whereabouts was interfering with her sleep and therefore medically undesirable.

'We understand Max's father is not in a position to contact us, but any help you could give us in locating his son would be very much appreciated. Any information will be treated in utmost confidence—doctor-patient confidentiality is sacrosanct. But it's imperative that this child is located. Can I give you my private number? If there's any information at all, we'd very much appreciate it. If you can see your way to help us or if you could pass a message to his father to ring me...'

They'll think he's carrying cholera or something, she decided as he worked through the list. It sounded scary.

As long as it worked.

It wasn't working immediately. Time after time Alistair was met with negatives. 'But they're not absolute negatives,' Alistair told her. 'Lots of the numbers I'm ringing are private numbers and a few wives and girlfriends of your stepfather's mates have been answering. They sound concerned. They seem to know Max and I've got them worried. Most of them have written my number down and have promised to get back to me if they hear anything. Hopefully I might have pushed some of them to ask the right questions.'

It was the best he could do. Georgie lay back and listened, letting the painkillers take effect, letting her fear for Max recede. Everything that could be done was being done. She didn't have to stir herself. She was almost asleep...

'Megan,' she said once, rousing, and Alistair touched her hand in reassurance.

'She's fine. Gina just came to the door and told me. She's awake and seems more alert already, and that's with the effect of the anaesthetic not worn off. We think we've won. When this list is finished, I'll check again.'

Wonderful. Megan would be OK.

She was so close to sleep.

The last phone call was made. She should tell Alistair to go. She didn't need him there. But...

But she didn't tell him to go. The sensation of someone picking up her burden of responsibility was so novel that she couldn't argue.

He was there. He was...nice?

She slept.

He should go. He'd finished the list. He'd done what he'd set out to do. Hopefully he had people asking questions all over the country, trying to find the whereabouts of one small boy.

Georgie was asleep. There was no point in him sitting beside her bedside any longer.

But he sat on. Outside was the chaos of the impending wedding. The wind was gathering strength—hell, he was starting to disbelieve the reports that this cyclone was blowing out to sea. How strong did wind have to get before it was categorised a cyclone?

He glanced out the window at the grey, storm-tossed sea and the palms bending wildly in the wind. This was amazing.

He glanced back to Georgie's bed, and he ceased thinking about the wind.

She was beautiful.

She was messing with his head.

She'd messed with his head six months ago, he thought grimly. He'd been happily settled, engaged to Eloise, paying a brief visit to Gina to make sure things were OK in his cousin's world. He'd met Cal and approved the match. He'd stayed on so he could make a family speech at their engagement party.

He'd met Georgie.

He'd actually met her earlier on the day of the party. She'd been sitting on the veranda of the doctors' house, drinking beer straight from the bottle. He'd talked to her for a moment. She'd sounded aggressive, angry, but also...frightened? It was a weird combination, he'd thought. He hadn't realised she was a doctor. He'd thought somehow then that she was a woman in some sort of trouble.

It had been a weird assumption, based on nothing but the defiant glint in those gorgeous eyes. He'd tried to talk to her but she'd been curt and abrasive, shoving off from the veranda, making it very clear that he'd been intruding in her personal space.

Then that night...she'd turned up to the party in a tiny red cocktail dress that would have done a streetwalker proud. It had clung so tightly that she surely couldn't have had anything on under it. She'd worn those gorgeous red stilettos, fabulous hoop earrings and nothing else.

She was so far from what he thought was desirable in a woman that he shouldn't have even looked. He liked his women controlled. Elegant. Like...well, like Eloise.

But he couldn't keep his eyes off her.

Then as the night wore on she approached him. He'd suggested—tentatively if he recalled it right—that they dance. She'd tugged him onto the floor, put her arms around his neck, started moving that gorgeous body in time to the music, close against him...

Alistair's world was carefully controlled. He'd learned the hard way what happened when that control was lost. How many times had he heard his father use that dumb line—'I just couldn't help myself.'

Yeah, well, he could help himself, until he held Georgie in

his arms, until he smelt the wild musk smell of her perfume, until he felt her hair brush his cheek...

He picked her up and carried her out of the hall. That, too, was partly at her instigation. 'Do you want to take me home, big boy?'

It had been a really dumb line. A total cliché. But it was an invitation he couldn't resist. She held him tight around the neck and she let her knees buckle so he had no choice but to sweep her up into her arms. And carry her outside...

It was just as well Gina saw them go. His cousin moved like lightning, furious with him, concerned for her friend, acting like he was some sort of ghastly sexual predator.

'She's in trouble,' Gina told him. 'She's not acting normally. She's vulnerable. Leave her alone.'

It was like a douche of iced water. Waking him up from a trance.

He left Georgie to her. He walked away, thinking he'd never see her again. But thinking...vulnerable? How the hell did Gina figure that out?

The next day, halfway through Gina's tour of the hospital, they walked into the midwifery ward and there she was. Georgie Turner. Obstetrician.

He'd assumed she held some sort of menial job at the hospital. But an obstetrician. He was stunned.

She didn't speak to him. He walked into the ward and she walked out. Once again he felt belittled. Guilty for a sin he hadn't had a chance to commit.

He should have got over it. And he was, he thought, gazing down at Georgie's face on the white pillow. He didn't want anything to do with someone as needy as Georgie.

But things had changed. When he'd returned to the States things had seemed different. His relationship with Eloise, seemingly so suitable, had suddenly seemed cloying. Dull?

A month later he'd told Eloise he couldn't go through with it. Not because of Georgie—or not directly because of Georgie. It was just that Georgie had showed him there was a life on the other side of control. He hadn't wanted it, but it hadn't been fair to Eloise to settle for her as an alternative. Eloise had hardly seemed disappointed, staying friends, accepting his decision with calmness. That had been great. That was why he admired her so much. He wanted that level of control.

He had it—except when he saw Georgie.

He couldn't stay to watch Georgie sleep. It didn't make sense. But he wanted to stay.

'It's no use wanting what we can't have.' It was his mother's whiny voice, echoing from his childhood. When his father had disappeared in a cloud of gambling debts, taking off with a woman half his age, his mother's voice had moved to whine and had never returned to normal.

'You keep your life under control. You make sure—make sure, Alistair, any way you know how that you never put yourself in the position where you can be humiliated so much you want to take your own life. I'm so close to suicide... All I have is you. Oh, Alistair, be careful.'

It had been a dreadful threat to hang on a child, but Alistair had known she'd meant it. If he'd threatened her nice stable existence—her pride in her son...

Well, he hadn't. He wouldn't even now, when his mother was long dead. So what the hell was he doing, staring down at this sleeping woman and thinking...?

He shook himself. He wasn't thinking anything that'd worry anyone, including him. This was jet-lag. Exhaustion after this morning's operation. Concern for a woman who had more than she deserved on her shoulders.

So get a grip, he told himself, but he let himself look at her for one long moment before he stood and walked slowly to the door.

And left her to her sleeping.

This wind was getting frightening. As Alistair walked out into the living room a shutter slammed off its hinges, hit the wall, broke off and tumbled crosswise past the house. He heard its progress, not falling but being blown. It was a big shutter.

One of the assembled bridesmaids screamed.

There were so many bridesmaids, still clustered. Apparently they'd dispersed to get their make-up done and now they'd re-grouped. How long did bridal preparations last? The photographer was trying to get them lined up but was having trouble.

Gina waved to him from the back row. He hadn't recognised her until now. Pink tulle?

'It's ridiculous,' she said, abandoning the photo set-up and sidling out of her spot to join him. 'Poor Em.'

'Didn't she plan this?' he said, staring at...pink?

'Mrs Poulos planned this,' she said. 'Sophia. Mike's mum. This is a big Greek wedding, just as she's always dreamed of. Em loves her too much to say no.'

'I never thought I'd see you in pink tulle.'

'Apricot,' she retorted.

'Right. Apricot.'

'Sophia wanted the men in apricot dinner suits with apricot and white frills on their dinner shirts. But Mike put his foot down at that. They're in black tuxes.'

'Cal, too?'

'Cal, too.'

'And for your wedding?' he asked in a voice of deep fore-boding, and she chuckled.

'If I asked you to wear apricot ruffles to my wedding, would you? Cousin?'

'No,' he said, revolted.

'Not even if I said please?'

'There's no love in the world great enough to encompass apricot frills.'

'Or red stilettos?' she teased him, and he stopped smiling.

'Gina...'

'I know.' Her smile widened. 'It's none of my business. But you and Georgie aren't slugging any more, I hope?'

'We were never slugging.'

'She's had such a hard time.'

'I'm starting to realise that.'

'Georgie's my only bridesmaid so you have to be nice to her.' She grinned. 'And, I promise, no tulle.'

He smiled back. He was trying to think of Georgie in tulle and failing dismally.

'She's OK?' Gina asked.

'She'd be better if she knew where Max was. I've been ringing through a list of her father's friends.'

'She let you do that?' Gina's eyes widened.

'I offered.'

'Yeah, but Georgie...' She hesitated.

'Gina, get back in line,' someone yelled, and Gina sighed and shrugged and smiled.

'Duty calls. Come and watch the wedding.'

'I'm not invited.'

'This is Croc Creek. Everyone's invited. Come at least to the church. It should be fun.'

And they all left, just like that. The photographer abandoned his work as hopeless and the car drivers ushered the girls out to the waiting cars. They were almost blown off their feet as they ran from house to cars.

Then they were gone, and the silence was unnerving.

What to do?

He'd already offered to help out at the hospital, thinking all the doctors would be at the wedding. But apparently two young doctors had arrived only three weeks ago—two eager and skilled interns on a working holiday from Germany. Herrick and Ilse were more than capable of taking charge and calling for help when needed.

Maybe he could go for a swim. But the wind made being outside unpleasant. The pool was protected, but even from here he could see the surface was littered with plant matter.

He should... He should...

Stay here. But… Georgie was sleeping off the bruise to her cheek, as well as making up, he suspected, for the sleep she hadn't had the night before. The thought of staying alone in the same house with the sleeping Georgie was somehow unnerving.

He'd head out onto the veranda to read. But just as he was making that decision, Mr and Mrs Grubb arrived. They swept into the kitchen to deliver a couple of casseroles—'for the doctors' supper if they get called away from the wedding, poor dears, and there's that nice young German couple as well need feeding up'. They were ceremoniously attired in their Sunday best. Dora's hat was…amazing.

'Why are you still here?' Dora demanded, and she seemed almost offended by the sight of him.

'Georgie's asleep.'

'All the more reason for you not to be here,' she snapped. 'Is that the only reason you don't want to come to the wedding?'

'I'm not invited.'

'That's a nonsense. Everyone's invited and it's not proper for you to stay here with Dr Georgie. You could be anyone.'

'As if I'm going to—'

'You're American, aren't you?' she demanded. 'I know your reputation. Overpaid, over-sexed and over here. Go put a suit and tie on and we'll wait for you.'

Some things weren't worth fighting. Deciding that defending his national dignity wasn't ever going to work, he decided on the second option. It seemed he was going to a wedding.

And so was Georgie.

It only took him a moment to change into his suit and when he returned to the kitchen Georgie was there. She was dressed, demurely for Georgie, in a tiny suit. In her beloved pillar-box red. And red stilettos. The skimpy skirt and jacket showed every curve of her gorgeous body. She'd applied make-up skilfully over her bruise, and it hardly showed under dark glasses. She was…gorgeous.

He stood in the doorway and stared.

She turned and saw him. And grinned.

'I overheard,' she said, and she chuckled. 'I decided I'd better come to the wedding. Maybe I needed Dora's chaperonage.'

'You need to be in bed.'

'I'm too scared to stay in bed. Over-sexed, eh?'

'You shouldn't be scared,' he said sourly. 'I'm going to a wedding.'

'Me, too,' she said cheerfully, and linked her arm through his. 'Overpaid too?'

'That's from the war,' Mr Grubb said, disconcerted. 'It's what we said about all the Yankee soldiers. They're not like that now,' he told his wife. 'At least this 'un isn't.'

'I can see that. How nice.' Mrs Grubb had changed tack, beaming at the unexpected expansion in her wedding party. 'You make a lovely couple. My mum's best friend, Ethel, ran away with an American sailor. He bought her silk stockings and they lived happily ever after.' She poked Mr Grubb in the ribs. 'Silk stockings. That's the way to a girl's heart.'

'We have other things than silk stockings,' Mr Grubb said with dignity.

'What things?' Dora demanded. Then she relented and giggled. 'Oh, well, I guess you are OK in the cot.' Then at the sight of Georgie and Alistair's stunned expressions she choked back her giggles and sighed. 'Oh, what it is to be young. Look at the pair of you. Ooh, I hear Cupid in the wings.'

'Dora,' Georgie said, quelling her with a look. 'I'm only going for the service.'

'Me, too,' Alistair said, and Dora beamed some more.

'Yes, dear. And then you can walk home together after. If this wind settles, like Sergeant Harry says it's going to settle—which it's not going to. It's going to be a biggie. I said to Grubb just before we got dressed, I said, it's going to be huge. I can feel it in my waters.'

'Um…what are your waters talking about?' Georgie said nervously, while Alistair said nothing at all. He was feeling like he was having an out-of-body experience and it was getting weirder by the minute.

'Cyclone, dear, that's what I'm feeling, no matter what Sergeant Harry's telling us. Veering offshore indeed.' Dora puffed herself up like an important peahen—or maybe peacock with that hat—gathered her shiny purse and took her husband's arm. 'But no matter. We've weathered cyclones before and we'll weather them again. Now, then, Grubb, let's all of us go to this wedding. Ooh, I do like a good wedding. Mind, one wedding breeds ten more, that's what I always say, and this one's no different.' She cast a not so covert look at Alistair and then at Georgie. 'I can feel that in my waters as well.'

'You have truly impressive waters, Mrs Grubb,' Alistair said, feeling it was time a man had to take control and move on. He took Georgie's arm just as possessively as Dora held Grubb, and he smiled down at her. 'Let's go see if they're right.'

Which meant that they were together. They were driven to the church together. In deference to Georgie's wounded face, Grubb insisted on dropping them off right at the church door before he went to find a parking place. Georgie and Alistair were practically blasted into the church together. Of one mind, they turned to the back pews, finding seats in the most obscure corner of the chapel.

'How come you're not a bridesmaid?' Alistair whispered as they settled in their back pew, and Georgie poked him in the ribs.

'Shh.'

The wedding hadn't started yet. Céline was singing 'My Heart Will Go On' at the top of her lungs, courtesy of Mrs Poulos, who was in control of the volume button. There was time for a brief conversation, even if Georgie didn't want it.

'But everyone else is,' he said. 'I thought you'd be a shoo-in.' Then he frowned. 'Isn't this the song from *Titanic*?'

She giggled. 'Nothing stops our Sophia. No little iceberg could get in the way of this wedding.'

'So why aren't you a bridesmaid?'

'Mike has three sisters and two cousins who, according to Mrs Poulos, would be offended enough to cause a rift in the family for generations to come if they're not bridesmaids. Em had already asked Susie so that made six, and enough was enough. However, one of Mike's sisters left coming here too late—the storm's stopped her—so Gina's taken her place. This is amounting almost to a plague of bridesmaids. I'm going to be Gina's bridesmaid and that's one bridesmaid experience too many in my book.'

'But you are Em's friend,' he said, watching the clutch of men around Mike at the altar. There were almost more wedding party participants than guests.

'I come from the other side of the tracks from Em,' she said, and he blinked.

'You mean there's a reason you weren't asked?'

'No, I...' She shook her head. 'I shouldn't have said that. Em doesn't care.'

'That you're from the wrong side of the tracks.'

'Yes.'

'You mean you're illegitimate?'

'I mean my family's dole bludgers and petty crims.'

'But you're not?'

'Maybe not,' she whispered dully. 'But you can't escape your family.'

He thought about his mother. And then he thought he'd rather not think about his mother. 'That's a hell of a chip on the shoulder you're carrying,' he ventured cautiously.

She glowered. 'Deal with it. I know when people are patronising me.'

'I'm not patronising you.'

'Right.'

'You know, I'm not exactly blue blooded either,' he said, eyeing her with caution. 'I'm not so far from the other side of your tracks that you'd notice.'

'Says the eminent neurosurgeon.'

'To the eminent obstetrician.'

She tried to glower. He smiled. She tried a bit harder to glower.

He glowered for her.

She giggled.

It was a really cute giggle.

The bride was about to make her entrance. Mrs Poulos did her worst with the control button. Whitney at her finest. 'I will always love yoo-oo-oo...'

The church was festooned with apricot and white ribbons, flowers and bows as far as the eye could see. It was...

'Very tasteful,' Georgie said, still giggling, and they rose to their feet as the priest motioned them all to stand. 'Someone should tell Sophia this is a farewell song. Why are you from the wrong side of the tracks?'

'Um...my parents didn't have much money.'

'Is that all? That's not the wrong side of the tracks. That's shabby genteel.'

'My dad went to jail. Embezzlement. He stole to feed a gambling habit.'

That made her pause. Her smile died. 'Your real dad?' she asked cautiously, and he nodded.

'Golly. You almost qualify.'

'Thank you,' he said dryly. 'So where's your real dad?'

'He lit out when I was four.'

'Mine lit out when I was fifteen. With a waitress from a burger joint, and a year's profit from AccountProtect First Savings.'

'Wow,' she said, and almost as a reflex she touched her face.

'He never hit me,' Alistair said. 'Did yours?'

'I... My stepdad did, yes.'

'So does that put you further on the wrong side of the tracks than me?'

She stared up into his eyes. Her gaze held. Suddenly her lovely lips curved at the corners and she chuckled again.

It was a good sound. A really good sound, he thought. And he felt pleased with himself. For just a minute she was putting aside her terrors for Max and her pain from her injured face, and she was enjoying herself.

And who could not enjoy this over-the-top wedding? Mike was standing at the end of the aisle, looking stunned. Nervous as hell, despite the array of assorted males supporting him.

This was ridiculous, Alistair thought. What a production.

And then the great front doors swept open. 'I Will Always Love You' had segued into a full orchestral rendition of the Bridal March and the guests turned as one to see the bride make her entrance.

Emily. The bride.

This was crazy. She was a powder puff of brilliant white sweeping into the church, with Charles Wetherby in his wheelchair beside her. Charles looked proud fit to burst.

Emily was seeing no one. She looked straight ahead until she saw Mike and faltered in mid-step.

Alistair turned to look at the bridegroom. And he saw the look that flashed between the pair of them...

The whole ridiculous bridal production faded to nothing. This was what it was all about, he thought, stunned. One man and one woman, committing to each other, with all the love in their hearts.

It was no wonder Em hadn't put her foot down over the apricot tulle. The apricot tulle was nothing.

This man and this woman loved each other.

He had been right to break it off with Eloise, Alistair thought suddenly with a flash of absolute certainty. Eloise would never have looked at him like that. And the way he'd felt about Eloise...

No. This was loving. Out-of-control loving, letting go, a leap of faith—and who cared about apricot tulle? It didn't matter. All that mattered was that they belonged together.

He didn't belong here, he thought suddenly. He felt like an impostor, an outsider privy to emotions he hardly understood.

Embarrassed—or maybe not embarrassed but caught in some emotion he couldn't begin to fathom—he turned away. He didn't want to intercept that look again.

He turned to Georgie.

She'd caught the look as well. Her face had changed. Her hands had risen to her cheeks as though to drive away a surfeit of colour.

Her eyes were filled with tears.

'Georg,' he whispered, but she shook her head fiercely, denying him the chance to say a word.

He wasn't going to say a word. He couldn't think of a word to say.

But tears were slipping down her cheeks. He felt in his pocket, produced a handkerchief and handed it over. Then, as she wiped her face, he took her free hand in his and held it.

What sort of man still used handkerchiefs?

It was a bit of an errant thought but it helped.

Why was she crying at a wedding? This was dumb. It was the stupid analgesics, she thought. It had nothing to do with the way Mike was looking at Emily.

She didn't do weddings. She didn't even do relationships. The only relationships she'd ever experienced had led her to disaster.

It was her own fault. She didn't know who she was herself. She was dumb. She'd go out with a lovely gentle fellow doctor. He'd treat her as if she were Dresden china and she'd feel... empty.

Did she want to be slapped around, as her mother had been?

Of course she didn't. But there were times when she'd be drawn into a relationship with someone...well, someone her stepfather might have thought a mate. Someone who treated her as she'd learned to expect. She hated that, and it never lasted but, still, at least she knew where she stood.

So she'd never fall in love with a good man?

That thought slammed home, alarming her. She'd been sitting a mite too close to Alistair and now she edged away. He turned and looked at her and he smiled.

He had a killer smile.

He was still holding her hand.

Alistair was one of the Dresden china ones, she told herself, feeling suddenly breathless. She knew from past experience that such men couldn't make her happy. She'd make them unhappy.

So stop smiling now!

Look at the bride and groom. That was why she was here. Not to think about Alistair-Good-Looking Carmichael.

And not to cry.

Pull your hand away, stupid, she told herself, but she didn't.

The bride and groom were making their vows, softly but with all the sincerity in the world. Mike was smiling at his bride, making Georgie feel...

Squirmy.

'Soppy,' she whispered, sounding as dumb as she'd felt for her tears, and Alistair grinned.

'Yeah, real Romeo-and-Juliet stuff. Bring on the violins.'

'They're happy though,' Georgie whispered, giving them their due.

'But we know this love bit's dangerous.'

She frowned, thrown off balance. 'Do we?'

'Of course. You need to decide with your head.' The priest was talking about the sanctity of marriage, but way back here they could whisper without fear of being overheard. The sound of the wind whistling around the old church was almost overwhelming, so bride and groom and priest needed the microphone to be heard.

'Decide what with your head?' Georgie asked.

'Your life partner, of course,' he told her, warming to his

theme. 'You and I are doctors. Scientists, if you like. We know the heart's nothing but a bit of blood-filled muscle. If it fails you might even replace it with a transplant.' He motioned to the bride and groom. 'So where do you think these two would be if their hearts were transplanted? Unless there's a fair bit of cool, calculated thought in the equation, then the marriage is doomed.'

'Hush.' But there was no need to hush. No one could hear.

But she needed to hush him. What was he saying—that she should choose one of the gentle ones? The guys her head told her were suitable, but her heart abandoned as they pushed the wrong buttons.

'So what do you—?'

'Hush,' she said again, becoming so flustered she wasn't sure what she was thinking. Concentrate on the wedding, she told herself. This was an overblown Greek wedding. The church was full of apricot and white tizz. The bride and groom were surrounded by a sea of apricot and white attendants.

It was over-the-top ridiculous.

It was lovely.

He was still holding her hand.

The head and not the heart?

Yeah, well, that was where she'd been in trouble in the past. The Croc Creek doctors' house was always full to bursting with medics from around the world. Doctors used this place as a base where they could put their skills to use in a way that was invaluable to the remote peoples of Northern Australia. Doctors came here to help. Or sometimes they came just to escape.

Like *her*?

Yeah, but she wasn't thinking about herself, she decided hastily. She was talking about potential lovers. So there were plenty available.

No one else seemed to feel a lack, she thought dourly, looking ahead at Mike and Emily. Maybe it was only *her* who'd never seemed to fit.

They were kneeling for the blessing. There was no need to say hush. Georgie blinked back more stupid tears.

It was only because she was weak, she told herself fiercely. It was because she was worried about Max. It was because her face hurt.

Alistair's hold on her hand strengthened. She gave a feeble tug but he didn't release it.

She didn't pull again. She sniffed and kept listening.

Then there was a break as someone played a Greek love song, with the volume on full to drown out the sound of the rising wind. Georgie didn't understand all that much Greek but the way all the old ladies in the church sighed and smiled, she guessed it had to be something soppy.

And then came the moment they'd all been waiting for.

'I now pronounce you man and wife.'

They rose as the priest gave his final blessing. The groom lifted Emily's veil and kissed her, oh, so tenderly.

It was just lovely. She was feeling...weird.

'Very romantic,' Alistair whispered dryly.

'Be quiet,' Georgie said for a final time, and to her fury she felt tears start to well again.

'I'm sorry,' Alistair said, and he sounded startled.

'There's no need to be sorry,' Georgie whispered.

'No,' he said, and squeezed the hand he shouldn't be holding. The hand she shouldn't be letting him hold. 'There's not.' He looked down at her in concern as she swiped angrily at her eyes with his handkerchief. 'We'll find him, Georg.'

But she hadn't been thinking about Max. Her eyes flew upward to Alistair's. And something...connected?

Their gazes held. He was comforting her, she told herself furiously, but she didn't quite believe it. For this wasn't a look of comfort and the confusion she felt was mirrored in his eyes.

She tugged her hand away with a faint gasp and turned her attention resolutely back to the bride and groom. They were being hugged by their respective families in the front pews.

A slate came loose from the roof above their heads. It crashed down—the sound tracking its progress on the steep gabled roof above their heads. She winced. Alistair tried to take her hand again but she wasn't having any of it.

She gripped her hands very firmly together and kept her attention solely on the bridal party. The Trumpet Voluntary rang out—played by Charles. His splinter skill. The trumpet's call was pure and true, almost primaeval against the backdrop of the storm, and once more Georgie found herself blinking back tears as the bridal party swept by them on their way out of the church.

But then, as the doors swung open and the wind blasted in, the bridal party stopped in its tracks.

Another slate crashed down.

The surge to leave the church abruptly ended.

'We might rethink the exit,' the priest announced in a voice he had to raise. Having left the technology of microphones to lead the couple out of church, he now had to raise his voice above the sound of the wind.

'This has to be a cyclone,' Alistair said, and Georgie blinked and bought herself back to earth. Earth calling Georgie... What the hell was she about, crying at weddings? She was losing her mind.

She didn't cry. She never cried. Crying was for wimps.

Alistair's dumb handkerchief was a soggy mess.

'We're still copping the edges,' she managed, hauling herself together with a massive effort. 'Despite what Dora's waters are saying, it's still only category three. Strong but not disastrous.' She winced as a particularly violent gust blasted past the church, loosening another couple of slates. 'Harry says the biggest problem is flooding inland. It's the end of the rainy season and the country's waterlogged as it is. We'll have landslips.'

'As long as that's all we have.'

'Scared?'

'Yeah,' he said, and he grinned. 'This wind is really terrifying for a man with a toupee.'

She choked. It was lucky the combination of wind and trumpet was overpowering because her splutter of laughter would ordinarily have been heard throughout the church.

He grinned.

Her laughter faded. He looked...a man in charge of his world. He was wearing his lovely Italian-made suit. His silver-streaked hair was thick and glossy and wavy, just the way she liked it. His tanned face was almost Grecian, strongly boned, intelligent...

A toupee...

She couldn't resist. She put her free hand into his hair and tugged.

'Yikes.' This time they were overheard. The people in the last pew—great-aunts en masse by the look of them—turned in astonishment. One started to glare but Georgie was giggling as Alistair clutched his head, and the old lady's glare turned to an indulgent smile.

'It's lovely to see the children enjoying themselves,' she said in the piercing tones of the very old and the very deaf. 'Look at the pair of them, canoodling in the back pew like a pair of teenagers. These will be next by the look of them. Sophie said this doctors' house makes them breed like rabbits.'

Georgie's mouth dropped open. 'Canoodling,' she muttered, revolted.

But Alistair was chuckling. 'Come on, rabbit,' he said, and nudged her to the end of he pew. 'Let's get out the side door before everyone figures that's the only exit out of the wind.'

'If we duck out the side door, the great-aunts will think...'

'Yeah, but we don't care what they think, do we, Georg?' Alistair said. 'We'll just get another tattoo and say damn their eyes.'

'How do you know I have a...?' She paused. She swallowed. Alistair's grin became almost evil.

'Aha! So where?'

'It's none of your business.'

'I told you about my toupee.'

'It's not a—'

'I just have very good glue.'

'I'll pull harder.'

'If you show me your tattoo, I'll let you pull all you like. I'll even let you canoodle.'

They were at the side door. He was ushering her through it, his arm around her waist as he propelled her forward. Behind them the entire wedding party was crowding round while they figured out the protocol of getting the bride and groom out of the church where the main door was suddenly unusable and slates might crash down on their heads. They'd have to use the side door. But not yet.

'Em and Mike...you'll have to go back to the altar and start the wedding procession again.' It was Mike's mother in full battle cry. 'Charles, start the trumpet again, from the beginning. Bridesmaids, back into line!'

'No mere cyclone's going to get in the way of Sophia's perfect wedding,' Georgie said, giggling, and then they were out the door, propelled into the instant silence of the vestry.

Alistair closed the door behind them. The silence was suddenly...electric.

'Hey. Um... Maybe we should go back and get in procession like everyone else,' Georgie said, suddenly breathless.

'But you're not like everyone else,' Alistair said, turning. He'd been holding her hand. By turning, she was against the wall and he was right in front of her, smiling down. 'You're different.'

'I'm not different.'

'Yes, you are,' Alistair said softly. 'You don't belong.'

She stared at him, confused. 'I do belong.'

'Why did you come to Croc Creek?' he asked suddenly.

'I got a job here.' He was so close...

'With your qualifications there's a job for you wherever you want to go in the world. Croc Creek's home for those who want to devote a couple of years to a good cause. Or those who want excitement.'

'That's me.'

'Or it's a refuge for those who are escaping,' Alistair said, as if he hadn't heard her. It was almost as if he was talking to himself. 'What are you escaping from?'

'I'm not.'

'I recognise the symptoms.'

'You're a neurologist, not a shrink.'

'I'm an escapee myself.'

'You...'

'I like a bit of control,' he admitted, sounding thoughtful. 'That's why I was engaged to Eloise. Only then I met you and I decided control wasn't everything.'

'Hey.' She was suddenly really, really breathless. 'How did we get to this? You're really saying I influenced you in breaking your engagement?'

'Of course you influenced me. Just the way I reacted... I'm not saying I want to take it further...'

'That's good because—'

'Shut up and let me speak,' he said, quite kindly. 'All I want you to know is that what happened six months ago was a really big thing for me. Huge. I don't usually proposition complete strangers.'

'You're saying that between us...'

'Something happened. Yes.' Something was certainly happening in the church behind them. They could hear Sophia giving directions right through the massive door. 'But I don't know what,' he said. 'And before you think this is a line, I need to say I'm not interested in doing anything with it. At least, I don't think I am. As I said, I like control and you don't make me feel I'm in control. But I also know... Georgie, I recognise you're running, so maybe you need to be honest enough to admit it to yourself.'

'Why?' She was suddenly angry. What the hell was he playing at, psychoanalysing her like this? For what purpose?

'So you can move on.'

'To what?'

'To...life? It's not all that scary.'

'Like you'd know.'

'I—'

'Look, I don't know what's happening here,' she muttered. 'You're talking about something I don't understand.'

'You do understand it,' he said, and before she could respond he tugged her into his arms. 'Or at least you understand that what's between us is...well, it just is.'

'It isn't,' she gasped.

'It's not?'

She should fight. Of course she should fight. This was crazy. What was she doing, standing in the vestry with the wedding party on the other side of the door, letting him tug her against him, letting him lift her chin, letting him...?

No. She wasn't fighting. For every fighting instinct had suddenly shut down.

Everything had shut down.

He was going to kiss her and she wasn't going to do a damned thing about it.

Alistair.

And that was her last sane thought for a long time. His lips met hers and everything faded to nothing.

Everything but him.

The feel of him... The strength of him... She was standing on tiptoe to accept his kiss—despite her stilettos, she was dwarfed—but he was holding her so strongly that it was no effort to stand on tiptoe. He was lifting her to meet him.

Alistair.

It was like some magnetic force was locking her body to his. This was how it had felt six months ago when she'd danced with him. He was a great dancer. So was she. The dance had been Latin swing, and they'd moved as if they'd been dancing together for years. But every time he'd tugged her against him, preparatory to swinging her away, twirling her, propelling her into the next dance move, she'd felt exactly as she was feeling now.

As if his body was somehow an extension of her own.

No wonder she'd wanted him to take her. No wonder...

But the time for remembrance was not now. Here there was only room for wonder. Room for him. He was kissing her urgently, as if he knew that this kiss must surely be interrupted. As indeed it must. But his fierceness seemed entirely appropriate. It was a demanding kiss, a searing convergence of two bodies, a declaration that this was something amazing, and how could she deny it?

She couldn't deny it. She allowed his mouth to lock onto hers. Allowed? No, she welcomed it, aching for his kiss to deepen. Her arms came around his solid, muscled body and held him to her. She kissed back with the fierceness that he was using as he kissed her.

Her whole body felt aflame. Every nerve was tingling, achingly aware of him. Every sense was screaming at her to get closer, get closer, here is your mate...

Her lips opened, welcoming him, savouring him, wanting him deeper. Deeper. The kiss went on and on, as if she was drowning in pure pleasure, and she was, she was.

Alistair.

He was all wrong for her. For so many reasons he was wrong. But for now he was right and she was taking every ounce of pleasure she could get.

Alistair.

But suddenly he was drawing back. He was holding her face in his hands, forcing them apart so he could look into her eyes. The confusion she saw in his matched her own.

'Georgie,' he whispered, and there was confusion there, too.

'Don't stop,' she begged.

'We can't—'

'Just kiss me,' she begged, and she linked her hands behind his head and tugged him down.

'Georg—'

'Just kiss.'

He smiled, that achingly wonderful smile that had her heart doing handsprings.

He kissed.

The sound of the trumpet crescendoed behind them.

The door of the vestry flew open.

And here was the wedding procession, diverted from the main door.

The priest came first. Then came bride and groom, as if propelled by the mass behind. Then bridesmaids and groomsmen and pageboys and flowergirls and guests after them, tumbling into their private space, funnelled into the vestry with the door to the outside still not open.

The priest stopped in shock. As did the bride and groom. There was a moment's blank astonishment.

Then...

'Hey, get in the queue, guys,' Mike growled as he held his bride close. 'Today is our day. Gina and Cal are next Saturday. You two can take the Saturday after.'

CHAPTER SIX

THE MUDDLE FORCED them apart. Blushing furiously, Georgie disappeared into the crowd and Alistair let her go. She might be confused but he was even more so.

He fell back to the edge of the crowd and then made his escape.

He wouldn't go to the reception. He was too...disoriented? Plus he hadn't been invited. It was one thing to go to the wedding ceremony and sit unnoticed in the back of the church, he thought. Not that he'd been unnoticed, but this was the theoretical etiquette scenario he was talking himself through. It was quite another matter to go to the reception, where he'd be eating food prepared for other guests, mingling with people he didn't know...

Staying near Georgie.

And that was the deciding factor. As the wedding party had forced them apart, Georgie had paled. She'd looked up at him with such horror that he'd been unable to think what the hell to do.

Maybe he should have taken her aside, tried to discover what the horror was about and see if he could defuse it.

But she'd backed away as if terrified, and he'd thought...well, did he have any reason to inflict himself on her?

'Yes, because of the way I feel,' he told himself, battling the fierce wind as he made his way back to the hospital. The wind was blasting so hard against him that it hurt. There was rain just starting, and raindrops so hard that they felt like pellets. But in some strange way it made him feel better. He felt like fighting—but he didn't know what, and he didn't know why.

'If she makes me feel like that then maybe I need to get the hell out of here,' he muttered, but he knew he couldn't go back to the States. Not until after Gina's wedding. Next Saturday.

'As soon as this wind eases I'll go down to Cairns and just come back for the wedding.'

That made him feel how?

In control? Maybe, but control was ceasing to seem very important. What seemed important was the way Georgie made him feel. Like there'd been an aching void which he'd suddenly figured could be filled.

He was so confused. He'd go to the hospital. Medicine was a way of burying himself, he thought. It left him in charge of his own world as he tried to fix the messes of everyone else's world.

He pushed open the nursery door and Charles was there. Charles Wetherby, still in his tuxedo.

'Why aren't you at the wedding?' he asked, and Charles looked up from Megan's cot and grinned.

'I've done my duty. I gave the bride away and I played the trumpet twice. I'll put my nose in at the reception later but one of the very few pluses of using a wheelchair is that if you say you need to excuse yourself for a bit, no one ever asks you why.'

'You were in the wedding procession.'

'Not me,' he said cheerfully. 'I hopped it—or wheeled it—out through the priest's changing room as soon as I finished playing. Not even Sophia saw me sneak away. Oh, Jill and Lily will come and find me soon and drag me back, but for now I'm sticking here. Using an invalid's prerogative. What's your excuse?'

'I wanted to check on Megan.' But Megan was sleeping soundly and there was no way he was waking her up.

'Megan is great. Ilse and Herrick have been keeping bedside vigil, but there's little need. Ilse brought Lizzie through in her wheelchair and she's had a cuddle. Thanks to you.' He put out his hand, took Alistair's and shook it firmly. 'We're more grateful than I can say. You know, we could really use a neurologist here. I know we could never match your US salary but...' He grinned. 'There may be other compensations. So any time you're free...'

'Thanks but, no, thanks.'

'I'm not asking for an answer yet. Give it more than a cursory thought before you refuse.' He eyed Alistair speculatively. 'So why aren't you at the reception?'

'I'm not invited.'

'You know that makes no difference. And Georgie...'

'Yeah,' Alistair said heavily. 'Georgie.'

'So you're figuring it out,' Charles said, straight-faced.

'Figuring what out?'

'That you two are dynamite together.'

'Hey, there's no way. We've only just met.'

'You met six months ago.'

'For one night.'

'And Georg went round with a face like thunder for days. She'd take that bike out on the back roads south of here and come back with her gas tank empty and her bike and herself covered in mud. We had no idea what was driving her...'

'Her brother had gone.'

'Yeah, but that had happened before. She'd never been like that.'

'Charles...'

'Yeah, I know, butt out.' His pager sounded and he glanced at it, sighed and smiled. 'Women. That's Lily. My foster-daughter. It seems she's stowed boxes of confetti in the pouch at the back of this chair and my presence is required immediately. Or my confetti.' He wheeled back from the cot, smiling. 'OK, I'll head off to the reception. You know, Georgie isn't much of a one for parties,' he said thoughtfully. 'I might send her back to join you.'

'Don't.'

'She got one hefty slug yesterday. As her treating physician, I've advised quiet time. Sitting in the nursery with you should be just the ticket.'

'I'd prefer—'

'To be alone. Yeah, wouldn't we all? But look at me. I walked alone and now I have a partner and a child and all the accoutrements of life. They just sneaked up on me while I wasn't looking, and aren't I glad they did.'

'I don't want—'

'You don't know what you don't want,' Charles said enigmatically, and wheeled to the door. 'Keep Megan safe. And do consider my offer.'

'Offer?'

'Of a job,' he said patiently.

'I don't want—'

'You don't know what you don't want,' Charles said again. 'Think about it some more.'

And he disappeared, leaving Alistair alone with his thoughts.

It was dim and quiet in the ward. Megan was the only child in the nursery. Ilse came in and talked to him for a bit, but her English was poor. She kept throwing longing glances at the desk and finally he checked what she'd been glancing at and grinned. The title might be in German but he could recognise a romantic novel when he saw it.

'Go back to your book,' Alistair said, handing it over with good humour.

'It's that it's so quiet,' she said apologetically, smiling back at him. 'Herrick is bored as I. Everyone is at the wedding or—how you say?—banging wood on windows. Is there to be a cyclone?'

'I don't know.'

'I think a cyclone will be exciting,' she said, with the placid pleasure of the young. 'But you…you need to be at wedding. I can take care of Megan.'

'I'll go in a minute.'

'We have money,' she said, and she smiled. 'Ten dollars my Herrick has put.'

'Ten dollars?'

'Dr Luke has started…what you call…a book,' she said. 'That you and Georgie by the end of the week… Two to one.'

'What—?'

'So you need to go back to wedding,' she said. 'Because ten dollars is ten dollars and I don't want my Herrick to lose.'

'Go back to your romance,' he growled.

'And you, too,' she said, and grinned. 'Doctor.' And she buried her nose in her book before he could think of a suitable retort.

Weddings sucked.

Oh, as weddings went, this was a good one. Mike and Emily were a match made in heaven—even cynical Georgie had to admit that. The Pouloses' over-the-top enthusiasm was infectious, their generosity amazing, and it would be a strange person who couldn't be drawn into the fun and excitement. Even the wind, blasting around the little hotel in ever-increasing strength, seemed to be there specifically to form a backdrop to the band.

Georgie danced until her legs ached. She threw the odd plate with gusto. She ate a little.

She didn't want to be there. She wanted to be…with Alistair?

Don't do it, she told herself fiercely. You don't do love. You don't do commitment. You don't know if he's a gentle one or a bully, but they always turn out one way or the other in the end, and you know you can't bear either.

It could be fun to find out.

No.

Her current dance partner, Bruce, the local wildlife officer, spun her in a clumsy attempt at waltzing. She thought back to

Alistair's expert dance techniques and that had her even more confused.

So why don't you want to find out? she asked herself.

'Because he's perfect right now.'

'Pardon?' Bruce broke into her conversation and with a start she realised she'd been speaking aloud. 'Who's perfect?'

'Um…' Not him, that's for sure, but how to say it and not hurt him? Bruce was a nice guy. One of the gentle ones. Except in the dancing department. Her toes had been squashed more times than she cared to think about. 'The little girl we operated on this morning,' she said, and he nodded.

They were approaching the corner of the room. Time for a tricky manoeuvre. Bruce put his tongue out just a little, his forehead puckered in concentration, and he swept her round.

There went another toe.

'I keep thinking of my work, too,' Bruce told her. 'Did you know Big Bertha laid her eggs right near the town bridge? Now I'm gonna have to fence off that part of the river till they hatch. Nothing like the vengeance of a mother croc if anything threatens their kids.' He paused, deciding to wait while another couple spun past them. 'Speaking of which…where's your little tacker? Where's Max?'

'With his dad.'

'Yeah, but Harry said—'

'Harry shouldn't have said anything,' she said curtly.

'Well, he didn't, so to speak, but of course he told Grace and Grace told Mrs Poulos and Sophia told me. You know things can't be kept quiet in this town. Hell, Georg, if you want a hand to hunt the bugger down…'

He would help, too, Georgie thought, forgiving him her squashed toes. This whole town would. They were all there for her.

The music ended. Bruce looked eagerly toward the bar. 'You want a drink, Georg?'

'No. Um, my face is hurting a bit. I might go home,' she said.

'There's still the speeches.'

'No, I think I'll go.'

'Alistair's back there, is he?'

She took a deep breath. They knew. Of course, the town knew. Any hint of gossip was around the town practically before it happened.

'I'm going home to bed,' she said with an attempt at dignity.

'Yeah?' He grinned. 'But I was asking—'

'I know what you were asking. Don't.'

'Course I won't. OK, I'll be off and find myself a beer. You don't want a ride home?'

'No.'

'Good, 'cos this is a great party. See ya,' he said with his accustomed good humour. 'But, you know, I've laid money the other way, so I'd prefer it if you could keep away from Carmichael. Ten quid's worth keeping.'

She turned around and Alistair was there.

'Hey,' Bruce said cheerfully. 'She was just going home to bed and you. Seems she doesn't have to.' He gave Georgie a friendly push toward Alistair, chuckled and left them to it.

The band started again. Fast swing.

'Hi,' Alistair said. 'Would you like to dance?'

'Dancing with you is dangerous.'

'I know,' he said, and he smiled. 'We both know. But what's life if we can't live dangerously?' And suddenly she had no choice at all. Alistair was tugging her into a rumba and she simply let herself go.

There was nothing like dancing with an expert. There was nothing like dancing with Alistair.

Dancing was wonderful.

Georgie's mother had loved dancing. From her tired, life-battered mother, dancing was the last thing anyone might expect, but May had loved it. She'd given up on hoping for dancing skill—or even interest—from the various no-hoper men she'd ended up with, but as a toddler Georgie had learned to be her mother's partner. When things had got too ghastly she'd learned to turn on the radio and plead with her mother to dance.

In the end illness and poverty had taken the dancing out of her, but May had left her daughter with a legacy she loved.

And Alistair's skill matched her own.

They danced like competition dancers. Every move he made she knew and matched and melded with. They didn't speak. She was laughing, abandoning herself to the joy of the dance, every fibre of her being responding to his.

Others on the dance floor were falling back, clapping in time, cheering. She was hardly aware of it. She loved it. She loved…

No. She didn't love…anything. Just the dance…

The music ended. She was exhausted, having danced to her limit, laughing up at him while the room erupted in cheers.

'Where did you learn to dance like that?' she demanded.

'My dad insisted on dance lessons when I was a kid,' he confessed, smiling, and he knew she loved it as much as he did. 'Pretty silly, eh?'

'Not silly at all,' she said. 'We ought to have introduced your dad to my mum.'

'And added a few more complications to our lives?'

Her smile faded, just a bit.

What was she doing there? Bruce was watching her from the bar. She'd told him she was going home.

She should go home.

'I thought you weren't coming,' she said.

'So did I,' he said. 'But Charles said the dancing was excellent.'

'Yeah?'

'And you were here,' he said simply, and as the music resumed—this time a slow waltz—he took her into his arms again. 'I'm not sure where this is going but I sat over there and figured that if I stayed there and you stayed here then I might miss my chance to find out.'

She gasped. She tried to break away. But he was holding her

tight against him. Her treacherous body was moving in time with his, melding to his.

She succumbed to the dance.

She succumbed to Alistair.

And, as if on cue, the lights went out.

Just like that, the room was blanketed in darkness. The sound system died and the last twangs of music from the band sounded tinny and echoing.

'Is this a hint?' someone said from the floor. 'Is it time for the bride and groom to go to bed, then?'

There was laughter but it sounded a bit nervous. For all the assurances they'd had that the cyclone would miss them, the locals were starting to make up their own minds.

Alistair didn't release her. For some dumb reason she didn't want him to. She stood in the centre of the room while everyone else grew scared, and she felt…safe.

Within the secure hold of Alistair's arms she could look out and see what was going on.

'Harry…' It was Charles, calling from the doorway, and his tone was urgent.

There was still some dim light—each table had a candle. Some candles had gone out, but people were using the lit ones to relight others. Soon there was enough light to see by.

Cal came through from the veranda, seeking them out specifically.

'What's wrong?' Georgie asked, seeing by his face that there was real trouble.

'There's been a bus accident up in the hills behind the town,' he told them. 'Martha and Dan Mackers saw the Mt Isa bus go past half an hour ago. Just after it passed they felt what they thought was an earth tremor. Given this weather, it's a wonder they ventured out at all but they thought they'd take the Jeep down and check. They didn't get far. The road's collapsed just south of their place and the bus is on its side down the cliff. That place is a dead spot for mobile coverage so the report's been brief—Dan had to get back to his place to phone in. So we have no idea what we're facing. Charles is briefing Harry now. Can you two get back to the hospital?'

'I'll come with you up the mountain,' Georgie said, hauling herself out of Alistair's arms and stepping forward. 'Of course I'll come.'

'No,' Cal said. 'I was with Charles when the call came and we talked it through. Yes, we'll want medics on the mountain, but we want only the experienced emergency guys. We've had an upgrade on the cyclone. It's veered. We're right in its path and we're expecting to be hit by morning. The hospital has to be prepared for multiple casualties and the code black disaster response is activated right now.'

'Code black?' Alistair queried.

'The big one. Major external threat. I'd rather go,' Georgie said.

'Not going to happen,' Cal snapped. 'Not with that face. Charles wants you here, Georg—apart from him, you'll be the most senior doctor staying put if I have everyone else I want. Alistair, can we count on your help?'

'Of course,' Alistair said, as if it was a no-brainer.

'Then the reception's off for now,' Cal said ruefully. 'Every able-bodied man, woman and child in this town has a job to do right now. A cyclone with a crashed bus thrown in for good measure...'

'Oh...' It was a wail from Sophia Poulos, mother of the bride-groom. She'd been standing open-mouthed as Charles had explained to people at his end of the room what was happening. But Sophia's wail caught them all. 'Oh... This is bad.'

But the mother of the groom was nothing if not resolute. She took a deep breath, gazed fondly at the bride and groom and nodded. 'But of course you need my boy,' she said. 'And our Emily. Who else can look after these people? Emily, let me find you something else to wear.' Another deep breath. 'All this food,' she said, and she clucked. 'All this lamb. I'll tell the chef to start making sandwiches.'

At least she didn't have time to think of Max. Or Alistair. Though even that thought meant that she was thinking of them both. Back at the hospital they were in full crisis mode. The back-up generators meant they had power, and they needed it. Every available person was set to work, securing anything that could be an obstacle. Boarding up the windows was the first line of defence, but it was assumed that they might break open and nothing in the wards was to be loose to become a flying threat.

A receiving ward was set up fast. Any patients not on the critical list were sent home if their homes were deemed secure, or moved to a safe haven—the local civic hall—if they weren't. Of the remaining patients, those in the wards with the largest windows were shifted to the south side, out of the direct blast and hopefully more secure. The storerooms in the centre of the buildings that had no windows at all became the wards for the most seriously ill—the patients who, if the worst came to the worst, couldn't get out of bed and run for cover.

The theatres were windowless but Charles wasn't giving them over for ward use.

'Even if there are no injuries from this bus crash, if this turns into a full-blown cyclone we'll have trauma enough. I want additional linen, stores and pharmacy supplies in Emergency, Intensive Care and both theatres. Move.'

A big storeroom at the back of the doctors' house was used for back-up medical supplies. Charles wanted everything brought into the main building. Everything.

'I don't want to run out of bandages and not be able to get at more,' he growled. There were six elderly people in the nursing-home section of the hospital. Charles had them sorting and stacking as if they were forty instead of ninety, promising them they could rest at the civic hall when they'd finished.

Amazingly they rose to the occasion. Everyone did. Including Alistair. Georgie was supervising storage, making sure she knew where everything was so it could be easily reached. Alistair was one of those doing the ferrying of gear from the doctors' house. He was using a car to travel the short distance but even so he was soaked to the skin. Every time she saw him his clothes were soggier. His beautiful suit would be ruined.

They passed each other without speaking. There was no time for speaking. The threat was rising with every howl of the wind.

She couldn't locate the oxygen cylinders. Where were they? The normal storeroom was now a ward, housing Lizzie and her four children. Megan's cot had been wheeled in there as well, and Georgie paused in her search to check on her little patient.

She was still sleeping but she was looking great. A quick check on the notes at the end of the cot indicated she'd woken up and had a drink and smiled at her mother. Fantastic. Thanks to Alistair.

But there were problems. Lizzie was sitting bolt upright in bed, looking terrified. 'Georgie, is the jail secure?'

'You're worried about Smiley?'

'I don't want him to be killed,' Lizzie muttered, and Georgie abandoned her task and crossed to the bed to hug her. She included Davy and Dottie in her hug.

'Of course you don't,' she said, understanding. 'Smiley's the kids' dad. He's been your husband. Of course you're worried.'

'I don't hate him enough to want him killed.'

'We checked.' Help was suddenly there from an unexpected source. Alistair was standing in the doorway, dripping wetly onto the linoleum. 'Charles has had people contact everyone this side of the creek, letting them know what's happening, making sure they're safe. Harry told him the holding cell's a prefabricated makeshift building and he's worried about it. So he's let Smiley out for the duration. Harry has the feeling Smiley thinks he might skip town, but he's not too worried—there's no way out of here until this is over.'

'But—' Lizzie said, and Georgie answered her fears.

'Don't worry,' she told her. 'Look where we put you. Smiley would have to walk through two wards to reach you, and the whole town knows his story. He'll be too busy saving his own skin to worry you now.'

'Do you care about him?' Alistair asked, and Lizzie flashed him a look of astonishment.

'Of course I care. He's the kids' father.'

'And you don't want to waste your time worrying about him,' Georgie said, understanding the young woman's fear. 'Which you would if you knew he was in danger. So now you can put him aside.'

'So where's your Max?' Lizzie asked.

Georgie froze. She'd been watching Alistair in the doorway. Looking at the way his shirt clung wetly to his chest. Just looking. But her thoughts were dragged sideways to her little brother.

'One of the nurses said Max was in trouble,' Lizzie said shyly. 'It's only... Davy got into a fight at school last year and Max stood up for him. I hate to think of him out there in this.'

'He's not out there.'

'No, but the nurse said you didn't know where he was.'

'He's with his father.'

'And his father's on the run? Oh, Georg...'

'We do get ourselves into trouble,' Georgie said, and gave her another hug. 'Who needs men? What a shame Max and Davy and Thomas will grow into the species.'

'They'll be nice,' Lizzie said stoutly. 'My Davy and my Thomas will be nice, caring men. I won't let Smiley turn them into thugs. And I bet your Max will be great, too.'

'He will be,' Georgie said.

'Georg, where do you want the extra stretchers?' Alistair asked, and if his voice sounded strained she was going to ignore it.

Back to work.

'In the corridors. We'll stack them near the entrance so they can be grabbed easily by whoever needs them.'

'You think it's going to be big?' Lizzie asked.

Georgie shrugged. 'I hope not. We should miss the brunt of it.'

'But you think—'

'I think we have to be prepared. Do you need help with the stretchers, Dr Carmichael?'

'No.' He looked at her for a long, hard moment. 'I'm fine by myself.'

He disappeared the way he'd come.

'He's sweet on you,' Lizzie said, and Georgie felt herself change colour.

'No.'

'He is.'

'It's no matter whether he is or not,' she snapped. 'Like you, I always fall for losers. So if he's falling for me, he's a loser by definition.'

And then the casualties from the bus came in.

This was no minor accident. The driver was dead. The first grim-faced paramedics told them that, and told them also to expect more deaths and more life-threatening injuries.

It seemed they had a major disaster on their hands before the cyclone even hit.

The first ambulance brought in a woman with multiple fractures and major blood loss and an elderly man who was drifting in and out of consciousness and showed signs of deep shock. Query internal bleeding? X-rays, fast.

X-Ray was in huge demand. Mitchell Caine, their radiologist, was supposedly on holidays, but his locum had been delayed by bad weather. Mitch had been dragged in that morning to assess Megan's scans, and now he was back again.

'I shouldn't be doing this, ladies and gentlemen,' he said as he worked his way through the queue of patients needing urgent assessment. 'I'm so tired I'm not dependable. Just double-check any results I give you before you operate. If I say right leg, check I'm not talking about an arm.'

But his X-rays and reports were solid and dependable. Nothing like a code black to make a man forget about holidays.

Hell, this situation was impossible, Alistair thought. One overworked radiologist and no one else for three hundred miles?

'No one's going to sue here,' Georgie told him as they worked on. 'Everyone does what they have to do.'

Which was why twenty minutes later Alistair, a neurologist, was in Theatre, trying to set a fractured leg well enough to stabilise blood supply to the foot. With Georgie, an obstetrician, backing him up.

There was no time to question what they were doing. They just did it.

With the blood flow established—Alistair had worked swiftly and efficiently and their patient could now wait safely until a full orthopaedic team was available to fix the leg properly—they returned to the receiving ward to more patients.

The second ambulance was there now, and a third, and there was a battered four-wheel-drive pulling in behind it.

There were patients everywhere, some walking wounded, suffering only bruising and lacerations, but others serious.

For all the chaos, the place was working like a well-oiled machine. Maximum efficiency. Minimal panic. Charles had divided his workforce into teams, but the teams were fluid, doctors and nurses moving in and out of teams as an individual needed specific skills.

Every medic in Croc Creek was on duty by now, including a nurse heavily pregnant with twins.

'Don't mind my bump,' she said cheerfully as they worked around her. She was cleaning and stitching lacerations with skill. 'Yeah, I'm ready to drop but I've told them to be sensible and stay aboard until this is over. Just hand me the stuff that can be done sitting down.'

There was more than enough work to hand over.

This was emergency medicine at its worst. Or at its best.

'You know, if this had happened in my big teaching hospital back in the US, I doubt if we'd do it any better,' Alistair muttered as they worked through more patients, and Georgie felt it was almost a pat on the back.

For all of them, she said hastily to herself, but it didn't stop a small glow…

She was carefully fitting a collar to a man who'd been playing it hardy. 'I'm fine, girl,' he'd said. He'd come in sitting in the front of one of the cars but now he was white-faced and silent. Georgie had noted him sitting quietly in a corner and had moved in. Pain in the neck and shoulders. Query fracture? Collar and X-rays now, whether he wanted them or not.

There was a flurry of activity at the door and Cal was striding through at the head of a stretcher. 'Alistair, can we swap duties?' he called across the room, and Georgie intercepted the silent message that crossed the room with his words.

Uh-oh. Alistair was a neurosurgeon. If Cal wanted him, it'd be bad.

It was.

'Head injury,' he said briefly. 'We had to intubate and stabilise her before bringing her in. Mitch has already run her through X-Ray. His notes and slides are here. Georgie…' She was near enough for him not to have to call her. 'Can you assist here?'

'Mr Crest needs X-rays.'

'I'll take that over,' Charles called. He'd just finished a dressing and he wheeled over to take Georgie's place. He glanced across at Cal's patient and saw what they all saw. A laceration to the side of her face. Deeply unconscious. 'Jill,' he said to their chief nurse, 'you work with this one, too. That's all I can spare. Do your best.'

'She'll need you all if she's to pull through,' Cal said gravely. 'The notes are there, guys.'

Jill was already wheeling the trolley swiftly into a side examination cubicle where they could assess the patient in relative privacy. Alistair was working as the trolley moved, while Georgie skimmed through Mitch's notes.

The woman—young, blonde, casually dressed but neat and smart by the look of it—was limp on the trolley, lying in the unnaturally formal pose that told its own story. Her breathing was the forced, rasping sound of intubation. Such breathing always sounded threatening, Georgie thought as she read. As it should. It meant the patient wasn't breathing on her own.

'Show me the films,' Alistair said.

Jill flicked on the light on the wall and held them up.

He winced.

'We're looking at interthalamic haemorrhage.'

'Yeah,' Georgie said grimly.

'Glasgow scale?'

'It was five half an hour ago,' Georgie said, referring again to the notes. 'But Cal has it now improving. It might have been initial shock that drove it so low.'

'Either way, I want an EVD in now,' Alistair said.

An EVD. A line to drain bleeding into the brain to prevent build-up of pressure. It was in many ways a repeat of the operation he'd done that morning on Megan.

But that morning they'd had six in theatre. Now...

'Let's find out if we have anyone else spare,' Alistair said grimly, reading her thoughts. 'But we move regardless. If pressure builds up any more, we're looking at major brain damage. We may be too late already.'

And in the end it was all down to Alistair, Jill and Georgie. In another life Jill had been a theatre sister in a teaching hospital that housed the major neurological centre for the state. She proved invaluable here. She had to be Jill of all trades. Surgical assistant. Charge theatre nurse. Junior. Everything else.

Because, to her horror, Georgie had to give the anaesthetic.

'You can do it with your eyes closed,' Alistair told her.

'Are you kidding? I can't—'

'We have three operations running consecutively,' Alistair said bluntly. 'You know that so let's stop the objections and just do it.'

So she did it, and she needn't have worried. She'd done the basics of anaesthetics in medical training and she'd performed almost as many gynaecological operations in Croc Creek than she'd had hot dinners. Up until now she'd had an anaesthetist every time she'd operated, but she'd watched what they'd done and enough had soaked in to make this almost instinctive.

But as well as that she had Alistair. She'd watched him work on Megan and his skill had stunned her. This was more of the same, and the woman under his hands had just as much chance of survival as if she'd been transported to a major neurological surgical team within minutes of the accident occurring.

The response team out in the field had intubated the woman and administered drugs to reduce the swelling of the brain as it haemorrhaged. They'd saved her life, and now Alistair was doing his damnedest to save her intellect.

He worked swiftly, referring to the CT scans again and again, making sure he was working on the source of the bleeding, his fingers moving with the instinctive speed of the highly skilled. The magnificently skilled. And every time Georgie faltered about anaesthetic dosage he snapped orders before her question was framed.

And finally it was done. The woman was as safe as they could make her. As Alistair applied the dressings and the pressure eased, Georgie checked the woman's pupils once again. There was a flicker of response.

'Hooray,' she said in a voice that was none too steady. 'This might just work.'

'We'll keep her asleep for a while,' Alistair said. 'We'll leave her in an induced coma. We'll check with one of the anaesthetists before we do that, though. All I know is that I don't want her feeling any pain. If she surfaces now, she'll emerge to confusion and I'm not risking any movement.'

'We still don't know who she is.'

'That can wait, too,' Alistair growled, and he stepped back from the operating table and let Jill run a swab over his forehead. He'd been sweating while he'd worked. He'd done the work of a team of doctors, Georgie thought.

He was...

One of the nice ones, she told herself, feeling more and more...strange? Weird. Here she was in one of the biggest medical crises of her career and she was thinking about Alistair? And she wasn't just thinking about him medically.

'Nice work, Turner,' Alistair said, and he gave her a grin across the table that might just as well have been a caress, the way it made her feel.

She didn't fall in love with nice, gentle medics, she told herself fiercely—desperately. They didn't keep her happy.

Even if they were Alistair.

By the time they emerged, the chaos had faded to a more manageable rush. The anaesthetist had finished working with another compound fracture and was free to take over the care of their unknown patient.

Georgie and Alistair were able to take a break.

Maybe even to go home. The emergency room was clear.

'Charles got everything sorted fast,' Jill told them as they emerged. 'This cyclone's moved now so we'll get hit directly. They're saying by morning at latest. We'll all be wanted again then so Charles is saying if you're free now, go to bed. He wants as many of his staff rested as possible.'

'That's fine by us,' Alistair said, and took Georgia's arm and led her out into the corridor. She should resist. She should...

But she was capable of doing no such thing. She let his hand stay exactly where it was.

Nice.

The entrance was crowded, but not with people. Here was the baggage from the bus—a muddled heap of sodden belongings. Alistair steered her past and she barely glanced down.

But she did just glance. And saw...

'Oh, God.' It felt like her heart had stopped beating.

'What is it?' Alistair asked, but she was already fumbling through the pile to reach what she'd seen.

She wasn't wrong. She lifted a bag gingerly from the pile, using one finger as if it might disintegrate before her eyes. It couldn't be.

'Max,' she whispered, and suddenly Alistair was beside her, holding her under her arm, looking down at her face in alarm.

'You're white as a ghost. Hell, Georg, what's happening? Are you ill? We shouldn't have let you work.'

'This isn't about me,' she whispered, and she had to fight to get her voice to work. 'It's Max. This is his backpack.'

'Are you sure?' he asked incredulously.

She'd pulled away, squatting on the floor, unzipping the bag with fingers that trembled. She peered in, then upended it entirely. A pair of faded pyjamas. A ripped windcheater with the name of a sports team on the back. Bulldogs. A couple of pairs of a child's underclothes. One teddy bear. Ancient. Minus an eye and with stuffing coming out one knee.

'Spike,' Georgie said. She lifted the little bear into her arms. 'This is Spike,' she said, and her voice had steadied. It was strangely calm. She turned to Harry, who'd just approached. 'Max was on that bus,' she said. 'His dad must have put him on in Mt Isa. Dammit, he should have rung. Harry, have you found any kids?' Her face suddenly blenched even more than before and she staggered backward so she was sitting on the floor.

'He's not...he's not one of the bodies, is he? Oh, God, please...'

'He's not,' Harry said, kneeling on the floor and gripping her hands. 'Georgie, I've been up there. We found no kids.'

'His dad... Ron's on the run. They might both...'

'I know Ron, Georgie,' Harry said. 'He wasn't on the bus.'

'But he might be hiding. He might—'

'Georg, any person in that bus would be far too battered to be thinking about hiding. And the wind's terrific. Your dad might be afraid of jail but there's worse things than jail, and staying out in the rainforest tonight would be one of them.'

'But Max is definitely there,' Georgie faltered. She looked up at Alistair. 'He is,' she said dully. 'This is Spike. Max has just stopped carrying Spike around but Spike's never far from him.'

'But there's also the shoe,' Harry said slowly, and behind them the phone rang.

'The shoe?'

'There's a child's shoe. It worried the guys at the bus. Hold on and I'll fetch it. I think we might have left it at the front desk.' He turned and walked swiftly away from them.

He should go, Alistair thought. He might be needed.

He wasn't leaving Georgie.

Georgie was staring straight ahead. 'I know he's there. I need to go.'

'You can't,' he said, appalled.

She looked up at him mutely and clutched the bear.

'I...'

He stooped to hold her. 'No.'

The phone was getting to him. Hell, it was two in the morning. This was the emergency entrance. He crossed to the desk and lifted the receiver.

'Dr Carmichael?' a woman demanded.

'Yes.'

'Charles said you were in Emergency,' she said. 'This is Fiona. I'm manning the phones here. I have a woman on the line who needs to talk to you urgently.'

'To me?' he said blankly, and then he thought, Two in the morning, it'd be someone from home. Eloise? Some drama with the team at home?

He glanced down at Georgie. She was holding the teddy like

it was a talisman, staring out into the night, as bleak as death. But her face was closed. She walked alone, this woman. When she was hurt she closed herself off.

'Put her through,' he told Fiona, not taking his eyes off Georgie.

'Is that Dr Carmichael?'

'Yes,' he said. The woman sounded as if she was whispering.

'You rang me earlier asking about Ron's son. Max.'

'Yes,' he said, becoming more alert. 'Yes, I did. Can you give me any information?'

'It's on the radio,' she said. 'I couldn't sleep and I was listening to the radio. They said the Mt Isa bus has crashed. They're talking multiple casualties. They say—'

'Are you worried that Max is on the bus?' he asked, cutting to the chase, and Georgie stared up at him, her attention caught.

'He is. My husband said Ron got rid of the kid. I was just...' She paused and took a deep breath. 'Well, I never thought... not for a minute, not really, but Max and his dad stayed here a while back and he's such a little boy. Him and that dog. And Ron didn't care. So when he said he'd got rid... Anyway, I told my husband that if he didn't tell me what Ron had done with him I'd go to the police, so help me. My husband knows me well enough now to know I don't stand up to him very often, but when I do I mean it.'

'When Ron said he'd got rid of him,' Alistair prodded, and Georgie was right beside him.

'I didn't think...well, he is his father after all, so he wouldn't... But if he had then I would have killed them both. But he said that Ron put him on the bus to his sister. Georgie. Max talked about Georgie all the time. Ron hated the dog but Max said Georgie would like him.'

'So Max is on the bus from Mt Isa,' Alistair said.

'That's what I said.' The woman was crying. 'Ron's on the run and we took him in for a bit and I hated it but I put up with it because of the kiddie. And my hubby wouldn't let the kid stay here. So he said he'd got rid of him and I made him tell me—'

'He was on the bus last night?'

'I don't know.' The woman was weeping. 'I nearly told you this afternoon when you rang but I was so scared. But he left here on Thursday and we're... Well, I'm not saying where we are, no names, but it fits and if he's on the bus, someone should know.'

'Thank you so much,' Alistair said gently. 'You wouldn't like to tell me your name?'

'No,' the woman said. 'I wouldn't.'

And the phone went dead.

Alistair turned to look at Georgie. 'It is him,' he said, but she already knew.

'Here's the shoe,' Harry said, walking swiftly back into the room. 'But it has to be too small to belong to Max.' Georgie grabbed it before he was two steps into the room. Harry was right—the shoe was tiny. It looked hand-painted, with a red painted fish whose eye was camouflaging a small hole.

'It's not his,' she said.

'Then whose?' Harry demanded. 'The guys found it up the back of the bus. But we've searched at least a hundred yards in all directions and in that country no one's likely to have gone further, least of all a child.'

'But it's not Max's,' Georgie said stubbornly, and shook her head. 'No matter. The backpack's his. I'm going out there now.'

'Are you kidding?' Harry moved swiftly between Georgie and the door, blocking the way.

'Max is up there,' she said. 'Get out of the way, Harry.'

'Georg, there's a cyclone hitting within hours. There's no way we're letting you go out to the bus site, even if you could get through, which you can't. A huge tree crashed down just as we got the last of the passengers out. We were lucky to get out ourselves. If I thought it was possible I'd go myself—walk in if

I had to, maybe take a team in—but I can't leave the town right now. No one can. We don't know when this storm's going to hit.'

'I'll take my dirt bike,' she snapped. She tried to shove Harry aside but he wouldn't move. He held her as if she was a feather-weight, and her karate knowledge did her no good at all against the big policeman's superior strength.

'No,' Harry told her. 'You said yourself it's not his shoe.'

'Then there's two kids,' she snapped, and shoved him again. 'Let me past.'

'We have no proof, and it's suicide, Georg.'

'We do have proof,' Alistair said gently from behind them. 'Harry, we've just had phone confirmation that Max was defi-nitely on the bus. Suicide or not, there's a child's life at stake. I'll go with her.'

The pushing stopped. Georgie whirled to face him, her face a mixture of anguish and fear. 'You can't.'

'Don't you start saying *I* can't,' he said. 'Harry, the tree's blocking the road, right? Who else in town has a dirt bike?'

'I have one,' Harry told him, making a decision and mov-ing swiftly into organisational mode. They now definitely had one child out there, and maybe another. That was worth tak-ing risks for.

He'd go himself, Georgie realised, if the safety of the rest of Crocodile Creek wasn't resting squarely on his organisational shoulders.

'It's in the shed, Georgie, fuelled up, key above the door...'

But Georgie wasn't listening. She was staring at Alistair. 'You really can ride?'

'I can ride.'

'You'd better not hold me back.'

'Stop arguing, you two, and get going. You don't have long,' Harry said. 'Watch your footing off road. These hills are old gold country and the place is littered with disused mine shafts. Don't take a step until you know it's safe. You've got a radio,

Georg? Of course not. Take mine and I'll pick up a spare at the station. Your cellphone won't work out there.'

'We're going,' Georgie said. 'I have to get out of these clothes.'

'Stilettos might be a bad idea,' Harry said gravely, but he was saying it to their backs. They were gone.

Leaving Harry looking after them. With a tiny shoe still in his hand.

Could Alistair really ride? She hardly believed him but by the time she'd changed swiftly into leathers and sensible shirt and boots and fetched her own bike from the sheds at the back of the doctors' house, Alistair was in the sheltered forecourt of the hospital, complete with bike.

The bike was an oldie but a goodie. It'd handle rough stuff.

And maybe so could Alistair. To her further astonishment he was dressed as sensibly as she was—in leathers as well.

'Borrowed plumage,' he said as she wheeled up beside him. 'This stuff was by the bike and in this wind we'll need all the protection we can get. And I've organised gear.'

It seemed he had, and he'd rallied the troops. Jill came rushing out of the main entrance as he spoke. Crocodile Creek's charge nurse had a white coat covering her wedding finery, but she'd defiantly repinned an exquisite orchid corsage onto her lapel.

She was carrying two emergency services backpacks.

'Charles told me to equip these for you,' she said. 'Your bikes aren't geared for baggage. Energy drinks, emergency saline, painkillers, a small oxygen canister, collars—everything you might need but we hope you don't. Also there's a decent radio that will get through to here. Charles says it stays on your back whatever happens and keep us informed. Harry also said to tell you he had to abandon a vehicle on the far side of the road block. He left the keys in it so you might be able to use it or take cover there if the wind gets too strong. But Charles says get in there,

take a look and get out again fast. And no heroics.' She paused
for breath. And swallowed. Her fear was palpable.

'You're all right here?' Alistair said, feeling torn. He'd done
all he could to alleviate cerebral pressure on the woman with
the head injury but he was aware that there was maybe a score
of other patients. But Max… And maybe another child. What
could be more urgent than that?

'We're under control,' Jill said, recovering, and he could
tell by her voice that she'd guessed his thoughts. 'Charles con-
curs. This takes priority or he'd never let you go. We've got so
many doctors from this wedding that we're OK. Your job is to
look after Georgie. And yours,' she said, turning to Georgie
and giving her a swift but fierce hug, 'is to find Max. Charles
says he'll move heaven and earth to get you custody from now
on. Our Lily loves him. CJ loves him. We all love him. Bring
him home safe.'

CHAPTER SEVEN

THAT WAS IT. The time for talking was over. It took all their concentration and more to keep the bikes on the road. The road up into the mountains was steep, and that helped a little. The road had been cut into the mountainside, forming a sheer cliff to their left. The cliff gave them a little shelter—not much, but without it riding would be impossible. Even under the lee of the cliff, debris was already piling up. Rain was slashing into their visors. It was like a scene from a nightmare—and the cyclone hadn't yet hit!

Alistair rode ahead, inching his way through the mess, and Georgie was content to let him. It had only taken minutes for her to realise that he could do more than just ride a bike. The man was an expert.

So why had he refused her offer of a ride on the back of a Harley when she'd collected him from the airport?

Pride, she thought, trying to keep her mind on anything but the thought of Max somewhere out in this storm. In his gorgeous suit Alistair would have looked pretty silly.

OK, one to Alistair. She was ready to forgive him anything right now. She'd have come alone, but now all she had to do was keep her bike on track behind his, keep him within sight, letting him do the initial assessment of the road and the obsta-

cles in their way. To come here alone would be terrifying. But
to have him in front...

Careful, she told herself. She didn't do dependence. Alistair
was one of the gentle ones, intelligent, caring, nice...

Oh, cut it out. The man was a loner. As if he'd be interested...

And if he was, then she wasn't. Happy families? She didn't
think so.

Where was Max?

Twenty minutes from home they found the tree. A massive
gum blocked the road entirely. They pulled to a halt, propped
their bikes and checked it out.

They didn't speak. The wind was terrific, hurling leaf litter
everywhere, and the rain was almost blinding them. The sound
of the wind was almost deafening in itself and taking off their
helmets to make it easier to listen would be crazy.

Alistair grabbed her hand and towed her. She let him. The
wind was so strong she felt she might be blown off the mountain if she didn't hold onto something.

And holding onto Alistair was...well, OK.

There was a way around. At the base of the tree, where
the massive roots had ripped their way out of the rain-sodden
ground, the land must have initially been almost clear. There
was a passage of sorts around the roots. They could take their
bikes through.

They walked it first, emerging on the other side to see, as
promised, one of the hospital's four-wheel-drive trucks. If Harry
had been driving it, he was lucky he hadn't been ten feet further along when the tree had crashed, Georgie thought. Hell...

'Will we go the rest of the way in the car?' she yelled to
Alistair, and he shook his head.

'If one tree was down a few hours ago, there's bound to be
more down by now. The bikes are our only chance. But stay
close to me. Don't drop back more than ten feet.' He'd been
yelling, too, and a sudden drop in the swirling wind made his
voice echo. He grinned and, seemingly on impulse, undid his

helmet clips, pushed up her helmet, did the same to his, tugged her close and kissed her gently on the lips. Then replaced his helmet as if nothing had happened at all.

'We'll find him,' he said softly. 'Come on, Georg. Let's go.'

The bus scene was chaos.

They'd been given careful directions but it wasn't hard to find. Ten minutes of careful riding past the fallen tree and there it was.

Or there it wasn't. The entire roadway had slipped, the slide having started from the cliff above, leaving the road a mass of sodden rocks and soil.

There were chains anchored to trees, disappearing down the slide. There were the marks of people—lots of people. The start of the slip was scarred with a mass of footprints, heavy boots, the signs of rescue workers involved in a massive re-trieval operation.

They still kept their helmets on—it'd be crazy to take them off. Propping their bikes on the sheltered side of the road, they inched their way to the edge of the landslip, shining the pow-erful flashlights they'd been provided with.

Twenty feet below was the bus.

'It's stable,' Alistair yelled across the wind. 'The guys said it's securely fastened. They used cables to make it safe.'

'I'm going down.' And she was sliding down in the mud, not caring what Alistair was doing, forgetting Alistair completely. She felt sick. Somewhere here was Max. Somewhere…

If he'd felt like hiding when the rescuers had come then maybe he'd be back in the bus by now. That'd be the sensible place for him to be. Please…

She tried to hurry but Alistair was behind her, gripping her shoulder, hauling her back.

'You fall and break your ankle and there's all of us in a mess,' he yelled. 'And remember what Harry said about old mine shafts. We do this carefully and sensibly, Georg, or not at all.'

She tried to brush him off but his hand still held her.

'What's it to be, Georg?' he yelled. 'If you start being crazy, I'll pick you up and tie you to a tree till I'm done, and I'll search the place alone.'

'You wouldn't...' She whirled to face him, trying to shove his hand away.

'Try me,' he said.

She stared up into his face—and she knew she'd met her match. His face was implacable. Either she started being sensible or he'd pick her up and put her where she'd be safe. What he'd do to keep her there she didn't know, but this man wasn't to be crossed.

'OK,' she said, trying not to sound as shaken as she felt. 'But I stay in front.'

'No,' he said, and grabbed her hand. 'We do this side by side, Georgie, or not at all.'

So side by side it was.

Even when they got to the bus he stuck by her. The teams before them had smashed out the front and back windows, or maybe they'd been smashed in the slide. The bus was sprawled on its side, its floor facing the road. They reached the front window and Georgie put her hand on the frame preparatory to climbing in.

'No,' Alistair said, and hauled her back. 'Not until I check the cables. The guys said they were OK but I'm not taking anyone's word on it. I want to know this baby's secure.'

'You check the cables and I'll go in,' she screamed into the wind, desperate to find out, even if it meant finding out the worst.

For answer he simply tugged her sideways and took her with him.

The cables were OK. The bus seemed solid, but by the time Alistair finally acquiesced to climbing aboard she was almost ready to scream.

Inside, the bus was appalling. People had bled here. People

had died here. There'd been no thoughts of clearing the mess—the rescue teams had moved as fast as possible to get everyone out and get off the mountain. Therefore the detritus of the rescue effort was still here. Dressing covers. Blood-stained clothing. A damaged saline bag, still half-full. And the rain was blasting in, soaking everything.

It looked like the scene of a massacre. They clambered inside and stood up as best they could and gazed around them.

Nothing.

No Max.

'Do you suppose he's under the bus?' Georgie asked, her voice faltering. Here inside the bus the noise of the wind was almost bearable.

'Harry says not,' Alistair said. There was no need now for him to be holding her hand but he was definitely holding it. It seemed a link that they both valued. 'The driver was caught underneath. They had to do a bit of levering to get him out—they did that last thing. But as they worked the bus moved again. It shifted over a tree stump before settling and they got a clear look underneath. They're almost a hundred per cent certain that it's clear.'

'But they're not absolutely a hundred per cent certain,' she said, swallowing.

'Let's not look for more trouble than we already have,' he said, pulling her with him as he checked every seat in turn. Making absolutely sure a small body wasn't wedged somewhere it could have been missed.

No one. Nothing.

The radio crackled into life in Alistair's backpack. He let go of Georgie's hand to drag his pack off and retrieve it. He watched Georgie all the time, as if concerned she'd bolt. 'Yes?'

'It's Charles.' Charles Wetherby was curt at the best of times and he was brief now. 'You two OK?'

'We're in the bus. There's no one here.'

'We've been thinking. If it's Max, there has to be a reason why he'd run, right?' Charles snapped. 'He's a sensible kid.'

'Yes,' Alistair said cautiously. The radio was powerful—he didn't have to hold it to his ear and they could both listen.

'We've been talking to patients from the bus. Most of them seem to have been asleep when it crashed and there were a few stops along the way, so trying to figure who was on the thing is impossible. And the driver's dead. But there's an old lady who says she was sure there was a boy sitting up the back on his own. And there was another child with one of the women, though she can't remember who. But she said the two kids were playing with a dog. Harry found a dog lead in the pile of belongings. He's checked all the baggage now and he's saying there's a smaller child's clothing. So we treat it as confirmed. We have two kids missing, and it's too late to send in more searchers. But it's the dog I want to talk about. I'm guessing here, but if the bus crashed and the dog took off in fright, maybe the kids went looking for it. It's a long shot but it's all we have. If we'd known this earlier, I would have sent in a team regardless. Two kids in the bush in a cyclone doesn't bear thinking of, but you're on your own.'

'The woman who phoned,' Alistair said, thinking it through. 'She mentioned a dog. It fits.'

'Max doesn't have a dog,' Georgie said.

'We assume he has one now,' Alistair said. 'It's odd to think he'd have run away for any other reason, and the only other option is that somehow he's buried somewhere underneath the bus. We'll go with the dog option. Thanks, Charles.'

'Keep me informed and move fast,' Charles said bluntly. 'They're saying three hours before the worst of this hits, but it may be less, and I want you out well before that. With or without kids. I know it's hard but look after your own skins first. Georgie, I know you can't make that call so, Alistair, I depend on you to make it for her.'

And the radio went dead.

'OK,' Alistair said. 'Where do we start?' But it was a rhetorical question. He was already moving back the way they'd come in—the smashed front window. The normal entrance to the bus was somewhere under their feet. Useless.

'Hurry,' he said, and she didn't need to be told.

Then they were outside the bus. Even in the time they'd been inside the wind had worsened. The cliff was protecting them from the worst of its force but the treetops were being blasted. Within two minutes of emerging, they heard the splintering of branches.

'This is crazy,' Alistair yelled. 'Surely they'd have returned to the bus. They must be lost.'

Georgie was shining her torch around the scene, taking her time now, knowing she had to be careful. It was so dark. To find anything before morning seemed impossible

They had to try. 'If I were a dog...' she muttered, thinking it through.

'What?'

'I was thinking... If they were up the back of the bus, chances are they'd get out through the smashed rear window. So let's check the rear.'

They did. Nothing there. But...

'The land up to the road is really steep here,' Alistair said, shining his torch around. The bush seemed impenetrable. 'If I were a terrified dog, I'd head for the nearest exit.' His torch swung slowly, searching, and Georgie joined hers with his. Then...

'There,' he said.

It looked like a creek bed. Or some sort of basic waterway. There were rocks along its base and there was a trickle of water under the stones. But the stones were big and packed close together, making it almost a track.

'If I wanted to get away in a hurry, that's the way I'd go,' Alistair said, and grabbed her hand and tugged her.

She went willingly.

But not as swiftly. Alistair was surefooted and fast. She'd thought he was a swank city surgeon, with his gorgeous suits and carefully groomed hair. But now…in his borrowed leathers and heavy boots he was as fast and as fit as any of the emergency service personnel Georgie knew in Crocodile Creek. He'd ridden the bike like an expert.

'Where did you learn this?' she demanded as they climbed swiftly from rock to rock. Every few feet Alistair stopped, shone his torch in all directions and yelled. Georgie tried it once but her voice was about a hundred decibels lower than Alistair's roar.

'College choir,' he said, shining his torch into the bush again. 'First baritone.'

'I meant the hiking. And the riding.'

'Abseiling's a hobby,' he told her. 'And there's not a lot of places you can abseil for joy without a bike.'

'Abseil for joy?'

'Abseil where you don't have half the enthusiastic amateurs of the country waiting for you as you haul yourself over the top.'

'You abseil alone?'

'I'm not an idiot. I do it with friends.' Her foot slipped a bit and he caught her before she hit the water. 'Careful.'

She didn't have to be careful when this man was here, she thought. He just took control. He just…

'But you do karate,' Alistair said. He tugged her up and her body met his momentarily as he steadied her. 'We're birds of a feather, Georg.'

'I'm not,' she said instinctively, and she felt rather than saw him grin.

'Deny it all you like,' he said. 'But it's there for all that. Damn.'

He stopped. She was slightly behind him. He still held her hand, and he tugged her absently against him as he shone his torch ahead. 'OK. Path ends here. What now?'

Maybe they ought to go back. The wind was screaming so

hard that if they hadn't been in the comparative shelter of the forest floor they wouldn't have been able to hear themselves speak.

Up until then the creek bed had formed what seemed almost a natural footpath. But now the stones stopped abruptly and the ground rose again. Alistair's torch picked out the flow of water and followed it. There was a natural cleft in the rising ground, and stones and water disappeared, almost buried.

'The water goes underground,' Alistair said, and raised his torch to shine it round. 'They must have left the path here.'

It seemed Alistair wasn't thinking of giving up yet, and neither was she.

'Surely they wouldn't have come this far.'

'If the dog got frightened and they were following it...like us, they'd have thought if they'd come this far they couldn't go back without trying to find him.'

'But where...?' Her torch joined his.

'There,' Alistair said, aiming the torch behind them and up a bit. There was a small break in the timber. 'We go in until it's blocked again and then we stop. Agreed?'

'OK.'

'You're worried about going in?'

'I'm worried about stopping,' she said, and tugged him forward.

Twenty yards. Thirty. The way was possibly the path of animals coming to drink—small animals. The path was clear to almost waist height but no higher. Alistair was using his hands to bush-bash, shoving the undergrowth aside to let her through. Georgie was holding both torches.

There was a crack like a shot from a rifle and a branch broke off above their heads, crashing its way down through the rainforest canopy to land ten feet ahead of them.

A cry.

Not theirs.

Georgie stopped as if struck.

Alistair had heard it, too. They stood frozen, almost afraid to move.

Nothing. Nothing but wind screaming above their heads and the driving rain.

Maybe it was an animal.

'It was a child,' Georgie said. 'I swear.'

'Wait,' Alistair said. He took his torch back from her and gripped her hand.

She waited. She was learning to trust him.

She'd come a long way in two days.

The wind was shrieking, making it impossible for them to hear anything else. Nothing. Nothing. But then came what Alistair had been waiting for. A tiny gap in the wind blasts, as if the wind was catching its breath to blast again.

'Max,' he roared into the night. 'Georgie's here. Yell back.' It was a yell to wake the dead and Georgie jumped almost a foot.

'Sorry,' Alistair said as the wind took up its screaming again. 'I should have warned you.' He gripped her hand again, warning her to stay silent.

She needed no second bidding. They stood hand in hand, waiting for another break in the wind. Alistair's arm came round her waist and he tugged her against him. Holding her steady.

No. Just holding her.

Waiting. Waiting.

The wind caught its breath…

And there it was. A yell, high and shrill, screaming through the bush.

'Georgie, Georgie, Georgie.'

Max. Dear God, it was Max.

The wind took over again but they'd heard enough. Close. To the right and up a bit. Past a break in the path…

Alistair was inching forward and Georgie was pushing him.

'Don't,' he growled, and his body formed a barrier so she couldn't go past him. She couldn't go faster.

And then...

'Hell,' Alistair said, and stopped dead. Then he was on his knees, on his stomach, lying full length on the ground, inching forward.

Astonished, Georgie followed him with her torch. And saw...

It must have been almost invisible. It still was. There was a mass of branches and leaf litter over the path, but there was a slit in the midst of it.

A yawning hole. It would have been disguised by leaf litter until someone had...someone had...

'Hold onto my belt,' Alistair ordered. 'And find yourself some purchase. I need to find the edge.'

She needed no second bidding. She knelt, grabbed the solid trunk of a sapling with one hand, then reached over and grabbed his belt with the other.

He was feeling with one hand, shining his torch with the other.

'There,' he said, tugging away a heap of leaf litter as Georgie helped to pull him back.

He'd exposed the edge.

A mine shaft.

The path they'd followed must indeed have been a path, made maybe fifty years ago when men had mined these mountains.

'Max,' she said, and it was a whisper. And then again but this time it was no whisper. 'Max.'

'Georgie.' It was half cry, half sob, and it came from deep within the mine. And then came the fierce yap of a dog.

Max. And dog.

Another blast of wind, so fierce this time that it rocked them, even in this sheltered place. There was another crack of splintering timber.

'Max, Georgie's here and I'm Georgie's friend. I'm Alistair.' They didn't need to discuss who was going to do the talking— Georgie's voice was way too weak. Pathetic, she told herself. She ought to do voice training.

'Max,' she yelled, doing her best. 'Max, I'm here.'

'Georgie…' It was a sob of terror.

'Who's down there?' Alistair boomed.

'Me and Scruffy and another kid.' Somehow the shaft made Max's voice echo, enabling it to be heard.

'Are you hurt?' Georgie yelled, and Alistair repeated it.

'Scruffy's got a sore leg. He keeps yelping. And it's cold.'

'The other kid? What's his name?'

'I dunno. It's dark.'

'Is he OK?' Alistair yelled. 'Is he talking?'

'He doesn't talk.'

'Is he asleep?' Oh, God, what was he asking? But Georgie knew what Alistair was asking, and she thought she didn't want to hear the answer.

But it seemed she did. 'He's hugging Scruffy,' he called. 'We…we sort of held hands for a bit when I cried. He's OK.'

Georgie saw Alistair's swift intake of breath. *'When I cried…'*

'Did you fall?' she yelled. Dear God…

'Scruffy fell in. The kid fell in after him. I stayed on top for a while and then I got really scared and I got too close and I sort of slid down on top of them. I hurt my knee a bit but it's not bleeding. But we can't climb out.'

Slid. Not fell. Georgie's breath went out in a whoosh. If they'd clear fallen…

'Max, is there another hole near you?' Alistair called into the shaft. 'I know it's dark but can you feel? Could you fall any further?'

'The bottom's made of rock,' Max yelled back. 'It's really hard.'

'Is there any water in there?'

'It's dry.'

She closed her eyes. How lucky had they been? They'd fallen into a shaft that had bottomed on rock and then been dug no further.

But how deep were they? Not so deep that she couldn't hear Max above the wind. Not so deep... Ten, fifteen feet?

'So you're all safe?' Alistair asked.

'We're stuck,' Max said in childish indignation that Alistair wasn't seeing the clear picture. 'And we're hungry. And Scruffy's hurt his leg.'

There was another explosive crack of timber. Too close for comfort.

'I need to get a bit further out so I can look down,' Alistair said. 'Can you hold me?'

'Of course.' She could have held back a ten-ton truck right now if it meant getting Max to safety.

'Let's just check my belt buckle's tight first,' Alistair said, and wriggled back a bit to check. 'This is Harry's gear and Harry's a bit wider than me. I don't fancy plummeting down, leaving you holding onto Harry's leathers.'

He was smiling. In a situation like this...he was smiling?

Maybe he had cause, Georgie thought, letting a little of the tension ooze away. The kids were safe. In this fearful wind the bottom of a mine shaft was probably the safest place for them.

And it seemed Alistair agreed. He wriggled forward while she held on for dear life. He shone the torch down and then he wriggled back again. He'd hauled off his backpack and he reached for hers as well.

'Provisions,' he said.

'Provisions?'

He was hauling out a couple of bottles of drink, high-energy orangeade. A fistful of chocolate bars.

'Jill's done us proud,' he said. He was tugging off his jacket. 'They can both huddle under this.'

She stared at him. 'Don't be stupid. We'll get them out...'

'Not for a while. You want to donate your jacket as well?'

'I... Of course.' She tugged off her jacket. Damn, she only had a skimpy top on underneath. Alistair had a long-sleeved shirt.

Maybe she needed to do a rethink on her clothing.

But Alistair had moved on, shoving the jackets and provisions out to the edge of the shaft. 'Right, Georg, hold me again.'

She did so. He shone his torch down, carefully assessing.

'I can see you guys,' he called. 'Max, hi. Scruffy, hi. And you...' He was obviously talking to the second child. 'What's your name?'

No answer.

'He wasn't talking on the bus either,' Max said. 'I don't think he can.'

'But you're OK?' Alistair asked, and then seemed to relax. 'Max, I want you guys to push yourselves as far as you can away from my torch beam. I'm tossing you a few things to eat and drink, and two jackets to put on.'

'We want to get out,' Max quavered.

'See, the problem is,' Alistair called apologetically, 'that a cyclone's about to hit. A really nasty storm. Any minute, in fact. That's why the bus crashed—the storm before the cyclone washed the edge of the road away. Georgie and I had to come in on bikes, which means we haven't got ropes. We'll have to get some. But you're safe where you are. What Georgie and I will do is leave you this food. We'll go and find somewhere to keep ourselves safe, but as soon as you hear the storm ease we'll be back with rope to get you out. We promise. It'll be a few hours—maybe until daylight—but you have to be brave. There's no choice.'

'Don't go,' Max called, and it was a sob.

Georgie was still gripping Alistair's belt as if her life depended on it, but she was appalled. 'We can't.'

'We don't have any choice,' Alistair called back to Max, ignoring her protest. 'Max, this storm is awful. You and your friend and your dog are in the safest place in the country right now. If we could, we'd join you, but you're pretty squashed as it is, and I'd need rope to lower us down. So we have to leave.'

'Georgie,' Max sobbed.

'I'll go down to them,' Georgie said, but Alistair had pulled back. As Georgie pushed forward, he caught her and held her, as one might hold a child.

'No,' he said. 'You and I are going back to the truck near the road block.'

'The truck? Are you crazy?' She was pulling away from him but he was holding her with ease. 'I'm staying with Max.'

Another branch split above their heads.

'This is bad,' Alistair said. 'And it's going to get worse. It's mostly branches and litter flying now, but if it's a real cyclone it'll be trees.'

'But the boys...'

'Help me now,' he said. He'd moved to the edge of the path, where an ancient log lay rotting. 'We push this across.'

'No.'

'Don't be stupid, Georg,' he said. 'Push.'

She stared at him, blind with fear, but his face was implacable.

'Push,' he ordered.

There was no choice. She pushed. Under their combined weight the log slid sideways. 'There'll be a few leaves and stuff falling down,' Alistair yelled to the boys. 'Stand hard against the side, cover your heads with your hands and push your faces against the sides. Right?'

'R-right.' Max sounded terrified but game.

'One more push,' Alistair said, and the thing was done. The log was right over the shaft, anchored by ten feet of wood at either end. As it shifted, the rotten under-edge crumbled a bit more, making it sit flat on the ground.

'No cyclone's going to shift that baby,' Alistair said in satisfaction. 'And it's still strong enough to deflect anything that falls on it. Right, that's the boys safe.' He grabbed a roll of crêpe bandage from his backpack and attached one end to his torch.

'What are you doing?' she whispered.

'Leaving them some light. It's too scary otherwise.' And his torch was pushed through the crack of shaft entry left at the side of the log, and lowered.

'Got it?' he yelled.

'Got it.' Max's cry was more muffled now that the shaft was covered. 'We like the jackets. But Scruffy's whimpering. I reckon his leg's broken. Now I can see…it's bleeding a bit.'

Alistair was at his backpack again. 'Aspirin,' he said. 'Charles is great. Ask and you shall receive.'

He tossed a small blue packet down the shaft.

'Max, give Scruffy a quarter of one of these,' he yelled. 'Not more. Just a quarter of one and put the rest where he can't get to them. Put it in a chocolate so he'll eat it. Or if he won't, then hold his mouth open, ask your friend to pop it right at the back of his throat and then stroke his throat until he swallows. If his leg keeps bleeding, use the dressing on the torch to bandage his leg. Keep him still and tug the bandage really tight. You can rip the bandage with your teeth if you have to.'

'But you'll be gone.'

'I'm not…' Georgie started, but Alistair caught her to him, held her fast and put a hand over her mouth.

'Yes, we'll be gone, and it might be a few hours before we're back. Max, I have to keep your Georgie safe.'

'I don't want you to go.'

'We don't want to go either,' Alistair called. 'But we need to. You tell each other stories. Eat the chocolate and keep drinking. Make some of the foil round the chocolate into a cup in your hands and give Scruffy a drink. Look after the pup and we'll be back as soon as the storm lessens and it's safe to get you out. OK?'

'Uh, OK.' It wasn't but it had to be.

His face grim, Alistair eased back from the shaft, hauling Georgie with him.

'No,' she sobbed, and he lifted her in his arms and hauled her further back.

'Yes.'

'No!' OK, what he'd said was reasonable but she was beyond reason. Every inch of her being was screaming that to leave Max alone during the storm was crazy. Criminal. Appalling.

The combination of weariness, shock and fear was overwhelming. Crazy or not, she thumped her hands against Alistair and contorted her body, fighting to get away from him.

In answer he simply cradled her tightly against him and started pushing his way back to the creek bed. As if she were a child. A burden of no note.

To fight him was useless. The hysteria of fear finally faded. Alistair didn't speak until she'd stopped fighting him, then he said mildly, 'You're carrying the only torch.' He stumbled a little. 'It'd help if you shone it ahead instead of using it to thump me.'

She was crying, helpless tears of anger and terror. 'Put me down. I'm staying. Please, Alistair, I'm not leaving him. In a cyclone... We don't know how long it'll be. I can't. I can't.'

'I know you can't, which is why I'm carrying you,' he retorted, keeping right on walking. 'Georgie, point the torch.'

'I can't.'

He stumbled. He sighed. He put her down in front of him and held her by the shoulders.

They were far enough from the shaft now for the boys not to hear. He could say what he needed to say.

'Georg, if I thought you'd fit, I would have let you slide down with them,' he said grimly. 'God knows, it looks the safest place anyone can be right now, and the shaft's not horizontal—it's mostly a steep slide rather than a fall. But there really is no room, and I'm not letting you stay up top. What use are you to Max if you're dead?'

'He'll be terrified. I'll just stay. I wouldn't be dead.'

For answer another limb cracked off a tree above their heads.

'You want to bet on it? We go back to the car. It's right next to a fallen tree, the tree's vast and it's protecting the car from the worst of the wind.'

'But if we can't come back… And if the storm's hours…'

'We're much more likely to be alive to come back if we get to safety now.' He'd caught her hand and was tugging her after him. 'If we stay here we'll be dead, and what use is that?'

'Oh, God…'

'I know,' he said more gently. 'You love him. But love has to make hard choices, Georg, and this is one of them.'

'Love? What do you know about love?'

'I'm just starting to find out,' he said grimly, and kept right on tugging.

CHAPTER EIGHT

BY THE TIME they got back to the crashed bus the wind had reached the point where speech was almost impossible.

Georgie had ceased to fight. OK, he was right. She knew he was right, but it made it no easier.

At the bus she paused but Alistair shook his head.

'I don't trust those cables,' he said briefly. 'And I'm damned if I want to be in that thing if it hurtles right down to the valley floor.'

Fair enough. He tugged her on, but she was moving with him now, accepting she had no choice. They reached the bikes and used them to get back to the car. That was a hair-raising ride, where they hugged the cliff side of the road to get what shelter they could from the windbreak it formed, avoiding as much as they could of the mountain of debris starting to form on the far side of the road.

Georgie had cause to be thankful they were both wearing full-face helmets. The rain made her almost blind. She needed windscreen wipers, but even if she'd had them, they'd have been useless. They needed their jackets. They were being whipped by debris every inch of the way and her arms were a mass of scratches.

But giving the boys the jackets had been a master stroke of

Alistair's, she conceded. It was a comfort to think the little boys were as protected as they could make them.

But finally they reached the truck. Here in the lee made by the combination of the cliff and the massive fallen log, the wind was almost manageable. They wedged their bikes in behind the log, then fought their way against the wind to the back of the truck.

This was a work vehicle. A big four-wheel-drive, with the whole back clear for cargo. There was a blanket tossed into a corner and a crate containing some sort of work gear. Alistair shoved the crate aside and spread the blanket over the bare metal floor.

'Welcome to safety.'

She hadn't realised the full strength of the wind's force—how hard she'd been leaning into the wind. As Alistair tugged her inside she almost fell.

He caught her, steadied her, set her on her knees beside him.

It was too small, she thought, winded, exhausted, shocked. Much too small.

And how long did a cyclone last? They'd radio to find out but, no matter how long it would be, it'd be much too long when Max was stuck out there in the wilderness.

And it'd be too long when she was stuck in the back of a truck with Alistair. He made her feel… He made her feel…

Just cut it out, she told herself breathlessly. She was feeling dizzy and more than a little sick. To find Max and then to be forced to leave him had almost torn her apart.

'I'm running the truck hard against the cliff,' Alistair said. 'That way if it's blasted it can't topple.'

'Can a cyclone really push a truck over?'

'I have no idea but I'm not willing to find out. I want it wedged securely.'

He moved it, blessing Harry for having the forethought to leave the keys in the ignition. Within two minutes he'd backed the truck further toward the cliff so it was edged in a V, with cliff on one side and the fallen tree on the other. Only the front windscreen of the truck was exposed.

There was a cargo screen between the front windscreen and the rear. They should now be safe, even if anything blasted through the windscreen.

How long till the cyclone hit in its full force? Who knew? She surely didn't.

Max.

Oh, God, she'd go mad.

'Drink,' Alistair said, and handed her a bottle. 'Damn, what we really need is a decent whisky. Or any whisky. What the hell is this?'

'Glucose-enriched sports drink,' she said. 'To give us energy. I thought you gave it to the boys.'

'Jill sent us with four bottles. I'm sharing. Handing over all drinks when we might be stuck here for twenty-four hours would have been dumb. And I may be heroic enough to hand over my jacket and enough chocolate to keep the boys happy, but all the chocolate would be ludicrous. So eat some chocolate.' And then as she looked at the bar with distaste, he unwrapped it and handed it to her again. 'Eat,' he said, softly but forcibly. 'Last time you ate was at the wedding and you've been working all night. Eat and then sleep.'

'How can I—?'

'Just do what comes next,' he told her. 'Max won't thank you for collapsing before we can get him out. Hell.'

A particularly violent gust was shaking the truck. Georgie shivered and Alistair tugged her close.

'Drink your drink and eat your chocolate and don't worry about it,' he said.

'Don't patronise me.'

'I would never do that.'

'You just did.'

'By telling you not to worry?'

'As if I could.'

'I know it's impossible,' he said, his voice softening. 'But they're as safe as we can make them. So we just focus on getting through this next few hours.'

'We shouldn't be here.'

'No,' he said equitably. 'We should be safe back at Croc Creek. But our best chance of retrieving the boys as soon as possible is to stay right here.' He was opening his backpack again, hauling out the radio.

'We should have left the radio with Max,' she said fretfully.

'And if he hadn't been able to use it? We'd have half Croc Creek thinking we were dead. Use your brains, Georg. Let's tell them we're safe.'

'We're not safe.'

'We're as safe as anyone within two hundred miles is right now. Charles?'

Another gust rocked their safe haven. The radio crackled into life. 'Carmichael. Where the hell are you? Carmichael.'

By mutual consent they'd turned off their remaining torch. The batteries should last the night but they had no need of them so why push their luck? If this storm was so bad that they were trapped for longer...

Don't go there.

'We're OK,' Alistair said into the radio transmitter and Charles's sigh of relief was loud enough to be heard over the wind.

'Where the hell have you been?'

'Finding the kids,' Alistair said.

'You've found them?'

'We have. Three of them. There's Max, a dog called Scruffy and another child, a boy of about five.'

'Do we know who he is?'

'We don't know,' Alistair said patiently. 'He doesn't talk.'

'He's hurt?'

'He doesn't seem to be. He's just silent. They both seem OK.'

'So you're on your way in now? How—?'

'We're staying put.' Briefly Alistair outlined the situation. When he finished there was a moment's pause before Charles spoke again.

'You're sure they're safe?' he said at last.

'As safe as we can make them.'

'They'll be terrified.' He paused. 'Well, we can't help that. We're all terrified. In some situations it makes sense to be scared. The full force is coming in now. I was contacting you to say get off the road fast. But you're protected where you are?'

'As protected as we can be.'

'And Georgie's being sensible?'

'Of course.'

'No, of course about it. This is Georgie.'

'I'm being sensible,' Georgie yelled, frustrated and incensed, and Charles's chuckle sounded through the static.

But then the chuckle faded. 'We're in for it,' he said, and his voice was now grim. 'Starting now. You guys stay safe. We can't get to you to help. As of ten minutes ago I ordered everyone inside and no one's moving. I just hope to hell...' He paused. 'OK. Enough. God be with you.'

And the line went dead.

'Um...' Georgie whispered.

'Um?'

'Did Charles just say, "God be with you"?'

'He did.'

'He's never said anything so...personal in his life. I didn't think he knew how.'

'Desperate times call for desperate measures,' Alistair said, and tugged her against him again. 'OK. The way I see it is the worst that can happen to us is the truck goes over. But we're protected—the downed tree will deflect anything else that falls. So we sit and wait it out.'

'I need to go to the bathroom,' she said, and he stilled.

'You don't.'

'I'm a girl. Girls don't have bladders like boys.'

He sighed. 'There's no argument about that one. You want the torch?'

'I'm not going more than four feet from the truck.'

'Very wise.'

'So, yes, I want the torch and I want you to turn your back and close your eyes.'

'Yes, ma'am.'

'Then I'll do the same for you.'

'You're sounding bossy again,' he said, and she switched on the torch in time to see his grin. 'Go ahead. My eyes are closed tight.'

That was the end of laughter. Fifteen minutes later the full force of the cyclone hit. Georgie had been lying in the dark, listening to the wind, thinking of Max, growing more and more fearful.

She was desperately tired but she couldn't sleep. No way. The wind sounded terrifying.

And out there was Max.

She lay rigidly in the dark, willing him to be safe, willing the storm to be not as bad as they feared, willing everything to be OK.

Alistair was right beside her. She was acutely aware of him—too aware of him—and it made things worse. She, who had spent her life fighting to have things under control, was suddenly so far out of her comfort zone that she felt like her world was tilting.

Alistair let her be, seeming to sense she couldn't talk. That she needed to be as far away from him as she could get.

And then she didn't have room to think anything.

She'd thought the wind had been terrifying. With the first blast of the full cyclonic force she was on the other side of the truck and in Alistair's arms and every single scruple was blasted right out of her mind.

She didn't speak. There was no point in speaking. She simply held on for dear life while the wind screamed like the hounds from hell, and the truck rocked back and forth on its axle as if it could take off any minute into the storm.

But it didn't take off. The wind was catching the nose of the truck and shoving it backward, pushing it further into its tight V. Alistair's reasoning had worked. But, still, the force of its rocking was appalling enough. To hell with being alone. To hell with staying in isolation. She buried her face in Alistair's chest and clutched him close.

But who was giving comfort to who? He was holding her as tightly as she held him. There was no choice. In the face of this shared threat there was nothing to do but hold each other, hold and hold...

How long she stayed rigidly fearful, locked against him, she didn't know. The wind didn't lessen and neither did the rocking, but the human body could survive on adrenalin for only so long. The terror that the world would end was fading. But still she stayed where she was. She lay holding tight to Alistair, letting his arms hold her, feeling the beating of his heart against her face. Letting her world settle on a new kind of axis.

Where terrifying was normal.

Where being held by Alistair was normal. Safe.

And something more.

He kissed her hair.

At first she thought she'd imagined it. But, no, she pulled back a little and saw that he was indeed kissing her.

She could see now. There had been no glorious sunrise—the deep black stormclouds made it still almost as dark as night—but not quite. There was sun somewhere behind these stormclouds and there was enough light now to see. It was morning?

And Alistair was smiling. Unbelievably, Alistair was smiling.

'If you've known how long I've wanted to do this,' he murmured against her ear. 'Six months, to be precise. Six long months.'

'You didn't...'

'Georgie, I fell in love with you the moment I saw you.'

'No.'

'No. It's not a good time now to say it,' he agreed, his smile giving way to gravity. 'It's a crazy, dumb time to say it. But I've been lying here feeling like I've never been so afraid in my life, and suddenly I thought that if the wind finally does manage to pick this truck up and transport us to Kansas, I'd never told you. And I've been thinking and thinking, in between worrying about saving our skins, you understand, that I really ought to tell you that I've fallen in love with you.'

She was having trouble breathing, much less speaking. 'You haven't,' she whispered finally, and she wasn't quite sure that she made a sound at all.

'It's too late to say that now,' he said apologetically. 'I'm thinking that I must have fallen in love six months ago. I just never knew I had. I knew you'd attracted me as no other woman had, but I thought it was crazy—that it was just some sexual need.'

'Gee, thanks.'

'See, here's the thing,' he said. 'What I felt then was so strong that when Gina interrupted us that night I could have wept. Afterwards I called myself all sorts of names, but I couldn't figure out how to get rid of how I was feeling.' He was whispering right into her ear. Any further away and she wouldn't be able to hear him. It was the most intimate sort of speech. She should pull away, she thought, but she couldn't. She couldn't.

'And then I walked off the plane two days ago and there you were,' he said. 'Just as I remembered you. And when I carried you away from Max, I felt sick. Because I knew you were torn apart and there wasn't a goddam thing I could do about it, but I would have torn my own heart out to spare you pain. Anyway...' He shifted slightly so he could kiss her, a feather kiss on the tip of her nose—no more—and then moved back so his lips were against her ear again. 'I lay in the dark and it hit me like...well, with the force of a cyclone, that what I'm feeling is this love thing that the world raves about and I've never even believed in. Until now.'

Her heart twisted.

It had been wrenched every which way in the last few hours, she thought, suddenly angry. Love. Terror. Hope.

Love. She loved Max. Her one true thing. They said love could extend to fit all comers. It surely felt like that. The way she felt about this man holding her close was surely something like that. This man she'd thought a manicured wimp in a classy suit, who was suddenly a biker and an abseiler and who'd lifted her as if she weighed nothing.

'Alistair, I always change my mind.' She had to be honest here. He deserved that at least. 'Please, don't fall for me. I'm not... I don't even trust myself.'

'Why not?' Maybe they were getting accustomed to the wind. Or maybe it was that they were so close to each other. They'd relaxed a little now, lying face to face, their mouths barely inches apart. Their noses were practically touching. The most intimate of settings...

'I fall for the violent ones,' she whispered. 'Like my dad. Like Ron. And I can't...do anything about it.'

'So you're saying you can't fall for me.'

'Yes, but that's just the problem.' She barely understood this herself—how to explain it to him? 'I have fallen for you. You said you felt this...thing. Well, I do, too, but I don't trust myself. How can I trust you?'

'How can you not?'

'See, if I fall for you, I don't know how you'll be,' she said, and she knew she was sounding pathetic but she didn't have a choice. 'And if you ever hit Max...'

'I would never hit Max,' he said, astounded. 'And what about if I ever hit you? Georgie, do you think I could do that?'

'No.' But she bit her lip and shook her head. 'Yes. I don't know. You see, all my values—they're all over the place. I can't figure out how to trust anyone because whenever I do it's all wrong. I came to Crocodile Creek to get away from stuff...'

'To get away from someone?'

'From a whole string of someones,' she said desperately. 'Guys I thought might be the one, only every time I did they just...they just...'

'Hit you?'

'I'd never let them,' she said with an attempt at dignity. What was it about this place, this situation, that was letting her expose herself so completely? 'Do you really think I'd let anyone hit me?'

'Only Smiley,' he said, smiling softly into her eyes. 'Only if it was absolutely necessary to put someone in jail.'

'I'm good at defending myself,' she said. 'I've had to be. But if you were great to me...'

'You'd think I was soft?' He was trying desperately to understand, she thought, and it made it worse.

'I can't figure it out myself.'

'You don't think you could give it a chance? Let me into your life a little and take it a step at a time?'

'You're leaving straight after Cal and Gina's wedding.'

'See, here's the thing,' he said, almost apologetically. 'Charles has offered me a job.'

She felt like her breath had been punched out of her. A particularly violent blast rocked the truck, but she was getting more fearful of what was happening right in here.

'You'll never do it.'

'Would you hate it?'

'I... It's nothing to do with me.'

'If I stayed, would you run again?'

'I can't,' she said, and her voice was a wail. 'I have Max. Max has all these friends. Gina's little boy, CJ. Charles's adopted daughter, Lily. Mrs Grubb. They all love Max to bits and he loves them. How could I walk away?'

'But you're so fearful of me that you might?'

'I don't know,' she whispered.

Another crash. Something hard and solid crashed down on the top of the truck. She shivered and Alistair was holding her tight again.

She should fight him. She should...

She couldn't.

'One day at a time,' he said, whispering against her ear. 'Let's just do it like that. I know I've added to the pressure—I shouldn't have told you but, you know, I thought maybe this might be the only chance I ever have to say it so, damn, I'm going to say it. Georgie, like it or not, take it or leave it, I've suddenly figured it out. I love you. And unless you object very, very loudly, so loudly that I can hear you above this damned cyclone, I intend to kiss you into the middle of next week. Right here. Right now. Any objections?'

Any objections?

Of course she had objections. She had a thousand objections. She just couldn't quite manage to voice them. She just couldn't quite manage...

He kissed her.

CHAPTER NINE

THE EYE OF THE STORM, when it came, came so swiftly that for a moment Georgie thought she was dreaming.

She'd been fast asleep. Wise or not, dopy or not, she'd been sleeping in Alistair's arms. The blast of the wind had been dulled by the beat of his heart. His declaration had been crazy. It had frightened her. But she'd been honest, she told herself. He knew where he stood.

So when he'd kissed her, what was a girl to do but respond? What was a girl to do but take comfort where comfort was offered?

What was a girl to do but to savour every single moment of his kisses? Of this time she'd held him tightly. Before the world had blasted its dreadful reality back against her.

So she'd gone to sleep, and maybe he had, too. She woke up feeling warm and safe and cherished. And the wind had stopped.

She opened one eye and then the other.

'Alistair.'

'I'm hearing it,' he said, and she could feel the rumble of his voice as well as hear it. Nice.

Very nice.

'The eye of the cyclone,' he said.

'You mean it'll come back.'

'Yeah, but we may have time.' He set her away from him, but then he smiled, tugged her back and kissed her, briefly but hard on the lips. A man claiming his own.

'Let's see,' he said, and reached for the radio.

Charles answered in seconds.

'You guys are safe?'

'We're safe,' Alistair snapped. He was hauling the box of gear forward to inspect its contents. Georgie moved to help him. He talked into the radio while she tugged open the lid.

'It's hell here,' Charles said, 'but the hospital's still standing.'

'As bad as that?'

'Maybe worse,' Charles said grimly. 'I can't spare anyone to help you.'

'You don't need to.' Alistair had discovered a coil of rope. He ran his hand along its length. Twenty feet? Maybe a little more. 'We have everything we need.'

'But the kids...'

'We'll get them out now.'

'You have maybe an hour, tops,' Charles snapped. 'Don't take any risks.'

'We won't take any more risks than we need to,' Alistair said gently. 'But even by being in the hospital back at Crocodile Creek we'd be taking risks. The guys are saying the eye might give us an hour's break?'

'That's the outer estimate.'

'Then we need to move,' Alistair said, and he replaced the radio in the backpack and hauled open the truck doors. To chaos.

The rainforest was a tangle of smashed timber, debris flung everywhere, the remains of trees mixed with the broken shards of others. It was like a huge crazy game of pick-up sticks.

The silence was eerie.

They hardly talked as they hauled the bikes out from their cover. They'd pushed them almost completely under the fallen tree, and the wind had pushed them further. But they were essentially undamaged.

Could they ride them? Maybe, in the lee of the cliff.

'We'll try,' Alistair said. They'd never get back to the mine shaft without them. Not in time.

And somehow they did. It was a feat of pure riding skill, Georgie thought, but it wasn't her skill. Alistair rode first, and she merely placed her bike's wheels in the tracks made by his.

Even so, it was a ghastly ride, with them half pushing, half riding through a mass of tangled undergrowth, a crazy jumble of smashed forest. The lee of the cliff had deflected some of the mess but not all, and it hadn't deflected water. Their wheels were sliding in pure slush. How much rain had there been? A flood? At times the road was more like a river, and there was nothing for it but to get off and push through.

But somehow they did, with Alistair's fierce determination to push through more than matching her own. As they reached the crash site and came to a halt, she felt like her insides had been put in a mouli mix.

There was still no wind. Not a breath, and it was still almost dark.

Ominous was too good a word for the sensation she was feeling, and she'd gone past terror. But fear had to be put aside. What they were attempting might seem crazy, but the alternative was to leave the kids in the shaft longer. And the land was now waterlogged. If there was another slip...

Don't think about it. Just think about putting the next step in front of the last. Alistair was off his bike, fighting his way through broken branches to the edge of the road. She fought her way through to join him and stared down.

The bus was no longer there.

For a moment she thought she was dreaming. The cables holding the trees hadn't snapped, but the trees to which they'd been attached were no longer there either.

The bus had presented a vast mass of metal, its broken windows opening it to the elements. The result must have been inevitable.

And she'd wanted to shelter in it?

'Oh, God,' she whispered, and Alistair's hand caught hers. He gripped, hard.

'Come on. We have work to do.'

Max. Please, God, Max.

It was lucky they had the old creek bed to follow, otherwise they'd never have found them. This was no simple walk, as it had been only hours ago. It was a mass of tangled timber they had to climb through, clamber over, creep under. And the creek bed was now just that—a torrent of tumbling water.

'The time,' Alistair murmured, and she glanced at her watch. Twenty-five minutes since the silence had started. They had an hour at most before the force started again. Oh, God.

She stumbled and Alistair caught her and steadied her yet again.

'We can't go any faster than we're going,' he said. 'Come on.'

At least he wasn't suggesting they go back. And, Georgie thought, that's huge. This wasn't Alistair's little brother stuck in the shaft. Alistair had had every right to stay back in Crocodile Creek. Right now, the sensible thing to do to protect himself was to stay in the truck and wait for the second blast to finish.

But that might be another half a day and he'd know—he'd know!—that she couldn't bear it. That running for safety even for those first hours had almost killed her.

He was doing this for her and she felt sick.

'I had no right,' she said, and he glanced across at her in concern. He'd managed to get over a half-rotten tree trunk, and he was helping her over.

'Sorry?'

'I had no right to drag you into this,' she said, louder this time and more strongly.

And, unexpectedly, astonishingly he chuckled.

'See, that's just it,' he said. 'What we were talking about. This love thing. You'd better get used to it. I love you, Georgie

Turner, and from now on you don't drag me anywhere. From now on, you'll just look behind and I'll be following.'

It was such a huge statement it took her breath away. She didn't... She couldn't...

'Don't get your knickers in a twist,' he said, and he grinned still more. 'We go down together, Georgie, or we don't go down at all. How romantic's that? But if you don't mind, I prefer the latter option so we need to move ourselves quite sharply.'

She gulped. She swallowed. He grabbed her hand still more tightly and led her forward.

Once again, if they hadn't known exactly where to go, they'd have been lost. The landscape was so different it was weird. The rainforest canopy had been swept to the forest floor. There were mountains of litter. Mountains.

But somehow they kept to the track. Somehow. And then...

'Here,' Alistair said. 'This log.' And then he raised his voice. 'Max.'

There was a moment's deathly silence when Georgie's heart forgot to beat. Then, magically, wondrously from below them...

'Georgie?' The yell broke in the middle into a sob, and Georgie thought her own heart would break. But this was no time for emotion.

'I'm here,' she yelled back. 'We promised we'd come. Max, are you OK?'

'J-just scared. It was so noisy. We weren't game to use our torch much in case it conked out. And there's water in here now, right up to our knees. Can you get us out now?'

Water. Oh, God.

'Sure.' Or she thought they could. She hoped they could. Alistair seemed to know what he was doing. He was looping the rope he'd brought around a vast tree trunk that had crashed right by the shaft.

Rising water.

It didn't bear thinking of.

'How's the other little boy?' she asked.

'He still won't talk. He's cuddling Scruffy.'

'Is Scruffy his dog?'

'Scruffy's my dog.'

'Why aren't you cuddling him?' she asked, trying to figure things out.

'My arm's sore.'

Her heart stilled all over again. 'Has it been bleeding?'

'A bit of stuff came down just after you left,' he said. 'It hit me. But the kid bandaged me up with some of the bandage you tied on the torch.'

'So he bandaged you with the same bandage you used on Scruffy's leg?' Alistair was knotting his rope, forming a loop in the end.

'The kid tore it with his teeth,' Max said. 'I was… I was crying.'

'Oh, Max…' And who was this strange kid? She wanted to hug him.

Why was she up here?

'Are you coming down now?' Max obviously felt the same way she did.

'Alistair is,' she said, as Alistair slid the looped end of the rope into the shaft.

'No,' Alistair said. 'You are.'

'Me.'

'You can't pull me out but I can pull you out,' he said. 'It makes sense. And if I go down and get stuck, I can't see you sensibly going back to the truck and waiting again.'

'I… I would.' Maybe.

'I'm not risking it,' he said. 'Put your foot in the loop. See the knots? They're to hang onto—they'll give you a better grip as I lower you. You go down and we'll figure out who comes up first when you're down there. Just hang onto it, relax and I'll pull.'

'You can't.'

'Watch me.'

* * *

She trusted him. There was nothing else to do. She put her foot into the loop and slid over the side.

The kids at the base were shining their torch up.

'Lean against the far side of the shaft and put your faces against the wall again,' Alistair warned them. 'There'll be rubble falling.'

She was on her way down. He was lowering her with the ease of a mechanical lift, as if such a weight was no problem at all.

But then she forgot about Alistair as she reached the base and Max was in her arms. He was wet and cold and shivery and he clung to her fiercely. Her Max.

It was such a tight fit. There was no room for them all, but Max was huddled into her, sobbing, and her arms enveloped him and then because there was no room and there was a need here as well, she was enveloping the other kid as well, and the dog...

The dog was licking her face.

'Move,' Alistair said above them. He was shining his torch down and his voice sounded a bit wobbly. 'Come on, Georg. I know this is a reunion but every second counts. Hugs are for when we're safe.'

Right. She gulped and pulled away a little.

'Littlest first,' she said. 'Can you hold onto the rope?' she asked the small boy.

He nodded.

'Will you tell me your name?'

Silence.

'He could hold Scruffy 'cos he's the lightest,' Max volunteered, and they all looked at Scruffy and then the silent child reached out and took him and held him. Tight.

It was a big ask for a little boy to put his foot in the loop, to hold Scruffy in one arm and the rope in the other, but there was that silent look of determination about him that told Georgie he could do it.

She smiled at him, gave him another swift hug for good measure and sent him on his way.

One boy and one dog rose smoothly to the surface.

The rope came down again. 'Max's turn,' Alistair said from above them.

'Georgie,' Max said, and gulped back a sob. But there was no time for hesitation.

'Go,' she said, and pushed him upward, then waited in the dark shaft for the rope to return. She was standing calf-deep in water, but at least her leathers and biker boots were keeping her dry.

The boys had been soaked. To have been stuck down there for hours... It didn't bear thinking of.

But there was no time to think. A moment later the rope was lowered again. Alistair tugged her up as if she weighed nothing. She rose smoothly into daylight, and Max and the kid and the dog and Alistair were all waiting for her. They grasped her under the arms as she came over the side and she wasn't sure who was doing the pulling.

But she was safe and here it came. The hug. Ten seconds of pure group hug—the whole lot of them. She felt so overwhelmed she couldn't do anything but hold and hold and hold.

'Right,' Alistair said, in a voice thick with an emotion he couldn't conceal. 'Enough emotion. We have a cyclone to outrun.' He turned the little boy to face him—their nameless child. 'You'll come with us?'

The little boy nodded, but Georgie thought it was great that Alistair had asked.

'What's your name?' she asked him again. He looked like a little owl, freckly and wiry and filthy, and, oh, so serious. 'You've been so brave. Can you tell us who you are?'

Nothing.

'Well, let's call you Rowdy,' Alistair said, and gave the kid another swift hug. Man to man. 'It's a man's name because you've just been as brave as a man.'

'Why did you choose Rowdy?' Max asked.

''Cos he's the rowdiest man I know,' Alistair said. 'Rowdy means really, really noisy. All this noise… I don't know how we stand it.' He chuckled and suddenly they were all smiling. 'So, Rowdy, will you come with us?'

Another nod. And another small smile.

'Great,' Alistair said. 'But you're taking a ride. On my back, Rowdy, mate.' He tugged his backpack around to his front and swung the little boy onto his back. The child was wearing only one shoe, and under the grime of a filthy, wet sock they could see a smudge of bloodstain. 'Georg, can you carry Scruffy?'

'Of course I can,' she said. She picked up the little dog, she grabbed Max's hand—and they ran.

Or they clambered. They moved as fast as they could over the rough terrain.

By the time they reached the road the wind was building up again. It was whistling eerily through the trees. The trees were starting to moan.

Please, please, please, Georgie thought. They had to get back to the truck. They must. She knew what the force was like now and she knew that Alistair was right. To be out here with no protection meant death.

They'd reached the bikes. Alistair didn't hesitate. By the time Georgie had pulled her bike to point back towards the truck he was on his bike, Rowdy was in front of him and he was holding his hands out for the dog.

'You can't,' she said, and he grimaced and motioned to his backpack.

'I took everything out. The dog goes in.'

'He won't,' Georgie breathed.

'He does or he'll stay here,' he said grimly, and before she could protest again he'd slipped the little dog inside. As if he knew exactly what was expected, the dog hunkered down so only his nose was sticking out. Alistair grinned and slung the pack carefully over his shoulders.

'We're all being sensible here,' he told Georgie. 'Max goes behind you. Go.'

How they made it she'd never know. It was hard enough for her to have Max behind her. Dirt bikes weren't meant for passengers. But Alistair hadn't been able to put Rowdy behind him because of Scruffy in the backpack. So Rowdy was huddled against his chest.

The set-up on his bike looked somehow...heart-wrenching? The wind was really rising now and Georgie had to concentrate fiercely as they pushed on, but there was still a part of her that was far too aware of Alistair Carmichael.

This man was about as different as it was possible to be from the slick, professional doctor she'd met from the plane two days ago.

He hadn't shaved for at least twenty-four hours. He was wearing borrowed leather pants, a ripped shirt and an ancient helmet, battered and filthy. *He* was battered and filthy.

He had a kid cradled against his breast and a dog in a backpack. He'd won Rowdy's trust with instinctive ease. He was riding a mud-splattered dirt bike with skill and precision.

He was heart-meltingly, life-changingly gorgeous.

He'd been offered a job in Croc Creek.

Life-changing? Could she change her life for him?

Now was no time for decisions. She slowed as he did, ducking and weaving around timber felled by the storm. Max was holding on for dear life behind her. She was aware that he was holding her tighter with the right arm than the left. What was the damage?

She should stop and look, only the blasts of wind were terrifying on their own now. To stop except for the times when she had to get off and shove her bike through water or around some obstacle was suicide. She'd fallen twenty feet behind Alistair's bike as it was.

There was a massive crack of splintering timber from above her head. She slammed her brakes and stopped inches from the trunk of a falling forest giant. For one heart-stopping moment she thought Alistair and his precious cargo were underneath. Oh, God... But then, almost before the last of the branches had sighed and settled, there was a hoarse shout, so loud it could be heard above the wind.

'Georg...'

There was such fear there that she caught her breath. Alistair was afraid. For her?

And she'd felt the same, she thought, dumping her bike and gathering Max tight against her. The little boy had come to the end of his resources. He was a mass of trembling fear, sobbing against her, hugging her close.

She gathered him tightly against her and hugged, but she had to yell back.

'Alistair.'

'Georg.' It was a shout of near relief—almost relief but still there was fear.

'It missed us,' she yelled. She'd been daydreaming, she thought. As fearful as this situation was, she'd allowed her attention to stray a little. She'd fallen back a little behind Alistair.

That moment's inattention had saved her life.

The mound of fallen timber in front of her was massive, but the wind was already shifting it again. She had to get over...

Max was going nowhere. His feet had gone from under him. 'We have to go beneath and around,' she told him, but he was incapable of moving.

'Max...'

She couldn't carry him. She couldn't...

'Georg...' How he'd got there so fast she didn't know, but Alistair was there. He'd gone down the hill from the road and clambered around, underneath the roots of the fallen tree. There was a trickle of blood slipping down his cheek. His face was white and shocked. He reached them and gathered them hard against him, and swore. And swore and swore.

'Max can't walk,' she told him, taking strength from the sheer bulk of him.

'Of course not.' He swung Max into his arms. 'Max, you're a hero,' he told the little boy. 'But you've done enough. The rest is up to me.'

As it was. Max may have run out of resources but Georgie was a close second. She followed numbly as Alistair retraced his steps but she was aware that he had to slow his steps not to draw ahead. It took them three times as long as he'd taken to get around the uprooted stump.

But finally they made it. Rowdy and Scruffy were huddled where they'd been put—right underneath the mound of fallen branches, with the bike shoved in after them to protect them from the worst of the blast.

The wind was so fierce now that it was an effort to move at all. Left to her own resources, Georgie might have stayed where she was. She'd have had to—there was no way Max was moving.

But Alistair was made of sterner stuff.

'Move,' he said. 'We ditch the bikes here but I'm thinking we're only minutes from the truck. Georgie, can you carry Rowdy?'

She took a deep breath. 'Of course I can.'

'Of course you can,' he said, and he smiled. 'My Georgie.'

And they did. Ten minutes later, battered beyond belief but essentially still in one piece, they reached the truck.

It was still as they'd left it, wedged firmly between cliff and tree.

It was all Georgie could do not to kiss it.

The windscreen was smashed. A branch had hit it, piercing it, but, instead of leaving it open to the elements, more foliage had been blasted against the front, making it a rigid shelter that nothing could now reach.

Including them. It took Alistair five minutes to pull enough of the rubbish away for them to enter. Georgie couldn't help—she sat and cradled two terrified children to her until he'd cleared the path in. He hoisted his backpack in first—with dog—and then motioned for them to precede him.

They were home.

She climbed in, tugging the kids in after her.

Alistair climbed in and pulled the doors behind him.

Safe.

The word was so overwhelming it was all she could do not to sob. But Max was already sobbing and Rowdy was so white she thought he might pass out. And the dog had crawled out of its backpack and was cringing, its belly flat on the floor, its eyes huge, its tail flattened. Georgie couldn't bear it. She lifted the pup into her arms first and then tugged Max against her, and then Rowdy looked so terrified as well that she tried to fit him against her as well, but it didn't work.

Or it did work.

Because Alistair had gathered the child against him and he was holding Scruffy and Max as well, and maybe a bit of her, too.

A sandwich squeeze. Five of them taking comfort, giving comfort, not able to speak for the moment—not a able to do anything except hug and realise that they were alive and that there just might be an afterwards.

The second blast of the cyclone was worse than the first but it couldn't reach them.

For the first hour they hardly moved. This was no time for assessment. It was simply time for reassurance and comfort and holding.

But then, as the little boys grew used to the rocking of the van, as they accustomed themselves to the screech of wind against the metal, they ate a few more of the chocolate bars that were still miraculously in Georgie's pack and the children drifted toward sleep.

They couldn't have slept at all in the long hours down the shaft, Georgie thought. It must have been a special kind of hell.

The boys needed to be examined, but for now comfort was of paramount importance, even for the little dog. He'd included himself in their sandwich squeeze and they were pleased to have him. Georgie and Alistair lay on either side of the kids and the dog, but they weren't rigidly side by side. The kids were sprawled over them like a litter of puppies, and so was Scruffy.

'Yeah, I love you, too,' Alistair told him as the little dog gave him a slurpy kiss and Max even gave a sleepy giggle.

Even Rowdy smiled a little.

What was it with the child?

'There doesn't seem to be a physical reason why he's not talking,' Alistair murmured as both children relaxed even further into heavy sleep. 'I thought at first he must be deaf, but he was responding to my directions on the bike.'

'Max says he hasn't said a word.'

'I did a fast check of his mouth as he came out of the shaft,' Alistair said. 'No damage.' He stirred, seemingly reluctant to break their hold. 'We need to check them completely.'

Which they did—sort of, though not so comprehensively that they'd wake them. Max had a long, ugly scratch on his arm. It had bled through the dressings Rowdy had put on, but when Georgie carefully unwrapped it she thought it didn't need stitches.

'And cleaning can wait until we're out of here,' Alistair said. 'We'll give him a dose of antibiotic but I'm not waking him for germs.'

Rowdy had got off even more lightly. A few scratches and bruises, with a couple of deeper scratches on his foot. He'd been wearing only one shoe. They tugged both the kids' shoes and socks off, getting rid of water that might well be contaminated. Weren't gold mines full of stuff you didn't want to think about?

They couldn't worry about that now. Rowdy seemed fine. He was huddled against Max, supremely trusting. The little boy's pockets were still stuffed with the chocolate bars they'd tossed into the shaft, and as she tried to remove them he whimpered and clutched at them as if they were important. But he wasn't still hungry. What was his story?

Georgie thought back to the bus passengers she'd seen. Who had been with this kid? No one who'd been capable of missing him, obviously.

One of the DOAs?

'Don't think about it,' Alistair growled, and she looked across at him and grimaced. This man could read her thoughts. It was a really scary ability.

'We need to make a splint.' He'd unwrapped Scruffy's back leg. This was a wound that needed proper medical attention. 'How's your animal husbandry?'

'Lousy,' she said.

'Mine, too. But this leg's fractured. Hell, he must have dragged himself over those stones, running away. Poor little rat.'

'Yes.'

'Will you let Max keep him?'

'Of course I will.' Some things were no-brainers.

He grinned. 'There you go. Georgie of the huge heart, expanding to fit all comers. Bear me in mind when you're working out how far you have to stretch.'

'Alistair...'

'I know,' he said, and he smiled at her with a look of such tenderness that she almost gasped. 'Much too soon. But inevitable, my Georg. Let's just work on it as a given.'

CHAPTER TEN

EVEN WHEN THE cyclone was past, their ordeal wasn't over. The cyclone had torn apart the district, wreaked its havoc and then swept out to sea, but there it paused and hovered, threatening still and keeping the land buffeted by gale-force winds.

There was no single moment when they thought, Now it's over, now its safe.

But as the worst of the wind died, the water damage made itself felt. The road where the truck was parked slipped a little and the truck lurched sideways. Not very much, but enough to force their decision to search for another place to shelter.

Georgie knew the area. Dan Mackers's banana plantation was the closest. Dan had evacuated himself and his family as they'd brought out the bus-crash victims, but surely somewhere there they could find refuge. The Mackerses' main house was up past the bus-crash site, but there were a couple of smaller huts used for itinerant workers that were closer to where they were. Georgie had delivered the Mackerses' children and she'd been to several Mackers parties. She knew where the huts were—or she hoped she did.

It was now impossible to use the bikes. Carrying Rowdy and Scruffy and helping Max all they could, they fought their way on foot through the mess that was the road and found one of the cottages still standing. Almost. Its outhouse had disappeared, but who needed outhouses?

The roof was intact, the place was dry and, best yet, there was bedding, canned provisions and bottled water.

'And mashed bananas for as far as the eye can see,' Alistair said in satisfaction.

They were safe, but they were stuck. There was no telephone—all lines were long down. In that last mad dash, taking the boys back to the truck, Alistair had transferred his radio from his backpack to his pocket. Somehow his whole pocket had been torn away, and the radio had been lost.

Charles would be frantic, Georgie thought as the hours wore on, but then she thought, No, he'd guess, or at least he'd hope. The weather was too wild for anyone to institute a search.

They settled down to wait.

They treated the boys' needs properly. They stripped them of their wet clothes, cuddled them and told them silly stories. They resplinted Scruffy's leg and kept him dry and warm and still.

They slept.

There were only two single beds in the hut. The boys and Scruffy had one. Alistair and George shared the other. No impropriety—how could there be in such close proximity to the boys?—but Alistair hugged her to sleep and there was no way she was objecting. No way at all.

He felt so right. Could she make room in her life for him? she found herself wondering. Could she learn to trust?

She didn't know, but more and more she knew she had to try.

And then, at midday on the day after the storm, the chopper came sweeping in from the east. First it headed for the main Mackers place—the obvious place to search. It hovered overhead for maybe twenty minutes as those in it obviously searched unsuccessfully for a place to land, and Alistair and Georgie fretted impotently and wondered whether they could make a fire with saturated green wood and no matches.

But then those on the helicopter obviously decided to give up and fly instead to check the outer huts.

There was no need for the helicopter to hover and search here, for they were out of the hut, waving and shouting, the little boys yelling louder than they were, and Georgie thought she was probably crying but, hell, who was watching?

Cal was at the controls. And Mike was up there, too. Mike, who must be having the most tumultuous introduction to married life anyone could imagine. And Harry. Her friends.

They were yelling and cheering and Georgie and the kids were yelling and cheering, too, but Georgie had tears running down her face she couldn't stop. Alistair's arm came round her waist and he gripped hard.

'I don't have a handkerchief any more,' he said, and she choked on a chuckle. And she didn't move away from his embrace.

It didn't matter what the guys on the chopper thought. She'd worry about that tomorrow.

There was no place to land. They'd have to be retrieved by harness but that was fine by all of them. The little boys had recovered enough to be brave—even excited at such a form of rescue. Harry lowered himself down in the harness for the first retrieval and Georgie let go of Alistair and ran forward and hugged Harry.

For the normally emotionally contained Georgie this was well out of character, and she could see Harry's astonishment.

'Hey,' he said, and hugged her back. Then he turned to Alistair and held out his hand. 'And hey to you, too. All of you. You're all safe?'

'We're all safe.' Georgie was struggling to get her voice to work. 'You know Max,' she managed. 'And this is Rowdy. Scruffy's inside with a broken leg.'

'Scruffy?'

'Max's dog,' Georgie said, and grabbed Max's hand. 'Our dog.'

'Max,' Harry said, and shook his hand. 'And Rowdy.' Alistair had his hand on Rowdy's shoulder. Rowdy was pressing hard against Alistair—a small boy in a big unknown world. But he was brave. Harry shook Rowdy's small hand and Rowdy gave him a small smile. 'You have no idea how much Charles has been sweating on you guys,' Harry said, still smiling down at Rowdy. 'What happened to your radio?'

'They should make those damned things windproof,' Alistair said. 'Can you take us home?'

'That's what we're here for,' Harry said, and proceeded to do just that.

And twenty minutes later they were in the air. Alistair, Georgie and their brood were safely tucked in the rear of the helicopter, but they could see down to the cyclone-ravaged land.

The damage had been appalling. It was still appalling. By the time they landed Georgie was so overwhelmed she could hardly speak.

Whole forests had been flattened like matchsticks. Plantations destroyed. Buildings were simply no longer there. The swollen river was crammed with debris.

'How many dead?' she asked as they landed and Harry and Mike helped them out.

'Ten that we know of,' Harry said soberly. 'That's including the bus-crash victims. But there's lots of places we haven't checked yet.'

'Oh, Harry...'

'At least you guys are safe,' he said, and turned to take Rowdy as Alistair lifted him from the plane. 'We were all going nuts.'

And, giving truth to his statement, here came Gina. She'd been on the veranda of the doctors' house—one of the few buildings not obviously damaged. She'd shielded her eyes from the sun as the chopper had landed, seemingly hoping against hope that it was...

And it was. She squealed her delight and came tearing across the intervening ground as if she was running for her life. Yelling.

'They're back. Our Georgie's back. And our Max and our Alistair. And there's new guys. They're back. They're safe back home.'

And before Alistair found himself enveloped in a bear hug that practically knocked him off his feet, he had the forethought to steady himself by hanging onto Georgie.

Our Georgie. Our Max. Our Alistair. And there's new guys.

It felt like a family, Alistair thought, and he pulled back to check that Rowdy wasn't too overwhelmed.

A family.

It felt really good.

He just had to get Georgie to agree.

A family.

The fuss was almost over.

Well, hardly. There was still the huge clean-up that had hardly started as yet, but for tonight Georgie could lie in her own bed and think about what had happened to her. Max was right by her side, and Rowdy was on the other side of her. Scruffy was in a basket under her bed.

Her world had expanded. They still didn't have a clue as to who Rowdy was, but that could wait.

If no one claimed him, maybe she would, she thought dreamily. Mum to two kids and a dog?

It sounded great.

And Alistair?

He'd let her be. They'd separated to have glorious hot showers—the water supply here was fantastic. Alistair had been needed in the hospital—Megan and the patient he'd operated on from the bus crash both needed his care. He'd been accepted as one of the Croc Creek doctors. Everyone was treating him as one of them.

Except her.

He loved her.

She just had to trust.

It was such a big thing. Huge. She couldn't even explain it to herself.

She loved him. Or she thought she loved him. If he left right now she'd break her heart.

So throw your heart in the ring. Take the plunge.

'It's Max, too,' she whispered, hugging her little brother close. 'To entrust Max…'

She could.

Head and heart were warring. How could she trust?

Max muttered a little and moved away a bit. It was muggy, close, and her cuddling was making him sticky.

She was cuddling him for her, not for him.

She let him move away a little and felt a stab of loss.

Oh, for heaven's sake, go to sleep. Go to sleep!

She couldn't. She stared up into the dark for a long time.

There were sounds on the veranda. Footsteps. Someone else wasn't sleeping. One of the other doctors?

Alistair? His bedroom was right next door. Maybe…

Maybe she'd be dumb to find out.

But the thought was irresistible. Carefully she slid out of bed, inching out so quietly that even Scruffy in his basket under the bed didn't stir.

She lifted the latch and walked out into the moonlight, turning and carefully latching the door after her. If Alistair was here…she'd want to be able to talk. She'd want to be able to…

She turned, smiling already at the thought.

'You,' a voice said, and she froze.

Smiley.

He was right in front of her. Maybe he'd been checking the rooms, maybe searching for her. Before she could react he'd moved with lightning speed, grabbing her, hauling her around and shoving his hand tightly across her mouth.

'Bitch,' he said, and her head swam.

She could fight. She'd been trained to fight. But he'd moved too fast, shoving her down hard on the ancient settee, seizing her arms and dragging them up behind her.

'You make one sound and I'll kill you, and then I'll go in and kill that kid,' he said. 'I swear. Yeah, I'll go to jail but I'm going to jail anyway. Maybe ten years, they're saying. Well, what's a few more years added to ten? If I'm going to spend time inside then every minute I'm in there I'm going to think how much I hurt you.' He'd twisted something around her wrists—some sort of length of rubber. He twisted so hard she cried out involuntarily, and he grabbed her hair and hauled at it.

'I told you. One more sound and I kill you now. I could break your neck just like that. Maybe I will. Or I have a knife. Hmm, what will I use? But that's not for here, and if you scream now the kid gets it as well as you.' And he tugged her to her feet.

She was helpless. He had her by the hair with one hand, the other he was using to tighten the bands at her wrists and push her toward the stairs.

'Georgie...'

Oh, God, it was Max. Max... No!

'Georgie...' His tiny body launched at Smiley as if he were a missile. 'Georgie...'

Smiley released her hair and struck Max, hard. The crash of his fist made a dull, sick sound and Max crumpled on the steps.

'You bastard...'

Alistair launched himself out of the darkness with such ferocity she didn't at first know it was him. Smiley's fist had crunched into Max with force but it was nothing to the force Alistair used. One moment Georgie was being held by the wrists, the next Smiley was hit so hard that he was propelled right over the balustrade into the garden below.

Alistair was over, too, launching himself at Smiley with unbelievable force.

'He has a knife,' she screamed, and there was another sickening crunch.

'Not any more he doesn't,' Alistair breathed, and then grunted as Smiley obviously made contact with him.

'Help.' Georgie's lungs were right there. Her only weapon. Unable to be used when Max had been attacked, she used them to full effect now. 'Help.' But she was huddled over Max. 'Max…' Dear God, he was so still…

Lights were going on inside. 'Help,' she screamed again, for good measure, and the veranda lights flooded on. She could see…

Max was conscious. He was stunned. A trickle of blood oozed from just beside his ear but he was looking up at her, wondering…

She wanted to hold him close but couldn't because her hands were still tied. Then she remembered—Alistair… She hauled herself up.

He had Smiley. Somehow Alistair had him tight, hauling him to his feet, swearing…

'You…'

Smiley's foot smashed down onto Alistair's, crunching so hard Georgie could feel his pain.

People were spilling out onto the veranda. Gina. Luke. Rowdy. Oh, Rowdy…

She turned back to Alistair. She felt his fury. Thump him, she thought, screaming in her head. Thump him back.

But he didn't. He gripped Smiley's arms so tightly that Smiley couldn't move, and he propelled him forward into the solid base of the veranda.

'Come and take him before I kill him,' he said to his friends. He wrenched Smiley forcibly against the balustrade. 'If I do what I really want, I'm done for. There's no way I'm letting this scumball say I used undue force.'

He stood motionless, holding Smiley in a grip of iron until Cal got himself together, and Luke, and suddenly Harry was there, too—where had he come from? All she knew was that Smiley was immobilised.

She turned back to Max, and Alistair was by her side, releasing her hands then holding her tight, looking down at Max with eyes that were as fearful as her own.

'Max...' His voice shook.

'I'm OK,' Max said, and his voice wobbled. 'He just punched me.'

'W-we're used to it,' Georgie said, turning to hold Max.

'Well, get unused to it,' Alistair growled, and his voice wobbled a bit more. But then it firmed, and strengthened, 'No more. That's it. You guys have been punched for the last time. I swear to you... Georgie, I want to marry you but even if you won't, I swear I'll stick around and make sure that no one touches you again. I swear. The violence ends. Right here. Right now.'

The violence ends. Right here. Right now.

She looked up at him with eyes that were bright with unshed tears. What had he said? *I want to marry you...*

It was enough. The trust started right then and there.

How to fall in love with someone because they hadn't hit out?

Alistair had hit with a force she couldn't believe. He'd used violence to protect his own. But then it was finished.

Smiley had hit him. And she'd felt that crunch on Alistair's bare foot. He was wearing boxer shorts and nothing else. How could he ever have thought he'd win against Smiley?

But he had won—not only with force but also with lack of force.

Her Alistair.

Soon she'd check out his foot. Soon she'd attend to the bruise already swelling on Max's face.

But for now...

'You'll stick around?' she whispered.

'Yes.'

She swallowed and hugged Max some more. 'Max, what do you think of me and you and Alistair being a family?'

And then she thought...family. Max. Maybe Alistair hadn't factored that into the equation.

But it seemed he had. He was gathering her into his arms, and because she was holding Max he was gathering him in, too. And then Rowdy, white-faced and obviously terrified, was limping down the steps, and Scruffy was clunking down on his splint, too. They were all gathered in as well.

'Welcome all comers,' Alistair said, in a voice Georgie failed to recognise. 'I once thought I wanted control. I even once thought isolation was the way to go. I must have been mad. Georgie Turner, biker, obstetrician, dancer, sister of Max, friend to Rowdy and Scruffy, will you and your wonderful entourage do me the honour of accepting my hand in marriage?'

And what was a girl to say to that?

She gazed up at their audience. Every medic in the doctors' house, plus anyone taking refuge there, and there were quite a few, Harry, Luke, Cal, Gina—this whole crazy community was waiting for her answer with seemingly just as much interest as Alistair.

Even Smiley, snarling between his captors, was being made to wait and listen, for there was no way Harry was taking him away before he'd heard her answer.

So she'd better get on with it.

'Yes, my love,' she said, with all the force she could muster, so her voice rang out over the dying wind, carrying around this old doctors' house which had seen so much and had been the hub of so much pain and pleasure.

'Yes, my love,' she said again, and she smiled up at Alistair with all the love in her heart. 'Yes, I'll marry you. But only if you kiss me. Right here. Right now.'

And who knew what the audience did then?

Georgie Turner didn't care.

* * * * *